Published by Comicker Press
https://comickerpress.com/

Cover design & Artwork by: Hagalazka
ISBN: 978-1-968826-01-7
First edition

For more information, visit: [www.comickerpress.com]

Dragonkin Saga

Addernotch

Written by: Brian McKee
Artwork by: hagalazka

I would like to give thanks to the Voice in The Water (you know who you are,) who was one of the few to read the early drafts of this work from start to finish. I would also like to give thanks to my Aunt Laurie, and my editor of Airy Words, who both scoured later drafts and picked apart my mistakes. Further thanks I wish to give to my Mother, Father, and Brother, without whom the little kobold boy named Skunk never would have come to be in the first place.

Dragonkin Saga
Addernotch
Book 1

Table of Contents

Dragonkin Saga
Addernotch
Book 1

Table of Contents

Sybhrod Mountains
Actancirum
Ruined Structure
Leoroch Plains
Karajene Village
Leomar Forest
Port Natha
Addernotch
Aigeth Plain
Map art by: hagalazka

hatchling

"Come on, Seto!" Amelia Lanswel called back over her shoulder as she vaulted effortlessly over a fallen tree, her leather hiking boots thudding against the fern-smothered forest floor with an almost inaudible thump. She looked back over her shoulder, her green eyes scanning the trees for any sign of her traveling companion.

He came around the bend a moment later, his black-feathered body shimmering with sweat, and his long beak hanging open as he panted for air. The aging krauven staggered to a halt a few paces away from Amelia and leaned up against a tree to rest his weary legs. "Slow down, Amelia!" he gasped, rubbing his forehead with a clawed hand that was more like talons. His brown eyes flicked up to glare at the human woman. "Gods. A moment. I just need a moment to catch my breath."

Amelia shook her head with a sigh, sending her long brown hair swishing between her shoulder blades. "Seto, really. We don't exactly have *time* to wait around. If we don't get to the stone soon, someone else will find it first, and then all of this will have been a waste of our time."

Seto clacked his beak, a display of emphatic emotion. "Yes, I know that. But I'm not as young as I used to be," He pointed out as he righted himself. As if to punctuate his point, several audible cracks sounded from his back. He grunted in discomfort and shot her another look. "And I haven't gone sprinting through dense forestry in *years*."

Amelia just smirked at him. "Excuses," she teased lightly.

Seto cawed at her.

She laughed at that. "Alright, alright, fine. Take a minute to catch your breath, but then we have to *move*."

Seto did not say a word. He ruffled his long black tail feathers and leaned against the tree again. Amelia observed him for a moment, then turned to keep her eyes on their surroundings. The Leomar Forest was full of life, and not all of it was friendly. She would be damned if she let any of it sneak up on them today. With barely a sound, she withdrew the bow from her back and nocked an arrow.

She cast her eyes about the forest as she waited. The leaves were full of the colors of spring — vibrant greens accompanied by bright flowering buds of every color under the ring. She could just make out small animals hiding among those colors, slinking this way and that through the underbrush. Harmless things. The occasional mouse or squirrel, an adder snake or two. Nothing with which to concern herself.

Above her, the air was alive with the chirps and whistles of birds. The thick, pungent aroma of oak, pine, and spruce hung all around her, blocking out most other smells. Somewhere far off in the distance, she thought she could hear the babbling of a small stream.

Despite the potential dangers, Amelia took a slow, deep breath.

"The forest is beautiful this time of year," she thought out loud, her voice low.

"Aye, that it is," Seto agreed as he came away from the trunk. He dusted off his back as well as he was able. He gave Amelia a small nod and smile. "Alright, I think I'm ready to go. Thanks for waiting."

Amelia returned the smile. "Think nothing of it," she said before turning to lead the way. "Come on. The stone fell over here-"

Amelia stopped when something moved in the underbrush nearby, larger and decidedly less appealing than the squirrels. It moved quickly, slithering along like a snake and closing the distance with long, light steps that barely made a sound. A spike of adrenaline flashed through Amelia's veins, and she was already going into motion before Seto even realized that anything was amiss.

With practiced swiftness, Amelia loosed her arrow just as the scaly shape leaped for Seto. A wet, meaty thud echoed through the trees, accompanied by an animalistic shriek.

Seto cried out in alarm, his back slamming into the tree he had just left as the slitherbounder crashed into the dirt at his feet. Amelia's arrow was lodged firmly in its eye socket. Its body twitched and spasmed on the ground, a horrid gurgle bubbling from its throat for a second before it fell still.

Amelia glared at the small beast. It was like an unholy union between a snake and a kangaroo, with a long serpentine body and powerful multi-jointed legs tipped with viscous claws. A mouth full of razor-sharp teeth and a head topped with a crest of crimson feathers completed the look of the signature nuisance of the south crater heartlands.

Seto's hand rested over his heart, his eyes wide with shock. He was short of breath for an entirely different reason now. He lifted his eyes to Amelia. "Thank you," he said again, his voice shaking.

Amelia nodded as she pulled her arrow out. "Don't thank me yet. We're not in the clear. These things hunt in packs. Where there is one there will be more." She explained while examining her arrow. To her relief, it was still perfectly usable. She wiped the blood off on her trousers before putting it in her quiver.

Seto clacked his beak, his expression darkening. "And after a ringstone fell nearby, they'll be agitated," he mused, tip-toeing around the corpse to stand at Amelia's side. "Which means..."

Amelia nodded. She could handle one angry slitherbounder easily enough. She was confident she could even manage a few of them. But If a dozen of them came at her at once, riled up and hungry?

She turned and beckoned for Seto to follow. "We need to hurry. We've got worse than competition to worry about, now."

Seto did not argue. He fell into stride beside her, making sure to keep close.

Amelia slowed her pace down so that Seto could keep up with her.

She'd enjoyed rubbing in how out of shape he was, but the time for such banter had passed. They made their way deeper into the woods, heading in the general direction they had seen the stone falling. It would be impossible to miss it once they found the crater. Finding the crater, however, would prove tricky. They had to deal with angered animals and the dense foliage of the forest, not to mention the risk of other people looking for the same thing they were.

Pieces of the pale ring fell to Aurus all the time. On most days, they would burn to ash long before they reached the ground. But sometimes, larger stones would survive the descent and reach the ground. Whenever this happened — particularly when it happened close to civilization — people would scramble for the crash site, each one hoping to be the first to collect it. That meant there would be competition. And in Amelia's experience, competition could turn violent.

Thankfully, though, there did not appear to be any sign of trouble yet. No more slitherbounders crossed their path, or anyone else for that matter. As they slowly began to relax, Amelia led them up a ridge that would provide a high vantage point that would make it easier to spot their quarry.

"There!" Seto suddenly cawed once they were at the top, pointing. "Down there!"

Amelia followed his talon-like finger, squinting into the forest. She spotted a fallen tree a moment later.

Looking at it, 'fallen' might have been an understatement. The trunk had been blasted apart halfway up, leaving behind a shattered, smoking stump that was still bleeding a thin veil of black smoke. Beside it, the earth had been torn open into a wide trench for several dozen yards before finally tapering off. Shredded leaves, sundered branches, and shattered rocks lay scattered all about the impact site. The unmistakable marks of a fallen ringstone.

"Looks like we're first on the scene, too," Amelia noted with relief. She kept her bow drawn, just to be safe. She began down the slope at a swift run, eager to claim their prize and quit this place. "Come on! Let's make sure we're first to *leave*."

"Again with the running," Seto groaned, electing to descend at a more measured pace.

Amelia snickered but kept her eyes trained on the surrounding woods. She waited at the base for Seto, then kept watch while he went to collect their prize. Now that she was paying attention, she noticed that the woods were quieter here. No doubt most of the animal life had scattered when the stone had fallen. All she could hear were the creaking of treewood and the rustling of the leaves.

She heard Seto letting out a triumphant caw and turned to face him. He emerged from the impact site, the ringstone cradled in his hands. It was roughly the size of an apple, blackened with burn marks from its descent. Even so, the silver light of luma beneath shone through, bright and resplendent. Seto held it up to her, grinning. "And here we are! A fine find, I think."

"Do you reckon the Assemblage will be pleased?" Amelia asked.

Seto dropped the stone into his pouch. "They usually are. I don't see why they wouldn't be this time."

Amelia clapped him on the back, grinning. "Glad to hear it. Shall that be all?"

Seto drew himself up with a nod. "Yes, I think so. And thank you."

Amelia tilted her head. "For what?"

Seto smiled at her and thumped his fist against her shoulder. "For watching my back out here. It's been too long since we've done something like this."

Amelia blinked, then smiled, fondly remembering an earlier chapter in her life. She returned the gesture. "I was just glad for the chance to spend time with you again, danger or otherwise."

"And give me hell over the fact that I'm getting old, apparently."

Amelia's smile turned into a smirk. "We *always* gave you hell, Seto. It's part of the fun of having you around."

Seto glared at her. "What do you mean?" he asked suspiciously.

Amelia poked him on the tip of his beak. "You poof up when we pick on you."

As if to prove her point, the feathers around Seto's neck and on the back of his head rose up, giving him a decidedly 'poofy' look. He gave her a sour glare and cawed in her face.

This only served to make her laugh.

Seto threw his hands up. "Bah! You know what? I take it back!" he huffed, walking past her. There was no hiding the smirk in his voice, though. "Why did I miss you when you moved out here?"

Amelia followed after him. "Maybe it was my good looks?" she asked.

Seto snorted. "Oh, please. You know damn well I find you featherless humans unattractive."

Amelia was undeterred. "My charming company, then. Don't deny it, I saw that smile a moment ago."

Seto cawed again and gave Amelia a harsh glare. She met the glare with a coy grin.

The two stared each other down for several long seconds. Amelia waited patiently, knowing full well what was to come. Sure enough, Seto's composure broke before hers, and he broke down into a fit of laughter. One which Amelia happily joined.

"Fine, you win," Seto relented, giving her a playful shove.

Amelia's grin widened. "Of course I do."

Their laughter slowly began to die down, and they got back into motion. They fell into a companionable silence as they followed an old game trail through the foliage of the forest. Amelia glanced up every so often, tracking the light of the sun with her eyes.

"The ring is beautiful here, isn't it?" Seto suddenly remarked as they passed through a small clearing, drawing Amelia's attention. She glanced over at him to see he had come to a stop, his head tilted back to stare at the sky. Curiously, she followed his gaze.

There, in the skies above, was the pale ring. From here it appeared as a band of perpetual silver light reaching across the sky from one horizon to the other. But to those with the means and will to study it, it was known to be a circle of precious stones that slowly orbited the entire world of Aurus. It glowed constantly, bright enough to be seen clearly even at the height of day, and enough to navigate the world even in the dark of night.

"So it is," Amelia mused quietly, stepping up beside her friend. She glanced at the sun, noting that it would be passing behind the ring within the hour. She hummed quietly. "The hour of short night will be soon."

Seto folded his hands behind his back. "How is it in this region? I've been cooped up inside so much I've not had the chance to watch it yet."

"Beautiful. As it is everywhere else."

Seto hummed quietly but said nothing for several minutes. The two just stood there, watching the sky. Eventually, Seto clacked his beak and turned to Amelia. When he spoke, his voice had lowered considerably. "This is another thing I missed. Watching the sky with you all from the spire's balcony."

Amelia frowned. "It *was* nice, wasn't it?" she mused, thinking back. She recalled how she would sit with Seto and Tamaya on one of the Attuner's Spire's many balconies and watch the world shift through all the colors of dawn and dusk during short night. It was always a quiet reprieve from the danger and the chaos of the assignments the magi would give them. A moment of peace and tranquility where the three friends could simply sit and exist with one another.

A pang of nostalgia hit her, and she turned to Seto. "We should make some time before you have to return to Underbridge. For old time's sake."

Seto perked up. "I would like that very much. If we could get Tamaya to join us, we'd have the full team."

Amelia's smile faded. Her hand ventured briefly to her lower belly, a tingle of discomfort traveling across it. "That would be easier said than done," she muttered. "She's devoted to her tribe these days. We can't pull her away from that."

Seto let out a low whistling noise, a Krauven's sigh. "I know, I know. Still, a man can wish."

The two were quiet for a moment. A gentle breeze washed over them, sending the branches swaying overhead. Amelia looked up, wanting to get in one more look at the ring before they got a move on.

But then she spotted something. A needle-thin streak of light coming from the ring. It shot across the sky, flaring brightly.

"Another falling stone," she said in a whisper. Seto followed her eyes, but by the time he was looking, the shard of the ring had already burned away, leaving only an afterimage burned in Amelia's vision.

Seto grunted. "Bah. I missed it," he grumbled. He turned to Amelia. "The wish is all yours, then."

Amelia turned to him with a quirked brow. "Wish?"

Seto nodded. "According to some old books I read recently, it was considered a sign of good fortune to see a ringstone fall from the sky in ancient times. They were called 'shooting stars,' and it was a custom in some cultures to make wishes upon them."

"And did anything ever come of such wishes?" Amelia questioned.

"Not to my knowledge. Wishes being granted by distant magical forces are the stuff of children's stories," Seto said with a shrug. He turned to Amelia. "Still, there's no harm in being childish every so often, don't you think?"

With that, Seto started into motion for the village. Amelia watched him go, her brow furrowing at his choice of words.

Her hand pressed tighter against her shirt, and a shiver threatened to go down her spine. She looked down for a moment. "A little bit of childishness, you say...?" she asked in barely even a whisper. Seto was right. What could it hurt?

She closed her eyes, her fingers curling into the fabric of her shirt, and she focused on the tingling of her skin. She allowed old memories to wash over her, to bury her in the joys and the regrets of her old life. Then, with all of the conviction she could muster, she turned her eyes to the pale ring and silently made her wish.

The wind stilled around her for a moment, almost as if to listen, and Amelia's heart skipped a beat. She held her breath, waiting for something else. Something more.

But nothing happened. The wind returned a moment later, howling among the trees as if even the forest was disappointed.

Amelia let out the breath in a sigh and turned to follow after Seto. She shook her head at her own foolishness, ready to forget the whole ordeal.

But then a sound reached her ears.

Amelia paused. She turned, listening. It was distant, muffled by the wood. Whatever it was, it was high in pitch.

It came again a moment later, and Amelia felt something she couldn't describe. An instinct she could not name flared within her, compelling her to investigate. Before she realized what she was doing, Amelia had broken into a jog in the direction of the sound. "Seto!" she called back as she went, drawing the Krauven's attention. "This way! I hear something!"

"What? Amelia?" he called after her, moving to follow. "What is it? What are you doing- Come back here! *Amelia!*"

She wasn't listening. She ran through the forest, weaving expertly between trees and bushes that had long since become as familiar to her as the back of her hand. She vaulted effortlessly over another fallen log and ducked to slide under a thick root that arched above the ground like a gateway, all without losing any speed.

As she drew closer, the sound became clearer in her ears. It was a cry of distress — although it was decidedly *not* coming from a human. An animal of some sort, perhaps? If so, she could not place what type. The sound was unfamiliar.

There was something else, too. Another sound, quieter but more numerous. As she drew nearer, the new noise resolved into airy snarls and snake-like hisses that made her blood run cold.

Slitherbounders.

She should have known they weren't done with them yet.

Her path soon brought her to the lip of a natural bowl in the terrain. Coming to a stop by the edge, she knelt and looked down at the source of the sound. At the bottom, she saw an animal carcass. Blackened fur with white stripes and an enormous fluffy tail marked it as a skunk. It was massive, too, easily the largest skunk she had ever seen. She reckoned its fur would be large enough to make a cloak for a thick-bodied dwarf in the right hands.

The skunk was surrounded by slitherbounders, four by her count. They circled the body, teeth bared and tails lashing in excitement. Amelia knew this behavior. They were toying with their prey. But why would they be toying with a creature that was already dead? It made no sense.

She saw one of them step forward to snap its jaws at the dead animal. In response, she heard the cry of distress she had heard before.

Her eyes widened. They weren't toying with the skunk.

One of the slitherbounders moved out of her way, and she realized that the fallen animal's belly had been torn wide open. A mound of still-moist innards was piled on the ground nearby, and she realized that the animal had been hollowed out. The stench of rot and decay hit Amelia's nose like an avalanche, though she did not flinch at the familiar smell.

Even had she registered the stench, however, her attention was fixated entirely on the small creature that lay curled within the skunk's hollowed belly. It was reptilian, its body covered in scales the color of bright green moss. Two small ivory horns curved up from the back of its head. Tiny clawed hands clutched the tip of a thick tail, which it had wrapped around itself like a protective blanket.

This was the source of the sound.

This tiny creature.

It was crying.

Its bright yellow eyes darted around, shimmering with fear and confusion as the slitherbounders preyed upon it.

Amelia stared at it, dumbstruck. She knew what that creature was. Even if she hadn't encountered its kind before, she would still have recognized it. Anyone and everyone with an education would.

This creature was a kobold. Judging by its size, it was no more than a hatchling.

But what would a kobold hatchling be doing here in the middle of the woods? To Amelia's knowledge, the creatures lived in vast underground colonies far away from the civilizations of mankind. What was this one doing so far from its home? And further, *where* was its home?

Or its parents?

Another slitherbounder stepped forward to snap its jaws at the baby kobold, drawing another terrified scream out of it. The noise snapped Amelia out of her trance. Her questions could wait. For now, she had work to do. Without a word, Amelia drew out her bow, nocked an arrow, and fired right as one of the slitherbounders decided it was time to go in for the kill. Her arrow punctured its long neck right before it could reach the hatchling. It gurgled and spasmed as it fell off to the side, toppling lifelessly over the skunk with a thud.

Amelia stepped forward, drawing another arrow and giving the loudest, angriest scream she could in the hopes of scaring the slitherbounders off. The three that remained spun to face her, teeth bared and hissing in response. One of them scraped its feet along the ground before kicking off at her in a direct charge. She turned her arrow on it and fired right as it leaped. The arrow punched through its skull between its eyes, sending the feral beast sprawling to the ground at her feet.

She stepped over the twitching corpse, her eyes darting between the two that remained. They backed away from her, turning their bodies sidelong to make themselves appear larger and more intimidating. Good. They were afraid of her. Just not quite enough to abandon their meal.

Not yet.

"Get LOST!" Amelia screamed at them, taking a threatening step forward and nocking another arrow.

That seemed to do the trick. The remaining slitherbounders determined that whatever meat they could find here was not worth the risk that Amelia represented. With their tails lashing behind them in frustration, they turned and scampered off into the woods, shrieking over their shoulders at her as they went. Amelia kept her arrow trained on them as they ran, and she did not drop her guard or her arrow until she was sure that they were gone.

When at last she could no longer hear them, Amelia took a deep breath, then another. Her heart began to slow, and the adrenaline in her veins depleted, replaced with a surge of lethargy. She slumped in place with a weary sigh. Then, swallowing heavily, Amelia turned toward the fallen skunk. The baby kobold was still crying.

Moving as slowly and as quietly as she could, Amelia approached the tiny dragonkin. She kept one hand hovering over the hilt of her dagger, just in case the creature became aggressive. The other hand was kept firmly on her nose to keep the odor at bay.

As she drew closer, the kobold poked its nose out of its bloody home. It looked around for any sign of the slitherbounders, then spotted her. It let out a frightened squeak and squirmed back into the guts of the skunk.

Amelia knelt beside the skunk and looked into the open cavity. The kobold was tucked into the back, its prior wails replaced with faltering whimpers and tiny hiccups. Its eyes reflected the light at her in the same way a cat's would. They glistened in the darkness, and she realized that the kobold was crying.

She knelt before it, just staring.

"What are you doing out here little guy?" she whispered. Curious, she reached a hand out toward it.

The kobold whimpered fearfully but did not flinch away. When her hand was close enough, it lifted its head from its tail to sniff at the tips of her fingers. It must have liked what it smelled, as the tip of its tail began to thwap softly against the earth like a dog's. The kobold let out a quiet trill, and Amelia had to admit, it was adorable.

"Hey there," she whispered, her lips curling up into a smile. She couldn't help herself. Her fingers wandered a little closer to the kobold, their bare tips brushing softly against the kobold's nose. It flinched back from the contact for a moment, sniffed her fingers again, and then pressed its face into her hand like a cat demanding pets of its owner. She couldn't help but laugh, scratching the tiny thing between the horns. "That's it. I'm not gonna hurt you," she whispered.

Alas, the moment had to end.

"Amelia!" Seto's voice drew her from her trance. She turned back to see the krauven as he finally arrived at the edge of the bowl. He staggered to a stop, gasping for breath. "Guh! What did we say about the running?!"

The kobold immediately withdrew back into the viscera, crying out in fear at the sudden loud noise. Amelia noticed as its mouth opened that the little creature had no teeth. She also spied the shattered remnants of a large egg in the back of the hollowed-out animal.

She turned back to Seto and held a finger up to her mouth, urging him to shut up. He blinked at her in confusion, tilting his head farther than a human could before his eyes landed on the baby in front of her.

"What...?" he breathed, venturing timidly into the hole. He came up to Amelia's side and knelt next to her, staring inquisitively. "A kobold? Here?" he questioned.

"I'm just as surprised as you are," Amelia whispered. "Don't Kobolds live underground in large groups?"

Seto nodded. "They do — and they are *exceptionally* community-driven. For one to be born all on its own — and above ground, no less..." he said. His attention turned to the dead skunk and the egg inside, his brow furrowing. "I can only assume it was left here on purpose."

Amelia frowned. "So someone killed this animal and left the kobold egg inside of it? For what purpose?"

Seto shrugged. "I'm a scholar, not a psychic. I don't know."

hatchling

The two were quiet for several seconds. Slowly but surely, the kobold poked its head out of the carcass again. Its yellow eyes, massive relative to its body, stared up at Amelia. Its fear was slowly fading away, replaced with curiosity. Its slit pupils widened out to take in more of her. She couldn't be sure, but she thought she could see a flicker of hope in the baby's expression. It reached a hand out toward her, and on instinct, she held her hand out. Its tiny fingers curled around the tip of her index finger.

Amelia smiled, warmth pooling in her chest. A moment passed before her smile faded. "What do we do?" she asked. "I'm not an expert on kobolds."

Seto was quiet for a moment. He rubbed at his beak in thought. "Well, most of the time, when you encounter an animal in dire straits in the wilderness, you're not supposed to interfere with nature's course."

Amelia frowned. "That's what you do for an *animal*. But this is a kobold. Kobolds are still people."

Seto hummed. "There are not many people who would agree with you on that."

Amelia grimaced, thinking about what she knew of kobolds. They were the servants of dragons — or at the very least, they often worshipped dragons. They came in a wide array of colors that denoted the dragon they belonged to. This one was a green scale — and more often than not, green scales were enemies of mankind. There were countless stories about the savagery and barbarism the dragonkin were capable of, and Amelia knew that the stories at least had a base in reality.

Entire villages burned to the ground, with anything and everything of value stolen, and every man, woman, and child slaughtered or hauled away to be eaten. Travelers waylaid and torn to pieces to decorate little-used roadsides. Water supplies poisoned, unmaking entire communities, like what happened in the city of Threne some years ago. She recalled a man she had met back in Underbridge who had described green scales as 'rabid animals with an agenda.'

But staring at the kobold in front of her, she couldn't imagine it being capable of such things. It was so small, so fragile, and so, *so* scared. It didn't even have any teeth. Its massive eyes bored into her, wide with terror, but shining with hope. It was practically begging her to save it.

Her hand drifted to her belly, and her frown softened. She made up her mind.

"It's just a baby," she said before reaching in and gingerly pulling the kobold out of the viscera. It let out a few high-pitched squawks of alarm, flailing in her grasp. But as she stood up and held the tiny thing up to her chest, cradling it like the baby it was, it ceased fidgeting. It stared up at her, eyes wide with awe and wonder.

She smiled at it, the warmth returning to her chest again, and she was unable to keep herself from laughing softly through her nose.

It was just such a shame that picking the kobold up meant having to take her hand away from her nostrils.

The stench hit her full force, and she just about retched on the spot.

The kobold blinked at her as she tried to regain her composure. As she did, cheeks now just a little greener than before, she gave him a weak smile.

"You stink," she croaked matter-of-factly.

The kobold apparently liked the sound of that, because it giggled.

Seto narrowed his eyes, the terrible sense of smell of his kind leaving him unfazed by the odor. "What do you intend to do with it?" he asked. "The people of Addernotch won't be happy that you brought *dragonkin* into their midst."

Amelia shrugged, finding her voice as she made it a point to breathe through her mouth. "I... I do not know. Not yet. But I can't just leave him here."

Seto opened his beak to offer some rebuttal. But when Amelia met his gaze, the words died in his throat. He shook his head in defeat a moment later. "Very well. Far be it from me to tell you what to do," he finally said, giving her a warm smile. "If you are certain this is the path you wish to walk."

Amelia returned her eyes to the kobold cradled in her arms. "I am certain."

The kobold curled up into a ball, gurgling at her before stuffing its claws into its large mouth. A tiny bit of drool came out of the corner, though it did not seem to notice or care.

Seto turned. "Come. We should quit this place," he said. "If we linger too long, we'll be late getting back."

Amelia nodded. She didn't want to be here if the bounders rediscovered their lost bravery, anyway. Wordlessly, she turned and fell into step beside Seto. As they walked, the kobold kept squirming in her arms. It looked up at her, then past her at the forest canopy. Its eyes followed the trees for a moment before slowly drifting closed. It happened so quickly that she almost missed it. The kobold fell asleep.

"He'll need a name," she mused absently.

"You're planning to keep it around that long?" Seto questioned.

Amelia paused. The words had left her mouth before she'd even thought about them. She shrugged a moment later. "Perhaps. Perhaps not. All the same, it will make it easier to talk about him if we have something to call him other than 'the kobold'."

Seto nodded along. "Fair enough, I suppose."

"Any ideas?"

"Not a one."

Amelia flashed him an irritated frown before looking back down at the kobold. He was adorable, sleeping in her arms like that. The stench hit her again, and she looked off to one side as she gagged.

Seto snickered at her. "And for once I am *glad* I don't have your human sense of smell," he said. "If only he didn't smell like a dead skunk, eh?"

Amelia might have made a jab at Seto for that, but it died on her tongue. She came to a total stop, her mind stilling amid a sudden flash of inspiration.

Up ahead, Seto realized she had stopped and turned to face her. He tilted his head. "Amelia?"

Amelia smiled at Seto for a moment. "That's it," she whispered before looking down at the kobold. She held him just a little closer to her chest, feeling his warmth against her. "I know what to call him."

Seto faced her more fully. "What?"

Amelia was quiet for a moment longer, thinking the name over. It was perhaps a bit degrading, but somehow, it just felt right. She leaned her head down and spoke in a hushed whisper. "Hello. It's good to meet you... Skunk."

It seemed that the kobold approved of his new name. For as Amelia carried him slumbering in her arms back to Addernotch, Skunk smiled.

Addernotch

Eighteen years later.

The village of Addernotch, nestled comfortably in a break in the expansive Leomar Forest, was no stranger to the comings and goings of wolf packs. The people that lived there were all too familiar with them — and in turn, the problems they could cause when they became too bold. Every so often, wolves would slip into the farmlands, bringing down livestock that wandered a little too close to the fences.

And if the wolves — or any wild animal — could snatch up an animal once, they would be emboldened to do so again. This had the potential to evolve into a serious problem, as the people of Addernotch relied on their crops and livestock to see them through each year and pay their dues to the Duke in Underbridge.

That being said, the people of Addernotch were not so foolish as to think that the mere sight of a wolf was cause to raise the alarm. The animals played a vital role in the region's ecosystem, just like any other. They had their place, and it needed to be respected. It was only when the wolves chose to intrude in the territory of man that action had to be taken.

And so, on a cool day in early autumn, not too far from the forest's edge, one such wolf, alone and tired, ambled up to the edge of a small stream. Its head swiveled around, looking for any signs of a threat, its ears perking up. When it was sure it was safe, it knelt down, plunging its muzzle into the cool water to slake its thirst.

In the blink of an eye, the wolf's life was snuffed out.

A near-silent whistle. That was the last thing the wolf heard before a well-aimed arrow punctured its throat from the side. It didn't even have time to yelp. It took a single step to the left before collapsing onto the ground, breathing its last breath.

Not far away, on a small ledge that overlooked the stream, a green-scaled kobold poked his head up from the bushes, bow in hand. His lips curled up into an enormous grin as he beheld his handiwork. "Ha! Mom! Mom did you see that?!" he asked in a yapping voice, hopping in place. "That was such a clean shot! He didn't even suffer or anything!"

Amelia emerged from behind a tree not far behind him, dressed in brown furs and covered in branches that had helped keep her out of sight. She gave Skunk a warm smile and patted him on the head, right between the long ivory horns emerging from the back of his head. This, in turn, made him gasp with delight. So great was his joy, in fact, that he dropped his bow. He let out an embarrassed trill before scooping it back up and clutching it to his chest with a small blush.

Amelia laughed. "I saw. Nice shot."

Skunk grinned at her, putting his impressive teeth on display and wagging his tail like a happy dog. He had grown considerably in the last eighteen years, coming in at just over four feet when relaxed. He'd be a little taller if he stood upright.

Amelia patted him on the back, then nodded at his kill. "Come. Let's not wait for the slitherbounders to smell our prize."

"Right."

The two slipped down the slope, Skunk taking the lead and bounding on all fours with natural ease. With his lithe figure and lightweight clothing, he leaped over the ten-foot stream in a single effortless bound. Amelia moved at a more leisurely pace, affording him a moment to himself.

Skunk slid to a stop by the fallen wolf and knelt down beside it. The fur was surprisingly lush for a creature all on its own. He surmised it had either only left its pack recently, or this wolf had simply been a *very* good hunter. He gingerly placed his hands on the side of the beast, running his dark claws through the fur.

His eyes lingered on his left hand for a moment. It was covered from the tips of his fingers all the way to his wrist in thick white bandages, hiding the scales underneath. He flexed his fingers for a moment, and his thoughts briefly drifted back to the first time he had seen a wolf this close. The skin of his middle finger tingled at the memory.

He shook his head, chasing those morbid days away from his mind, and focused back on the kill in front of him.

"Sorry about this," he muttered. "But you were too close to our territory. You know how it is." A moment passed, and Skunk frowned. Something was off. Leaning in, he sniffed curiously at the wolf.

All at once, his mind came alive with an array of scents.

The crisp spice of dry grass and the bland grit of old dirt.

The sticky, coppery residue of blood, mixed into a pungent cocktail with sweat and saliva.

There was something more. A strange, heavy musk. Like burning coals and citrus, buried under dirt and stone.

For a moment, Skunk felt a pang of recognition. It faded as quickly as it had come, though. Skunk leaned back and away from the carcass, frowning.

"Huh... You're not from around here. You're a long way from home, buddy," he realized. He sat upright, crossing his arms over his chest in thought. "You're from way up north, aren't you? What are you doing all the way down here? Hunting not so good back home? Did the ry'thar get your friends?"

Sadly, corpses were not in the habit of revealing their secrets. Skunk shrugged. He'd just have to live without knowing.

It was at this time that Amelia emerged from the water and knelt beside him. She gave the wolf a once-over, then smiled. "A fine kill. And none too heavy, either," she said before taking the carcass in her arms and rising to her full height.

Skunk huffed, his brow furrowing. "Show off," he grumbled, glaring down at one of his arms. His light brown shirt clung tight to his scales, custom-tailored to fit his hunched frame. It was comfortable but did little to hide how scrawny his arms were.

Amelia rolled her eyes at him. "You're still young, Skunk. Give it time. And maybe do some pushups," she teased before turning back for Addernotch.

Skunk huffed. "Hey! You know pushups don't do anything for me!" Skunk called after her, scampering to catch up. "I *naturally* run around on all fours! It's not impressive or hard when I do it!"

Amelia shot him a glance, a twinkle in her eye. "I could always drape this wolf over your back, and then we could see how that goes."

"Do that and I'm gonna eat 'em."

Amelia snorted. "You'd better not do that until the meat's been cooked."

Skunk rolled his eyes. "Yeah yeah, mind my manners, it's rude to eat the meat raw, blah blah blah," he complained, though there was no missing the smirk on his face.

Amelia chuckled at him. She nudged him with her foot. "None of the cheek, young man!"

"What, like this?" Skunk asked before puffing his cheeks out as far as he could. And given how long his face was, and his sharp cheekbones, there was a lot of cheek to go around.

Amelia laughed. "You are such a smartass."

"And whose fault is that?"

"Mine for not disciplining you enough?"

Skunk nodded sharply. "Uh-huh! Not like you'd do that anyway. You love me too much."

Amelia paused at that. The two had reached the top of the ridge. She turned to look down at Skunk. He just smiled back up at her, his tail wagging.

Amelia smiled wider. "Yes, I suppose I do."

Skunk grinned widely in approval before scampering ahead, eager to get back into town. The sooner they were in town, the sooner some of the wolf's meat would be sent his way. Amelia did not match his enthusiastic run, opting instead to move at a brisk but measured walk.

Skunk waved back at her as he reached the top of another hill. "C'mon, slowpoke!" he called before continuing ahead. He didn't need to watch his mother to know she'd keep up with him. Or rather, he wasn't bold enough to go so far away that she couldn't. He just had too much energy to be comfortable moving at a slow pace. And so he ran, nose low to the ground and sniffing around.

It wouldn't be a long walk to get back to Addernotch — half an hour, at most. Around twenty of those minutes would be spent within the forest. This gave Skunk plenty of time to find things. Grubs, mushrooms, anthills, bones, birds.

Speaking of birds...

Skunk came to a stop and stood upright, having just heard a high-pitched chirp above him. Curious, he looked up. He stood beside a fairly young tree, its leaves starting to shift hues from green to gold. On the lowest of the branches, tucked up against the trunk, he saw a bird's nest.

He could hear the babies chirping from here, but he couldn't see any sign of the mother. Nor could he see what the baby birds looked like. They must have been tiny, though, given the pitch of their voices and the size of the nest.

I wonder what they look like, he thought. And it was that single thought that triggered his curiosity. Without a second thought, Skunk dug his claws into the trunk and climbed.

It only took him a few seconds to get to the nest. With a grunt, he hoisted himself up onto the branch beside the nest and peered inside. There, four little yellow baby birds looked back up at him, eyes wide. They chirped and trilled, squirming uncomfortably in place.

Skunk's eyes shone with delight. "Aaaaww! You guys are adorable!" he said softly, lowering his belly to the branches. "Look at you! Where's your mama?"

"Skunk! What are you doing up there?!" Amelia's voice called out to him, drawing his attention. She was coming into view from behind a cluster of shrubs, moving at a surprisingly brisk pace, considering the literal dead weight she was lugging around.

Skunk waved at her. "I found some birds! They're cute!"

Amelia quirked a brow at him, then looked at the nest. Her frown deepened. "Don't bother them, Skunk. They're just babies."

"I know, I know," Skunk called back, looking into the nest again. "I'm not gonna touch 'em."

The birds kept squawking at him. It seemed they were starting to recognize that he wasn't a threat to them — not right now, at least — but they still didn't care much for his presence.

Amelia came to the base of the tree. "Skunk, come down from there. We don't have time for side tracks. Besides, if their mom sees you, she's going to-"

"SQUAWK!"

Speak of the feathered devil, and she shall appear.

Skunk turned his head when he heard a shrill, furious battle cry. He barely had time to let out a yip of alarm before a feathery ball of yellow death slammed into his face. He flailed uselessly, covering his head as well as he was able as the mother bird's sharp beak pecked relentlessly at his unprotected scalp. He swung his arms out, trying to scare her off, but only succeeded in throwing himself off balance. A fact he only realized when the world pivoted around him and his stomach went on a holiday to his pelvis.

Skunk yelled as he toppled from the tree and came crashing back down onto the hard earth below, kicking up an impressive cloud of dust. Pain flared up in his chest and shoulder, eliciting a pained groan.

Amelia stood over him, an unimpressed look on her face. "I warned you."

Skunk moaned in dismay, covering his snout with his hands. "Shut up," he said before hauling himself to a sitting position. He shook his head and looked up at the nest, fearing the mother might pursue her attack. Instead, she just stood on the branch, shrieking and cawing at him. If he could understand bird, he was certain he would be hearing a very colorful string of expletives right about now.

He narrowed his eyes at her. "That was mean! And where did you even come from?!" he demanded.

"SQUAWK!"

"That is not a helpful answer!"

Amelia hefted the wolf in her arms. "It is to be expected. A good mother is never far from her babies."

Skunk sighed and hauled himself back to his feet. He gave her a smile. "Just like you, right?"

Amelia paused for a moment before a tender smile crept across her face. "Exactly. Just like me."

Skunk tilted his head. *She's doing it again.*

It was odd to him. Sometimes Amelia would get this far-away look in her eye when talking about their family. He could never get a read on her when it happened. He couldn't tell if she was happy, sad, or something else. Whatever the emotion was, though, it was potent, and it ran deep. And the fact that he couldn't identify it bothered him greatly.

Amelia shook her head a moment later before continuing on her way. "Now come on! We don't want the meat to go bad."

"Right," Skunk agreed, giving the mother bird one more look. A second later, he smiled at her. "Sorry for bothering your kids. You're a good mom. Keep 'em safe!"

The bird squawked at him again, and he was fairly certain she was saying 'Get the hell out of here!' Taking that as his cue, he made sure he hadn't dropped anything before scampering off to catch up with his own mother.

It wasn't long before Skunk and Amelia emerged from the Leomar Forest. The woods covered a series of gradually sloping foothills and shallow mountain peaks that separated the Aigeth plains in the south, and the Leoroch plains to the north. As a result, coming out of the forest's southern border provided one with a beautiful and largely unobstructed view of the landscape for miles and miles. The lush green fields were dotted with small copses of trees and river streams that wove elegantly between the hills as they flowed for the ocean to the west. The sky was largely clear today, save for a smattering of fluffy white clouds, and the pale ring.

Skunk took a deep breath, savoring the fresh air. There was a very faint salty smell today, no doubt brought this way by the winds from the sea. It wasn't often that the smell made its way this far east, and Skunk seemed to be the only one who ever noticed. He took a moment to enjoy it before turning his attention down to Addernotch.

To an outside observer, the village would be utterly unremarkable. The settlement straddled one of the many streams that wound through Aigeth, with numerous bridges constructed to accommodate foot traffic. The homes were simple but sturdy, built from wooden logs and planks gathered from Leomar. Some were lucky enough to have stone foundations — such as the lumber mill and Seto's schoolhouse.

The most notable facet of Addernotch would have to be the cobblestone road that cut through the village from east to west. Merchant caravans coming to and from Port Natha to the west often passed through on that road, bringing with them coin and news from abroad.

Such concerns were never of interest to Skunk, however. Whatever else the pit-stop village may have been, it was home. He didn't want or need it to be anything else.

The return trip was made in peaceful silence, and soon enough the duo were back on the road that cut through the heart of the village. A handful of people were out and about today, and some of them gave Skunk and his mother friendly nods and waves as they passed.

Amelia adjusted their kill in her arms and gave Skunk a small nod. "Why don't you run along to the schoolhouse, Skunk? I'll take care of the wolf."

Skunk turned back to her, his tail drooping. "Wha- awww, come on!" he complained, stamping his foot in childish defiance. "I never get to come along!"

Amelia rolled her eyes. "Skunk, if you went with me to the slopper *or* the butcher, you and I both know it would take the entire militia to get you to *leave*. And there are more valuable uses of your time than standing around drooling at uncooked meat."

Skunk opened his mouth to offer up a scathing retort, only to realize that his mother was absolutely right. So instead, he clamped his mouth shut, crossed his arms, and stuck his nose up into the air, puffing up his cheeks in a childish huff. "Mmph. No fair."

Amelia laughed. She set the wolf down for a moment and leaned down to plant a quick kiss on Skunk's head, right between his horns. That done, she hefted up their kill and started down the road. "I'll see you at the house, Skunk. And tell Seto I said hello!" she called back over her shoulder.

Skunk watched her round the bend, and then he was alone. A tiny, rebellious part of his brain told him to sneak after her anyway, but he was quick to shut that notion down. She'd learned how to tell when he was getting up to mischief, and it never went his way. Giving in, he turned and made his way to Seto's schoolhouse.

It only took a few minutes for it to come into sight. A long, narrow building with a high shingled roof sat near the western edge of town, cordoned off from the rest of Addernotch by one of the streams. A wide bridge made of stone and wooden supports spanned the water, serving as the main entrance to the grounds. The fields to either side of the house were fenced-off, creating wide but controlled spaces for the children to burn off energy between lessons.

Not wanting to disturb anything, Skunk opted to look in through one of the windows before heading in. Wooden tables had been neatly on either side of the room, leaving a central lane clear for traversal. Children sat at each table, watching and pretending to listen as Seto walked up and down said lane. Some looked bored, some looked intrigued. One was picking his nose, and Skunk stopped looking at that one pretty quick.

Determining that nothing of *immediate* importance was happening, Skunk let himself down from the window. He dusted himself off, made sure there wasn't anything from the forest stuck in his cloak, and then gave three sharp knocks on the door. He waited a second before pushing through and stepping in.

Seto had paused his lecture, and his eyes lit up as the kobold entered. "Ah! Skunk, my boy! I was wondering if you were going to come by today," he said by way of greeting. His eyes shot immediately to the bow slung over Skunk's back. He clacked his beak. "I take it your mother took you out hunting this morning?"

Skunk nodded, closing the door behind him. "Uh-huh. Gothard told us there was a big wolf stalking a little too close to the farms the last few nights, so mom and I went to take care of it."

One of the kids sat up a little straighter. "Did you shoot it?"

Skunk grinned. "Right in the throat!"

"Cool!"

Seto blanched. "Wha- Skunk! Come now, young man, don't encourage him!"

Skunk shrugged. "Hey, he asked."

"Yeah!" the boy chimed in. "And this is a school! Aren't we supposed to ask questions?"

Seto pressed his hand to his face, letting off a tired croaking noise. "Oh, Five have mercy," he moaned in mock despair.

Skunk chuckled before moving forward to wrap the aging krauven in a warm hug. "Heh. Good to see you too, gramps."

The air rang with the amused snickering of the children, and Skunk couldn't help but grin as Seto squirmed in his arms. Still, he beamed when he felt the old bird return the embrace. "Yes yes, good to see you, too, young man. Now stop hugging me so tight. These hollow bones were brittle even before I got old."

Skunk pulled back after giving the man one more squeeze. "Sorry. So, got anything for me to help out with?" he asked, eager to make himself useful.

Seto nodded a moment later. He turned and gestured with his beak toward the far end of the room. "Yes, actually. I just received a shipment of goods this morning from a few old colleagues of mine back in Underbridge. Manuscripts, tomes, scrolls, and the like. Unfortunately, I haven't had a chance to get them sorted yet."

One of the children, a little girl, thrust her hand into the air. "Oh! And it's also because Mister Seto's eyes are absolute trash!" she declared. The other children, once again, broke into amused snickers at their teacher's expense.

Seto turned to the girl with a quirked brow. "Laugh all you like, young missy. But mark my words; one day, you too will be old and barely able to tell a signpost from a spear shaft. And when that day comes, know that I will be laughing at you from the grave!"

The girl stuck out her tongue at Seto, to which he simply cawed at her. Again, the children laughed. Seto shook his head and turned back to Skunk. "The children of today. I fear for our future, Skunk, I truly do."

Skunk tilted his head. "Aw, c'mon, they're just having a little fun, gramps," he said.

Seto waved at him dismissively. "Bah, don't you join them. I have Sylvia working on putting away the shipment right now. I am sure she would be delighted to have your help. If you would be so kind?"

Skunk's face lit up with the widest grin he'd had all day, and any temptation to tease the old bird about his age was swept from his mind. "On it!" he exclaimed, already bounding for the door to the back room.

Seto smirked at the display. "Just try to keep it down, please. I *do* have a lesson to give," he cautioned after Skunk.

Skunk threw him a sharp salute before stepping into the back room.

It was a dimly lit affair, about half the size of the main classroom. The left wall was populated with shelves, each one loaded down with old books, scrolls, and the occasional relic that Seto had somehow managed to get his talons on. Nearly all of these things had been sent here by Seto's old associates from the Assemblage in Underbridge.

Farther back, three wooden crates sat against the far wall. And there, sitting at a desk, was Sylvia. Her back was to him, affording him a view of her plain white dress and long, messy blonde hair. She turned in her seat, having heard him coming in. She brushed a lock of hair aside, revealing her pale complexion and gentle features. She smiled as she saw him, her dark blue eyes shining even in the low light of the room. "Skunk. Hello," she greeted in that low, gentle voice of hers.

"Hi!" Skunk said, scampering across the room to join her. Her scent hit him all at once. Straw and hay, cotton and grass blades, lavender stalks and honeyed porridge. He looked down at the crates, seeing each one was filled with books. "Seto said you needed some help with these."

Sylvia nodded and placed her hand on his back. "I'd like that," she said, her voice low and quiet, like a gentle spring breeze.
Skunk felt himself relaxing almost immediately.

"Alphabetical, I assume?"

"That's right," Sylvia nodded. "I'm up to B."

"So does that mean you're busy as a bee?"

Sylvia giggled softly, but she didn't say anything else. Not that Skunk minded in the slightest. Pulling over an unused stool, he took his place beside Sylvia, close enough that their shoulders were touching. He went to reach for the first book, but Sylvia had already picked it up and was now holding it to him. He flashed her a small smile, one she returned, and took the tome in his hands.

The two fell into a companionable silence. The only sounds were the muffled echoes of Seto delivering his lecture in the classroom and the occasional chirping of birds outside. It was peaceful. Serene, even. Skunk didn't even mind the monotony of the task at hand. It was simple, repetitive work. In any other circumstance, he would have been bored out of his mind. But the company made it cozy and comfortable. Seconds turned into minutes, and if they went uninterrupted, Skunk was certain they could sit like this for hours.

His eyes flicked to Sylvia as they worked. Her expression was plain and muted, as always. Yet he had learned long, long ago to read her emotions in her eyes. She was content in their silence, just like he was.

Outside of the room, Seto's lesson went on. "Now, children. Please raise your hand if you can tell me the nature of the pale ring? You, Kelton."

"O-oh, uh. T-the pale ring is, er... it's the thing that magic comes from?"

"Correct, very good. The pale ring is the birthplace of all magic in Aurus. The white light it emits is known as luma — shortened from 'Luminescence'. It is *this* light that serves as the bedrock foundation of all forms of spellcraft. And all known forms of life have at least a tiny spark of it buried deep within them. Many great people study for years, learning how to connect the Luma inside of them to a shard of the ring. These men and women are known as magi, and by calling upon the luma of their attuned stone, they are able to bend the world around them, sparking fire where none existed before, imbuing a man's body with enhanced strength, and even granting a flightless fox the ability to soar through the skies. So long as their attuned ringstone remains intact and within their reach, a magi can work wonders."

A moment. Seto spoke again. "Yes, Amadalie?"

A girl spoke. "Um, my mum told me that sometimes, the ring sends us pieces of itself."

"And your mother would be correct. You see, the pale ring is not like the wedding ring your mothers and fathers wear. It is a collection of countless thousands of individual stones, some as small as a pebble, and some even larger than the mountains. They are forever traveling around our world, and every so often, these pieces smash into one another, breaking apart. When this happens, it is not uncommon for the smaller shards to fall down to our world as shooting stars.

These 'ringstones,' as we call them, are highly sought after by magi, enchanters, and collectors."

"Skunk?"

Skunk blinked, snapping out of his trance. He realized with some small embarrassment that he had zoned out while listening to Seto's lecture through the door. He turned to Sylvia. She was looking at him.

"You alright?"

Skunk nodded, glancing back down at the next books to sort. "Yeah, I'm fine. Sorry 'bout that. I just zoned out a little," he said before hauling up the next few books from the crates. "Ooh, looks like this is the last batch!" he said as he set them down on the table.

Sylvia nodded as the two got to work. They worked in silence again, and Seto's lecture wandered off into other subjects that Skunk found far less interesting. Devoid of that distraction, he was free to focus on his work — and his company. Without even realizing he was doing it, he leaned into Sylvia's side. If the woman minded the contact at all, she did not show it.

As the minutes dragged on, and Seto continued his lectures, Skunk found his eyes drawn towards the room's sole window. He could see a small sliver of the pale ring in the sky from here, nestled against the horizon.

A strange sense of calmness came over him, even more profound than what he felt being with Sylvia. He relaxed in his seat, his weight settling comfortably against Sylvia's side. "The ring's pretty today," he mused quietly.

Sylvia followed his gaze. She smiled knowingly. "You *always* say that," she pointed out warmly. "It's *always* beautiful to you."

Skunk gestured at it. "Well, yeah. I mean, just *look* at it. The thing's gorgeous! I can't help it!" he said unreservedly. His smile faltered a second later, and he frowned. "Though... sometimes when I look at it... It's weird. Sometimes it makes me feel kinda sad."

Sylvia turned to Skunk, her brow furrowed in confusion. "How come?"

Skunk shrugged. "I dunno. It's like... Uh, what's that word? You know, for when you're remembering stuff from when you were really little? Nostalgia?"

"That's the word, yes."

"Yeah. It's kinda like that," Skunk said, gesturing vaguely. "I look at the ring, and it's like I'm looking back on some old faded memory. A happy one."

Sylvia followed his eyes up to the ring again. She hummed and pulled him close in a warm side hug. "And do you have any idea what that 'faded memory' could be?"

Skunk shook his head. "Nope. Not a clue," he said plainly. He returned Sylvia's hug from the side. "But I don't think I really need to know. It's not important."

Sylvia nodded quietly. Eventually, the two disentangled from each other and got back to work. The remaining tomes were put in their place, and the two stepped back out into Seto's schoolhouse to assist the aging krauven in whatever manner he needed. Skunk gave himself over to the work wholeheartedly and with a smile on his face. But every so often, his eyes would drift out the nearest window and back to the ring.

It was a strange thing. That feeling of 'nostalgia' he felt when he looked at the ring was stronger than usual today. And there was something else, too. A faint tickling sensation in the back of his skull, as subtle as a blade of grass brushing against an exposed thigh. Subtle but somehow intense at the same time. Skunk shuddered, scratching at the back of his head and focusing back on the work ahead of him.

But the tickle did not go away.

Dragonkin

Skunk was dreaming.

At least, he thought he was dreaming. There was no other way to describe the strange images assaulting his mind. He had no body, no voice, no breath. None that were his own. He was only a spectator, staring out at a landscape he had never seen before through the eyes of someone else. Even so, it felt painfully familiar.

Rolling hills of pearly white stone stretched out before him as far as the eye could see, emitting a faint, heavenly white light. Countless craters and cliffs peppered the land, while bottomless ravines around them like the blue veins of an aging human palm. Everlasting reminders of long-past collisions.

Were that not strange enough, the sky was devoid of the pale ring. And without that shine, the unimpeded sparkling of millions of stars filled his vision. There were so many, in fact, that they wove together in long, sparkling currents of sapphire blue and amethyst purple.

It was an alien sight, and Skunk felt that he should have been frightened by what he was seeing. But, strangely, all he felt was contentment. Otherworldly as it was, this land was peaceful. Serene. A captured moment of perfection, impossible in the real world. He could stare at it for hours and hours. If he had any say in the matter, he would have.

But he did not have a say.

As he stared, his vision began to drift slowly toward one of the nearby cliffs. There, a creature of impossible majesty emerged, its eyes narrowing as it oversaw its domain. It was gargantuan, easily dwarfing Seto's schoolhouse with its muscular, green-scaled form. Eyes as yellow as the sunset peered across the land, and wings that could envelop the sky twitched on the beast's back.

A dragon. Skunk had never laid eyes on one before, but there was no mistake. It wasn't even a point of intellect or past knowledge. He couldn't describe it, other than that he just... *knew.*

The dragon looked up, and Skunk followed its gaze.

If he still had eyelids, he would have blinked in surprise. *What is that?* He wondered.

Against the obsidian backdrop of the starry sky, a shining blue marble, half framed in shadow, spun lazily overhead. He could see white clouds traveling across its surface, traversing the expanse between oceans, mountains, lakes, forests, and deserts.

An entire world, seen from an angle he never could have dreamed. It was beautiful.

So why, then, did it fill him with such terror?

Crack.

A sharp needle of pain shot through Skunk's mind. The blue marble began to grow, and an unseen force pulled on him. The ground trembled, and the great fissures splitting the land wrenched open even wider. Thunderous booms and groans filled his mind, the deafening cacophony of shattering stone. And underneath that deafening cacophony was a chorus of anguished roars and cries of rage.

And then came more images. Flashes of humanoid creatures dressed in crimson robes, their faces hidden behind empty masks of copper, gold, and silver, their four arms raised as if to cradle the white marble that floated in *their* sky. He saw mountains bursting into flame, cities of gold and granite folding in on themselves as the earth opened to swallow them whole. He saw waves of water swallow continents. He saw gnashing fangs, blood on the stones. War, death, and anguish, all in a swirling haze.

Crack!

He wanted to cry out. To scream for help, for his mother. But he had no mouth. He had no voice. All he could do was watch and listen. Watch as this beautiful world was torn asunder, listen as it screamed for mercy against a tide that harbored none.

Finally, he forced himself to give voice to his fear. Emotions he could not describe swelled in his breast, surging up a newfound throat, longer and thicker than he remembered, before tearing past scaly lips in a primal roar. The voice was not his own, and the despair and anguish in it sent a chill down his spine. A thousand voices like it answered his call.

The ground shattered beneath him. Something woke up.

And he knew no more.

Skunk awoke with a scream. He sat up, clutching his chest to calm his pounding heart. It thumped wildly in his ears, drowning out everything else. He looked around, his eyes wide and frantic as he took in his surroundings.

Slowly, his panic began to subside. He was in his bedroom, a cramped but cozy affair with a bundle of furs and hides arranged like a nest on the floor. His bed. The first rays of morning sunlight were coming in from his room's only window, bringing with them a gentle warmth.

"J-just a dream," he mumbled to himself, taking several deep breaths. "Just a b-bad dream."

Footsteps thumped rapidly across the floor outside his room before the door suddenly slammed open. A *very* sleepy-looking Amelia came half sprinting, half staggering into the room. "Skunk!" she slurred, looking around with bleary eyes. "Are you alright?! What's wrong?!"

Skunk gave her a weak grin. "It's okay, mom. I'm alright."

Amelia promptly enveloped him in a bone-crushing hug, forcing an indignant squeak out of him. "Oh, thank heavens! I heard you screaming. You just about gave me a heart attack."

Skunk rolled his eyes and returned the hug. "Just about gave myself one, really," he said quietly. "But I'm okay. It was just a bad dream."

No sooner had the words left Skunk's mouth than he doubted them. It *had* been a dream, yes. But somehow, saying that just felt *wrong* to him. Insufficient. He couldn't put his finger on why. But he had no other way to describe it, so he put it from his mind. He turned to look out his window. He could just make out the edge of the pale ring from here.

There was that tickle in the back of his head again...

Amelia was quiet for a moment before standing up. "Well, with all of *that* excitement, I somehow doubt we're going to be getting back to sleep," she remarked with a chuckle.

Skunk looked away sheepishly. "Sorry. I didn't mean to wake you."

"None of that, young man. Come on, let's put some food in your belly."

Skunk would never say no to food. He took a minute to get dressed, throwing on a simple pair of brown slacks and a plain white shirt, then followed Amelia to the dining room. Soon enough, the house was filled with the smell of cooking meat. Choice cuts from the wolf they had hunted the previous day and some strips of dried pork Amelia had purchased before that.

The moment Skunk had his plate, he began the most common ritual in the Lanswel household. He ravenously tore into his breakfast like he was a starving animal — snarling and all. He knew it was rude, but he just couldn't help himself. Even in esteemed company, he had never been able to hold back when eating.

Not that Amelia seemed to mind anymore. She called it 'endearing.'

The first time she'd said that, Skunk thought she meant he was going to turn into a deer, and freaked out an appropriate amount. He had been a child, though, so it was an understandable misunderstanding.

But as he was tearing into his food, snarling and growling like the most adorable of angry gremlins, he couldn't help but notice that Amelia wasn't tending to her food with the same sort of enthusiasm she usually did. She was looking out the nearby window, a thoughtful frown on her face. Skunk paused his eating to speak. "Mom?" he asked through a mouthful of food.

Amelia turned to him, jumping in her seat. "Huh? Yes, Skunk?"

Skunk swallowed his food. "What'cha thinking about? You're being kinda quiet."

Amelia gave him a small smile after a moment then turned to look out the window again. "It's probably nothing, but the ry'thar are late this season."

Skunk followed his mother's gaze. He didn't know much about the ry'thar. He'd only laid eyes on them a handful of times and never spoken with one directly. They were tall, strong lion folk who kept to themselves in isolated clans and tribes. He knew that Amelia had a good relationship with the clan that lived to the north, the Karjene, though the nature of that relationship was one she had never elaborated on. She only ever said she was good friends with them. Every so often a small band of ry'thar would come to Addernotch with a haul of herbs, furs, horns, and other such things to trade.

He turned back to his mother. "Do you think something's wrong?"

Amelia pursed her lips. "Hard to say. I don't know what is happening with them until they turn up. But they are usually quite punctual. They were supposed to have come to trade weeks ago. For them to be *this* late…"

Amelia trailed off for a moment, and an uneasy feeling settled over them. She dismissed it with a shrug. "Bah. Pay me no mind. I'm just being paranoid. Finish your breakfast."

Skunk didn't need to be told twice. With a happy grin, he looked down and tore into what remained of his breakfast, putting any thoughts of the ry'thar out of his mind. Had he not been so engrossed in his meal, he would have noticed Amelia's expression darkening again.

Once Skunk was done with his breakfast, he made his way to the schoolhouse. There wasn't going to be any hunting today as far as he knew, and Skunk wouldn't be of much use to her in any of her other work around town. Not that he minded. Working at the schoolhouse was nice. He got to spend time with Seto and Sylvia, and he liked the kids. Their curiosity and energy reminded him of himself, even though he was a solid decade their senior by this point.

This time, he was there for the start of the lesson. Skunk's job was simple: Hang in the back, and if a child needed help with something, he or Sylvia would go and help them if Seto was otherwise occupied. Simple things like basic maths, how to spell certain words, and so on. If particular materials or books were needed, Skunk or Sylvia would retrieve them.

In short, they were Seto's little helpers.

"Now, children. If you all have been paying attention and taking notes as I asked, then I should hope one of you can tell me the name of the current Duke of Underbridge?" Seto said, finishing off a long-winded explanation of the distant city's founding.

There was a brief pause. A boy spoke up. "Cedric the Stargazer?"

A girl piped up. "Nuh-uh! That was the *first* Duke!"

"No, that was Ceodore!"

Seto clacked his beak, a sharp sound that cut through the argument before it had the chance to start. Once he was sure that he had the children's attention, he spoke up. "I am afraid the young lad has the right of it, Jana. Cedric Lonentel *is* the current Duke of Underbridge. That being said, *Ceodore* is the one who harbored the title of 'Stargazer,' not Cedric."

There was the scratching of quills on parchment as the children took notes. Jana and the other boy quipped under their breaths in hushed tones that Skunk was pretty sure the others couldn't hear. He could hear it just fine, though, and their semi-serious bantering put a smile on his face.

A moment later, Seto nodded. "Now, it is almost time we break for lunch and play. Before that, however, does anyone have any questions?"

Immediately, a hand shot up. A freckle-faced boy with a mess of brown hair. Seto nodded to him. "Yes, Albert?"

Albert fidgeted in place before nodding at Skunk. "Um, It's not about Underbridge, sir, but uh, What's Skunk?"

Skunk blinked. "Huh?"

Albert went on. "You've told us lots 'bout krauven and dwarves and ry'thar and all that. But I dunno what Skunk is."

Seto hummed, clicking his beak again. "Ah. I see. I would have thought you'd have been told by now. Curious that you haven't. Skunk, would you like to do the honors?"

Skunk grinned and stepped forward, his tail swishing eagerly behind him. "Sure! I'm a kobold."

The boy blinked. "A... kobold?"

Seto nodded, placing a hand on Skunk's back. "Aye, a kobold. A race of dragonkin that largely keep to themselves in deep underground burrows and dens."

Jana leaned forward. "Wait, dragonkin? So, is Skunk a dragon?" she asked.

Seto shook his head. "No, no, not a dragon. But Kobolds are *related* to dragons. Not much is known about the relationship between them, however. Most Kobolds tend to keep to themselves in isolated communities called 'hordes.' Not many are known of, and of those that are, even fewer are inclined to speak with the people of Aurus. All we can say for certain is that kobolds tend to live under the rule of dragons. Not unlike how we the common folk are the subjects of lords and kings."

Albert nodded along. "Woah. But, if kobolds live under dragons, then why is Skunk here?" he asked curiously.

"Al! Don't be rude!" Jana snipped at him.

"I'm not being rude! I just wanna know!"

"You can't just ask someone why they live where they live, stupid!"

Skunk chuckled and lifted his claws placatingly. "Hey, hey, easy kids. It's no big deal, I don't mind answering. My mom found my egg out in the woods, and she brought me back home with her. I'm a kobold, yeah, but I was raised here in Addernotch. It's as simple as that."

Seto nodded sagely. "Quite right. And I am glad that she did. For a finer kobold the world has never known," he said, rubbing the space between Skunk's horns affectionately.

Skunk grinned, his tail wagging happily behind him. "D'aw, thanks gramps!"

There was a moment of silence. One of the other children spoke. "Aren't dragons bad, though?"

Skunk's tail stopped wagging.

Seto turned to the boy, his expression souring. "Nothing is ever quite so clear-cut, young man. Even as the races of man have the capacity for good and evil in equal measure, so too do the dragons."

The boy hummed along quietly. "I guess. But there are so many stories about big bad dragons burning entire cities to the ground," the boy pointed out. "That sounds pretty evil to me. And kobolds serve dragons, you said."

Skunk took a step back. "I... I'm not..."

Another boy spoke up. "One time, I heard old Freya say that Skunk tried to eat-"

Seto clacked his beak so loud it made the children flinch. "Not another word, lad!" he barked, his natural crowlike caw bleeding through into his typically smooth voice.

The schoolhouse fell silent. Skunk barely even noticed. A phantom sensation was dancing along his tongue. The taste of copper. Alongside that taste came a string of voices echoing from the depths of his memories.

"What's the matter, little dragon?! Aren't you gonna breathe fire?! Steal all my stuff?!"

"Ha! Look at him cry! He's a freak and a coward!"

"What are ya gonna do about it, huh?!"

"H-hey! Get off him!"

"Help! Someone help me!"

"SKUNK! Get off him!"

Skunk screwed his eyes shut and shook his head to banish the memory. His left hand tightened into a fist, tingles running up and down the middle finger. A moment later, he opened his eyes.

Seto was looking at him, his expression darkening. He turned back to the class. "Listen, children. You have to understand that the stories you have heard up to now were written to *be* simple. They are not reflective of the real world. Many dragons are hostile toward the people of Aurus, yes. For example, there is the red dragon Korthul, whose horde conducts routine raids on the people of Lasuun in the deserts far to the south. Centuries ago, The green dragon Azada terrorized the men and women who would one day go on to found our nation. But she would be slain *by* a dragon. That dragon's name was Thalgrum, and he was a kind-hearted blue dragon who relinquished his own territory to our founders and *defended* them from Azada's wrath."

A moment passed. A new voice cut through the room. It was Sylvia. "And whatever stories you might have heard from Freya, put them far from your mind," she said with surprising confidence. She stepped past Skunk, placing herself between him and the view of the children. "It was a long time ago. Whatever Skunk may have done wrong, he has more than made up for it."

Seto smiled warmly. "Quite right. Skunk has been a devoted member of our community ever since his mother found him, so let's not let ourselves get carried away by the stories of one disgruntled woman, shall we?"

The boy looked down, visibly ashamed. "Yes, sir. I'm sorry, mister Skunk."

Skunk looked off to one side, idly rubbing at his left middle finger. He licked at his lips in an effort to dispel the lingering taste of copper. "It's okay," he said quietly. "You didn't know."

Seto nodded in approval. "Good. Now that that's settled, class is dismissed. Head out and get some fresh air. We'll reconvene here in a while for the next lesson. Sylvia, would you mind taking care of Skunk?"

"Of course," Sylvia said.

As the children began to put away their things, she came up to him and took hold of his hand. Her fingers were cool and soft. She tugged at his wrist, gently but firmly. He did not resist as he was led into the back room.

The door closed behind them with a heavy clunk. Skunk went for the nearest chair and fell heavily into it, his hands pressing against his face. The old wood creaked in his ears like the rumbles of a thunderclap.

"Skunk? Look at me," Sylvia said softly, drawing his attention. Skunk lowered his hands to stare into her eyes. They were shimmering with concern. "Are you okay?"

"Y-yeah. Yeah, I'm uh, I'm okay," he mumbled hoarsely. "Thanks for standing up for me."

Sylvia said nothing. She took hold of his hand and gave it a firm squeeze.

Skunk was quiet for a moment. Then he threw his head back to let off a low groan of frustration. "Gah, dangit! I thought we were done with all that!"

"Skunk."

It was only a single word, but it immediately stilled Skunk's tirade before it could go any further. He looked down at Sylvia and slumped in his seat. "Right. Sorry."

Sylvia smiled. "Don't apologize. You did nothing wrong."

Skunk felt a little bit of warmth in his chest at that. He sat up a little straighter. "I just don't like being reminded of- well, you know."

"I know," Sylvia agreed quietly. She gave him a reassuring hug, running her hand down the back of his head. "Don't let it get to you. You're a good person."

"You sound awfully sure of that," he managed to half-joke.

Sylvia leaned back slightly to look into his eyes again. Her expression had hardened. "If you weren't, Skunk, then I wouldn't be alive right now."

Skunk was quiet for a moment. He looked down. "I guess."

The two sat in silence for a little while. A thought occurred to Skunk, and a small smile tugged at his lips. "Is it just me, or has this *always* been what it's like for us?" he asked softly.

Sylvia tilted her head, a curious glint in her eyes, but she said nothing.

Skunk went on. "Whenever I got upset or whatever, and mom wasn't around to take care of me, it was you who'd always come in to save the day. Heck, that was how we *met*."

Sylvia hummed softly, pulling her hands away from him. "I remember. It was cold that night. But it was you who protected me."

Skunk laughed weakly. "I just wish I didn't need you to come and protect *me* so often."

The two were quiet as Sylvia gave Skunk an appraising look, her eyes drifting up and down his form. Suddenly, she stood. "Close your eyes."

Skunk did as he was asked without even thinking about it. Only after his world was plunged into darkness did he think to question it. "Uuh, why?"

Sylvia said nothing, though she did giggle. Skunk heard her walking away, the floorboards creaking faintly under her subtle weight. He heard one of the chests click open, and Sylvia procured something. She came back a second later and stood before him.

"Hold out your hands," she instructed.

Skunk frowned. "Sylvia, c'mon, I'm not a little kid!" he protested. Despite his protests, he still held out his hands.

Sylvia giggled. "Oh, then you're going to *hate* this."

Something was set down in his hands. His fingers closed around it automatically, feeling the texture and the shape. It was small, easily cradled in his palms. Whatever it was, it was soft, but with a faintly rough texture. Some sort of stuffed fabric.

A few seconds passed. Sylvia's finger poked Skunk on the nose. "You can look now, you know."

Skunk went just a little rigid, and he felt a tiny bit of heat creeping into his cheeks. "...Oh."

Sylvia laughed again, and Skunk opened his eyes. Looking down, he saw that Sylvia had given him a cloth doll — and he knew what it was meant to be almost instantly.

"It's me?" he asked in surprise, pulling at the black cloak with the skunk-skin pattern running down its back.

Sylvia nodded. "Mhmm."

"Wow. It's really good," he said, turning it over in his hands. Sylvia had always had a fine attention to detail, and this was no different. That said, it *was* a little on the creepy side. The spare buttons she had stitched into the face to serve as his eyes stared back at him, wide, dark, and eternally unblinking.

He tugged at one of the arms, finding the stitching was sturdy and competent. He smiled for a second, then frowned in confusion. "It's really neat. But uh, what's it for? I mean, I'm not gonna play with it. My claws would rip it apart."

Sylvia hummed softly at that. She reached out, gingerly cupping her fingers under and around Skunk's hands as if to help him support the weight of the doll. She ran her thumb back and forth over his. "It's not for playing."

Skunk quirked a brow but said nothing.

"Look here," she continued, pointing out something on the doll. Skunk looked and realized that it was one of Sylvia's hairs, coiled around his horn like a decorative golden string.

"It's so that if ever we're far away, and you need me but I can't get to you, you'll have a little part of me with you. I *was* going to save it for a special occasion, but, well…"

Skunk blinked, carefully running his thumb over the horn. "That… is *so* incredibly corny," he joked with a small laugh. "Like, that is fairy tale levels of corn."

Sylvia rolled her eyes but said nothing.

After a moment, Skunk held the doll to his chest. "But it's really sweet. I love it. Thanks, Sylvia. I dunno what I'd do without ya."

Sylvia reached out to lightly stroke Skunk's cheek. "I'm sure you would do amazing things, Skunk. Amazing things."

"What, like eat all the meat in a fifty-mile radius?"

Sylvia chuckled. "Well, I mean, that *would* be an amazing achievement."

The two shared a laugh, and the last wisps of Skunk's discomfort finally faded away. He held the doll a little closer before giving Sylvia his warmest smile. He was just about to open his mouth and speak when the door opened up and Seto came walking in.

He closed the door behind him and let out a tired whistle of a sigh before making his way for Skunk and Sylvia. "I am so terribly sorry about that, young man. Are you feeling alright?" he asked, kneeling beside Sylvia.

Skunk nodded, his tail wagging happily off the side of the chair. "Much better now, yeah. Sylvia cheered me up. Like always."

Seto visibly relaxed before reaching his hand out to pat Skunk on the shoulder. His talons might have felt alarming to someone else, but Skunk had long grown used to their sharpened tips. Besides, his scales were harder to pierce than *that*.

"I am glad to hear that. Do you think you'll still be alright to work today? Or should I send you home?"

Skunk shook his head. "Nope, I'm good to go, don't worry."

Seto nodded slowly, not looking entirely convinced, but he did not press Skunk. "Alright. If you're sure."

Skunk grinned wider. "I'm sure," he assured the old krauven before hopping out of his seat. He gave Sylvia another appreciative look. She smiled back.

He looked at the doll one more time before tucking it into his pocket.

Willard whistled an aimless, meandering tune as he and Mumphrey meandered down one of the dirt roads on the outskirts of Addernotch. The sun had long since vanished behind the horizon, leaving just the constant glow of the pale ring to see by. Not that the aging man minded the dark. He spent the majority of his days tending to his crops out in the fields, breaking his back for an honest living, before ambling back to his little house, where his cranky wife Matilda would find some new subject to rant and rave at him about.

She was a wonderful woman and he loved her dearly, but Suna's breath, she could get just a little *too* noisy. Sometimes Willard wanted peace and quiet after working himself half to death. And so it was that he often left the house after the sun went down to walk around town with his dog. It served two purposes: Award himself with some quiet and let Mumphrey burn off any leftover energy so he could sleep at night without going into a tizzy when an owl scratched the roof.

The softer shades in the world that came out under the ringlight were far easier on his eyes, too. As gorgeous as Addernotch was, the colors could get a bit bright. Especially when one had to work under the sun for hours on end. But the gentle breeze, the crisp night air, and the relative silence were just what he needed to soothe his often overworked senses.

The duo had been walking for close to an hour, now. Willard was starting to feel the burn in his calves as they came around a small bend on the path. The forest loomed ominously to their right like a waiting tiger, separated from them by a field of tall wild grass and scattered bushes. To their left, a simple fence cordoned off Willard's land. He paused by a post and looked off toward his house. He hadn't been trying to loop back around for it, but it had just worked out that way.

We've been out here long enough, he figured. *Might as well head back.* He let off a grunt. "Alright, boy. C'mon. Let's head inside, eh?" he said, lightly tugging on Mumphrey's leash.

The loyal hound, however, didn't seem to hear the command. His nose was planted firmly in the dirt, sniffing incessantly. Something had clearly caught his attention, though Willard couldn't even begin to guess what it could be. Not that he cared — he wasn't one to give a damn unless it became important.

And important it became, as suddenly, Mumphrey looked up toward the forest and arched his back, hackles rising, and let off a low, warning growl. Willard paused, looking down at his faithful friend. "Huh? What's wrong, boy?"

Mumphrey took a step back, teeth showing in a vicious snarl while his tail tucked between his legs. He let out a series of ferocious barks before darting forward, only making it a few steps before the leash went taught and arrested his momentum.

Willard grunted, digging in his heels to keep the dog from sprinting off. "Woah! Hey! Mumphrey, what the hell?!" he demanded, pulling on the leash to bring his dog back. But Mumphrey wasn't listening. He just kept barking, louder and louder.

Cursing under his breath, Willard looked past his dog to the treeline, trying to figure out what the mutt had spotted.

Something was looking back at him.

Yellow eyes with slit pupils glared back at him from the darkness, shining with reflected ringlight. The eyes narrowed. He heard metal scraping on metal and saw a flash of steel in the darkness. A rush of adrenaline flooded his veins, and he opened his mouth to shout for help, already turning to run.

He didn't even make it a step before the arrow found the side of his neck.

A heavy thunk rattled all of Willard's senses, and suddenly, he could no longer breathe. His dog was forgotten as his hands flew up to his throat, a horrified gurgle all that could make it past the blood flooding his windpipe. He toppled to his knees, his heart pounding frantically in his chest. Darkness crept in around the edges of his vision, and in a matter of moments, he was toppling forward into the dirt, his mind fading away. The last thing he heard before he died was the sound of clawed feet stomping through the dirt toward him and Mumphrey squealing in terror.

Relics

Skunk went to bed early that day. Though Sylvia's gift and kindness had chased away the worst of his discomfort, the incident at the schoolhouse still left him feeling tired and out of sorts by the time he got home. After an early dinner, he tucked himself straight away to bed. He slept well, with no strange dreams or visions of otherworldly landscapes to distract him—just pleasant, peaceful slumber.

When Skunk woke up, he felt refreshed and energized. He lifted himself from his nest with a languid stretch, his lips parting into a large yawn and his back emitting a few pops. He spent a few minutes tidying himself up and getting dressed before stepping out into the house.

He shot a glance through the nearest window as he emerged. It was gorgeous outside, with bright sunlight and the chirping of birds. Through the walls of the home, the faint aroma of the town in motion reached his nostrils. Distant pig sweat and healthy moss, the passing wafts of people he knew and didn't. Muscle and fabric, dirt and grass, the occasional hint of iron. He took in a deep breath, savoring the familiar scents.

And then he realized that something was wrong.

Addernotch was by no means a bustling town. By the reckoning of many, it was a very sleepy place, especially during winter. But even with that typical, easygoing atmosphere, there was always, *always* someone talking out on the main street just outside of Skunk's home, and there was always a lively tone to the conversation.

Today, the conversation was almost non-existent, and Skunk realized with a pit forming in his stomach that the tone was very different. It was low. Solemn. Anxious. And there was something else, too. Something in the scent. He sniffed again, trying to parse it.

Someone else was in this house. Someone besides him and his mother. The smell was strong, a lingering hint of potent alcohol and sharp spices hanging over the metallic tang of iron and steel.

Then he heard voices coming from the dining room. Skunk turned, the last bleary remnants of his slumber forgotten. One voice was recognizable as his mother's. The other was low enough that Skunk couldn't put a name to it just yet. Curious and concerned, he advanced into the dining room

Amelia sat at the dining table, already dressed, her expression dark and serious. Her eyes were narrowed with grim contemplation, her elbows resting on the table's surface, her fingers steepled together in front of her lips.

Sitting across from her was a man that Skunk did not see very often. He was older than many in Addernotch, sporting a shiny bald head, a needle-thin mustache, and his fair share of wrinkles. He sat upright in his seat, radiating an aura of authority and dignity. He was dressed in simple padded armor with a yellow insignia woven onto the front of his left shoulder, marking him as the captain of the Addernotch militia.

"Gothard?" Skunk asked, stepping further into the room.

The aging man turned to him, the last vestiges of a similarly grave expression to Amelia's replaced with a warm and friendly smile. Strained, but genuine. "Ah! Skunk, young lad. We didn't hear you get up. How are you?" He asked, his mustache twitching with every movement of his lips.

Skunk stared at him, then at Amelia. His mother's hardened expression did not change. She just looked at him for a moment.

Skunk turned back to Gothard, frowning. "What's wrong?" he asked slowly, taking a few steps forward.

Gothard's smile strained before fading altogether. He nodded slowly. "Nothing gets past you, does it?" he grumbled before turning back to Amelia and gesturing at her. "He's your boy. You want him to know?"

She lowered her hands, folding them together on the table, and affixed Skunk with a firm look. "There's been an attack."

Skunk's eyes flew wide in shock, his jaw dropping open. In a flash, he was at the side of the table, claw tips sinking into the wood in a white-knuckle grip. "What?! Is everyone alright? Who attacked us?!" he demanded, forcing himself onto the tips of his toes to better look into their eyes.

Gothard let off a tired sigh. "I am afraid we do not know. Not for certain. But Willard Stantonfeld's gone missing. As has his wife, and several of their animals."

Skunk felt a stirring of horror in his chest, as well as a flood of primal instincts he did not have the words to describe. His tail scraped against the floor in a display of nervous energy. He couldn't claim to know Willard all that well, but from what few words he had traded with the man, he seemed to be a good sort. The thought that he had been attacked...

Gothard offered Skunk a sympathetic look. "Unfortunately, we don't know much else. There are clear signs of a struggle near Willard's property. There are blood stains, drag marks, footprints, and the like. There is also the fact that his dog was found on site, partially..." Gothard drew up short, his lips pursed together and his brow furrowing with uncertainty. His eyes shifted as he hunted for the right words.

Skunk's claws dug a little deeper into the table. "What? Partially what?" he asked, his tail thumping against the floor in agitation. "Tell me!"

Gothard sighed and shook his head. "Partially devoured."

Skunk's eyes flew wide. He swallowed heavily, his stomach turning. "W-what?" he asked, his voice coming out strangled. "What could have..."

Gothard turned his attention back to Amelia. "We don't know, yet. That's why the militia is being mobilized to maintain the village perimeter tonight."

In all of Skunk's time in this town, he had only heard of the town militia being mobilized a scant handful of times, usually in response to spontaneous incidents such as a child going missing in the woods. It was always search and rescue back then.

"I take it you're not here just to notify us of the situation," Amelia pointed out. She raised an eyebrow at Gothard. "If that were the case, you wouldn't have asked to come inside. You want something from us."

Gothard smiled at Amelia. "Like mother like son, eh?" he asked, impressed. "Very well. To the heart of the matter. I am hoping to enlist your aid in this matter. Specifically, your boy."

Skunk's eyes widened. "Wait, me?" he asked in surprise. "You want *my* help?"

Gothard gave him a warm smile and a nod. "I do, young man. You've got a better nose than some bloodhounds I've met, and you've done plenty of hunting since you started living with us. You are skilled with a bow, and you can see in the dark better than anyone under my command. Combine that with your mother's experience, and the two of you make a potent team. I want you two to lend the militia what aid you can until this situation is resolved. Just in case our 'visitor' decides to return."

Skunk swallowed heavily. Despite the grim scenario, a small part of him couldn't help but feel excited. This was his chance, an opportunity to *really* make himself useful. He stood up taller, puffing out his chest. "I'm in. Just tell me where you want me, chief."

"Slow down, Skunk," Amelia said, shooting him a disapproving look. "This isn't a regular hunt. Whatever did this was bold enough to come into Addernotch itself — and *clever* enough to avoid detection. This is going to be dangerous. Maybe it would be for the best if you sat this out."

Skunk frowned, any small hint of excitement he felt fading away. He spun to Amelia, his tail thumping against the floor in disapproval. "No way! You heard Goth! Whatever did this *hurt* someone! I'm not just gonna sit around and let 'em do it again if I can help it!"

Gothard frowned, idly playing with his mustache. "Goth?" he echoed under his breath.

The others ignored him.

Amelia stared long and hard at Skunk, her expression shifting to a look that he never much cared for. A stern, cold, and utterly unreadable expression that made him feel like she was peeling back the layers of his soul to peer at the truth buried deep within. She rarely used it, but whenever she did, he knew that things had just gotten serious.

Still, Skunk held his ground, matching her gaze. "Please. I want to help," he stressed, his claws digging slightly deeper into the wood of the table. "I *have* to help. I gotta protect my people. What good am I if I can't?"

"Skunk..." Amelia whispered. She searched his eyes a moment longer, still searching for something. Finally, she seemed to find whatever it was she was looking for. She gave Skunk an approving look and a slow nod. "Alright. You can help," she finally relented.

Skunk relaxed, his expression softening with relief. "Thank you, mom."

Amelia smiled and gave him a pat on the head before turning her attention back to Gothard. She rose to her feet. "What do you need us to do?"

Gothard rose as well, holding his hand out for Amelia to shake. "The militia will be meeting up in front of the town hall at short night, so make sure you're there," he said heartily. He gave Skunk another warm smile and clapped the kobold on the shoulder before making his way out of the house, leaving Skunk and Amelia alone.

The second the door closed, Amelia strode purposefully around the table and up to Skunk's side. Her expression was hardened, an unfamiliar gloom hiding behind her eyes. "Skunk? Are you sure you want to do this?" she asked.

Skunk hesitated for a second. He had thought he'd made his stance pretty clear a moment ago, but if it was more assurance his mother needed, he'd give it gladly. He stood up as straight as he could and met her gaze. "Absolutely. I'm not gonna sit on my tail while my pack gets hurt."

Amelia frowned. "You don't have anything to prove, you know. If this has to do with what happened at Seto's-"

"Mom," Skunk cut her off, shaking his head. "Please. That has *nothing* to do with this. My people need help, so I'm helping. It's as simple as that."

Amelia was quiet for a moment. Then she smiled. She knelt in front of him and put her hands on his shoulders. "That's my boy," she said, pulling him into a warm hug. Skunk blinked, taken aback by the unprompted embrace, but he was happy to return it all the same. When they came apart, Amelia rose to her full height and guided Skunk toward the stairs. "Before we go anywhere, there's something I need to give you," she said cryptically.

Skunk tilted his head as they went. "What is it?"

"You'll see," Amelia replied evasively, making Skunk puff up in indignation.

"Mooom!" he protested, pawing at her hip as they reached the top of the stairs. "You know I don't like it when you dodge the question!"

Amelia chuckled. "Yes, but you're cute when you pout," she retorted. "And if things turn out as dangerous as I suspect they might be, then I plan to milk all of the joy I can out of today."

Skunk threw his hands up with something between a feral growl, a childish whine, and a laugh. "Grah! You're the worst!"

Amelia grinned. "I'm your *mother*."

"Same thing!"

Amelia snickered again but did not tease him any further. She simply led Skunk into her room.

It was a humble affair, with a low ceiling and only a single window set into the far wall. Morning shafts of sunlight painted a grid of yellow light across the wooden floorboards. Dust particulates kicked up by the door danced lightly through the sunbeams, reminding Skunk of dancing fireflies. Pressed up against the wall to the right was his mother's bed, while a heavy wooden chest lingered against the wall to the left.

Skunk tilted his head at the chest as he was led over to it. "Huh. Ya know, I've never seen inside this thing before," he commented before giving it a sniff. He winced. It smelled strange, that was for sure. Unfamiliar metals and chemicals, stale from years of going undisturbed, were barely perceptible through the old wooden walls.

Amelia let go of Skunk and knelt before the chest. "There's a reason for that," she said as she procured a key from her shirt. With a heavy click, she unlocked the chest and opened it with a swirl of ancient dust and stale air. The muted smells Skunk picked up a moment ago resolved into something *much* sharper, making him sneeze. *This thing hasn't been opened in years,* he thought.

Amelia rested a hand on the rim of the chest, staring down at the contents inside. "You see, before I came to Addernotch, I led a *very* different life," she said quietly. She reached in, pushing a few things aside. "I picked up a lot of things in that time. Most are mementos and keepsakes. Trophies, if you will. But some of these are things I keep in case I need them again."

She moved aside one more object before finding her target and pulling it out. It was a sword sheathed in a finely made brown scabbard that reminded Skunk of the polished wood in the mayor's house. The end of the scabbard was capped with shining silver metal, and the hilt of the sword was wrapped in reddened leather. Strange runes were engraved upon the crossguard in a language Skunk did not know.

Amelia examined the sword for a few seconds, a distant look in her eyes as if she was suddenly somewhere else. Somewhere far away. She turned it over in her hands. "This old thing..." she said softly, running her fingertips gently along the length of the scabbard.

Skunk leaned forward slightly, tilting his head. "Woah... I didn't know you had a sword like that," he said, eyes wide with childish fascination.

Amelia's expression sobered up quickly. "It's a relic," she said simply.

Skunk turned his attention from the blade to his mother's face. She almost looked pained to be holding it. Uncomfortable. Her brow was furrowed, and that unfamiliar gloom was hiding in the usually radiant shine of her eyes again. Skunk felt a stirring of concern, and couldn't stop himself from placing a clawed hand on her arm. "Mom?"

Amelia jumped at the sound of his voice, then turned to him, smiling. She turned the blade over in her hands. "This sword served me well on many occasions, Skunk. It saved my life more than once. But when I came here to Addernotch, I felt I didn't need it anymore. I wanted nothing more than to throw it away and be done with it, but sentiment demanded I hold onto it. So I buried it and everything else from those days in this chest. And now?" She held the sword with an almost reverent look on her face before presenting it to Skunk. "Now I want you to have it."

Skunk stood upright in surprise. "Wha- really?!" he asked, taken aback. He knew how to use a sword, of course. Amelia had given him training in the basics, but that had been a long time ago, and they had been using wooden practice swords. He'd never held a real one before.

Amelia nodded. "You're old enough. And if anything happens in the coming days, I want you to be ready to defend yourself."

Skunk nodded slowly. He curled his fingers a few times before reluctantly taking hold of the sword in his hands, one hand on the hilt, the other on the scabbard. Amelia released it into his possession, then stepped back to give him some room. Curious, Skunk pulled the sword free to better examine the blade.

The first thing Skunk noticed was that the steel was gorgeous. Years spent inside of that stuffy old chest had done nothing to dull the sword's pristine shine or mar its razor-sharp edge. The second thing he noticed was its size. In the hands of a human, the blade was clearly designed to be wielded with one hand. Lightweight and easy to wield, perfect for quick cuts and light thrusts. But for him, it was more appropriate to call it a broadsword. Despite this, though, it just felt right in his hands.

He grinned up at Amelia. "Is it magical?" he asked, a sparkle of hope in his eyes.

Amelia snorted. "Ha! Oh, I *wish*. Unfortunately, no, it is not enchanted. Just very finely made," she said, thoroughly crushing Skunk's hopes and dreams in one fell swoop.

Skunk frowned. "Aaaaw... Still, this is..." he said, lowering his voice as he held the sword in front of him to admire it better. "Wow. You sure you wanna give me this?"

Amelia nodded. "I am. It's yours. Maybe you can put it to better use than I did."

"What do you mean?" Skunk asked curiously. "You just said it served you well."

Amelia's expression darkened. She sat back slightly, and her eyes shifted off to one side. "It *did* serve me well. Or rather, it served my *purposes*."

Skunk swallowed heavily. He took a tentative step forward. "Mom?"

Amelia shook her head. "It doesn't matter," she finally told him. She gave him a warm smile and placed her hand on his shoulder. "The past is the past, and I would have us both focus on what lies ahead. It is my sword no longer. It's yours. And I trust you'll make good use of it."

Skunk blinked at her, searching her eyes. Part of him wanted to start asking questions, to try and peel back the layers of mystery that covered his mother. But at the same time, he had no desire to stick his nose where it did not belong. Not with her, at least. And so, with a shrug, he slipped the blade back into its scabbard and held it out in front of him one more time. He gave his mother a big grin. "I will. And I'll take good care of it! Thanks, Mom," he said, his tail wagging again.

Amelia nodded. "So I should hope."

Skunk looked it over one more time, eager to get it belted to his hip so he could see how it felt. There was just one problem.

"Uh... how do I put this on?" he asked a second later, his grin becoming one of embarrassment.

Amelia laughed.

Far outside of Addernotch, on the road to the east of the small town and hemmed in on the north and south by towering trees, a dwarven woman straddled the back of her lumbering mount. The creature was no horse, however. It bore a striking resemblance to an elongated armadillo, its large, round body covered in segmented, bone-yellow armored plates. A long mammalian face emerged from the beast's front, tipped with a flowering nose reminiscent of a mole's. Broad-tipped claws ideal for digging through dirt and stone left gouges in the road as it passed, and a long, mace-tipped tail swished behind it with every step.

The woman on its back looked up at the pale ring, a light-skinned hand brushing a stray lock of her reddish hair out of her glaring green eyes. She paused momentarily as she caught sight of the symbol emblazoned on the back of her armored wrist guard. A symbol of a blazing sun entombed within a jagged mountain peak. The same sigil was etched into her thick breastplate and the shins of her plated boots. Her fingers, thick with the grime of the road, curled into a tight fist.

"This had better not be another dead end," she growled under her breath before lowering her hand to the twin-headed axe that lay secured comfortably at her side.

The beast beneath her snorted and warbled, slowing for a moment to turn its head back to face her. Its beady black eyes shimmered with concern, and she felt a stirring of emotion for her oldest companion. The woman smiled and patted the beast on the back, just beyond the saddle. Satisfied, the beast turned its attention to the road ahead.

The woman followed his gaze, and soon enough, caught sight of her destination. They were still a few hours away, but there, in the distance, just visible beyond hills of green past the nearing forest edge, was the small town of Addernotch. Danica eyed the settlement with a hard frown, and her grip on her axe tightened, while her other hand reached into her pack to withdraw a gently glowing ringstone.

    "I can hardly wait," she seethed, her eyes narrowing as long-buried hatred burned in her veins. The stone in her hand almost seemed to glow brighter in response to her conviction, and she allowed herself to become lost in the daydream of what was to come.

    "One way or another, I *will* have my pound of flesh. One way or another, kobold blood will flow."

Night Watch

Amelia spent the next hour or so giving Skunk a quick refresher course in swordplay. Due to his diminutive size and different body shape, the lessons were centered more around the fundamental principles of melee combat rather than any specific techniques. Basic parries, how to guard his vital areas, simple ripostes, practical stances, and a few tips on what *not* to do in the middle of a sword fight — like spinning.

But even with that activity, the seconds felt like hours to him. He often found his gaze drifting to the sun, marking its passage across the sky for the pale ring. It felt agonizing, but finally, *finally,* the sky began to darken with the onset of short night, and the world was painted in ominous shades of orange and purple.

With that, it was time to go. Skunk took a minute to grab his bow, a quiver of arrows, and throw on his black fur cloak before following Amelia to Addernotch's town hall. There was an eerie, tense atmosphere in the streets as they walked, and fewer people than usual could be seen out and about. Word traveled fast in a small town like this, and everyone was hunkering down in their homes in hopes of evading whatever foul creature had come knocking.

The town hall came into view soon enough. A modest, two-story affair that, to Skunk, was the pinnacle of luxury and status. Surrounded by a stonework fence, the town hall was sturdily constructed and edged with decorative patterns that ran up and down the beams and front-facing windows. A balcony jutted out from the second floor, overlooking the front yard.

Some twenty or so people, mostly human men, were gathered in that yard, each one dressed in padded armor and armed. Most held simple arming swords, spears, and wooden round shields. They were talking quietly amongst themselves, visibly tense — but also a little excited. Skunk could see Gothard standing on the front steps of the house, speaking with a withering, wrinkled old man that he knew to be the mayor.

The militia captain perked up on seeing Skunk and Amelia's approach. "Ah! There you are!" he greeted warmly. "That makes everyone. Let's get this briefing underway."

Amelia found a position by the fence gate and leaned against the stones, arms crossed over her chest. Skunk looked up at her, tilting his head at the grim expression she wore. It reminded him of the patient scowl of a prowling predator, and he did not care for it. Not on her.

Gothard's smile faded. He cleared his throat, stood upright, and spoke loudly to address the assembled troops. "Ahem. Alright, lads and lasses. In case any of you have had your heads buried in the dirt all day, here's the situation. Last night, an unknown force breached Addernotch's northern borders and made off with old Willard, his wife, and plenty of their livestock. We don't know what did it or why, but it's more intelligent than a desperate wolf or a family of hungry bears."

In the crowd, one of the men spat on the ground. "Pfah! My money's on it being the ry'thar!" he proclaimed with obvious contempt.

Amelia's expression hardened considerably. "I can assure you, it's not," she bluntly stated.

The man turned to face her, his stubbled face screwing up in disdain. "What makes ya so sure of that?" he demanded. "The lionfolk are a buncha brutes and scavengers who'd tan ya alive for lookin' at 'em funny!"

Amelia did not flinch. "If they tanned your hide because you looked at them, that says more about the quality of your face than their disposition."

A series of chuckles came from the crowd at that, and even Skunk couldn't help but laugh a little. The look on the man's face was priceless, red and puffed up with furious embarrassment. "Wha- hang on, you can't just-" he spluttered in protest.

Amelia, proving that she very well *could* and *would,* did not give him a chance to recover. "The ry'thar are different from us in many ways, but they are not brutes or savages. I lived among them for months, and am close friends with the daughter of the Karjene's current war chief. I know their ways, and this couldn't be farther from them."

Gothard added his voice to Amelia's. "And *besides* all of that, what would our neighbors stand to gain from a raid on Addernotch? They've enjoyed the benefits of trading with us for years now. Nay, Amelia's got the right of it. It's not the ry'thar. If it was, you can bet that there wouldn't be all of the secrecy. They'd have pounced, and we'd be dead."

With that, the man who spoke up looked down, thoroughly debated into submission.

Satisfied that the matter was settled, Gothard accepted a pouch from the mayor and descended the steps. "Truth is, we don't know *what* we're facing. But that is what we are here to figure out. All we know is they came from the north and were gone before we could find 'em. But our guard was down, then."

Skunk watched curiously as Gothard went from man to man, passing something out from the pouch. He realized after a few seconds that they were wooden whistles.

"We'll be splitting into teams of four," Gothard went on. "And establish a perimeter around the edge of town. We'll concentrate on the north, but we'll want a few of you to keep an eye on the other sides. If these guys come back and try to sneak around, we don't want them to find an easy way in. If you spot our wood-be assailants, or if you get into a fight..."

He held a whistle up high. "Then *blow your whistle.* Sound carries pretty far out here in the night, and these whistles are as good as they come. Blow hard, and backup will come running."

Skunk fidgeted in place, waiting to see if he and Amelia would be getting any additional instruction. Gothard came up to them and passed a whistle to Amelia. She eyed it for a second, an appreciative smile gracing her lips. "These are ry'thari whistles," she said.

Gothard nodded. "Aye. Part of our trade last spring."

Amelia ran a thumb over the whistle, then dropped it into her pocket. Gothard gave her a slow nod and a clap on the shoulder before making his way back to the steps.

"What happens if we don't find anything?" one of the troops asked, a younger man, barely in his twenties.

Gothard turned to him. "If nothing happens, then we go home and get some rest. The other half of the militia's on standby to take up a second shift if nothing happens on ours."

Skunk, tired of being quiet, took a step forward. "And if we find the bad guys?" he asked hopefully. "What do we do then?"

At once, all eyes were on him. Skunk quailed, suddenly feeling very small and out of place. The stares he was getting bored into him, and he quickly slinked back to his mother's side. He had forgotten for a moment that he was not a part of the militia. He was well and truly out of his element, and a tiny, scratching voice in the back of his head berated him for forgetting it.

Gothard came to his rescue, thankfully. His expression was grim, and the fiery ringlight did not seem to reach his eyes. "Then we fight them off. We protect our homes and our families. We can decide what to do after we're safe," he stated simply. "Juna willing, it won't come to that."

He turned his attention back to Amelia. "Amelia. I want you and your boy to have a look at the scene of the last attack. See what you can see and what your boy can sniff out."

Amelia frowned. "Did you not have your own men investigate it already?"

"Aye, I did. But my men aren't exactly trained for this kind of investigative work," Gothard shrugged. "They came up with a whole lotta nothing. You and your boy, on the other hand, might have better luck."

Amelia gave a dutiful nod as she came away from the wall. "Very well. Lead the way."

Gothard turned back to the rest of the assembled troops. "Alright! Briefing's over! Form up and move out! Try to keep within eyeshot of at least one other group at all times!"

There was a collective call of affirmation from the militia, and Skunk watched in amazement as they sprang into motion, rapidly coming together as coherent units. The organization among them was not something he typically got to see, and it stirred a primal feeling of satisfaction in his heart.

A feeling that swiftly spluttered out at the realization that he was not included.

Stifling a sigh, Skunk fell into stride beside Amelia as Gothard led the way for the north side of the town.

The stench was the first thing Skunk noticed. It struck him like a brick to the face long before the upsetting scene came into view. He knew what death smelled like, and it sent his emotions scrambling into confusion. Normally, that smell meant he'd just finished a hunt, and that meant a tasty snack or a hearty meal was soon to follow. But that feeling was muddied into disgust as he considered that the stench did not come from an intruder that had wandered into his pack's territory, or from what would be dinner that night. The small came from a dog that *had* been a part of his pack.

The scene was gruesome. Short night was ending by the time they arrived, the light of the midday sun returning to full strength. Skunk felt his stomach lurch. Willard's dog lay on its side in the dirt. The poor animal's side had been ripped open, exposing its insides. The air buzzed with a swarm of hungry flies, and the scavenger birds circling overhead had only been kept at bay by three militiamen posted to keep anyone from disturbing the scene.

Gothard led Skunk and Amelia past the waiting troops and gestured at the corpse. His eyes lingered on the dog with evident sorrow. "Poor mutt... was a sweet thing. Didn't deserve this," he said softly.

Amelia nodded quietly. She glanced down at Skunk, her expression contorting. Skunk met her gaze, eagerly awaiting instructions. A second later, his mother turned back to the dog. "Whatever did this, they probably left behind a smell. Skunk, sniff around, see if you can pick anything up," she told him curtly.

Skunk didn't say a word. He simply got to work.

Dropping down on all fours, his nose to the dirt, he started sniffing. His senses were bombarded at once by a barrage of smells that immediately struck him as odd and out of place. He cringed, trying to make sense of it. It was a jumbled mess, and it had been partially swept away by the wind and the passage of time. But still, there were details, subtle and faltering, that he was able to pick out as he crept slowly but surely around the area.

The first thing was a sharp, spicy smell. It reminded him of woodsmoke and burning charcoal. It was layered intensely with something cold and rough. Rock and snow? He frowned. There wouldn't be snowfall in Addernotch for a while yet. Why could he pick the smell out here? Shoving the question aside, he kept sniffing.

There were, of course, the scents of violence. Blood and gore, the stench of rot. He could smell something natural, musky, like body odor and dried sweat, heavily overpowering the other scents. Either Willard had been working hard and had yet to bathe, or whatever had attacked him had come in numbers. The tangy smell of tree sap and forest moss mingled with the sweat. It clung heavily to the other aromas, but not as thickly as it would have to an animal that called the forest home.

All of that was fine. But there was something else under it all. Something that Skunk found familiar, somehow. Unbearably so. It was like those times when a word got stuck right on the tip of his tongue. He pondered it for a few seconds, his brow furrowing.

And then it hit him.

This was the same thing that wolf smelled like, he thought, recalling his hunt from the other day. *But it's stronger here. Much* stronger.

Sadly, that revelation did nothing to tell him what it belonged to.

He stood up, crossing his arms over his chest. "Huh. Weird... I dunno what it is. I've only smelled it once before, on that wolf mom and I took out the other day," he relayed to the others. He turned back to them with a helpless shrug. "Whatever did this, though, there were a few of them — and I doubt they live in the forest. They don't smell right for that."

One of the nearby sentries gave Skunk a look of surprise. "You can tell all that by sniffing the dirt?" he asked incredulously.

Skunk gave him a big grin. "Sure can!"

Nearby, Gothard mirrored the smile and nodded at the soldier. "Told you."

The soldier returned the smile once his surprise wore off. "Damn! Think you could track them down?"

Skunk nodded sharply. "Uh-huh! Easily! The smell's really distinct, so it'd be cake to follow it home."

Amelia looked up. "Out of the question," she stated simply. Skunk turned to her, opening his mouth to protest, but the hard look in her eyes shut him down. She slowly shook her head. "We don't know what we're up against. Until we know more, chasing them is too much of a risk for you. Especially if they came in numbers."

Skunk felt a small blow to his pride but was quick to shrug it off. Having completed his task, he moved to join his mother by the dead dog. Amelia held up a hand, silently commanding him to stay put.

The grim look returned to Gothard's face. "What about you? Any ideas?" he asked quietly.

Amelia didn't answer for several minutes. She lightly paced around the edges of the scene, kneeling down in many places to examine the dirt and the signs of damage on the body. Every so often, her gaze flicked back to Skunk. Every time, she was visibly more and more distressed. Skunk had no clue why she would be worried about him, though. He was doing as he'd been told and sitting still.

Eventually, Amelia finished her examination and turned back to Gothard. When she spoke, her words came slowly and carefully, as if she were afraid of waking a beast. "Whatever launched this attack, they were organized, as you noted. And they were quick. There *are* prints in the dirt, but..."

She trailed off, her eyes turning to look at Skunk again.

He tilted his head at her, and his curiosity won out. "What is it?" he asked softly.

Amelia jolted as if she had been startled. She swiftly turned away and shook her head. "I don't know. But whatever they are, they are dangerous. If they come again, we will be in for a brutal fight."

Gothard hummed quietly, stroking his beard. "And the mutt?" he asked soberly. "What happened there?"

Amelia turned back to it. "Cut open with a blade," she stated simply. She pointed at the wound. "Look. The cut is clean and straight. A smooth stroke with a blade designed for that exact purpose."

"Could be bandits," one of the sentries suggested helpfully.

Gothard gestured to the dog. "It's not the usual modus operandi of common brigands to cut up a dog like this. Nor would they have been so quick and clean in their abductions. And I cannot see a tactical advantage in them deciding to withdraw without raiding the entire town. Not unless it was a really small group."

The sentry shrugged wordlessly and returned to his vigil.

It was at around this time that the rest of the militia emerged from Addernotch and took to the fields. Skunk looked around at all of them, fidgeting anxiously. "I don't like this," he murmured anxiously, an uneasy sensation pooling in his chest.

Gothard hummed. "Neither do I. Amelia, can *you* track them?"

Amelia turned to Gothard. "I think so. They left clear enough tracks to follow."

Gothard smirked. "Then let's go and see if we can't find out where our guests have pitched their camp, shall we?"

Suddenly, Skunk felt *very* offended. "Wha- HEY!" he protested, stepping forward. "Didn't you just say that it was too dangerous to go after them until we knew more?!"

Amelia turned to him with a hard look that immediately cowed him into silence. "Too dangerous for *you,*" she reiterated.

Skunk puffed up. "Oh, come on! I can take care of myself, and you know it!" he claimed, throwing his arms up into the air.

Amelia flinched, then offered him a small smile. She knelt in front of him and placed a hand on the back of his neck. "I know, Skunk," she said gently, nothing but love and affection in her voice. "But you're still a little green — if you'll pardon the pun."

Skunk puffed up his cheeks but did not dignify that with a response.

Amelia chuckled and shook her head. "Joking aside, I have a different job in mind for you."

Skunk was quiet for a second, still offended. But he couldn't stay mad at her, and he swiftly relented. "Alright, fine. What do you need?"

Amelia's smile brightened. She stood up and nodded toward the forest. "You have good eyes, especially in the dark. I need you to stay out here and join the sentries in keeping watch for the intruders. If they manage to get past Gothard and I, you will need to help with the defense effort. Think you can do that for me?"

Skunk latched onto the command with gusto, his prior offense almost instantly forgotten. He threw a sharp salute. "Yes, Mom!" he replied, his tail thumping against the ground for emphasis.

Amelia giggled softly and ruffled the kobold's head. "That's my boy," she said, her fingers sliding gently over the soft patch of scales between his horns. The gesture drew a quiet rumble of a growl from Skunk, which sounded vaguely like a big cat purring. With that, Amelia rose to her full height. She reached into her pouch and passed her whistle to Skunk. "Remember, if you catch sight of the enemy, blow on this and reinforcements will come running."

Skunk took the whistle in his hands. "Gotcha. You be careful out there, okay?"

"I will," Amelia promised. She knelt to plant a kiss on Skunk's forehead. "I love you, sweetie."

Skunk might have flushed red if his scales were capable, as he realized she did that in front of *everyone*. "Moooom!" he whined, batting her hand away. "C'mon, do ya gotta?!"

Amelia smirked. She didn't need to answer.

Skunk blew out a grumble, then relented. "Love you, too."

"There we go," Amelia said with satisfaction, then nodded to Gothard.

The man tried his best to hide his charmed smile, but Skunk could see it clear as day. A second later, the man turned to the sentries. "Form up, lads. Keep it down and do as the lady tells you. Until we get back, she's in charge!" He ordered.

The troops complied, swiftly falling into step behind Amelia as she led the way for the woods. Skunk watched them go, and slowly but surely, any satisfaction he had gotten from his task was washed away.

This whole situation didn't sit right with him, and in the silence that followed their departure, his unease only grew.

Fidgeting anxiously with the whistle, Skunk's eyes settled on a large tree with a wide and verdant canopy that rose out of one of the hills. Figuring it would provide a decent vantage point to overlook the fields, Skunk made sure he still had his lunch of dried jerky, then took off for the tree on all fours.

Skunk remained in that tree for the next several hours, attentively casting his eyes over the land. Not that there was anything to see but grass, bushes, dirt, and the militiamen making their rounds. Skunk watched them more often than not, listening as they chatted amongst themselves in high-spirited, friendly tones. They joked and laughed, displaying their camaraderie for all to see. But even as they talked, they stayed attentive, never taking their eyes off of the forest.

Whenever Skunk caught himself looking at the people instead of the forest, he would snap himself back to the task at hand. But, inevitably, his eyes would be drawn back to them, and the cycle would repeat. He couldn't help it. And every time, he felt just a little more uncomfortable on his perch. He looked left and right, becoming painfully aware of the fact that there was no one else on this branch with him.

The sun's journey toward the horizon continued at a slow and laborious crawl. Soon, the world began to tint gold with the coming of sunset. Skunk gave a glance toward the ring, its glow becoming noticeably brighter in the sky as the sun withdrew for the night.

He leaned back against the trunk of his tree, just staring at it, allowing himself to get lost in the sight of it. As it grew brighter above him, his inner turmoil slowly eased. The nostalgia came to him again, soothing and comforting, like the hazy, half-formed memory of an early birthday.

But there was something else, this time. That odd tickle in the back of his head. His brow furrowed. He'd felt it back in Seto's schoolhouse the other day. It hadn't bothered him, then, but he'd been distracted. Now, though? He sat up a little more upright, his face screwing up. *What* is *that?* He thought.

No answers came to him, however. Bit by bit, the trance he so easily fell into began to subside. The sky was being swallowed up, darkened by a veil of black clouds creeping in from the west. A distant crackle of thunder sounded, snapping Skunk back to the present. He frowned. He could already tell that tonight was going to be dark, wet, and loud.

Not that darkness was ever a problem to his eyes. Giving himself a little shake to awaken his dulled senses, Skunk returned his attention to the fields. He gave a quick scan for anything out of the ordinary. And then he frowned as something occurred to him.

Amelia and the others weren't back yet.

Now, a hunt could take a considerable amount of time, he knew that firsthand. Hours or even days could be spent tracking down a single target. But Amelia would not commit to a hunt *that* intense right now. The group hadn't brought any rations for a prolonged trip, and considering the security of the town was at stake, they weren't likely to waste time foraging. The stated objective had been to find the intruders, nothing else.

"They should have been back by now," he realized as he looked back up at the sky. With these clouds rolling in, and with the setting of the sun, Skunk knew that if all had gone well, Amelia would have doubled back long ago.

Something was *very* wrong.

Skunk felt his flesh tingling under his scales, and a thrill of anxiety ran down his spine. His instincts, suddenly alive with awareness, screamed at him to abandon this post and go after her. He shut those impulses down immediately, reminding himself that she had ordered him to stay back. He was not about to disobey that order. He held his position, but the stillness made his discomfort even worse.

The troops down below had lit up lanterns to help them see in the darkness. To Skunk's eyes, they all stood out like a lighthouse or a beacon fire. They might as well have been screaming 'I am here.' He would be able to see them from a mile away. The fact they were so visible didn't sit right with him. Doubly so when the last shafts of light from the ring were smothered by the clouds, leaving the world in absolute darkness.

Skunk huddled closer to the trunk of his tree, pulling his cloak around himself like a blanket. He scanned his eyes across the fields once again, his fingers idly toying with the hilt of his new sword at his side. Down below, he saw one of the troops moving away from the others for a particularly tall patch of grass. Skunk leaned forward, confused, wondering what this man could be up to.

A moment later, Skunk got his answer. He cringed in mild disgust and secondhand embarrassment. The man had sought the grass to relieve himself, based on his posture. Skunk politely looked away, turning his attention back to the forest. A chill wind blew by, sending the tall grass drifting with a gentle rustling noise.

Movement.

Skunk's eyes locked onto a spot in the grass, his pupils dilating to take in more light and identify the thing. He leaned forward, attentive. There was something in the grass, and it was moving *fast*, but he couldn't make out any details from where he sat. All he could tell was that it was heading straight for the oblivious soldier.

Skunk felt a rush of adrenaline. His hand flashed for his whistle while he reached his hand out. "Behind you!" he shouted at the top of his lungs. The soldier turned to him in surprise, the light of the lantern on his belt casting his flushing face in flickering orange light. The man opened his mouth to say something.

He never got the chance.

The thing in the grass rose behind the soldier. A clawed hand reached out and grabbed him around the throat. Skunk gasped, realizing with dread that the hand was tipped with sharpened claws.

Claws that dug into the militiaman's throat with ease.

Blood cascaded down the front of his padded armor and splattered against his chin.

"NO!" Skunk screamed. Instinct took over. The whistle fell from his hand as he pulled out his bow and drew an arrow, hoping to save him.

It was too late.

The unknown attacker hauled the dead man down into the grass and out of sight. Skunk fired his shot blind. He cursed under his breath as the arrow vanished uselessly into the darkness. He couldn't shoot like this, he'd never hit anything. The grass gave his target too much cover, and the brewing winds knocked his arrow far off course. It would take too long to compensate.

With a whimper of panic, Skunk drew his sword and slid down the tree, his claws leaving long gouges in the wood as he descended. The second his foot met the earth, he snatched up his whistle and blew into it as hard as he could. The ear-piercing shriek echoed across the plains, and his ears stung. As voices raised in the distance, Skunk kicked off into a wild sprint on all fours. It only took him a few seconds to cross the distance, but each one felt like an eternity, and the terror in his chest swelled with every step.

He slid to a stop a few yards from the grisly scene. He stood upright, the blood draining from his face and his stomach churning with revulsion. The soldier's body had already been brutalized.

He lay on the ground, his throat sliced open, the front of his armor torn apart. His chest had been rent wide and was now being torn into by some manner of monster. It snarled and growled, ravenous and uncaring of the bloody mess it was leaving with every clawful of meat it tore from the body.

Skunk knew he should have gone in for the attack while the monster's back was to him, but his fear left him paralyzed and almost silent.

Almost.

Skunk choked out a strangled whimper, feeling the need to retch. He took an uneasy step, the world wobbling around him.

His tiny vocalization caught the attention of the beast. It stopped its snarling meal and held still. A long, scaly tail swished behind it in agitation, and with a low growl, it picked up a cruel but primitive spear on the ground beside it as it began to rise. And as it did, Skunk began to make out more details.

The creature was slightly taller than him, but much broader. Its naked body was covered in hard green scales, its hands and feet tipped with blood-smeared claws. The back of its elongated head was decorated with two ivory horns that cursed for the sky, and its glaring yellow eyes glowed as they caught the lantern light. Blood and viscera dripped from its maw, a long tongue licking hungrily at its lips.

Skunk backed away, shaking his head in disbelief. He couldn't believe what he was seeing. "No... n-no, you can't be," he choked out, unable to find the words to finish the thought.

But it was.

A kobold.

Its body bulged with toned muscles as it rose to its full height before him. The sight of it drew another pathetic whimper out of Skunk as an instinct he had never felt before drove him to tuck his tail involuntarily between his legs. The kobold was obviously stronger than him, and he backed away in a sign of submission.

The kobold eyed him for a moment, noting his clothes and the sword in his hand. Its lips peeled back, affording Skunk another look at its yellowing teeth. Skunk was so absorbed by the sight that he barely even noticed when the sounds of battle and screaming began to rise up in the plains around him, accompanied by a chorus of whistles. The kobold growled again and uttered only a single word, its voice like fire and landslides.

"Traitor."

With that declaration, the kobold's mouth opened wide, issuing forth a horrific roar before it aimed its spear squarely at Skunk's heart and lunged.

Blood on the Grass

Skunk scrambled back from the taller kobold's lunge with a panicked scream, barely batting aside the oncoming strike. His parry did nothing to disrupt the kobold's charge, however. It barreled into him with its shoulder, bearing him to the ground and driving the air from his lungs. Skunk wheezed, his vision swimming as the monster fell upon him, a flurry of teeth and fangs going for his throat. He tried to force it off, but its larger bulk held him against the ground. Its teeth snapped dangerously close to his face, sending his heart leaping into his throat. A foul stench rolled across his face, hot and sticky, making him cringe.

The kobold, impatient, reared back and raised its sharpened claws to plunge them into Skunk's face. Thankfully, he was faster. Skunk jerked his head to one side, allowing the oncoming claws to harmlessly pierce the blood-slick soil. Then, with an animalistic snarl of his own, he bit down into his enemy's wrist. The scales offered a moment of resistance before yielding to his teeth, and warm blood gushed into his mouth.

Kobold blood.

He suddenly felt sick, and he almost retched. The sound of the kobold above him roaring in pain and anger only served to amplify the chaos of his confused emotions. Still, his survival instincts made their demands, and Skunk was powerless to disobey. He dragged his teeth along the other kobold's forearm, shredding glistening scale and rippling muscle. The kobold reared back with a scream, its wide eyes staring at its mutilated wrist in shock.

Skunk took the moment of weakness to squirm out and get away. He felt a whoosh in the air behind him as he scrambled to his feet, and something scraped against the back of his horn, knocking him off balance. He staggered forward several paces before rising and spinning back to face his enemy, bringing his sword with him in a clearing swipe. A wise move, as the strike knocked aside another thrust from the kobold's spear.

"Why are you doing this?!" Skunk shouted, his voice trembling in fear.

The kobold did not answer. It shook off the pain and pressed the attack, thrusting and swiping with its spear with only one hand. The attacks were slower and less precise, but the kobold had training and experience that Skunk dearly lacked. Every barely-parried swing forced him to retreat, and despite his efforts, his adversary left several shallow cuts in his scales where his guard proved lacking.

Eventually, the kobold came in with another charge, letting out a powerful roar that sent Skunk's instincts flailing. Barely stifling a whimper, he dove to one side in a clumsy roll. As he came up, he turned to face his enemy, his blade held in front of him. The kobold turned, digging its feet into the ground and gouging shallow trenches into the dirt. It pushed its good arm out, extending its spear to its full length, and brought it down in a wide, low-sweeping arc. Skunk gasped as the shaft of the spear smashed into his ankles with such force that it splintered and snapped.

He fell off his feet, crashing once again onto the ground. Grunting, he rolled onto his back. The kobold was lunging for him, its broken spear cast aside, its claws angled for his throat. In a flash of terror, Skunk held his sword out in front of him as far as he could. He looked away, screwing his eyes shut in preparation for the end.

A great weight slammed into his arms, jolting his shoulders, and something warm and wet slapped across his face. The smell of blood flooded his nostrils. But it wasn't his blood.

He heard the kobold gurgling above him, and he slowly opened his eyes. His heart skipped a beat, and his breath hitched.

The kobold had impaled itself on Skunk's sword, having not had time to alter course as it fell upon him. The blade was buried halfway to the hilt in its throat. Fresh blood dribbled over the crossguard and Skunk's trembling hands in thick streams. Its eyes locked onto Skunk's, wide and unreadable. It worked its jaw as if still trying to bite him. More blood fell from its quivering lips to splatter against Skunk's face.

As the strength left its body and its muscles gave out, it slid down another few inches. Skunk cringed as metal scraped through flesh and bone, and whimpered as the kobold's nose pressed against his. Its lips peeled back in a hate-filled snarl, and through the blood clogging its throat, it managed to utter a single word.

"Traitor."

And then it fell limp. Its heavy weight settled on top of Skunk, pinning him to the earth.

He lay there for a moment, frozen. He couldn't move or breathe or anything. He could only stare, slack-jawed and horrified at the corpse. Its dead eyes were wide open, dull, and glassy.

His stomach churned, and Skunk found his voice again. A strangled, raspy whimper escaped his lips as he tried desperately to force the body off of him, his muscles straining against its bulk, his lungs burning. It was hard to breathe through the stench of death. It was suffocating.

Gasping, Skunk began to squirm in a desperate bid to just get out from under this thing.

He had to get away.

He needed space, he needed *air!*

Using all of the strength in his legs and arms, Skunk finally managed to pry the corpse off of him. He was hyperventilating as he rolled onto his hands and knees. Irreconcilable feelings assaulted his mind. His skin was crawling under his scales, tingling and itching like a mountain of roaches. His stomach twisted, his heart hammered against his ribs, and blood surged through his veins. His instincts were in an uproar, screaming at him to run, to fight, to cower, grovel, beg, scream, and cry. Every command conflicted, leaving him paralyzed.

He heaved, the partially digested remains of his lunch and breakfast splattering against the ground, mingling with the viscera. "Oh gods," he gasped when he could speak again, his voice hoarse and his throat raw. He tried to rise, only to fall back on his backside. His hand found his chest as if he might somehow calm the pounding of his heart.

His eyes fell on the other kobold's corpse, and the pool of blood spreading across the ground beneath it.

Skunk was unable to look away. He had killed creatures before, and he had never enjoyed it. But never once had the act of taking a life left him feeling so awful. He didn't understand, and that only served to scare him even more. What was wrong with him?! Primal cries of distress escaped him, leaving without his permission.

The scream of another human being killed answered his cries, and Skunk realized with dread that the horrors of the night were far from over. Rolling back to his hands and knees, he looked out across the fields. The lights from the militia's lanterns were flailing wildly. Some of them suddenly snuffed out with the shattering of glass. Others suddenly tinted red as blood sprayed across the glass. The screams were accompanied by clashing steel, hungry growls, and the sharp shriek of whistles that ended far too abruptly.

The kobold he had killed wasn't the only one. There were *many*.

"Oh, gods..." Skunk breathed again, his stomach twisting into knots when he saw a pack of four of them bounding through the grass not far away. A man charged to meet them, roaring a battle cry with his sword and shield raised. The first kobold ducked to one side, dodging his swing, and buried its claws into the man's waist. He yelled, turning to try and pry it off of him, but this only left him vulnerable. The next three pounced, throwing the entirety of their weight against him and hauling him to the ground. Skunk could hear him screaming.

And then he couldn't.

The same thing was happening all over. Many of the militiamen that Skunk could see from here did not last long. Those who were able to fight off their attackers would not last for long. Against numbers like this, they would swiftly be overwhelmed.

It was a massacre.

"W-what do I do?!" Skunk stammered, trembling as he forced himself to his feet. He had been ordered to stay here, to help with the defense in case of an attack. But nothing could have prepared him for a fight like *this*. He had thought it was a small group they'd be dealing with! Not a small *army*! His thoughts turned to his mother and Gothard, and his heart dropped.

Against a force like this, what chance did *they* have?

Stay and help Addernotch, or run and help his mother. Those were the only options Skunk could see. He looked down at his blood-stained hands, then realized with a start that he no longer had his sword. He looked around frantically, and his eyes soon found it buried in the dead kobold's throat.

Whimpering guiltily, he rolled the corpse onto its back and pulled the sword free. The scrape and *shlick* of the edge leaving dead flesh sent a thrill of disgust down Skunk's spine to pool and tingle at the base of his tail. Holding the sword loosely, he turned to the battlefield.

The other half of the night watch that had been stationed around the other sides of town was arriving now, drawn by the sounds of battle. With their arrival, the enemy's element of surprise lost some of its edge. A proper defense was starting to come together. Still, they had suffered heavy losses in the opening moments of the ambush, and the enemy had undoubtedly broken past them. The forces in town didn't have time to prepare themselves. A fact that was made clear when Skunk saw the first signs of a spreading fire.

Sylvia and Seto were in there. They couldn't fight. They would be helpless.

At that moment, the choice was made for him. Skunk set his jaw, cleaned and sheathed his sword, lowered himself onto all fours, and broke into a sprint, his clawed feet kicking up sprays of dirt and grass as he ran. He tried to ignore the bodies he passed on the way, human and kobold alike. *Protect Addernotch,* he thought to himself. *Protect Seto. Protect Sylvia. Protect my pack. That's all that matters!*

Amelia grunted with strain as she drove her boot into the chest of the third kobold to try and kill her in the last minute. She maintained the momentum, pinning the kobold to the earth beneath her. Its eyes glared at her with vicious contempt, its sharpened claws reaching for her ankle. She did not give it a chance and loosed an arrow into its eye at point-blank range. Its life ended with a twang and a wet thud. Behind her, she heard Gothard's sword rending the flesh of his own enemy. She turned to see the old man doubled over, clutching at his chest and gasping for air.

He turned to face Amelia. He was speckled with blood, his padded armor torn in places where kobold spears and claws had managed to get past his guard. "Was that the last of them?"

"In this group, at least," Amelia growled, pulling her arrow out of the dead kobold. She looked around at the chaos that surrounded them.

Tracking their mysterious invaders back to their source in the woods had been easy enough, but it had taken time. They found a small campsite that could have housed no more than five or six. They had been traveling light, and Amelia assumed they had been living off the land as they made their approach to the town. The camp had been empty when they arrived, but the signs of their presence were clear enough, most prominently in the slabs of carved meat dangling over a burned-out campfire.

Human meat.

Their missing villagers.

Amelia had suspected what they were up against before they left Addernotch. The signs were clear enough. She'd figured they were dealing with a small band of raiders. It wasn't uncommon behavior for their kind.

Still, a small pack, while dangerous, was manageable. A plan had been drawn up to simply wait for the hunters to return to their camp and take them down in an ambush. Gothard had sent one of their number back to warn the rest of the militia what they were up against before everyone else spread out and got into position. Everything had been in place, and Amelia thought it would be an easy day.

But then the rest of the horde arrived.

The realization had dawned on them with a rising tide of dread. Their small team of kobolds returned, yes. But there were more with them. And then more. And *more*. Soon enough, it became clear that the camp they had found was not that of a small raiding party.

They were scouts working for a much larger force.

The moment that realization was made, Amelia motioned to Gothard's hiding place. They needed to *go*. They were in no way able to fight this many kobolds with the small numbers they had brought. He had agreed, and they attempted to withdraw without drawing attention. In retrospect, Amelia knew they would never get away without being noticed. If their sense of smell was anything like Skunk's, there was no hope of avoiding detection.

The remainder of Gothard's men were sniffed out only seconds after the order to withdraw was given. Amelia heard their voices rising in alarm, before being snuffed into dreadful silence. All that had been left to do was run and pray.

The resulting chase had not been as brutal as Amelia had expected. Spears, arrows, and gnashing fangs were at their backs for only a short while before breaking off. Distressingly, Amelia and Gothard had been forced to flee *north,* away from Addernotch. And with an increasingly large force of kobolds now ahead of them, marching the way they needed to go, they were forced to proceed at a plodding pace, unable to get back and warn the town — and they still kept running into straggling groups made of smaller, weaker kobolds that lacked the stamina to keep up with their bulkier leaders.

Amelia could only hope Gothard's messenger made it back in time.

Gothard growled, wiping his blade off on a rag before jogging up to Amelia's side. "I've never heard of a band of kobolds this large," he said under his breath. "Not without a dragon to command them."

Amelia frowned. "And the green scales are without a dragon," she pointed out. "According to Seto, at least."

"Well, whatever the case, we should just be grateful that they elected not to keep chasing us," Gothard pointed out. "Now come on. Who commands them won't mean much if we can't fight them off."

Amelia nodded and took in a deep breath to calm her nerves. Years of practice came into effect, and cold, calculating instinct took over. "The main force is ahead of us," she said clinically. "And Addernotch isn't far. What do you imagine the town's chances are?"

Gothard grunted, the two of them starting the return trek to the village. "Against a force like this, not great. If the kobolds get into the streets, a lot of innocent people will get caught up in the fighting, and I get the impression that's what these monsters want." Gothard growled, his hands clenched into fists at his sides. "Grah! This whole situation is a tactical nightmare! My people are good, but they were never prepared for a situation like *this!*"

Amelia shook her head. "Then we need to get back and help them."

They had to take a long way around and move agonizingly slowly to avoid running into the bulk of the enemy force, and even then their trek occasionally brought them into the path of another pack. It would be a simple matter for Amelia and Gothard to take them down, being the experienced fighters they were. But between the time it would waste and the risk of drawing more attention, they chose to hide and let the enemies pass them by.

By the time Addernotch came into view, the worst of the fighting had already broken out. Amelia came to a stop by the edge of the woods, a horrid feeling gripping her heart.

The messenger must not have made it. Or if he did, his warnings had been insufficient.

A sizable section of the village was already on fire, and the flames were spreading fast. She could see the silhouettes of their enemy against the firelight, carving through the streets in a relentless rampage. More silhouettes clashed with them while others ran in a desperate bid to get away. The militia seemed to be giving as good as they were getting, but that would only do so much for them. After all, the kobolds had so much more to give than Addernotch.

"It's bad, but it could be a *lot* worse," Gothard observed, his mustache quivering as he put on a tiny, proud smile. "And look. There's a clear line. The kobolds are trying to push west. I say we head in at the eastern end of town and work our way west, rally survivors, and hit them from the back."

Amelia, however, was barely listening. She watched the flames crawling along one of the rooftops, eating away at thatch and straw and wood. Her home may very well have already been swallowed by the flames. And Skunk was in the middle of all of that.

"Amelia!"

Amelia blinked and turned to Gothard, her mind processing what he'd said. He put his hand on her shoulder. "I'm sure your boy is fine. You taught him well. We'll keep an eye out for him, but for now, I need you to *focus.*"

Amelia took a deep breath, forcing her near-panic over Skunk's safety into submission. She steeled herself and gave the older man a grateful smile. "Lead the way," she said.

Gothard nodded before drawing his sword and charging ahead for town. Amelia nocked an arrow and fell in a short distance behind him, her old battle instincts returning to the forefront.

Hold on, Skunk, she thought. *I'm on my way!*

Skunk swapped back to his bow as soon as he was in the streets, trusting his aim at a distance over his lack of skill with a blade. He climbed up the first house he came to and ran along the rooftops, heading for Seto's place. As he ran, his elevated position gave him a very good look at the situation.

It was absolute chaos. Most regular people were scattering in terror before the advancing horde of kobolds. The slowest of them were run down in the streets, pinned down, and dragged out of sight by their ankles before anyone had the chance to help them. They kicked and screamed the entire way, powerless.

Others tried to defend themselves or their families, picking up whatever tools and weapons they could. Their efforts were valiant, but they lacked training, and in the end, most were overwhelmed and violently incapacitated. Some were able to capitalize on their larger size or grouped up with others to form a functional counter-offensive — but it wasn't going to last.

Others still hid in their homes, trying to keep the kobolds from knowing they were even there. They did not count on their enemy's sense of smell, sadly, and were often the targets of the invader's flames. They either burned alive in their homes or were forced to flee into the streets, where the enemy was waiting for them.

Skunk tried to help where he could, firing arrows at kobolds as he ran for the schoolhouse, but most of his shots missed. His confused instincts and the chaos around him threw off his aim. Every missed shot stung, each one a life he failed to save.

Skunk slid to a halt when he saw a man from the militia standing in an alley. Behind him, a woman was sheltering her child, their bodies pressed tight against the back wall of an emptied home. A trio of kobolds advanced on them with murder in their eyes, each one wielding a blood-stained bone club. The militiaman hid behind a round wooden shield while he leveled the tip of his halberd at his enemies.

"Get back!" he barked at the kobolds, swinging his polearm in warning. "I said get back! All of you!"

One of the kobolds snarled and lunged, drawing the man's attention. With a cry, he turned to drive the shaft of his halberd into the kobold's side, sending it crashing into the wall beside it. The swing left the man open, however, and the second kobold charged in with a delighted roar. He tried to lift his shield to catch it but was too slow. Skunk watched in terror as he was dragged to the ground.

"NO!" Skunk screamed, and this time, he didn't wait to fire his arrow. It shot through the air with a sharp whistle and punctured the kobold in the back of the head, allowing the militiamen to shove it aside and rise. The third kobold turned to look where the arrow had come from. It caught sight of Skunk and bared its teeth.

Skunk took an involuntary step back, his hand fumbling as he reached for another arrow. There it was again, that surge of conflicting instincts. *What is wrong with me?!* He yelled internally, frustration rising alongside his confusion.

Thankfully, the kobold's attention was on him, meaning it didn't realize until it was too late that the axe head of the soldier's halberd was descending onto its skull. Skunk cringed as the kobold's head was split open like a watermelon, brains and blood spilling forth as it crumpled to the ground.

At this point, the first kobold to charge had recovered from its untimely meeting with the wall. It saw a chance to get past the soldier and took it, springing at the woman and her child. The soldier turned after it, crying out.

Skunk grit his teeth and forced himself to focus through his confusion. He managed to draw and shoot his second arrow, but it came up short, only glancing off the kobold's foot. It reached the woman and swung its club. Skunk shouted, afraid he was going to see their blood and limbs scattering to the ground.

While he was relieved that didn't happen, his relief turned to dread when the kobold discarded his club and turned back to the man, the child clutched tightly in its hands, and its claws held up to the boy's throat. The woman lay limp on the ground behind the kobold, her hands clutching her head.

"Let him go!" the soldier shouted, keeping his halberd ready to thrust at a moment's notice.

Skunk heard the kobold cackling, a horrible sound that terrified and *thrilled* him. The conflicting emotions made him hesitate again, his hand hovering uselessly over his next arrow.

The kobold's grip on the boy tightened, and Skunk could hear his wails even from here.

"Give yourself up," the kobold growled. "Drop your weapon and the meat will live."

The man hesitated. Skunk could not see his face from here, but he could only imagine his eyes darting between the boy and the kobold threatening him. A moment later, the boy screamed, tears running down his cheeks before drying in the heat. "Dad, help! Don't let it hurt me!"

The soldier's resolve crumbled like a house of cards in a stiff wind. He slumped, dropping his halberd to the ground with a clatter. "Damn you, beast!" he shouted. "If you hurt Connor in any way, then I swear to all the gods-"

The kobold cackled mockingly, but it did not release its hold on the boy.

Nor, Skunk realized, did it see what he could. On the back of the soldier's hip was a sheathed dagger, his left hand hovering over it. The way his body was turned hid the motion from the kobold's sight. He was waiting for a chance to charge in and save the boy.

Skunk, seeing a chance to give the man the opening he needed, drew his arrow. The kobold saw him, though, and shifted, putting the boy between them. Skunk cursed under his breath. The kobold was shifting back and forth behind Connor, leaving Skunk incapable of taking the shot. He was good, but from this distance, he couldn't be sure he'd hit his target or hit the boy he was trying to save.

"You coward!" he screamed, lowering his bow with a huff of rage.

The kobold's smirk turned into a furious scowl, and it answered Skunk's accusation with an indignant roar. It spoke at him in a language he did not understand, the words harsh, guttural, and thick with bitter contempt.

Thankfully, its impassioned rant left it unable to hear the woman rising behind it. She held the kobold's discarded club in her hand, and with a scream of rage, brought it down on the kobold. Its movement made her miss its head. The blow instead came down on its shoulder. Even from here, Skunk could hear bones crunching.

The kobold gasped, its claws falling away from the boy's throat as its own bones tore apart its muscles. It turned dizzily back to the woman, only for her to follow up with a powerful blow to the front of its face. It staggered back against the wall of the alley, clutching at its bleeding muzzle with an agonized gurgle. The boy saw his chance to run, sprinting into his father's waiting arms.

Skunk had a clear shot. With a snarl of vindication, he fired his arrow. It sailed through the air, silent and deadly, and punctured the kobold's side. The shaft buried deep, and the creature dropped to the ground. It twitched once, looking vaguely in Skunk's direction, then fell still.

There was a brief moment of calm as the fight ended, and the mother ran out to join her son and husband, only wobbling slightly. Skunk shouldered his bow and slid down the wall of the house, digging his claws into the wood to slow his descent. Once he was on the ground, he ran to check on the family. "Hey! Are you alright?" he asked, gasping for breath.

The boy's eyes locked on him and went wide. He screamed, pressing himself tighter against his parents for protection.

Skunk drew up short, horrified by the looks he received. He felt as if he had just been struck. Shame and guilt washed over him as the parents turned to him, their eyes ablaze with a storm of emotions. Fear, confusion, hatred, and so many others. All directed at Skunk.

"Go away!" The boy shouted before his father could silence him.

Skunk's heart twisted in his chest. He took a step back, shaking his head with a stiff neck. "I... I'm not..." he tried, but the words died in his throat.

Somewhere nearby, someone screamed, and Skunk was reminded that he was in the middle of an active battlefield. He looked down for a moment, his hands clenching into fists. "Arm yourselves and get somewhere safe," was all he said. Then, without another word, he dropped to all fours and started running. He didn't dare to look back.

If he had, he might have seen the mother's hand reaching after him.

Skunk was fortunate enough to meet no further opposition on the way. Seto's schoolhouse came into view, free of fire for now. A handful of militiamen were stationed outside of it, forming a defensive line at the bridge with spears and shields. A duo of archers stood on the other side of the stream.

The soldiers saw him approach, and the archers were quick to draw their arrows. Skunk slid to a halt and quickly lifted his hands over his head. "W-wait! Don't shoot!" he called. "It's me! It's Skunk! I'm on your side!"

The soldiers hesitated for a moment, looking among themselves.

Before they could say anything, the door was thrown open. Sylvia stepped out, disheveled, pale, and in her nightgown, but unharmed. "Skunk! Come on, get inside!" she called, beckoning to him.

Skunk took that as permission to approach and started forward at a jog. On hearing the woman's voice, the soldiers saw no reason to bar his path. However, the furious, hate-filled glares Skunk received as he ran past them hurt far worse than any arrow or blade ever could. He tried to ignore them as he scampered up the steps.

The moment he reached Sylvia, he threw his arms around her as tight as he dared, as if she would vanish into smoke if he didn't. Shuddering, he buried his face into her shoulder. "Thank the Five. You're alright," he breathed. "I was so worried about you."

"Forget about me!" Sylvia protested, pulling back to look Skunk up and down with dawning horror. She reached a hand up to touch his face. "What about you?! You're covered in blood!"

Skunk shook his head. "I'm alright. M-most of it isn't mine," he tried to assure her.

"And that makes it better?" Sylvia rebuked.

Skunk was quiet for a moment, then sagged. "No."

Sylvia frowned but said nothing more. She turned and ushered him inside, closing the door behind them.

The schoolhouse was packed with children and their parents. Some gave Skunk wary looks as he entered, the parents in particular. He felt another stab of hurt at the accusations in their eyes, and the unspoken words behind them rang loud and clear in his head.

You did this.

This is all your fault.

You're one of them.

You monster.

He shook his head, trying to banish the irrational thoughts. He turned and tried to focus on finding Seto. The old krauven was in the back, kneeling beside a little girl sitting and crying in the corner. His hand was on her shoulder, and he was whispering something to her. Skunk felt himself relax, but only a little. He moved across the room, careful to keep his distance from everyone else.

Seto looked up and beamed with relief. He rose to draw Skunk into a hug of his own. "Oh, Skunk! Thank Suna, you are unharmed," he said, his old voice quaking with relief. "You *are* unharmed, aren't you?"

Skunk returned the embrace, nodding slowly. "A little scuffed, but I'm alright," he lied before turning to look at the rest of the building. "How bad is it?"

Seto frowned. "Bad," he said grimly. "This is a schoolhouse, not a refugee center. I just don't have the resources at hand to shelter this many people, especially without any warning. But the parents didn't know where else to go, so here we are."

Sylvia pursed her lips together. "I don't like it. The school is out in the open. We're exposed and vulnerable. Our only line of defense is the militiamen stationed outside, but they are few and just as scared as the children."

Seto shook his head. "I don't like it either, but where else *could* they go, hm? We're days away from any other settlement, surrounded by grassland in all directions. To flee into the hills would leave these families directionless and even more exposed than they are here. The enemy is coming *from* the forest, so heading there for cover is suicide. At least here there's a line of pikemen and walls between us and the creatures that want to kill us."

Skunk frowned, glancing out the window. He recalled how the kobold with the boy had demanded the soldier surrender. The more he thought about it, the more he began to wonder if killing them was what the kobolds were here for, or if something else drove their actions.

He did not voice those curiosities for now, though. Silence returned, bringing with it the anxiety and the crawling restlessness. Skunk growled under his breath, the claws on his feet digging into the floorboards as his toes curled. He reached up to take hold of his horns as the adrenaline began to wear off, and the dreadful reality of the situation finally began to set in.

His home was burning. His people were dying. They were pinned and trapped, and there was nothing they could do about it. People he had known since he was a baby were being eaten alive or dragged off into the night, and he had been powerless to save them. The one time he *had* been able to help, his efforts had been rewarded with fear and suspicion. He still had no idea where his mother was, and to top it all off, he had killed three kobolds tonight.

He felt dizzy. The sounds of the children crying and the fires raging outside were muffled into an indistinct white noise. Phantom screams and battle cries licked at the edges of his thoughts. His chest tightened, squeezing his lungs, strangling him. Breathless and light-headed, Skunk fell to the floor in a trembling heap.

"Skunk?!" he heard from above him, and he felt something cool and soft wrapping around his hand. He grasped it tightly, too tightly, his mind and world spinning. *Why is this happening? Why are they here? Why did they make me kill them? Oh, gods,* why *did they make me kill them?! Why?! Why?! WHY?!*

When some air finally made it into his lungs, it immediately left him in the form of a long wail of distress. He screwed his eyes shut to try and block it all out, but against the darkness of his eyelids, everything he had seen tonight surged back, vivid and clear. Gaping wounds, lifeless eyes, his home in flames, and blood on the grass.

"Skunk, hey. It's going to be okay," someone said above him. He was numbly aware of something pulling him up to lean him against the wall. Something wrapped around him, and his fracturing mind recognized it as a hug. Choking down his sobs, Skunk latched onto whatever it was for all he was worth. He felt a hand on the back of his head, and soothing sounds whispered into his ear.

Slowly but surely, the familiar motions began to chase away the anxiety attack. He heard someone urging him to take a deep breath, and he did. The old pattern came back to him easily. Inhale, hold. Exhale, hold. Inhale, hold. Exhale, hold.

Finally, Skunk's world began to come back into focus. Sylvia was the one holding him and stroking the back of his head. Seto knelt beside them, a hand on Skunk's shoulder. "You're going to be okay. I promise," he whispered. "We'll get through this."

Sylvia drew back to look him in the eyes.

The moment was broken by a commotion outside. Skunk's blood ran cold when he heard the soldiers shouting. Everyone went still as the sounds of battle broke out beyond the walls.

"Damnit," Seto growled before standing and striding through the room, speaking as loudly as he dared. "Children, hide! Under tables, in the back room, anywhere out of sight! Quick and quiet. Parents, help me barricade the door! let's go!"

Everyone was swift to obey, the children moving to hide in a flurry of frantic silence while their parents moved to push things in front of the door. Tables and chairs, mostly. Skunk, however, did not participate. His attention remained fixed on the door. It almost seemed to be growing in his vision, swelling and rotating to loom in front of him like the profile of some hungering beast.

He swallowed heavily. The sounds of battle carried on outside for a moment longer. He heard a soldier utter a horrified scream that abruptly cut off. And then it was silent.

Their defenses were gone.

Skunk shivered again. If the kobolds reached this building, they would just set it ablaze as well. The barricade would trap everyone inside. Even if they didn't die in the resulting inferno, there was nowhere to run, and Skunk knew well enough that they couldn't hide from a kobold's nose.

The instinct to protect his pack reared its head, overpowering his fear, and Skunk was on his feet before he even realized it. He turned to Seto, who was about to withdraw into the back room as well. The two made eye contact. Skunk took a breath. "I'll lead them away," he said, trying to project confidence he did not feel.

Sylvia turned to him sharply, her eyes blazing with disapproval. "What? Skunk, no-"

"If you all stay put here, you're dead. They'll just light the schoolhouse on fire if the door slows them down. The barricade's useless. But besides all of that... They're kobolds," Skunk reasoned. "And so am I. I'm... They think I'm a traitor. I'll be a more tempting target. I'll draw them away. While I do that, the rest of you *run*. Hiding won't work, trust me. They'll just sniff you out."

"But what about you?" Seto asked, crossing the distance between them.

Skunk turned to him. "I can look after myself," he said, though he was not sure he believed it. A moment passed. Skunk's expression softened. "Please. I have to help, somehow."

Seto gave Skunk a solemn nod. "Very well. If that is what you believe is best. Just be careful. And come back alive."

Skunk felt relief at Seto's allowance, but Sylvia was not so easily convinced. "Seto! They'll kill him!" she protested, coming up to Skunk and placing a hand on his shoulder. "Please, don't go."

Skunk turned to her, his lips curling up into a tender smile. "I gotta do *something*, don't I? You're my pack."

Sylvia opened her mouth to retort, but nothing came. She looked into Skunk's eyes long and hard, looking for something. Whatever she found, it convinced her she couldn't talk him down. And so, with a grim nod, she gave Skunk a quick hug and backed away. Skunk's hand twitched after her as she withdrew, knowing that there was a good chance that would be the last time he'd ever feel that embrace, and wanting nothing more than to pull her back in and never let go.

Steeling himself, he turned to the nearest window. He didn't look back at the others, fearing their eyes might make him reconsider. With a quick leap, he scrambled up the wall and climbed out.

He landed on the grass outside in a low crouch, his bow already in his hands. Moving as quickly as he dared, Skunk crept around the side of the schoolhouse and peered across the yard to get a better look at the opposition. He planned to shout at the kobolds, make a big show of being a traitor, and run off to lure them away. But what he saw in front of the school killed his plans before he could put them into motion.

The soldiers lay sprawled across the road on the other side of the bridge, dismembered in a brutally elegant fashion. None of the kobolds he had seen tonight had been capable of anything like that, and Skunk felt a thrill of fear at the idea of facing an enemy that *could*.

But he saw no kobolds. Only one creature, unlike any he had ever seen before. It stood upright, nearly seven feet tall, with a muscular body covered in green scales, just like the kobolds. Runes had been carved into the creature's arms, legs, chest, and even its eyebrows, each one glowing with the same light as the pale ring. A thin-bladed, curved sword was held casually in the creature's hand, the sort of weapon one might see in the hands of a fencer. Nothing like the crude and barbaric designs used by the kobolds. Still, the blade dripped with blood — presumably, the blood of the dead soldiers.

But most striking of all were the wings that stretched from the creature's back, unmistakably dragonlike in appearance. Its similarly draconic head, adorned with ridged horns, observed the fallen bodies with an almost bored expression. Its yellow eyes swept over the carnage with obvious contempt.

It was *wrong*. Skunk could not express why, but everything about this *thing* was incorrect. Disturbing. Aberrant. An overwhelming feeling of disgust formed in his gut as if the mere sight of this thing was a violation of his body. He let off an involuntary growl.

A sound he came to regret, as the creature lifted its eyes to stare directly at him.

First Fang

Skunk and the figure stared at one another for several long seconds, the only sound being the distant roaring of the fire and pitched battle. Skunk swallowed heavily, wishing for nothing more than to withdraw, but the creature's gaze held him, transfixing him. It slowly tilted its head, its eyes shimmering with curiosity.

Suddenly, it spoke. "Step forward, little one. Into the light, where I can see you."

Skunk blinked. Its voice was smooth and masculine, laced with a subtle accent he was unfamiliar with. It was not at all the guttural snarl he would have expected, nor was it the feral yapping of the kobolds flooding Addernotch. It sounded refined, like the drawl of a pampered noble.

For a moment, Skunk braced to flee, as planned. But something held him in place. He couldn't explain why, but suddenly he was emerging from the shadows to face the creature. He walked with slow, halting steps and shakily placed himself between the towering creature and the schoolhouse.

The creature quirked an eyebrow at him, sizing him up while looking over his nose at him. "A rather small one, aren't you?" he noted casually. "State your name, runt."

"Skunk," he answered before slapping a hand over his mouth. The answer had come unbidden, without his consent. *Does this guy have some sort of mind control power or something?*

The creature frowned. "Skunk? As in the animal with the wretched stench?" his expression soured. "Disgraceful."

Shaking off his anxiety, Skunk lowered his hand and spread his stance defensively. "W-who are you?!" he demanded, trying and failing to hide the fearful quiver in his voice. "I told you my name, now you tell me yours!"

The creature almost looked amused by Skunk's attempt at bravery. He took a few confident strides toward him, and the feeling of wrongness under Skunk's skin grew worse. Then the creature tucked one foot back and dipped into a graceful bow, its blade held off to one side.

"I am First Fang Karak, servant of the Emerald Fire. Charmed."

Skunk took a step back. His sweat-slick hands held his bow so tight they were trembling. "O-okay. A-and why are you here?" he asked a second later. "Why are you doing this? Why are you attacking Addernotch?! We've done nothing to you!"

Karak stood back up, tilting his head. "We?" he echoed curiously. "You mean to tell me you stand beside these... *things?*"

Skunk's lips peeled back in a vicious snarl. "This is my home! These are my people!" he shouted, barely holding himself back from firing an arrow from his bow.

Karak snorted. "A green scale? Living with humans? Ridiculous," he grunted dismissively before taking a step forward.

"Why are you here?!" Skunk shot back, drawing an arrow and aiming it directly at Karak's throat. "Answer me! *Why?!*"

Karak paused, eyeing the taut bowstring with evident boredom. "I *would* ask why it concerns you so," he said slowly before pointing his sword at Skunk's pounding heart. "But for daring to bear arms against me, you have forfeited such a courtesy."

Skunk didn't even have time to realize that Karak was on the move before the first swing came. His eyes widened with shock as Karak kicked off the ground, the runes in his scaled body pulsing with light. They hissed audibly like water drops sizzling on an iron pan. Karak was upon Skunk in a blink, his blade swinging from the side and carving effortlessly through the wooden shaft of the bow.

Skunk leaned back, barely keeping his head. He toppled back to the ground, thrown off balance as the release of the tension in his bowstring sent both halves of the weapon flying into the air. He went for his sword, only for Karak's clawed foot to smash into his face. A horrible *crunch* filled Skunk's head alongside a fiery agony. He might have screamed, had the air not then been driven from his lungs when his back mashed into the front steps of the schoolhouse.

Karak scoffed and advanced at a casual, measured pace, one hand folded behind his back and his sword held loosely off to one side. "Your reflexes are pitiful. No wonder you were abandoned."

Skunk sucked in a lungful of air, his hand once again reaching for his sword as fire burned in the back of his skull. A furious growl sounded from the bottom of his throat. "Shut UP!" he roared, drawing the blade free and throwing himself at Karak, aiming for the heart. His blade only found empty air, Karak side-stepping the thrust with insulting ease.

Karak's hand latched onto the back of Skunk's head and drove him down to the ground at the base of the stairs. Skunk screamed again as his nose struck the hard-packed dirt. Something gave way, and suddenly, he could taste blood. His sinuses were flooded with wet warmth and the smell of copper. He tried to get his hands under him to rise, but Karak's grip was impossibly strong, keeping him pinned.

"You do not lack bravery, I will admit," Karak mused, not even straining against Skunk's struggles. "But bravery alone does not give you value. You are small. Weak. Runts like you aren't worth the meat it would take to raise you. That the humans would invest in you is yet more proof of their ignorance."

Skunk managed to turn his head free of the dirt, one eye glaring into Karak's face with bitter contempt. The monster looked at him as if he were waiting for a child to be done with a temper tantrum. It was maddening, and all of Skunk's nerves lit aflame with indignant rage. He screamed his throat raw, ignoring the blood leaking out of his mouth and nose. "I said shut up!" he snapped. Thinking fast, he swung his tail up as hard as he could into Karak's hip. The blow carried little force, but it did draw the thing's attention. Karak turned to the offending appendage with a growl, his eyes narrowing with growing impatience.

That one moment of looking away was all Skunk needed.

With a grunt, he reversed his grip on his sword and swung back with all of his might, aiming for Karak's thigh. He felt a moment of resistance and a surge of pride as his blade found its mark, biting into Karak's scales and drawing blood. The dragon-man gasped, flinching away from the blow and releasing his hold on Skunk's head.

Snorting out some blood, Skunk forced himself back to his feet, gasping for breath through his ruined face. He turned to Karak and charged, instinct taking over. He couldn't let him recover!

Sadly, Karak's unnatural speed proved too much for the fleeting advantage Skunk's ploy had earned him. His blade swung around, batting Skunk's attack harmlessly aside. Before Skunk would course correct, Karak's hand curled into a fist and swung up, *hard,* into his chin. Skunk lifted off his feet, rising several feet into the air as stars exploded across his vision. His teeth clacked painfully together in his mouth. He felt a hand constrict around his tail, and the world pivoted around him.

Karak turned, using centrifugal force to hurl Skunk into the front door of the schoolhouse. The wood broke easily under the force of the impact, and Skunk felt something in his torso snapping, drawing another agonized scream from him. He could hear panicked voices echoing within the room as he crashed through the barricade before dropping to the floor in a gasping heap.

He heard screams all around him, and a rush of adrenaline forced Skunk to open his eyes. Karak was advancing, the boredom gone from his eyes. Replacing it was a dark glare of single-minded purpose.

"A clever tactic, boy," Karak complimented. "But insufficient."

Skunk tried to rise again, only to crumple to the floor, one hand flying up to his chest. He doubled over, giving wet, agonized coughs that left specks of blood on the floorboards. He felt hands on his back, cool and smooth, and he knew them to be Sylvia's. "Skunk!"

"R-run!" he tried to shout, but the words slurred in his throat, muffled by his own blood. He coughed it out before trying again. *"Run!"*

Karak's foot came down on the floor in front of Skunk. He lifted his head. The First Fang towered over him, one hand behind his back, and his blade aimed directly between Skunk's eyes. Karak's eyes shifted to Sylvia at his side. He sneered with revulsion. "You *care* for this one, runt?"

Interpreting a threat in the question, Skunk tried to knock Karak's sword aside. He didn't have his weapon, but maybe, if he could get a grip on the blade, he could-

Skunk screamed, white-hot agony flooding his palm as the tip of Karak's blade flickered back and drove itself through the top of his hand, pinning it to the floor. He heard Sylvia shrieking beside him, and he felt her scrambling away from the violent scene.

Karak snorted. "As I thought."

The blade withdrew from Skunk's hand, slick and reddened with his blood. He watched the blade rise, powerless to stop it. The tip rested against his chest, right over his pounding heart. Karak grunted. "Rest, now," he instructed and tensed to thrust.

Something came down on him from the side, forcing him to turn. He raised his sword just in time to catch the chair that Sylvia had swung at him. The sharpened edge carved cleanly through the wood, sending debris scattering across the floor. Skunk's eyes widened, and he realized a moment too late that Sylvia was wide open and exposed.

Growling in frustration, Karak lifted a foot and drove it into Sylvia's stomach. She folded like paper around the blow, her jaw flying wide, before crashing to the floor several feet away.

"Sylvia!" Skunk cried, a surge of more adrenaline forcing him to scramble after her. Karak didn't give him the chance. The First Fang grabbed onto the back of Skunk's shirt before turning to throw him against the far wall, once more driving the air from his lungs.

"Stay down!" Karak snapped, the formality gone from his voice. He turned to the rest of the room, where the children and their scattered parents were cowering, watching the scene unfold. Karak took a breath and ran a hand down his chest as if he were casually dusting himself off. "As for the rest of you. If you value your lives, you will offer no resistance."

"L-leave them alone!" Skunk called out weakly, trying once more to get up. "They're just kids!"

Karak didn't even flinch. "All are complicit," he said, his voice cold with unwavering contempt. "And all shall be held to account."

Skunk clutched at his chest, every gasp for breath rattling and gurgling in his throat. He could still feel blood dripping out of his broken face. "Please, just stop," he begged. "Take me if you want, but leave the rest of them alone!"

Karak turned to Skunk, frowning. "Did you not hear me? *All* are complicit. *All* shall be held to account. There are no exceptions."

"But we haven't even done anything!" one of the children cried out before being silenced by his mother.

Karak laughed under his breath as if he had been told a clever joke before looking up at the roof. "Once upon a time, I believed the same. But you shall see. I'll make sure of it."

Skunk groaned and looked around for his weapon. Sadly, there was no sign of it. He must have dropped it outside before Karak threw him in here.

Karak turned to face the room of cowering children and raised his hands as if to give praise to the gods themselves. "You will *all* see! You are poisoned by your ignorance, but no longer! In emerald flames shall you be purged of your sins-"

His words were suddenly cut off, silenced by a grunt and a meaty *thud*. Skunk blinked, his mind taking a second to realize that an arrow had appeared in Karak's back. The First Fang turned, his eyes alight with rage.

Gothard came charging through the door, sword and buckler raised. Karak turned to meet the coming assault with a snarl, lifting his sword into a fencing stance.

Another arrow came in, but Karak was ready for this one. His runes flared, and he swatted the projectile aside before meeting Gothard's overhead slash.

Acting quickly, Gothard issued a bellowing battle cry before lifting his foot and driving it hard into Karak's injured thigh. The blow sent Karak staggering back a few paces, before, with a growl, the dragon-man gave a flap of his wings, taking him back to the far end of the room from the door.

"Everyone out!" Gothard commanded, continuing his advance. "Go! Go! GO!"

The scattered civilians didn't need to be told twice. In a flurry of activity, the scattered children and their parents quickly made for the exit, screaming and crying out as Gothard crossed swords with Karak again. Skunk could see Sylvia in the mix, clutching at her stomach and being helped by Seto. The krauven gave Skunk a firm look and a sharp nod toward the exit.

Time to go.

Skunk couldn't argue. With another groan of pain, he finally pushed himself to his feet and moved as fast as his legs could take him to where the door had once been. The moment his feet found the stairs, he lost all sense of balance and toppled forward to the dirt with a grunt. The ground was still slick with his blood from earlier.

"Skunk!" A familiar voice shouted. He looked up, and through his blurring vision, he saw Amelia thundering toward him from the bridge. She fired another arrow into the schoolhouse before sliding to a stop next to Skunk, her eyes wide. "By the Five... Oh, my baby, what did it *do* to you?!"

Despite everything, Skunk was able to find it in him to smile. "He beat me up."

Amelia's face scrunched up, somewhere between frustration, distress, and amusement. Before she could speak, though, another clash of metal sounded from within the schoolhouse. She frowned and quickly nocked another arrow. "Move!" she ordered, backing away.

Skunk more flopped than rolled to one side as something came flying out of the schoolhouse. The color drained from his face when he realized that it was Gothard, being carried through the air by Karak. He was impaled through the chest by the dragon-man's sword. A few more flaps of Karak's wings carried them almost to the bridge, where he drove the militiaman into the earth, pinning him there.

"Gothard!" Amelia shouted, firing her arrow. Karak turned, ripping his blade up and out of the dead man to bat the arrow aside in another burst of impossible speed. Once again, Skunk noticed a pulse of light from Karak's runes coinciding with his sudden acceleration. Looking closer, Skunk realized that Karak was starting to breathe more heavily from exertion.

"What is going on with him?" Skunk groaned as he slowly rose to his feet, another wave of revulsion washing over him. He looked down and, finally, saw his sword in the grass. He bent to retrieve it, his body burning in protest.

"He's enchanted," Amelia noted, drawing another arrow and firing. Once again, Karak slapped it out of the air, and once again, the runes pulsed. Amelia growled, lowering her bow. "And the bastard has the stamina to match. Damnit, how do we beat something like that?!"

Panting softly, Karak smirked. "You don't."

Amelia snarled, then drew another arrow. "I wasn't asking for *your* opinion, you bastard!" she shouted before firing.

Another pulse of luma, another grimace, and Karak knocked the arrow aside like all the others. And then he was crossing the distance between them, closing on Amelia in a heartbeat. She reacted remarkably quickly, ducking down as Karak's blade darted out in a horizontal sweep intent on taking her head. Another arrow was in her hand, and she thrust it up for Karak's gut. He rolled aside, his runes pulsing once again, placing him directly behind her.

For a moment, Skunk thought that his mother was about to meet the same fate as Gothard. But to his shock and relief, Amelia proved that her reflexes were not to be underestimated. She turned, dodging the incoming thrust of Karak's sword by a mere inch and continuing her thrust with her arrow. Sadly, Karak's hand caught her by the wrist. With a snarl, his forehead snapped forward, cracking into hers with a loud *smack*.

Amelia staggered back, her bow falling from her hands, then quickly dove into a backward role that barely saved her life as Karak swung for her. She came up by Skunk's side, blood trickling from a new wound in her forehead. She reached down to her lower back and drew out a pair of daggers. She spared Skunk a glance. "Go. Catch up to Seto. Gothard and I rallied some reinforcements. I'll cover you!"

"I'm not leaving you, mom!" Skunk refuted, holding up his sword. He had to hold it in his off-hand, making him wilt with a lack of confidence. It felt clunky and unnatural, especially through the bandages covering his fingers.

Amelia shook her head. "I gave you an order, Skunk!" she shouted before moving forward, blades up and ready to plunge into Karak's gut. Skunk tried to follow her, to offer support, but his injuries prevented him from taking more than a step before he fell to his hands and knees, hacking up more blood. He heard the clash of steel, and both combatants grunted with effort.

More blood. His vision was blurring. A realization came to him, then, one that chilled him to the bone.

I'm dying.

There was no other explanation. Panting, he lifted his eyes to look at Addernotch, at his home consumed by flames. Was this really how it was going to end? So abruptly, and with no answers?

He could still see the fleeing children from here. Sylvia stood by a pair of collapsed houses, waving her arms to direct the children toward the militiamen that Amelia and Gothard had brought.

His stomach dropped when he saw a kobold emerge from the shadows of the alleyway behind her.

"*Sylvia!*" he screamed, his voice a gurgling rasp. "Behind you!"

Sylvia turned to him, hearing his voice even from here. For a moment, they made eye contact. Then she turned around.

The kobold leaped out of the darkness, tackling Sylvia to the ground before she even had a chance to scream. Its hands reached out, one covering her mouth while the other placed its claws to her throat.

"*No!*" Skunk rose to his feet, his grip on his sword so tight his hand might have bled. He took a step, but he didn't make it any farther. Something heavy slammed into him, sending him sprawling to the ground and crushing him under immense weight. Instinct took over, sending him squirming and thrashing. "Get off me!" he screamed at the top of his lungs. "Sylvia! *Sylvia! No!*"

"Skunk, calm down," Amelia's voice said from above him as the woman rose, and Skunk realized that she had been the thing to smash into him. As she stood, blood dripped from a gaping wound in her belly. One of her daggers was missing, but her expression was still set in a determined grimace. Skunk looked past her to Karak, whose open hand was smeared with Amelia's blood.

"I will confess, you fight well. For a human," Karak remarked as he advanced.

"Oh yeah?" Amelia asked, panting for breath. "And what the hell are you supposed to be that you can comment on that?"

Karak smirked. "Something more."

Amelia scoffed but offered up no retort. She squared her stance protectively in front of Skunk, sheltering him from Karak. Skunk took the opportunity to turn back to where he had seen Sylvia being tackled to the ground, hoping that there might still be a chance to get to her.

She was gone.

"No…" he choked, reaching out to where she had been. "Sylvia…"

His eyes turned slowly to Karak, his lips peeling back to show his teeth. With the last bit of strength he had, he forced himself to stand, ignoring the flares of agony all over his body. "Give her back!" he shouted in defiance, leveling his sword at Karak's throat.

Karak did not answer this time. He merely lowered into a battle stance, his runes flaring with light, and Skunk knew that this time, neither he nor his mother would survive the incoming attack. He braced himself all the same, intent to go down fighting at least.

A battle cry sounded from somewhere close, by the bridge, and a throwing axe came flying out of the darkness to crunch into Karak's side. The dragon-man folded to one knee with a cry of pain, the runes along his body flickering. He turned to where the axe came from, hissing.

Following his gaze, Skunk was surprised to see a lumbering creature as large as a horse bounding toward them. It was covered in natural armored plates and loped across the bridge in long, steady strides. A dwarf woman dressed in thick armor rode on its back. a large two-headed axe clutched in one hand and a throwing axe in the other. She reared back to throw.

Karak growled before flaring his wings. He kicked off, leaping into the air just in time to dodge the second axe. It thunked uselessly into the wall of the schoolhouse. The dwarf's mount came to a sliding halt just beneath Karak, warbling aggressively as the woman rose. At this distance, Skunk could see the fresh blood smeared on the blade of her axe, and the stench of kobold blood and old metal reached his nostrils.

"Get down here!" the woman roared, drawing forth her third and final throwing axe and hurling it at Karak with remarkable precision. With a grunt, he swatted the projectile aside. His movements were visibly slower than before, and his face was contorted with pain. The dwarf bristled in anger.

Karak glared at her, breathing heavily. With a growl, he pulled her axe from his side and tossed it away. Blood spurted free from the wound, and he rested a palm against it. A fiery glow came from his hand, and Skunk heard the sizzling of flesh. Karak loosed a quiet sigh, then turned his attention back to the dwarf. To Skunk's surprise, the corner of his mouth quirked up into a smirk. "Danica Flatstone. How curious that you of all people should be here," he said slowly.

The dwarf, Danica, lifted her axe and rested it on her shoulder. "You know me?"

Before Karak could offer an answer, the heavens flashed, and a rumble of thunder echoed across the plains. A moment later, a drop of rain splattered against the dirt, followed by another, and another. Karak looked up as a deluge of rain fell on the village. He frowned in disappointment, glancing first at the flickering runes on his arm, and then at the gathered remnants of the militia across the bridge. "Hmph. it would seem our time here is at an end," he mumbled. His teeth showed in an agitated snarl. "But it is no matter. We have what we need."

He threw his head back, and a roar that should only belong to a dragon blasted out of his lungs, echoing across Addernotch. The roar was so loud that Skunk's hands flew up to cover his ears, and an instinct he could do nothing to resist forced him to his knees.

And then Karak was flying away. Skunk watched him go, shocked and confused. *He's leaving?* Looking back into town, Skunk was surprised to see the silhouettes of other kobolds withdrawing for the woods. Many of them were dragging bodies behind them, or carting them in crudely built wagons. Some of the bodies were still moving.

Danica did not care about that if her reaction was any indication. She took a step after Karak, screaming with such volume that Skunk swore it rivaled the First Fang's roar. "You fucking coward!" she shouted, her voice muffled by the rising rainstorm. "Get back here and fight me!"

But Karak did not heed her. In a matter of moments, he was gone, vanishing into the blackness of the night sky. The sounds of battle rapidly dwindled, leaving just the white noise of the storm.

Amelia fell to the earth, catching herself with her hands and gasping for breath. Skunk saw her clutch at her stomach, and he remembered the visceral injury Karak had given her. He felt an impulse to go to her and reached out. But before he could even advance a step, he collapsed into what was rapidly becoming mud. With that fall, Skunk knew he would not rise again.

He was done.

The world was going dark around him, his vision tunneling. He saw Amelia turn to him without even a glance at her own injury. She said something, but the words were all a meaningless murmur. A pounding headache filled Skunk's skull, in time with the rapidly slowing beat of his heart. He lifted his uninjured hand for her, and she grasped it in both of hers. He barely felt it. She was shouting something, but again, he couldn't hear her.

"Mom," he whispered, his eyelids getting heavy. "Sylvia. They took Sylvia..."

Amelia said something. More murmurs. Meaningless noise. Skunk's head fell limply to one side, the final wisps of his energy fleeing him. The last thing he saw before darkness consumed him was Danica turning toward him, her axe in her hand and murder in her eyes.

Danica

In his near-death slumber, Skunk endured fractured, incomprehensible nightmares. Fangs, blood, fire, and glowing runes flashed through his mind like spinning shards of glass from a broken window. They came relentlessly, each one more disturbing than the last. He heard the excited chattering of the kobolds as they chased down their prey and the agonized screams of their victims. Over it all, reveling in the slaughter, was the all-consuming roar of a dragon.

He saw men, women, and children he had known for his entire life as mangled corpses on blood-soaked dirt. He saw their faces frozen in terror as they were dragged into raging fires and gnashing shadows. He saw open wounds, exposed bones, and ravenous kobolds feasting on the dead. In the middle of it all, grinning at him with cold contempt, was Karak.

And then, just as quickly as it had all started, it ended.

Skunk awoke with a start, his eyes wide. They immediately snapped shut as blinding white light pierced his retinas. He groaned in discomfort, rubbing at his face. He could feel a lingering sting in his muzzle and the palm of his hand, reminders of his injuries. His chest ached, and every breath brought with it a fresh swell of pain. But once he had a moment to think, he realized with surprise that none of it was nearly as bad as it had been before.

Opening his eyes again, slower this time, he looked at his hands. Both were wrapped in bandages, and the gauze over his right palm bore a dry red stain. Skunk frowned. He remembered being stabbed through that hand, and a morbid sense of curiosity compelled him to poke at the hole.

He blinked when his finger pressed against sensitive flesh and tender scales. There was no open cavity. He flexed his fingers in awe. *I've been healed?* Now that he thought about it, despite how sore his face was, he realized he could breathe properly. The disfiguration of his snout had been corrected. All of his injuries, previously life-threatening, were all but gone, leaving only a dull ache behind.

"What in the world?" he whispered, his voice a dry rasp. He coughed a few times, then let his hands fall to his sides and took in his surroundings. He lay in a bedroll under the roof of a large tent, and he was far from the only one. It looked like half of the militia was in here. Gaps in the fabric overhead allowed shafts of early morning sunlight to shine through, and Skunk could hear the breeze and the distant chatter of townsfolk. He could hear wood groaning, wheels clattering, and tools at work. The air was thick and damp after the previous night's rain, and the breeze that wafted through carried the stench of woodsmoke and rotting flesh.

Skunk groaned, moving to sit up. A weight on the blanket to his right stopped him. Looking down, he almost jumped out of his skin when he saw Amelia lying down beside him. She was out like a light, her crossed arms serving as a pillow. Her face was hidden from view by a curtain of unwashed hair. Her body was also wrapped in bandages, and Skunk recalled the grotesque slash Karak had left in her and breathed a sigh of relief.

He reached a hand out to her shoulder and gingerly shook her awake. Amelia murmured something in her sleep and lifted her head. There were dark bags under her bloodshot eyes, betraying her exhaustion. She blinked at him a few times, her mind not catching up with her senses. A moment later, her bleary wariness was replaced with a surge of elation.

"Skunk!" she cried, lunging forward and wrapping him in a gentle hug, careful not to agitate his injuries. "Oh, thank the Five, you're okay! Y-you are okay, aren't you?"

Skunk returned the hug as well as he could, relishing the physical contact. The tactile feel of his mother's arms around him, her fingers pressing into his back and neck, was of great comfort. Overcome with relief of his own, he nodded into Amelia's shoulder. "I'm alive," he said. "But... no. I'm not okay."

Amelia drew back, taking Skunk's right hand in both of hers and giving it an affectionate squeeze. "Me neither," she said quietly.

Skunk swallowed heavily. His smile faded, and he looked back up at the roof. He thought of Sylvia, and his relief faded. Her face flashed before his eyes, twisted with panic as the kobold took her. He could only imagine how she must have been screaming.

Was she still alive? He wondered. *Had it killed her? Had she been eaten like so many others?* Try as he might, he could not chase away these questions. They nipped at his mind like rabid dogs, and his heart twisted with grief. More questions about the attack joined them, and the complete lack of answers only served to amplify his misery.

He screwed his eyes shut, shivering uncontrollably. "They took Sylvia," he whimpered, his hand reaching to the pocket in his shirt where he kept her doll. To his relief, it was still there, and surprisingly undamaged. He pulled it out and held it close to his chest, trying to calm himself down.

Amelia did not say anything, though Skunk could hear her shuffling. She wanted to say something, but she could not find the words. Ultimately, she settled for wrapping her arms around him as if to shield him from the world with her own body. She ran her hand down the back of his neck. "It's going to be alright," she whispered. "It's all going to be okay. I've got you, Skunk."

A tiny part of Skunk wanted to feel offended. She was cradling him and whispering to him the way she had when he was a little child. That tiny voice of pride died almost as quickly as it manifested, though. He leaned into the embrace, trying to take what comfort he could from the embrace and his mother's murmured assurances. She hadn't led him astray in all the time he had known her, after all. This would be no different.

Slowly but surely and bit by bit, Skunk was able to get his trembling under control. He took a series of deep breaths, forcing his rampaging emotions back into line. When he was certain he could speak clearly, he lifted his face and opened his eyes. "How am I alive?"

Amelia pulled back, sitting cross-legged on the ground beside him with a hand still on his back. "It was a close call. You were on death's door for a while. But that dwarf woman, Danica, had a healing pearl on hand. She gave it to me, and I gave it to you. You needed it far more than I did."

Skunk blinked in surprise. He remembered the dwarf — mostly because of the barrage of profanities she had sent after Karak. He also recalled the look in her eyes when he had passed out, and it had not been the look of someone wanting to help him. He gave Amelia a weak smile. "Thank you," he said softly.

"You're welcome."

"What happened next?" Skunk asked, turning to face his mother directly.

Amelia paused for a moment, then sighed and looked away. "I can't say I know much. I've spent most of my time with you. What I do know is that everything's in chaos."

"It's been hell," a new voice suddenly interrupted them. Skunk jumped and looked up to see a human man approaching them. He looked to be in his mid-to-late thirties, adorned in a blood-stained apron and his long blonde hair tied back to keep it out of his pale face. He had just come inside and was cleaning his hands in a bucket of water.

He continued. "The militia's in shambles. Gothard and the mayor are both dead, so we've got no leadership. More people are missing than there are bodies to bury. No one has any idea what's going on or what to do. It's all a mess."

Skunk blinked. "W-who are you?" he asked cautiously. He'd seen the man around town before, but they'd never been properly introduced.

The man flinched, turning to Skunk directly. "Ah, ahem. Einwal. I'm the one who's been tending to the wounded," he said. There was a slight tremble in his voice that Skunk did not miss. It stung, but he chose to ignore it.

"So, I guess I gotta thank you, too, huh?" he asked a moment later.

Einwal slowly relaxed and closed the gap between them. "In part. That healing pearl has done the majority of the hard work. I've mostly been changing your bandages and keeping your wounds clean. Speaking of which," he paused by Skunk's bedroll, his hands flexing uncomfortably at his sides. "D-do you mind if I, uh...?"

Skunk shook his head. "No, not at all. Do your work. I don't bite."

Einwal cringed, and Skunk regretted his choice of words. Amelia's hand on his back slid to his shoulder and gave a comforting squeeze.

Einwal knelt a moment later to take a look at Skunk's injuries, starting with the bandage on his hand. He silently unraveled them, his eyes focused on the upturned palm.

No one said anything. The silence was thick and impenetrable, and Skunk did not care for it. It left his mind free of distractions, free to conjure worst-case scenarios. He swallowed heavily and forced himself to speak up. "Did anyone go after the kobolds? Are our friends alive?"

Einwal peeled the last of the bandages away from Skunk's hand. There was an ugly scar where he had been stabbed, but otherwise, the wound had healed nicely. "Not to my knowledge," he said regrettably. "It was all a mad scramble after the enemy left. Everyone who still had legs to walk on was busy just trying to put out fires. After that, we were all too busy seeing who was left alive and tending to the wounded. A lot of people died even after the kobolds left."

Skunk looked down, cradling his healed hand. "R-right," he mumbled, his tail thumping against the dirt in agitation.

"It would not have been a good idea to chase after the kobolds so soon regardless," Amelia noted. "Against any other horde, it would be a simple matter. But this force was well organized and well trained. That dragon-man, whatever he was, has made this horde into a force to be reckoned with. Trying to give chase now would be suicide, and our defenses would be all the weaker for it."

Einwal didn't comment. He examined Skunk's body for a few more seconds, then nodded in satisfaction. "The pearl's doing its work. You should make a full recovery in a couple of days at most. Don't do anything strenuous, eat plenty of food, and get plenty of rest. You'll be back to your old self in no time."

Skunk frowned. "I didn't even know there was such a thing as 'healing pearls.' What are they?"

Amelia smiled and pulled a ringstone from her pocket. Skunk looked at it, surprised. Its surface had been engraved with runes.

It was strange. Though he did not know the language, the letters nonetheless seemed familiar to him, like a half-forgotten memory or a fading dream. He gingerly took the stone in his hand.

Amelia explained. "A healing pearl is a type of enchanted item. A smooth ball, usually a little less than an inch across, and usually made of steel or stone. They dramatically accelerate your body's natural healing process. So long as it remains in your digestive system, it will help you recover *much* faster. This ringstone is what provides the pearl with its power. That's why I haven't left your side. I needed to keep the stone close."

Skunk blinked, and his hand found its way to his stomach. "So... there's a ball of steel in my guts right now?" he asked, his eyes widening slightly.

Amelia nodded.

Einwal piped up. "It's an effective treatment in a lot of scenarios, but it's slow-acting. Contrary to what you might read in fables and stories, you can't just swallow one like you would drink a 'potion' and be right as rain in seconds, and it's going to leave you ravenous," He explained before rising. "Now, I have other patients to tend to. Remember my instructions, now. The pearl's doing wonders, but you're still healing. Get rest, and eat plenty of food."

Skunk nodded. "Right. Thanks."

Einwal gave a short nod of his head, then went to tend to his other patients, leaving Skunk alone with Amelia. Neither of them said anything, and Skunk took the chance to lay back down and try to rest. He was still sore, and he was done talking anyway. He turned his attention to the world outside, just listening to it turn. He closed his eyes, breathing deeply, trying to find motes of familiarity in the town's scent.

The stink of the battle was all-consuming, but even through the thick miasma, he could still pick out tiny points of familiarity. He could smell fresh-baked bread, somewhere far off at the edges of his senses. The smell of tree sap and fresh leaves from the forest wafted over the destruction. It was enough to let him relax, at least a little bit. It meant they were still alive.

A moment later, he felt Amelia's palm against his forehead. Her thumb rubbed across his brow, and she began to hum. Skunk couldn't help but smile as the familiar melody swam into his thoughts.

He had heard it many times before — especially when he had been little. A soothing lullaby that had always soothed him. He was a full-grown adult now, but he didn't mind hearing the song again. The nostalgia helped him bury his concerns for the moment, and just like when he was little, he soon found himself drifting back to sleep. This time without the nuisance of nightmares.

Skunk awoke an hour later, and this time, he felt well enough to rise — but he was also starving. Einwal hadn't been kidding about that. A fresh pair of clothes and a bundle of assorted dried meats had been set out for him while he'd been asleep, courtesy of Amelia. His black fur cloak was still intact, thankfully, and the blood splatters had been cleaned out of it. Amelia waited patiently while he ate and got dressed, then handed him the ringstone to keep the pearl going. That done, they stepped out into the open air of Addernotch, and Skunk got a paralyzingly clear view of the damage.

An entire third of the village was gone. Where the homes had once stood along the northern edge of town, only piles of black-charred debris remained. Over half of what was left had suffered damage in the fighting. Some would be livable, but most were in desperate need of repairs. Bodies were still being collected, gathered into wheelbarrows and wagons by those who were left to carry out the gruesome work.

Skunk stared at it all, the air sucked from his lungs. "It's horrible," he choked.

"It is. We could never have been prepared for an attack like this," Amelia agreed from beside him.

Not far away, Skunk saw the body of a kobold sprawled on the ground, its limbs twisted unnaturally. A dirtied man came up beside it, kicked it viciously in the ribs, and lifted the corpse by the armpits. Skunk shuddered at the look in its dead, glassy eyes. It *hated*. Even in death, its eyes shone with malice, staring back at him as the body was hauled away to be burned. Its teeth showed in a feral grimace, dried blood caked onto its fangs and lips.

"Why did they do this?" Skunk whispered. "What did they want?"

Amelia did not answer.

After a few seconds, Skunk shook himself and set off at a brisk pace down the street, his tail swishing behind him in short, agitated flicks. He heard Amelia walking behind him.

"Skunk? Where are you going?" she asked.

"The schoolhouse," he answered, keeping his eyes forward. "I want to see Seto."

"Seto is fine," Amelia assured him, reaching out. "You can't push yourself. Let's get you home-"

"I want to see Seto!" Skunk cut her off, spinning to face her. "I wanna make sure he's okay! And he might've seen what happened to Sylvia!"

Amelia drew up short, and it was only then that Skunk realized how loudly he had spoken. He wilted on the spot, overcome by shame when he saw the suspicious and accusatory glares of the few people on the streets around him. He saw one of them drumming his fingers on the shaft of the shovel he carried as if he was just waiting for an excuse to use the tool as a weapon.

Amelia stared at Skunk for a moment, her eyes wide with surprise and hurt. After a moment, she relented. "Alright. Just take it slow, Skunk. You're still healing."

Skunk nodded, the wind in his sails dying in the wake of his outburst. "I know. I'm sorry," he mumbled.

Amelia put a hand on his head. "No. Don't apologize. You've done *nothing* wrong," she told him, and he knew she was talking about far more than just raising his voice with her.

Without another word, he turned and started down the street again, trying to ignore more than just the ruins. Try as he might, however, he couldn't dismiss the stares. He was used to being the oddity in town, sure. The one that all of the strangers and newcomers would gawk at every time he passed. But never before had those eyes been so *hateful*. These people were supposed to be his neighbors. His friends. His *pack*. And yet their eyes blazed with nothing but loathing. He wilted as he walked, trying to smile at one of them, a woman. She spat on the ground as he passed and went back to her work.

By the time he was at the bridge in front of the schoolhouse, Skunk felt ready to lay down and pass out, if only so he wouldn't have to endure the looks any longer. The front door had yet to be replaced, and a phantom pain tingled along his spine. The grounds were mercifully clean, all of the blood washed away by the rain.

Skunk paused by the end of the bridge, his eyes lingering on a patch of dirt. That was where Gothard had fallen. His body was gone, though.All that remained was a small hole, courtesy of Karak's sword.

Skunk screwed his eyes shut, trying to force the images out, then continued on his way to the school. As he ascended the steps, he could hear voices from inside the building.

"I'm sorry, ma'am, but I've told you everything I know. We've known for a long time that there have been green-scales living in the region, but we have no idea where they live, nor how many there are," one of them said. It was Seto. He sounded exhausted.

The voice that answered him was gruff but feminine. Danica, Skunk assumed. "And you never once thought to send someone to investigate?"

"What do you expect us to do? We're a small stepping stone of a village. We don't have the manpower or the authority to take the fight to kobold hordes. Besides, they mostly operated in the planes to the north. A large ry'thar tribe calls that region home, the Karjene. The few times kobolds have been sighted were not deemed important enough to disturb the lion-folk's territory over. We may be on good terms with them, but they would not take kindly to such an intrusion."

Skunk stepped into the doorway. Looking around, he saw that most of the tables had been removed, and the few that were left were pushed against the wall and loaded with supplies. Bedrolls were scattered across the floor with clusters of children huddled in small, silent groups. Some flinched when they saw him, but most seemed unresponsive.

Danica grunted, crossing her arms over her chest. "And here I thought you Assemblage mooks were supposed to know everything."

Seto frowned, clacking his beak in annoyance. "Miss Flatstone, I am a *scholar*. There is much I do know, but that does not mean I know *everything*. My friends in the city meant well to send you to me for answers, but just because I know one green-scale does not mean I am an expert on them!"

Danica closed her eyes. "So, in short, I have to track them down on my own. Typical," she snarled, her face contorting with frustration.

Seto shook his head, exasperated, but said nothing else.

Danica opened her eyes and finally noticed Skunk and Amelia standing in the doorway. She visibly tensed, a hand flying for one of her throwing axes. Skunk took a fearful step back, his heart skipping a beat. Danica paused, however, her eyes landing on Amelia, and she slowly relaxed.

Seto followed her gaze. His eyes shined with profound relief, and his cheeks lifted in the largest smile Skunk had ever seen from him. "Skunk! Oh, thank the stars!" he cried, crossing the distance in a few steps before enveloping the battered kobold in a warm embrace. "I was so worried for you. How are you feeling?"

Skunk managed to put on a smile as he returned the embrace. "Better, now that I know you're okay," he said, hugging the old krauven. A moment later, he pulled back, staring into Seto's eyes. "Sylvia. I saw her being taken."

Seto's smile faded, and he gave a slow nod. "She was. I wanted to help her, but there was nothing I could have done. If I had tried, they would have torn me to pieces, and the children needed me. I'm so sorry."

"Was she at least alive?" Skunk pressed desperately. "They didn't kill her, did they?!"

Seto shook his head. "No, no, she was still alive, last I saw. It's strange. The kobolds seemed to be more interested in taking prisoners than killing people."

Skunk slowly relaxed. There was a chance, then, slim though it may have been. Until they found a body, there was hope that she was alive. He breathed deeply to calm himself, his left hand wandering to the doll in his shirt pocket. "Okay... okay. We'll get her back. Somehow," He said, before looking up at Seto again.

Before either of them could say anything more, Danica's voice cut through the room. "Hey! Kobold!" All eyes turned to her. Her arms had crossed over her chest again, and her eyes had settled into a hard glare. She was staring directly at Skunk. "Your mother used my healing pearl to save you. You owe me your life, and now I expect you to repay that debt."

Skunk swallowed hard, taking an instinctive step back as the woman crossed the gap between them. Her wide build and thick armor made the earth tremble beneath her every heavy step. He felt like an ant standing before a mountain when she finally reached him, even though he was only a few inches shorter. He opened his mouth to say something, but Danica beat him to it.

"Tell me everything you know about the horde that attacked this town," she said, her words short and to the point.

Skunk recoiled. "Wha- huh?"

Danica leaned toward him threateningly. "Don't play dumb with me, kobold. You're from the horde that attacked Addernotch, so you're going to tell me everything you know. Plain and simple."

Suddenly, Amelia was by Skunk's side, placing a hand on Danica's shoulder. "Back off," she warned. "That's my son you're talking to. And he's still healing."

Danica scowled. "You're *son*? That thing's a kobold!"

Amelia took a threatening step forward. "Yes, he is," she growled.

Danica gritted her teeth and threw her arms up in the air. "Bah. Fine, whatever," she relented. She took a step back. "There. Personal space returned. Now answer my question, kobold."

Skunk stared at her for a few seconds. His first impulse told him to turn tail and flee. The woman clearly had no kindness in her heart for him, and he had enough to worry about. But something in her eyes halted him in his tracks. There was a tension in her face that was not in line with the anger she was putting on display. She looked almost desperate.

Skunk swallowed heavily, then shook his head. "I'm sorry. I don't know anything about them. They abandoned me in the forest when I was still an egg."

Danica quirked a brow. "Really? Why the hell would they do that?"

Skunk looked down at the floor. "I dunno. But that big one, Karak... he said I was a runt. He said I wouldn't be worth the meat it'd take to raise me. And the other kobolds were all bigger than I am."

Danica growled in frustration. "Bastards. That they'd abandon their own blood over something so trivial. How many of their own songs have they silenced prematurely...?" she wondered.

Skunk blinked. "Songs?" he asked.

Danica shook her head and focused her eyes on him again. "And that's *all* you know?" she pressed.

Skunk faltered, wanting to press her about the 'songs,' but chose against it. He shook his head. "That's it. I'm sorry."

Danica closed her eyes and took in a long, deep breath. She let it out in a heavy sigh. "Right. Thanks for nothing," she grumbled before shaking her head and marching for the door. "Out of my way."

Skunk let out a yelp as the fuming dwarf thundered past him. He watched her descend the steps and make for the bridge, all the while uttering profanities under her breath. About halfway down the path, Danica came to an abrupt stop. She stood still, looking up at the sky, and visibly began to relax.

Amelia and Seto were talking, but Skunk's attention was on Danica. He was curious about the woman, now. He watched with interest as she reached into a pouch and withdrew another ringstone, one that glowed far brighter than the one healing his wounds. She held the stone up to her chest, muttering under her breath.

Skunk knew he should leave her be, but he was just too curious. And besides, he still needed to thank her for her part in saving him. And so, slowly, he crept down the stairs and followed her, his tail dragging in the dirt behind him. As he approached, Danica's words began to come into focus.

"I'm so close," she whispered to herself, her fingers clenching tightly around the stone. "Just a little farther..."

Skunk drew to a stop a few yards away, watching Danica curiously. He put on a small smile. "Um-"

Danica jumped, quickly stuffing the stone into her pouch and spinning around to face him. Her eyes narrowed in frustration. "Juna's fucking tits, don't sneak up on me like that!" she shouted at him.

Skunk leaned away from her as if her shout carried enough force to knock him off balance. A moment later, he righted himself and kept smiling. "Sorry. I just wanted to say thank you."

Danica blinked, her anger replaced with confusion. "What are you talking about?"

Skunk took a step forward. "You drove off Karak. And you gave Mom the healing pearl. You saved our lives," he explained simply. His smile grew somewhat. "So, thank you."

Danica eyed him for a few seconds, not sure what to make of the expression of gratitude. She huffed. "Uh, yeah, sure. Whatever," she grumbled awkwardly before turning away.

Skunk took a step after her, his smile fading. "Hey, are you alright?"

Danica stopped, but she didn't look at him. "Look, kobold. I'm not here to make friends — especially not with one of *your* kind. I'm here to kill kobolds and take back what they stole from me and *my* kind. So just stay out of my way and leave me alone. Got it?"

Skunk flinched at the bitter contempt in her voice and slumped in place. "Oh. Okay. Sorry," he mumbled dejectedly.

Danica stayed still for a moment, and Skunk thought she was about to say something else. In the end, she left without another word. Skunk watched her go. *Well, that could have gone better,* he thought. He turned back to the schoolhouse and saw Amelia and Seto walking toward him. He wagged his tail a few times, but the movement did not last long.

Amelia glared past Skunk at Danica, her expression souring considerably. "What is her problem?" she hissed.

Seto shook his head. "As much as I hate to say it, I can't blame her."

Skunk stared after Danica, watching her take a turn down the street to disappear behind a half-collapsed house. The hostility in her voice echoed in his mind alongside the gnashing fangs of the first kobold he killed. He hugged himself and looked down. "I can't, either," he mumbled.

Amelia knelt and put her hands on his shoulders. "Hey. Come on. Let's go home. You still need rest."

Skunk nodded weakly. "Sure."

Beside them, Seto let out an exhausted whistle. The old krauven turned to Amelia. "Before you go, there has been a town hall meeting called for tonight, just after sunset. All are welcome to attend and lend their voice to finding a solution. I'd be grateful for your presence, Amelia. I fear the days ahead are not going to get better anytime soon, and your insights will be invaluable."

Amelia gave him a small nod. "We'll be there. You just focus on taking care of the children."

"I will," Seto assured her, then looked at Skunk. "And look after him, won't you? He was in bad shape even before Karak arrived."

"That's the plan. Take care, Seto."

With that, Seto gave a small nod of his head and went back inside, leaving Skunk and Amelia on their own as they walked through the streets.

Once again, the oppressive silence and misery left in the aftermath of the battle seeped into Skunk's scales. It burrowed down into his heart and his soul, burning him from inside. There were so many people missing, their voices gone from the background noise. It was wrong, and every fiber of him knew it.

Finally, he had to speak, just to try and drown the silence out. "We're going to get them back, right?" he asked at length, looking up at his mother hopefully. "We're gonna send the militia to rescue our people."

Amelia looked down at him. The look in her eyes was not what he had been hoping for. It wasn't a look of confidence or conviction, it wasn't defiance or determination. All he saw in her eyes was regret, sympathy, and pity. An uncomfortable feeling began to pool in his stomach.

He reached out to take her hand, gripping it tight. "We're saving our people, *right?!*"

Amelia turned away, unable to look him in the eye. "I don't know. I wish I did, but I don't. Everything's wrong right now, and I can't predict what's going to happen next. So for now, let's just go home," she said softly. "You still need rest, and I need to think."

The pit in Skunk's stomach deepened, swallowing up any words he might have used in rebuttal. His tail lashed behind him, and a small growl of frustration welled up from the bottom of his voice. Still, he knew she was right. That didn't mean he had to like it.

Just be safe, Sylvia, he thought as his mother guided him back to their home, thankfully still standing in the aftermath of the battle. *Please. We'll figure something out, I promise.*

Prisoners

The last thing Sylvia recalled was a clawed hand wrapping over her mouth and a heavy weight bringing her to the ground. Everything after that was a blur of noise and pain. She knew she had fought to free herself from her assailant, but she was no fighter. She had been powerless against them, and in the end, a blow to the side of her head sent her tumbling into nothingness.

As she came back to reality, the pain came back to her body. She was covered in numerous festering aches, lingering testaments of the beating she had received. Whimpering softly, she flickered open her eyes to see shafts of silver ringlight shining down through the canopy of a forest rolling by overhead. It was night, just past sunset by the looks of things.

As her other senses returned to her, Sylvia heard the rolling of wheels and the unmistakable chattering of countless kobolds. When she tried to turn and get a better look, she noticed thick, abrasive ropes around her wrists and ankles that dug painfully into her skin. She winced, gnashing her teeth together behind tightly pressed lips to contain an exclamation of pain.

She wasn't the only one in the wagon. Several other people — mostly children — were bound like she was. She could hear the occasional whimper from her company, but no one was speaking. Curious, she looked around beyond the edges of the wagon.

There were several others, each one filled with more prisoners and escorted by kobolds armed with spears, clubs, and brutal axes. The bigger, burlier kobolds pulled the wagons along at a surprising pace, demonstrating the impressive strength some members of their kind could possess. Seeing this, Sylvia knew escape would not be possible, and the silence told her that conversation would not be allowed.

And so Sylvia settled in to wait. As she waited, it dawned on her that she had never seen this part of the woods before. The land inclined before them, gradually growing steeper and peppered with large rocks. Sylvia felt her already dry throat tighten with fear. They must have been just on the border of the leoroch plains. How long had the kobolds gone without resting to cover this kind of distance in such a short time? Alternatively, how long had she been unconscious? It was a frightening set of questions to consider.

As afraid as she was, however, she did not succumb to panic. In her mind, she rationalized that if the kobolds had gone to such lengths to capture this many people, they must have wanted them alive. Similarly, the wagons implied they wanted their prisoners unharmed. Otherwise, they would drag their prisoners or force them to walk.

Time crawled by at a snail's pace. The unfamiliar landscape and frightening situation were swallowing Sylvia's attention, preventing her from resting. The wait was agonizing, and in time Sylvia found her mind drifting back to Skunk.

The last time she had seen him, he was on the ground, beaten, broken, and coughing up blood. Sylvia was no expert on medicine, but even she could tell that his wounds were potentially fatal. Her heart twisted in her chest, and she tried not to consider the possibility that he was dead.

After what felt like hours, there was a change in scenery. The trees thinned and faded, and Sylvia felt gravity shifting beneath her as the wagon rolled onto level terrain. The ground under the wheels changed from dirt and grass to hard stone. The air turned dry and chilly, a crisp breeze nipping at her aching flesh through her tattered dress.

"Enough. We rest here," the voice of the tall dragon-man called out from somewhere nearby. As the wagons rolled to a stop, the tired kobolds got to work. One of them came up to Sylvia and pulled her forcefully out of the wagon. She grunted in pain as she was unceremoniously dropped on the ground like a sack of potatoes. Taking a moment to breathe, she lifted her gaze.

A spear was pointed right at her face. She froze, her heart skipping a beat. The kobold snarled in warning, showing off its razor-sharp yellow teeth. She swallowed the lump in her throat and gave a slow nod of understanding. The kobold seemed to recognize the gesture, snapped a word at her in a language she did not understand, and then moved on to threaten the next line of prisoners being unloaded.

With the kobold out of her way, Sylvia gasped. An enormous golden grassland unraveled before her, stretching out for miles before subtly blending into foothills far to the distant north. Several narrow streams snaked between the hills in elaborate patterns and reflected the ringlight at her like diamonds. There were almost no trees, and what few there were did not look like any she had seen before.

These were the Leoroch Plains, a massive dale that received far less rainfall than Aigeth to the south. The Sybhrod Mountains surrounded the land on all sides save the south, blocking ocean rain clouds from ever reaching these elevated steppes. Somewhere among those golden fields, the Karjene ry'thar went about their business, whatever that may have been.

Despite the danger she was in, Sylvia couldn't help but admire the view. The kobolds had brought them onto an elevated ridge to make their campsite, the high altitude lending Sylvia an even greater vantage point.

"Feed the prisoners," the dragon man commanded, walking toward the edge of the rocky ridge. "The forest is rich with berries, nuts, and shrooms. Forage some."

Sylvia glared at him for a moment before turning her attention to the children. They were huddling together and shaking like leaves. Their eyes were wide with terror, darting from side to side. She recognized all of them.

One of them, a little boy with big freckled cheeks and messy red hair, looked up at her. He sniffled. "Sylvia? What's gonna happen to us?" he asked in barely a whisper.

Sylvia offered him a smile. "I don't know," she said truthfully. "But they won't kill us. They need us for something. Stay strong and do what they say. We'll be okay."

The little boy did not seem reassured. He tried to get comfortable, shuffling and fighting with his bound wrists and ankles until he was sitting on his knees.

Up ahead, one of the kobolds approached the dragon-man. It stood out from its fellows by its armor, a collection of leathers and hides marked with studs of bone. A nasty serrated sword was belted at its hip. "Karak," it said bluntly. "You seem troubled."

Karak turned to the kobold, half his face lit by the ring, leaving the other bathed in shadow. "Troubled? That is not the word I would use. But I do find myself pondering the outcome of our assault."

The kobold snarled, glaring back at Sylvia and the other prisoners. "We got what we came for," it snarled. "What is there to ponder?"

Karak turned back to look over the dale. His tail swung lazily from side to side. "There was a woman there. A dwarf. Danica," he said at length, drawing the kobold's attention. "I know her."

The kobold's eyes narrowed. "I trust you aren't having second thoughts, *First Fang?*" it asked, and Sylvia did not miss the disdain in its voice as it uttered the title.

Karak did not seem bothered by the disrespectful tone. "Hardly. Danica is no friend of mine, I assure you. But she is a stubborn woman at the best of times and will have ample reason to track us down. And if, as I fear, our enemies band together in response to our little operations, she may prove an annoyance if left unattended."

The kobold hissed. "Kssshh! She is but one stupid dwarf! You see infernos brewing in dying sparks!"

Karak's expression hardened, and to Sylvia's shock, he brought the back of his hand around to slap the kobold *hard* in the face. The kobold yelped like an injured dog as it was sent sprawling into the flames of the first campfire. Sylvia's eyes widened, and she expected to hear it screaming in agony as the flames consumed it.

Instead, the creature hauled itself from the flames, utterly unharmed save for a bruised pride. Its fellows issued frustrated yaps and chastisements at it, their tone no more serious than if it had just spilled a glass of milk across the table. Grumbling, they went to put the campfire back together.

When Karak spoke again, his voice had darkened into a warning growl. "Even a dying spark can light a fire when given fresh kindling, and you may be assured that her lust for vengeance will burn long and hot. You would be wise not to underestimate her. Such complacency has cost you and your people much in the past. Or have you forgotten Azada's fate?"

The kobold growled in frustration but said no more in defiance. "So be it. What then would you have us do, First Fang?"

Karak huffed and turned to look back out over the plains. His wings stretched on his back. "Assemble a team. Go back the way we came and prepare an ambush for Danica. If possible, take her in alive. If not, do not hesitate to kill her. She carries a ringstone with her — It is to be brought back to the Young Master."

The kobold nodded. "It shall be done. But we are tired after the battle and the climb. We need rest."

Karak didn't turn around. "Of course. Choose your team well and get some sleep. You depart at first light."

The kobold bowed its head. The agitated shivering of its tail and the tremble in its cheeks told Sylvia that it did not care for the commands. Whether it was due to disagreement, or a simple distaste for the one who issued them, however, was anyone's guess. Without another word, it turned and stalked off.

Then it was quiet. As the kobolds labored to build up their camp, Sylvia realized that this was not the entire enemy force. She had seen kobolds being cut down in the fighting, yes, but nowhere near enough for there to be so few left. By her count, there were less than twenty in this group.

Perhaps they had split up during their withdrawal? If the kobolds wanted these people alive, it wouldn't do to have *all* of their prizes in one place. Plus, traveling in large numbers meant a slower pace and leaving a massive trail. By dividing up their forces, they would make more trails to follow and increase the odds of at least one group making it back in one piece.

Eventually, the kobolds sent to scour for food returned. They made rounds through the camp, delivering a loose assortment of nuts, fruits, berries, and mushrooms — some of which were decidedly lethal, Sylvia knew.

"Eat!" a kobold commanded as it tossed her 'meal' at her knees.

Sylvia felt the urge to point out that the mushrooms would kill anyone who ate them but bit her tongue. The kobold was already moving on, and she imagined all she would get for her trouble would be a new bruise. Looking down at the loose pile of food, she winced as she realized they had been given no utensils with which to eat, and the food was on the ground.

Still, there were precious few options available to her. With a sigh, Sylvia knelt, straining her back, and carefully tried to pick out what bits of food she could without inhaling any dirt. Several of the children moved forward to do just the same, and thankfully, had the good sense not to eat the mushrooms. Seto's lessons in the local flora had paid off, it seemed.

One of the children, the one Sylvia had spoken to earlier, suddenly coughed and spluttered, spitting out the food he had been eating. He must have inhaled a pebble or some dirt. Either way, his timing couldn't have been worse, as one of the kobolds was stalking past at the same time.

"Quiet!" it snapped, cracking the butt-end of his spear across the back of the boy's head.

He cried out, curling up and squirming. "I-I'm sorry!" he wailed fearfully. "Th-there was a rock-"

Another blow, this time to his ribs. "I said *quiet!*"

Sylvia lifted her head, her eyes narrowed. "Please, stop! He's just a child!" she pleaded impulsively, knowing already that the effort would prove futile.

Crack.

The shaft of the spear found her head this time, sending her falling onto her side with a gasp.

The kobold loomed over her, its eyes blazing with fury. "QUIET!" it roared in her face. Its breath reeked of rotting meat and poorly digested meals. Spittle sprayed across the side of her face, making her cringe and close her eyes to keep it out. "One more word and I will—"

"You will do nothing!" Karak's voice suddenly barked. Like a candle snuffing out, the kobold's wrath evaporated. It scrambled away from Sylvia, tail tucked between its legs. She stared after it, then turned to Karak in confusion. The dragon-man stood over her, his hands clasped formally behind his back. His eyes darted to the kobold. "Be on your way. I would speak with this one."

The kobold growled but did not question the order. It scampered away, leaving Sylvia and the children alone with Karak. She blinked, baffled, and looked up at him.

To her surprise, Karak knelt in front of her and took hold of her shoulders, gently helping her up to her knees. His grip, despite his claws and the strength he had displayed so far, was remarkably gentle. He gave her head a thorough examination, then nodded in satisfaction. "A mild bruise, nothing more. You will be fine."

Sylvia stared at him, dumbfounded. Karak smiled and shook his head. "Do not misunderstand me. I do not ensure your physical health out of any form of affection. I merely have standards, a trait my companions are regrettably slow to take up."

Sylvia closed her mouth and narrowed her eyes. "How noble of you," she said sarcastically.

Karak's smirk persisted a moment longer, then grew. "I remember you. You attacked me. With a *chair.*"

"You were hurting my friend," Sylvia shot back without hesitation. "I had to help him."

Karak's smile faded. "I do recall the strange affection you two displayed for one another. He called you 'Sylvia,' did he not? It is a very pretty name."

Sylvia cringed in revulsion as Karak brushed a strand of her disheveled hair out of her face. She forced herself to hold still until he withdrew.

"He fought with respectable valor — and remarkable stupidity — to try and defend you," Karak added, his tone mocking.

Sylvia bristled as she recalled the brutal beatdown she had witnessed. She bit her lip to keep herself from verbally tearing Karak apart. No matter how much she hated him, she had no desire to invoke his wrath, especially since he seemed to be in a civil mood. She took a deep breath to calm herself. "You said you wanted to talk to me," she recalled.

Karak chuckled and shrugged his shoulders. "I have questions for you. About your friend. Skunk, was it? It is a rare thing to see dragonkin mingling with humans, especially with such intimacy. How did you come to know one another?"

Sylvia narrowed her eyes. "That's none of your business," she said simply.

Karak lost his smile. "You stand to gain nothing by defying me, girl. Answer my question."

Sylvia ground her teeth together but eventually gave in. She'd give him just enough to satisfy his curiosity, but nothing more. "We were both really little at the time. I don't remember much. I saw him running into the woods and I followed him. We sat under a log together to get out of the rain and we talked. The adults found us and brought us home. He's been my best friend ever since."

Karak hummed quietly, his tail lashing at the stone behind him. He clearly suspected she was keeping things from him. "And by what justification was he allowed to live among you?" he asked. "Kobolds do not mix with humans. They are like oil and vinegar, ice and fire. Forces in constant opposition."

"You're wrong. Skunk is our friend," Sylvia refuted. "He has a good heart, and he's always willing to help whoever needs it."

Karak's grin grew. "Ah, I see. So he is tolerated because he is *useful,*" he deduced, an edge of disdain creeping into his voice. "Little more than a slave or a servant, then."

Sylvia scowled, shaking her head again. "No! He's our *friend!* He helps teach the children at the schoolhouse, and he helps protect us!"

Karak barked out a condescending laugh, and Sylvia felt the hair on the back of her neck stand on end. "Allow me to correct you, dear. He *tried* to protect you. And he failed. Spectacularly."

"Why does it matter?" Sylvia demanded, trying to ignore the rising tide of anger she felt at hearing her dearest friend insulted and disparaged at every turn.

Karak made a show of considering the question for a moment, then offered another shrug. His smile returned, almost sheepish. "I confess, it does not. The runt is no threat to me, but he *is* an oddity. I was curious about him, and now my curiosity is satisfied."

Karak stood back up, a silent declaration that the conversation was over. Sylvia, however, was not going to let this chance slip her by. As long as she had the ear of the enemy's leader, she might as well see if she could get some answers.

"I have a curiosity of my own," She called as he turned to leave, drawing a few angered glances from the other kobolds.

Karak paused and turned to face her, tilting his head. He said nothing.

Sensing that he was listening, Sylvia continued. "Fair is fair. I answered your questions. Answer mine."

The kobold Karak had dismissed before growled and moved toward her.

"You do not ask questions—" it began to shout, but Karak lifted a hand, silencing it. He stared down at Sylvia for several seconds, then folded his hands behind his back.

"Very well. Speak."

Sylvia blinked in surprise. She hadn't been expecting that to work. She took a deep breath, trying to shake off the nervous jitters creeping up her spine. "Why do you want us?" she finally asked, the first question to come to mind. "There would be no point in keeping us alive unless you need us for something. And just a moment ago, you went out of your way to make sure your 'companion' didn't damage me too badly. So why? What do you want?"

Karak stared at her for a moment, then put on a large grin. "You are to be brought back to our home," he said plainly. "There, you will be given a choice. You will either cast off the shackles of your prior allegiances and join hands in common cause with us, or you will be cast into the flames as a sacrifice, that your flesh and soul might nourish the Young Master."

Sylvia blinked, horrified. "W-what?" she choked out. "Betray our friends or be sacrificed?! Why?! What for?! And who is this 'Young Master' you keep talking about?!"

Karak's smile faded. He stared her down for several long seconds, then looked up at the ring in the sky. "You will know all, in time. For the moment, all you need to know is that your service, or your sacrifice, is not done for the sake of bloodlust or malice. No, what I do, I do only so that justice is finally done, that the sins of antiquity are at last put right."

"What sin? What are you talking about? And how does murdering people put *anything* right?" Sylvia questioned, narrowing her eyes.

"The *ultimate* sin," Karak said, spinning to face her. "The sin of the Auriuns that brought dragonkin to the precipice of extinction upon which we *still* teeter. I will freely acknowledge that you, specifically, may have had no hand in the sin when it began. But by the mere beating of your heart, the *accident* of your birth, you perpetuate it."

"But we haven't *done* anything!" Sylvia shot back. "And we're not Auriuns! We're just farmers, *human* farmers! We would have been happy to sit by and leave you in peace, but *you* attacked *us!*"

"Your inaction does not absolve you," Karak said bluntly.

"Absolve us of—"

"Enough," Karak cut her off, shaking his head. "Your temper rises. Even were I to tell you all there is to know, you would not listen. If you did, you would not be able to understand. If you were able, you would choose not to. Your first curiosity is sated, but I will waste no more breath on this conversation. You will *all* be made to know the truth, in time, when you are *ready* to *listen*. But until then, I command you to be silent."

Karak turned away, folded his hands behind his back, and began to walk away. Sylvia watched him go, her teeth grinding together behind her lips. As much as she hated to admit it, he was right. Her temper *was* rising. Sylvia had never been an angry sort, she'd only felt angry once or twice before in the whole of her life. But this creature, his callous dismissal of their lives, the smug ease with which he promised to sacrifice them, was the last straw.

"You're blind," she said before she could stop herself. "And you're *wrong.*"

Karak froze and slowly turned to look at her over his shoulder. His eyes had narrowed dangerously.

Sylvia continued, knowing she'd already crossed a line there was no turning back from. "You say we're complicit in a sin? That we share the burden of some horrible crime? Even if that were true, do you think that gives you any right to commit sins of your own with impunity? Does that justify the blood on your hands? Does that justify the murder, the deaths, and the burning of our homes?! Does *our* sin absolve you of your own?!"

The silence and tension that lingered in the wake of her questions settled on her shoulders like a blanket as heavy as all the world. All eyes were on her. The townsfolk were horrified, not by her words, but by her boldness, while the kobolds stared at her with barely contained hatred, or at Karak with curiosity, wondering how he would answer.

Karak's tail swished. "Yes," he finally said in a matter-of-fact tone. "It does. For no sin I ever commit, no evil, could ever eclipse that which runs fresh in your veins."

Sylvia withered. She hadn't truly expected her impassioned speech to sway him, but as the adrenaline faded, and his unmoved stare bored into her, she finally began to realize what she had just done.

Karak turned to her directly. "You say I am blind?" he went on slowly, his voice like smoldering coals and smothering ashes. "No. I *was* blind, once. But then I was blessed to have my eyes opened to the truth. And I'll not shut them again."

He leveled a finger at Sylvia. "You, on the other hand, have proven your blindness to me. And I do believe I commanded your silence."

Sylvia heard something moving behind her. Before she could react, she felt a clawed hand grabbing the back of her head. She gasped, her face driven into the hard ground. Stars exploded across her vision, and she shrieked in pain.

"You should know, child, that it is unwise to disobey the command of your betters," Karak's voice reached her from above, cold and merciless. When he spoke again, it was to someone other than her. "Have your fun with her. Make an example of her. Show the rest of them the consequences of defiance. Just don't kill her. Dead meat is useless to us."

Ungentle fingers curled into her hair, hauling Sylvia back up with a painful jerk. Her vision was blurring, tearing up from the pain, and something warm and wet was dribbling out of her nose. She saw the terrified faces of the children nearby, watching her.

She tried to smile at them. "It's okay," she said to them. "It's going to be okay. I promise."

She heard the scraping of steel, and a sickening cackle behind her.

Her vision went silver, then black, and her world was pain.

Meeting

"Order, everyone!" Seto's voice, exhausted but steady, rang clearly over the front yard of the town hall. As one of the oldest people still alive after the attack, one of the most well-traveled, and as the teacher at the schoolhouse, Seto had been elected to direct and moderate this meeting. Given his skills at rallying the attention of unruly children, Skunk imagined that he would be a natural in the role.

Skunk looked on at it all from one of the far edges of the large space, his claws fidgeting anxiously over his heart. There were so few people here. Fewer than he had been expecting, even when considering the massacre. Was this all that was left? Or had others simply elected to stay home and let others sort everything out?

As if sensing his concerns, a hand pat the space between his horns. He looked up to see Amelia giving him a reassuring smile. He swished his tail a few times, appreciating the gesture. That small kindness did nothing to ease the tension in the air, sadly. Anxiety and dread were felt by all, cyclically feeding each other like a horde of snakes devouring each other's tails.

One person stood out in the crowd in this regard. Danica stood at the opposite end of the fenced-in yard, leaning against the wall with her arms crossed and her eyes locked attentively on Seto. A large leather-bound book was open in her hands. Skunk wasn't entirely sure she'd received an invitation to be here, but he certainly wasn't going to be the one to ask her to leave.

Seto called for order a few more times before the anxious villagers fell into silence. Once he was sure he had everyone's attention, he cleared his throat and clasped his hands behind his back.

"Thank you all for coming," he began, putting as much authority into his voice as he could manage. "I do not need to tell you that last night was, perhaps, the worst night in Addernotch's history. Our homes stand burned and collapsed, our friends and families dragged into the night, and our leaders slain before our very eyes. Against the might of our invaders, we stood little chance. Still, I believe Addernotch's militia may take some pride in the fact that they made our enemy bleed for every inch they took."

A general murmur went up from the crowd. Skunk eyed them, and he could see a handful of men and women who had fought in the battle perking up a little. The expressions on their faces ranged from forced pride in their effort, to disappointment that it had been inadequate.

Seto went on. "But now, at least for the time being, the battle is over, and we must decide what we are to do next. Now, I am but an old man, with little knowledge of the arts of war and battle. While I appreciate the trust you have all put in me to conduct this meeting, I am no mayor, and I am no marshal. I am merely to help keep the discussion civil."

"What is there to discuss?!" A man shouted from the crowd, a younger gentleman with his arm in a sling. He angrily stomped his foot. "Way I see it, our friends and families were taken, so we gotta get 'em back! Simple as that!"

Skunk did not know that man's name, but at that moment he decided he liked him.

The next person to speak, not so much. Another man, somewhat older, his hair short and graying, with lines of experience and stress set deep into his tanned face. His brow furrowed at the younger man. "And how exactly do you propose we do that, lad?" he asked, crossing his arms. "We were at our best, and we were *braced* for an attack, but the kobolds still tore us apart. We're utterly outmatched, and even if we weren't, we don't know where they went."

The first man scowled, his face reddening with anger. "Oh, so we're to just leave our neighbors to die?! Is that it?!" he shouted.

The older man shook his head. "That's not what I'm saying—"

The younger man jabbed a finger at him, cutting him off. "My *brother's* among the missing! I gotta assume the kobolds want them alive for some reason, but I'm not willing to put money on them staying that way for long!"

A handful of others raised their voices in agreement, shouting at the older gentleman. Skunk winced, hearing the word 'coward' thrown around more than once. Seto quickly raised his hands, letting out a series of sharp cawing sounds that silenced the rising chorus of discontent. "All of you, please, calm yourselves!" He called over the last vestiges of the clamor. "All opinions are to be heard! Squabbling and bickering among ourselves will get us nowhere."

There was a tense moment where no one said a word, everyone allowing their collective tempers to cool down a bit. The older man looked down and sighed. "I know how you feel, lad. Believe me, I do. I *wish* we could go after the kobolds. They took loved ones of mine, too. But you need to understand that our militia was devastated in the attack. Over half of the survivors are in no condition to travel, much less do any more fighting. Our battle-ready force numbers under twenty, by my count."

"I can still fight!" the younger man countered indignantly.

"Son, your arm is in a *sling.*"

"I got two arms!"

"You would get yourself killed."

The young man opened his mouth to continue the argument, then winced, his free hand flying up to his injured shoulder. A moment later, he conceded the point with an agitated grunt, kicking the earth again.

Another voice joined in the discussion, a woman this time. "Not all of us are fighters," she pointed out. "Most of us in this town 'ave always been farmers. We've got children, *bloody children,* huddlin' up in Seto's schoolhouse cause their folks up and got taken away. I don't like the idea of what's left of our militia goin' out there, leavin' our young defenseless, and maybe even gettin' themselves killed. There's been enough death already."

It took a moment, but more voices steadily rose to agree with her. Skunk listened to it all, and he felt his heart dropping. When he had come to this meeting, he had hoped that the consensus would be to plan a rescue. Go out, get their missing people, and bring them back as soon as possible. But that was not the tone of the discussion, and while he could recognize the logic, his heart could not accept it.

"Amelia," Seto suddenly said, drawing Skunk out of his reverie. He looked up to the birdman along with his mother. "Have you anything to add?"

Amelia was quiet for a moment. She looked around at the gathered townsfolk, and Skunk could see it on her face that she was torn on what to say. A second later, she turned to address the crowd.

"As much as it pains me to say it, we are in no fit state to send anyone after the kobolds, much less survive if the horde should launch another attack," she stated in a tone of resignation. Skunk looked up at her, his eyes flying wide in shock.

"Mom!" he protested.

Amelia flashed him a guilty look but kept talking. "Like the older gentleman said, we lost too many people. Sending our still battle-ready forces after our attackers would only end in more deaths, and leave the civilians undefended. I say that we call for aid from Port Natha and Underbridge. Dispatch messengers to those two towns, along with a one or two-man escort from what's left of the militia for each."

"But we're already short on swords," the younger man from before pointed out. "You're asking us to weaken our defenses even more?"

Amelia sighed and shook her head. "As I said, we won't survive another attack if the kobolds return even as we are now. At least this way our messengers have a better chance of reaching their destination, and more hands to pass their letter to if they come under attack."

The logic was sound, but that didn't make it any better in Skunk's ears. He turned back to the crowd, hoping desperately that someone might raise their voice to counter his mother's points. There was only more agreement.

Another man spoke up. "Those cities aren't exactly close. It'll take two days to reach Port Natha, if everything goes smoothly, and more for Underbridge. We'll be sitting ducks in the meantime."

"What about the ry'thar?" another woman asked. "Amelia, you got ties to them, don't ya? They're good in a fight. Maybe they can help us out."

Amelia nodded. "Yes, I have a good relationship with the tribe to our north. I can petition them for aid, but I cannot promise they will *answer* the call."

"And why the hell not?" the man with the sling asked. "We've been trading partners with them for years!"

Amelia turned to him. "Most ry'thar tribes are insular and isolationist by nature. The Karjene are no exception. They don't like to involve themselves in the affairs of others, especially in matters of war. Unless they perceive an immediate threat to their own safety from the kobolds, they will not be inclined to lend their spears to our cause. It simply would not be their fight."

"The kobolds seemed to be coming from the north," Seto observed a moment later, and a few murmurs went through the crowd as the masses caught onto his line of thought. "Do you think the kobolds and the Karjene may have already traded blows?"

Amelia shrugged. "It's possible. And it would go some way toward explaining why they haven't shown up to trade this season. But we do not know for certain how *far* north the horde's burrow is. They could very well have emerged from the ridges that divide our territories."

"And in the meantime," the older gentleman added. "Those of us still fit to do so can try to prepare the town for another attack. Traps, palisades, spike pits, barricades. Whatever we can craft to slow the kobolds down and force them where we have an advantage. They have numbers and speed on their side, but they're smaller and weaker than most of the militia. Funnel them into chokepoints and we might stand more of a chance."

Seto nodded. "Very well. Then I say we put it to a vote. All in favor of sending word to Underbridge, Port Natha, and the ry'thar for aid, say aye."

A chorus of "aye" rose from the crowd, with only a scattered few staying quiet. It was clear that the ayes had it.

Nowhere in their immediate plan of action were there any provisions to go after the missing villagers.

No one was lifting a finger to go after Sylvia.

For Skunk, that was the last straw.

Before he knew it, he had stepped forward. "No!" he shouted before he could stop himself. All eyes turned to him, the tempo of the discussion grinding to a halt. He hesitated for a second, intimidated by all of the eyes boring into him, but forced himself to continue. He leaned forward, holding his hands out in a pleading manner. "We can't just abandon them! Those are *our* people! They didn't stop being worth protecting when they were hauled away! We have to send *someone* to help them!"

The faces kept staring, and Skunk realized that their expressions were *not* welcoming of his opinion. Cold glares, skeptical scowls, and pitying frowns were all he received. Still, he had gotten started, and he was not about to give up. Not now.

"Skunk," Amelia said quietly from behind him, her hand finding his shoulder. He jerked forward, shaking off her grip. He placed a hand over his heart.

"S-send me!" he pleaded desperately. "I can track them down! I know what they smell like, and I can move faster than the rest of you! Send me to find them, and I will! The kobolds will be slowed down by their prisoners, right? I can—"

"Oh, would you just shut up already?! No one asked for *your* opinion, *monster!*" A new voice cut him off, sharp and bitter. Skunk shrank back, his words dying in his throat as he cowered against the ground. The owner of the voice, a tall and skinny woman with wild red hair and green eyes, emerged from the crowd, her wrinkled pale face set in a disgusted snarl.

Skunk knew her. He'd never be able to forget her.

"F-Freya," he choked out her name, already dreading what was to come next.

She came to a stop a few yards away and jabbed an accusatory finger at him. "You're one of *them!* Why in the world should anyone here listen to a thing you have to say?!"

Skunk took another step back, shaking his head. "Freya, please. I just wanna help my people," he tried.

Freya snorted. "Your people? Well, I dunno if you have the brains to notice, *kobold,* but *your people* are precisely what put us in this situation!"

"N-no!" Skunk protested loudly, not noticing how tightly his right hand was clenched around his left. A familiar, sickening tingle crept into the tips of his fingers, and the faint taste of copper was on his lips. "Please, just let me—"

"I said SHUT!" Freya shouted, her voice breaking with emotion, and again, Skunk went silent. Freya gestured at him as she turned to the rest of the crowd. "Look at it! This little bastard has been living in our town for years! I've been willing to put up with him all this time simply 'cause I was out-voted on the matter! But now a bunch of kobolds that look *just like him* turn up on our doorstep to kill and haul off our loved ones! Who's to say he hasn't been feeding them information about us!? I say we put him to the sword!"
There was no delay between that declaration and the chorus of angry voices rising to shut Freya down. For a fraction of a second, a tiny smile graced Skunk's lips. *At least some of them still trust me...*

Seto clacked his beak loudly, the sharp sound echoing across the yard like the strike of a gavel. "Freya, that is enough! Skunk put his life on the line to protect me and my students last night. I watched him practically sacrifice himself for our sake. He is not our enemy, and I'll not have you wishing harm on one of our own!"

Freya scoffed. "Oh, of course, *you'd* defend him!" she accused, waving him off dismissively. She turned back to Skunk. "But those monsters took my *son,* and I mean to see *someone* pay for it!"

Skunk's eyes flew wide. "Your son was taken?" he echoed in horrified disbelief.

Freya bared her teeth. "Oh, remember him, do ya?" she seethed, taking a threatening step toward him. "Figured you'd have put him from your mind, seeing as *you're* not the one who has to bear the scars!"

Skunk's left hand was burning at this point, and somewhere in the back of his head, he could hear the hungry snarl of a starving beast. He shook his head. "Freya—"

"My little boy is gone! And your kind, your flesh and blood, took him away from me!" Freya cut him off again.

Skunk wilted on the spot, overwhelmed by a rush of shame and guilt. He looked down, his eyes losing focus. "I... I'm sorry..." he muttered.

"Being sorry won't bring my boy back! And it won't make what *you* did to him any better! They should've killed you *years* ago!"

Suddenly, there was a rush of movement from behind him. Skunk looked up just in time to watch Amelia close the gap with Freya and punch her, *hard,* in the face. Startled shouts rose from the crowd as a sickening *crack* echoed through the air, and Freya fell onto her backside with a cry of pain.

Skunk's eyes widened. He lifted his hands to his mother, words already forming on his lips to try and tell her to stop, but Amelia beat him to it.

"*Never* speak to *my* boy that way again, Freya!" She shouted, her voice louder and filled with more fury than Skunk had ever heard before. "I can accept that you've never liked him. I can respect that you want someone to blame for what has happened to your son. But if you *ever* speak to *my* son like that again, I *will* break far more than your nose. Do you understand me?!"

"Mom, please," Skunk begged, snapping out of his trance. He grabbed her arm, drawing her eyes down to him. He flinched at the fire he saw in them, but it was impossible for him to truly be afraid of her. He squeezed her arm tight and shook his head. "Don't do this. Just let it go," he begged. "Please. It's not worth it."

Amelia looked down at him for several long seconds, her chest heaving. Everything around them was silent, everyone waiting to see what would happen next. Finally, Amelia let out a heavy sigh. She turned back to Freya. A moment later, she held out a hand to help the other woman up.

Freya eyed the hand warily. When hers came away from her face, Skunk saw with a guilty wince that blood was leaking out of Freya's nose. She wiped it away, then stood without accepting Amelia's hand. She glared down at Skunk, her eyes ablaze, and spat at his feet before skulking back into the crowd.

Against the wall, Danica scoffed. The large book in her hand thumped close with a muffled thump that seemed far louder than it should have. Skunk's sensitive ears picked out a word muttered under her breath that everyone else missed. "Idiots."

Seto clacked his beak. "Enough. I fear we'll make no more progress tonight," he called out, tired and resigned. "We reconvene tomorrow at first light to pick our messengers and their escorts. This meeting is adjourned. Get some rest, everyone."

Amelia had a hard time taking her eyes off Skunk as they filtered out of the yard and back out into the streets. The kobold's face was barren of his customary joy and optimism. In its place was a pall of dejection and disappointment. More than that, however, was the shame. It had fallen over his eyes after the confrontation with Freya. She knew her son's history with the woman well enough to know that the encounter had left him shaken and off-balance.

"We can't just leave them," Skunk insisted under his breath once they were a ways away from the town hall. He looked up at Amelia, his eyes shimmering with quiet desperation.

"We won't abandon them," Amelia assured him, kneeling to be at his level. She grabbed his shoulders, giving them a firm squeeze. "But you have to understand. This is a difficult situation. Everyone is scared and out of their element. We have to be careful, or we're just going to get more people killed."

Skunk looked down, sagging in place. "I know," he mumbled, kicking at a stray stone. "I just hate the thought of our friends waiting for rescue... of *Sylvia* waiting for rescue, and never getting it."

Amelia was quiet for a long moment. She sighed and ran her hand down the back of his neck, trying to comfort him. "I know, sweetie," she whispered before pulling him into a hug. "Once reinforcements arrive, we can plan a proper counter-attack. Until then, however, the safety of the survivors has to come first, and everyone will have a part to play in the days ahead. That includes you."

Skunk shuddered before gratefully returning the hug. "Just promise me," he began, his voice hitching in his throat. "Promise me we'll get Sylvia back."

Amelia opened her mouth but stopped herself just before the words could leave her throat. She silently reprimanded herself for the impulse, knowing that such a promise was not hers to make. Unfortunately, she knew the ways of the green scales better than he did. The odds of Sylvia, or anyone, still being alive by the time a counter-attack could be organized were slim to none.

"*Promise* me!" Skunk insisted, pulling back to look into her eyes. The look on his face broke her heart. There was so much pain in his eyes. So much fear. She had only seen that look in his eyes once *before*, and it had been the worst time in Amelia's memory. To see it again...

Amelia sighed, looking away. *I can't drag him down any further,* she told herself solemnly. *The truth shall have its due, of that I am sure. But for now...* She offered Skunk a reassuring smile. "I promise. I'll do everything i n my power to bring her home."

Skunk's tail swished a few times, and a tiny bit of light returned to his eyes. Thankfully, he seemed to miss how Amelia did not say she would bring Sylvia home *alive*.

Then Skunk blinked, his muzzle scrunching up. He sniffed at the air a few times and turned to the side. Curious, Amelia followed his gaze.

Danica was approaching them, leading her lumbering mount behind her. The smell Skunk had picked up reached Amelia, a powerful and earthy musk that could only have belonged to the curious beast.

"What *is* that thing?" Skunk asked, leaning back slightly.

Danica frowned at him. "His name is Lorok if you must know."

Amelia managed to chuckle, spying a chance to give Skunk a distraction. "He's a shelldigger. They're native to The World Below. They're often put to work by dwarven communities, serving as mounts or beasts of burden. See that armor? That and that tail makes them good in a fight, makes them tough. Their long strides make them excellent for getting around, and their big claws make them perfect for digging out tunnels."

Skunk's eyes lit up as he received this new information, his tail swishing a few times. "Woah... cool."

"You're educated," Danica grunted. "But I didn't come over here to discuss this big lug."

Amelia frowned and rose to her full height. Recalling the animosity of their previous encounter, Amelia carefully put herself between Skunk and the dwarf. Danica briefly quirked her brow, then shook her head and stood tall.

"You're going to the ry'thar to the north, are you not?" she asked, short and to the point.

"I am. Why?"

Danica hummed. She nodded once, then again, seemingly to herself as she came to a decision, then met Amelia's gaze again. "I want to go with you."

Amelia tilted her head in surprise. Her first impulse was to say 'absolutely not' and be on her way. Danica's treatment of Skunk had put the dwarf well and truly in Amelia's disfavor. But then she recalled how the woman had effectively saved both of them from Karak, and then there was the fact that it was Danica's healing pearl sealing up what was left of Skunk's wounds.

There is a debt to be repaid. Might as well hear her out, she decided, relaxing. "I say again. Why?"

"The ry'thar are supposed to be good hunters. They can track down the kobolds better than I ever could. But I need a guide to find them. You know them, and so you can guide me."

Amelia stared at the dwarf for a moment, crossing her arms over her chest in thought. "Even after what the kobolds did to this town, you would still chase after them?" she questioned in surprise. "I do not doubt you can handle yourself in a fight, but if you are planning to attack the burrow, it will only end in your death."

Danica shrugged. "This is far from the first green scale horde I've encountered. Trust me, I know my limits. The ry'thar can help me scout them out. Once I know what I'm up against, I can make a plan."

Skunk slowly inched out from behind Amelia, giving Danica a curious look. "You're really set on getting back what they stole from you, huh?" he asked in a low, curious voice.

Danica shot him a glare but nodded. "Yes. I've been fighting green scales for years now. It would carve shame into my line were I to give up now just because this horde is bigger than the others."

Amelia pondered the proposal. From the few things she had heard on the subject, Danica had been a fierce combatant when she had joined the fray last night, swiftly felling multiple kobolds with ease, and had been a large part of the relative success of Gothard's plan. Danica knew how to handle herself in a fight, and her near-obsessive commitment to finding the horde could prove useful to the people of Addernotch if given proper direction. And putting all that aside, Danica wouldn't be able to pick on Skunk if she was with Amelia.

And so she nodded her agreement. "Very well. You're welcome to accompany me to Karjene. I can introduce you to Tamaya. She's the war chief's daughter and my old friend. That should get you a foot in the door, at least."

Danica actually smiled, the first time Amelia had seen the woman do so. "Thanks," she said plainly. "When do we leave?"

Amelia glanced up at the sky. The sun had set some time back, and the night would still last for a while. Urgency demanded that she leave as soon as she could. But there was still the matter of Skunk's healing injuries...

She nodded and turned back to Danica. "Tomorrow, at first light. Meet me back here and we'll set off together."

Danica nodded without a word, then turned to depart, leading Lorok along.

Suddenly, Skunk spoke up. "Take me with you!"

Amelia turned to him, blinking in surprise. Skunk's posture was tall and straight, his eyes ablaze with a mixture of fiery determination and frantic desperation. He took a step forward. "Please! Let me help!"

Amelia swiftly shook her head. "No," she said simply. "I need you to stay here and help with the defense in case the kobolds come back."

Skunk gaped at her, his eyebrows furrowing with discontent. "What?! Mom, come on!" he exclaimed, spreading his arms out in a display of frustration. "You can't just leave me here! I can be more useful to you! I can tell when an enemy is coming, I can find their trail so we can track them later! I can find out if Sylvia is still alive! I can help keep you safe!"

Amelia knelt before him again, her jaw set. "No means no, Skunk. You're not leaving Addernotch."

Skunk shook his head in denial. "Mom, please—"

"Skunk, I am giving you an order!" Amelia said, raising her voice to emphasize the gravity of the situation. Skunk immediately went quiet, shrinking back. His eyes shimmered with hurt, and Amelia felt a sting of guilt. She forced herself to bury it and soldier on. *This is for his own good.* "Listen to me, Skunk. I understand how you feel, I do. But right now, I need you to stay *here*. I can look after myself, but these people need someone to look after *them*. That person is *you*. Do you understand me?"

Skunk worked his jaw up and down, fishing for some sort of retort or comeback, but in his exhaustion and inexperience, he found nothing. He let off a frustrated snort and kicked at the earth. "Damn it!" he shouted. Without another word, he turned on his heels, dropped to all fours, and sprinted down the street, swiftly vanishing from sight.

Amelia stood up, reaching after him as he ran away. She wanted to call out to him, but there was nothing she could say that would make this better. So she just watched as he rounded a corner and disappeared behind the burned remains of an old house.

Behind her, Danica shifted. "You confuse me," she grumbled. "From what I heard, he's good in a fight, and kobolds have a better sense of smell than anyone else. He's right, he could be useful. Far more useful with us than back here where everyone hates him. And you said it yourself. If the enemy returns, there is no hope of victory."

Amelia stared after her son. She did not turn to look at Danica. She took in a heavy breath. "You're right... but at the same time, what you and I are doing is dangerous. The Karjene are no friends to dragonkin, and Skunk shares the skin of our enemy, if not their heart. He'll be safer here." She looked down at the ground. "And besides, if we run into the horde, I cannot be sure that Skunk will be able to control himself. He means well, but he is impulsive. Reckless. He's emotionally driven, and after the events of the last few days, he is nothing *but* emotion. He wants his best friend back. If he sees a chance to rescue her, no matter how dangerous, he'll throw his life away to do it."

Amelia finally turned back to Danica and shook her head. "And I cannot allow that. Not with him. Here at least, he has the chance to run if the worst should come to pass."

Danica stared at Amelia for several long seconds, one eyebrow quirked. She looked past her where Skunk had run off. "You know he's never going to be able to take care of himself if you keep the leash so short. The boy proved himself in the attack, but you're suffocating him. Babying him."

Amelia frowned, a biting remark rising in her throat like bile, but she was quick to swallow it back down. Danica wouldn't understand. She *couldn't* understand. Amelia lifted a hand to her lower belly. "He *is* my baby," she stated simply before turning to follow her son back home. "And if it meant keeping him safe, then I would gladly give my life."

Behind her, she could just make out Danica's muttered response.

"Then for both of your sakes, I hope you never have to prove that."

Obedience

Skunk had the nightmare again. Addernotch ablaze, kobolds running rampant, blood and bodies littering the streets of his home. But there was something else, this time. Something deeper. A memory began to manifest.

Like a drop of ink spreading through a cup of water, the burning form of Addernotch was slowly replaced by a forest in the middle of the night. Rain poured down all around him, and Sylvia sat at his side, her cheeks flushed from the cold, her palms caked in dirt. The children huddled together, shivering in fear under the protective cover of a fallen tree.

A beast stalked toward them from the darkness beyond the rainfall curtains, shriveled and mangy. Its eyes, wide and crazed, caught what little light there was and shone with bloodthirsty anticipation. It bared its fangs.

Skunk returned the gesture in kind.

Under it all, somewhere far away at the edges of his senses, a voice called out to him.

No. Not calling. *Roaring.*

The starving animal lunged at him, and Skunk matched the charge despite his terror. Fangs and claws met, and liquid red mixed with the rain—

Skunk awoke with a start, the roar echoing loudly in his ears. He sat up, his eyes darting around in a groggy half-panic. As his senses caught up to his thoughts, he realized that he was in his room. He could hear almost nothing through the walls, and judging by the light, he figured it was still early.

Skunk groaned and flopped back into his nest of a bed. He stared blankly up at the ceiling as his heart began to calm itself, then closed his eyes. His thoughts wandered.

Mom's gonna leave this morning. He thought with a grimace. *She's leaving me here. Alone... in a town that hates me.*

He sucked in a long, deep breath before summarizing the entire situation in two words.

"This sucks."

After a few minutes, his stomach growled at him, and Skunk realized that he would find no more rest this morning. Groggy and grumpy, he hauled himself out of bed, got dressed, and stepped out of his room.

Early dawn sunlight spilled in through the front windows, painting the interior in autumnal shades of orange. He sniffed at the air, easily picking up Amelia's scent. The fatty, salty savor of fresh bacon accompanied it. Skunk hesitated for a moment, not really in the mood to trade words with Amelia, but his stomach growled at him again. The decision made, he stepped into the dining room.

Unsurprisingly, Amelia was already prepared for travel. Her daggers were strapped to her side and her bow was slung over her shoulders. Her usual garments were gone, replaced by a suit of dark padded armor similar to what the soldiers of the militia had worn. What set hers apart was the visible age, wear, and tear it had collected. It was darker in color, being almost black, and wrapped around her body as if it had been custom-tailored to fit her.

Another relic of her old life, Skunk supposed.

Amelia looked up as he entered and tried to smile. "Skunk. You're up. Did you sleep well?"

"No," was all he said. He sluggishly dropped himself in his chair and focused on the grain of the table.

He heard Amelia shifting in front of him. "Me neither," she confessed.

Neither of them said a word for the longest time. The air was thick with tension, and Skunk had no idea how to deal with it. So he just sat there, staring at the table and wishing he could turn back the clock to a few weeks ago. Eventually, Amelia dared to break the silence. She cleared her throat and spoke. "How are your wounds?"

"I'm fine," Skunk grumbled, propping his chin on a palm and tracing circles in the wood with a clawed fingertip. Danica's pearl had finished passing through his system last night shortly before he tucked in for bed. A few aches and pains notwithstanding, his wounds were all healed.

Amelia, sensing that he was not in the mood to talk, let off a quiet sigh. "Skunk, listen. I know you're afraid for Sylvia. I am, too. But—"

"Don't!" Skunk snapped, his lip twitching up to show off his teeth. "Just don't. I don't wanna hear it."

Amelia flinched back, her eyes wide. "Skunk," she breathed, lifting a hand toward him.

"I said *don't!* I get it. You already explained it to me. I don't need you to explain it *again.*"

Amelia looked like she wanted to say something else, but no words came. In the end, she set her hand down on the table and went back to eating.

Skunk's lips pressed tightly together. A small voice in the back of his head was screaming at him to apologize. It was buried under another, far more powerful voice. Primal, bitter, and *angry.* He could only imagine it was the dragonkin in him. It halted the words in his throat, leaving him silent for a long time. Eventually, though, he managed to push out a question.

"When are you leaving?"

Amelia looked out the nearby window, her brow furrowing. She sat back in her seat. "In truth, I should have left already," she confessed quietly. She looked back down at Skunk, and a tiny smile crept onto her face. "But I had to make sure you would be okay, first. I couldn't leave in good conscience if you were still hurt."

Skunk grunted. "You should get going, then," he said, just wanting this conversation to be over.

Amelia stared at him for a few seconds, her smile withering away. There was no hiding the hurt in her eyes. That little voice screamed again. And again, it was beaten down.

After a moment, Amelia stood up. "I have something for you, first," she said quietly. Stiffly. She walked past Skunk, drawing a confused glance from him. He turned in his chair to watch as she marched for the back of the room. It was then that Skunk finally noticed the bow and quiver of arrows leaning against the back wall. Amelia lifted them both and presented them to him. "Here. To replace the ones you lost."

Skunk took the bow and looked it over. It was plain and simple, utterly void of the elaborate and elegant flourishes of the sword she had given him. Still, it was well made. The wood was sturdy and had a good bend. He plucked the string a few times and found it satisfactory. "Where'd it come from?" he asked, genuinely curious.

"It used to belong to a soldier of the militia," Amelia explained. She looked away, her expression darkening. "He won't be needing it anymore. At least this way it will be put to good use."

Any pleasure Skunk may have felt at receiving this gift evaporated into mist. He frowned at the bow and ran his thumb over it with a newfound reverence. Sniffing it, he could just pick up a hint of garlic and pepper mingling with body sweat and greasy hair. He recalled the scent, albeit faintly, though he had no name or face to put to it. He set it down on the table and nodded. "I'll take care of it," he said, almost as if he were speaking to whoever had wielded the weapon in the past.

"I just want you to take care of *yourself* while I'm gone, alright?" Amelia said, reaching out to pull Skunk in for a hug, but he pulled back out of her reach.

"I wouldn't have to if you just *took me with you*," he grumbled irritably.

"You know why I can't do that," Amelia muttered, reaching out for him again. Not for a hug, but just to rest her hand on his shoulder. Skunk allowed it.

"Oh, you can," Skunk countered. "You just *won't*."

Amelia winced again, but then her expression hardened. "Skunk, listen to me—"

"No, you listen to *me!*" Skunk cut her off in a shout, his frustration at the whole situation finally boiling over the lid of his patience. He slammed his hands onto the table and stood up. He glared fiercely into her eyes, his teeth showing. "I'm not an idiot! I know you're not leaving me here because you want me to keep the town safe! I *can't* keep the town safe! I could barely keep one child safe! I *tried* to save people, and I just couldn't! But maybe I can help keep *you* safe! So why can't you just trust me to *try?!*"

"Skunk, that's not—"

"Do you think I'm weak?! Is that it?!" Skunk went on, shaking his head violently. "Do you think I'd slow you down?! What do I have to do to *make you trust me?!*"

The silence that followed was beyond heavy. Skunk blinked, his heart shriveling in his chest as his words echoed in his head. His wrath evaporated like the morning mist, and as he looked up into Amelia's eyes, he could only feel fear and dread.

Amelia's expression was utterly unreadable. "All I want is for you to be *safe,*" she finally told him, her tone even, measured, and ice-cold. "Nothing is more important. You have no idea how much you mean to me, Skunk. You *don't.*"

Skunk looked down and to the side, the last remnants of his anger conjuring up one final spitting remark. "You're right. I don't. But do you?"

If Amelia had an answer to that question, she did not voice it.

Skunk followed Amelia out of the house to link up with Danica a short time later. Neither of them had spoken since Skunk's outburst. What was there *to* say? Skunk already knew that any pleas for his mother to change her mind would fall on deaf ears. She had made up her mind, and if anyone was more stubborn than Skunk, it was the woman who raised him.

Might as well not waste my breath.

Danica was waiting for them by the town hall when they turned up, joined by her shelldigger mount and a brown horse. She stood with her arms crossed over her chest and an impatient frown on her face. She looked up as Amelia approached. "You're late," she called bluntly.

Amelia nodded toward Skunk. "Apologies. I was making sure my son was alright before setting out," she explained while heading for the horse.

Danica turned to the kobold. "Speaking of. My healing pearl?" she asked, holding out a hand.

Skunk flinched at the tone in her voice. He reached into his pocket and withdrew the metal sphere and the ringstone that had powered it. He turned them over a few times in his hand before giving them to Danica. "Here. It's been cleaned," he assured her.

"It'd better be," Danica grumbled as she pocketed them. She hoisted herself easily onto her strange beast's saddle. "Alright, Lorok," she said as she got settled. The beast tilted its head in response to the name, letting off a low snort. Danica smiled affectionately, patting it on the back of its head. "Let's go."

Amelia swung her leg over her horse's back as if she had done it a thousand times before. Thinking about it, Skunk figured she probably had. He looked up at her, feeling even smaller than before. His tail swished through the grass a few times, and one last time, he considered trying to convince her to let him come. He shut the impulse down, however.

Amelia looked back down at him, her eyes faintly shimmering in the early dawn light. "I'll be back soon, Skunk. You have my word. Take care until then. I love you."

Skunk opened his mouth to return the sentiment, but the words caught in his throat, silenced by his frustration.

Amelia waited for a few seconds, her eyes lowering with disappointment. She turned to Danica. "We ride north and west," she said simply. "It will be slow going until we reach the leoroch plains. But then we cut west until we reach the river, then follow it upstream. The Karjene make their camp on the bank, though where exactly they are will depend on the time of the year and the movement of the herds. It may take us several days to find them."

Danica nodded. "Lead the way."

Amelia hesitated. She gave Skunk one last glance, staring deep into his eyes. Time seemed to freeze around them, and Skunk felt a tugging in his chest. A familiar sting of guilt made itself known, finally overpowering his anger. "Just... stay safe," he begged in barely more than a whisper. "*Please.*"

Amelia held his gaze a moment longer. "I will," she promised. Then she looked ahead and spurred her horse into motion, cantering through the streets to the north. Danica gave Skunk a glance of her own, more skeptical, before following her. Lorok let out a happy warble as he went into motion.

Skunk watched them go. Every impulse screamed at him to give chase, but he refused to heed them. He stood in silent torture, watching his only family ride off with a stranger until, at last, both of them vanished into the forest to the north.

A bone-chilling breeze blew by, making Skunk shiver. He pulled his cloak tighter in a bid to keep warm. All at once, he felt suddenly and awfully alone. It was a feeling he was not accustomed to, and he did not like it.

The town began to come alive around him. Townsfolk were getting up and going about their days, and the shrieking of roosters greeting a new day rang out over the rooftops.

Skunk started walking. He couldn't stay still. He *hated* staying still. Being still meant he wasn't doing anything productive, and now more than ever his people needed him to make himself useful. He made his way to the one place he knew he could be useful, and the only place he knew he would be welcomed.

His mind was empty for most of the walk, and he did his best to ignore the rubble around him. Efforts were well underway to clear out the debris and get the town ready for what was to come. By the time Seto's schoolhouse was in view, Skunk could already see the occasional group of people moving about to try and set up defenses. There would be trenches, spike pits, barricades, and walls set up wherever it made sense.

Seto stood in front of the schoolhouse speaking with a couple of militiamen as Skunk crossed the bridge. Judging by Seto's narrowed eyes and the tension in his stance, the discussion was not going his way.

"I understand, sirs, but there are children here," Seto was stressing to them, his voice heavy with fatigue. "They lost their homes — or worse, their families — in the attack. They're scared and jumpy, and they have nowhere else to go. Is there nothing you can spare? Extra sheets to keep them warm, or even just some bread?"

One of the men shook his head regretfully. "I'm sorry, Seto, but the answer's final. Everyone's struggling right now, and the children aren't doing all the hard labor. They'll get what they need, but nothing more."

Seto clacked his beak several times in a display of agitation, then let off a low, resigned whistle. "Very well. We'll just have to make do, then," he grumbled, not bothering to hide his irritation.

The two militiamen nodded, then turned to leave. They caught sight of Skunk and stiffened, their hands flying for their weapons. Skunk came to a stop, his heart jumping into his throat and his hands raised in a placating gesture. The soldiers slowly relaxed, recognizing him. Still, the hateful fire in their eyes remained. Skunk cringed with hurt but tried to smile and wave.

"Bah. Leave him," One of the soldiers spat. Skunk sagged as the two walked by him, then grunted as one of them bumped him with their shoulder as they passed. Skunk turned to watch them go, a flare of anger in the back of his skull. His left hand curled into a fist, his scales tingling and burning under the bandages. He took a deep breath and forced himself not to react.

He turned back to Seto. The old krauven closed the distance to him, glaring after the departing soldiers. "The nerve," he hissed before looking at Skunk. "Are you alright, son?"

Skunk nodded tiredly. "I'm okay. I overheard what you guys were talking about. Things are pretty bad, huh?" he asked, hoping to take his thoughts away from how his people were treating him.

Seto sighed, running a hand down his face and beak. "Very. These children are scared for their lives and need every comfort I can get them. But practically speaking, what comforts there are to go around would be put to better use elsewhere."

Skunk looked back at Addernotch. The stink of the attack still hung thick in the air. Combined with his already festering frustration, it was enough to draw an involuntary snarl out of him.

Seto placed a hand on Skunk's shoulder to comfort him. "But what about you? How are you holding up? I can only imagine how hard the last few days have been on you."

Skunk kept his eyes locked on the town for several long seconds, trying to find the words to adequately describe his emotions. Finally, he brushed Seto's hand away. "I don't know, Gramps. It's just... *wrong*. Everything's wrong," he said, allowing his bitterness and frustration to creep into his voice, oblivious to how it was rising. "Everyone's hurting. *I'm* hurting! I'm sad, I'm anxious, I'm scared, I'm *angry!* I want to make it better, but I don't know how, and Mom left me behind, and I *hate it!*"

There was a moment of quiet, and Skunk realized with a blink that he'd started shouting. He looked up at Seto, expecting to find stern disapproval.

Instead, all he found was a solemn but understanding nod. Seto placed a hand on Skunk's back. "I understand how you feel, but I would urge you not to mistake the *feeling* of helplessness for being *truly* helpless. There is much work to be done here, and I can think of none better suited to help me."

Skunk looked down. "Sylvia would be."

There was a pause. "We'll just have to make do," Seto murmured.

Without a word, Skunk allowed himself to be escorted inside. The interior was much the same as it had been yesterday, the debris from his confrontation with Karak cleared out to make room for the children. There was a little more energy this time, thankfully. The children had gathered together in small groups scattered across the room, talking in hushed voices. There was still a pall of fear hanging over them, but it seemed the worst of the initial shock had passed. Skunk was pleased to see that there were at least a couple of little smiles here and there.

He glanced up at Seto. "Okay. What do you need me to do?"

Skunk put all of himself into the various tasks that needed doing over the next few hours. The work was monotonous and dull, and when combined with the profound lack of company, he found his mood dropping further with every task he completed. Time crawled by at a snail's pace, making things so much worse.

Still, he threw himself into all these tasks and more with vim and vigor. Sorting books. Clearing rubble. Repairing damage. The more physically demanding tasks were a blessing in disguise. He was not physically strong, so the extra effort he had to put into them gave him less room to get lost in the quagmire of his mind.

But underneath it all, there was no denying his dissatisfaction. This work was important, yes, and he would do it. But it *felt* meaningless to him. Trivial. Just mundane busywork absorbing his time and his energy. Time and energy that would be put to better use elsewhere. But he had nowhere else to *go*.

And then there were the stares. Most of the children couldn't help but watch him as he worked. Some would shy away from him as he passed, or whisper among themselves when they thought he wouldn't hear. They were scared, and he couldn't be mad at them for it. How could they feel any differently after what they'd all been through? Still, it upset him deeply, and that drove him to push himself all the harder.

And so he worked. And worked. And *worked*. His muscles ached from strain, his lungs burned for a reprieve, and his stomach snarled at him for lunch, but he did not relent. It was the most productive he had ever been in the schoolhouse. It hurt, and he latched onto that, letting it drive him on.

Skunk was outside, hammering away at a plank of wood to patch up the hole in the front of the schoolhouse when Seto emerged. He looked exhausted, his posture drooping and his eyes half-open. He gave Skunk's work an appraising look, then nodded. "That will do, Skunk. Take a break."

Skunk released the plank and took a step back, panting. He leaned against the wall he had just patched up and gave Seto a curious glance. "A break?" he asked, incredulous. "But there's still so much work to do."

Seto nodded, the worry evident on his face. "I know. But you've been running yourself ragged. It's almost noon, and I don't think I've seen you stop to catch your breath *once*. You're going to hurt yourself if you keep this up."

Skunk shook his head, turning back to the wall. "No, no. It's fine. There's a lot to do. Just—"

Seto's hand took him by the shoulder. Skunk blinked as the old man looked intensely into his eyes and slowly shook his head. "Skunk. Please. *Rest*. For my peace of mind, if nothing else."

Skunk wanted to argue the point and get back to work, but a twinge of pain in his shoulders and thighs shut him down. Agitated as it made him, he couldn't deny Seto's point. He *was* exhausted. The hammer slid out of his hand and thumped against the ground. With a growl, Skunk brushed away from Seto and dragged himself to the stream.

He groaned, sitting down by the water's edge and letting his bare feet fall into the stream. The cold water sent a shock of awareness through his system, dispelling some of his lethargy. He stared at his reflection.

His own face never used to evoke any kind of powerful emotion in him. But now? In his mind's eye, his face was replaced with that of the first kobold he killed. Lips quirked into a bloodthirsty grin, eyes alight with murderous glee, scales smeared with the viscera of a dead man. A feeling like fire boiled in Skunk's blood.

Shouting in anger, Skunk kicked his reflection. Water splashed up and around the blow, and the image was disrupted. A moment later, it returned, and he saw the bitter scowl on his face.

A lump formed in his throat. That wasn't how he was supposed to look.

"Skunk?" Seto called gingerly behind him as if to avoid scaring a frightened animal. "Are you sure you're feeling alright?"

"I'm fine," Skunk lied.

Seto clacked his beak. "Are you lying to me?"

"...Yes."

"I thought so," Seto chuckled softly. He sat down beside Skunk, dipping his feet into the water. He withdrew a few slices of bread and a cut of dried meat from a pouch at his side and held the meat out to Skunk. He accepted it with a quiet grunt. The two ate in a quiet, companionable silence.

Skunk looked down at the meat in his hand. He knew what Seto was doing. He was waiting for Skunk to start talking and venting. But even if he wanted to talk, he wasn't sure where he could begin. So he just nibbled on his lunch, letting his thoughts wander where they would. Eventually, he said the one thing that kept coming up in his thoughts over and over again.

"They hate me."

Seto draped a feathery arm over Skunk's shoulders. "No, they don't, Skunk. But they *are* scared," he said gently.

Skunk scoffed. "Yeah, *scared* of *me.*"

"They're just children," Seto insisted. "They don't know any better. But give them some time. They'll—"

"I'm not talking about the kids, Seto," Skunk cut him off. "Even the *adults* look at me like they wanna kill me. Hell, Freya *called* for everyone to kill me."

Seto cringed at that. He hummed, and his hold on Skunk tightened. "She did. But nearly everyone protested when she did."

Skunk sighed and shook his head. "That doesn't stop them from *glaring.*"

"Emotions are running high," Seto reminded him. "It's to be expected. You're not the only one suffering right now."

"Do you think I don't know that!?" Skunk suddenly snapped, shoving himself away from Seto's grasp and turning to face him. "I *know* that everyone's suffering right now! All I want is to do something about it, but I *can't!* All I can do is— is *sit* here with everyone else, twiddling my thumbs and *wishing I could do more* and— GAH!"

Skunk spun on his heels, raking his claws through the nearby guardrail of the bridge, leaving a series of deep, ugly gouges in the wood. Silence fell over the two, and Skunk realized with another pang of guilt just how childish he was acting. Flushing with embarrassment and shame, he quietly cleared his throat and turned around. There was no judgment on Seto's face. Just sympathy.

"I'm sorry," Skunk apologized. "I'm acting like a brat."

Seto shook his head. "No, no. Don't be sorry, Skunk. I was condescending to you. I'm the one who should be sorry."

Skunk was quiet a moment, then looked back down at his face in the water. He let out a heavy breath, sat down, and shook his head. "I just feel so *useless* right now. It's driving me nuts."

"I know, Skunk," Seto said softly, placing his hand on Skunk's back. "Believe me when I say I wish there was more I could do, too. Hell, were I still in the prime of my youth, I would have aided in the defense myself."

He shook his head sadly and looked down at Skunk. "But my youth is long behind me. The best I can do is look after these children."

Skunk closed his eyes. "It's not the best *I* can do."

Seto hummed quietly beside him. He patted Skunk on the back a few times. "No. Perhaps it isn't," he agreed. Skunk glanced at him, confused, but the krauven said nothing more on the subject. Instead, he stood up and offered his hand. "Come. Let's take a walk."

Skunk blinked, accepting the hand and rising to his feet. "A walk? Really?" he questioned. "But there's still so much work to do! And the kids!"

"The children will be fine, Skunk. They can manage on their own for ten minutes, and the work isn't going anywhere," Seto told him reassuringly. "You'll be much better equipped to handle it if you have a chance to clear your head."

Skunk wanted to argue, to stress that he wanted to get back to work, but in truth, he just didn't have the energy for it. Seto smiled at him, and the two set off at a slow pace through the streets of Addernotch. Seto led the way, keeping them on the southern border of the village. If Skunk were to guess, it was a deliberate move to keep them out of sight of the townsfolk going about their work, and far away from the forest.

He looked to the south, across the rolling fields. It was strange. It was all so pristine in that direction. Verdant greens, touched only by the slightest onset of the reds and golds of autumn. Clear blue skies, fluffy white clouds. The last colorful flowers of the summer season were just barely visible as tiny dots of color. If he stopped sniffing at the air and just drank in the view, he could almost imagine that there hadn't been any bloodshed.

Seto noticed Skunk looking and came to a stop. "Quite the view, isn't it?"

Skunk nodded. "I guess. Been there my whole life, though. It's not anything special to me."

Seto chuckled weakly. "I suppose that's fair. Still, you can't deny that it's pleasant."

"I guess."

A second passed, and Seto's cheeks lifted in a smirk. "Amelia chose quite the place to settle down. But you know, when I first moved here after she took you in, I *hated* it here."

Skunk looked up at Seto in surprise. "What? Really? Why?"

"I come from a jungle, Skunk. I was born in Orovyr. And then a large chunk of my life was spent in Underbridge, or out on the road. I was used to either being in motion, or surrounded by towering trees, or walls and ceilings and throngs of people. Some may have found it claustrophobic. Me? I found it comfortable. Securing. When in place, I had plenty to hold me down. On the move, I didn't have to worry about it. But to stay idle in a tiny place like this, surrounded by empty wilderness for miles in every direction? I felt loose. Untethered. Like I'd get swept up in the wind and drift off into a horizon I could never find my way back from."

Skunk tilted his head. "Then why did you stay?"

Seto smiled down at him. "Well, for one thing, I got used to it with time. But the main reason I endured it was for your mother's sake. The weeks after she took you in were not easy on her. Nobody knew the first thing about raising a kobold hatchling, and she needed someone to back her up when everyone else wanted her to get rid of you. I endured the hardship because I wanted to be there for my friend."

Skunk nodded along slowly, looking back out over the grassland beyond Addernotch's southern border. He folded his hands behind his back, his heart sinking as he thought of his mother.

He knew she could take care of herself, but he was still worried. And as he thought of her, his mind turned to their last interaction. He remembered shouting at the woman who raised him, who loved him unconditionally, and who had advocated for him every time his nature became a problem. His heart twisted in his chest, and he closed his eyes. "I wish I could be there for her," he mumbled dejectedly. "I wish she'd let me help her."

Seto was quiet for a few seconds. Without a word, he placed a hand on Skunk's back and gently urged him into motion. "Try not to be too angry with her, Skunk. All she wants is what's best for you."

Skunk was quiet for a few long seconds, recalling how their last real conversation ended.

"You have no idea how much you mean to me, Skunk. You don't."

Skunk frowned. In the moment he'd been too angry to process what she'd been saying. But now that he was thinking back on it, he realized there was much more to those words than he realized.

"Seto?"

"Yes?"

Skunk bit his lip for a moment, unsure of how to voice his question. "Before we left the house, Mom and I argued a little bit. And she told me that 'I have no idea what I mean to her.' Do you know what she meant by that?"

Seto looked forward, his hands folding behind his back. His face tightened with thought as if he were trying to measure just how much he should say. "Your mother is a complicated woman, Skunk," he began soberly. "She has more going on than you understand — and it is *not* for me to tell you. You'd have to ask her yourself."

He paused and faced Skunk, catching his gaze. "But I *can* and I *will* tell you this: Amelia *loves* you. She loves you more than life itself. She put everything on the line for your sake, and she has done every day you've been in her life."

Skunk looked off to one side, his regret mounting more and more. "I know that. I'm grateful, really. I love her, too, but... I dunno. I just wish she'd listen to me more."

Seto hummed. "Do you believe she needs to?"

Skunk blinked up at him. "What?"

Seto smiled and kept walking. "Just a thought. Don't mind me."

Skunk frowned, wanting to press the matter, but elected not to for the time being. The two fell back into silence, continuing their walk.

Eventually, a smell reached Skunk's nose. He paused, cringing at the stink of rot and decay. It would have been overwhelming had it not been somewhat smothered by the smell of freshly turned soil. Curious, his eyes followed his nose.

A graveyard, brand new, was being built along the southern end of the village. There had been so many bodies that the old graveyard simply wouldn't cut it anymore. Freshly filled graves were spaced out in roughly even rows, each one temporarily marked with simple wooden posts. One grave stood open, a collection of people standing around it as a body was lowered in. One man and three children.

A family. And judging by who was present, it was painfully apparent who they were burying.

Skunk came to a stop, his mind stilling. His senses focused on the family burying one of their own, and he could pick out the words. The father was kneeling to face his youngest child, a little girl who was only a few years old.

"Mommy's not coming back, sweetheart."

A lump formed in Skunk's throat. He rubbed at it anxiously. A moment later, one of the other children, a boy, spotted him. He whispered something and pointed, and all eyes landed on Skunk. He took a step back.

A tiny voice in the back of his mind sneered at him.

You're intruding.

They don't want you here.

They blame you.

You don't belong here.

Leave.

Seto sighed quietly. "We've been away long enough. We should turn back," he said, placing a hand on Skunk's shoulder.

Skunk, however, did not move. He remained rooted in place, his thoughts spiraling into a storm. *They lost their mother*, his mind echoed, the thought loud and all-consuming. *She was murdered. They are going to miss her. Did they have the chance? To tell her they loved her? Did they take it?*

Skunk began to stiffen. His guilt and regret swelled into absolute *shame*, spreading like a wildfire he was powerless to put out. His earlier behavior resurfaced, every misstep and regrettable decision replaying behind his eyes. He had interrupted her when she'd tried to comfort him. He'd snapped at her. He'd *snarled* at her, *bared his teeth* at her. He hadn't thanked her for the new bow she had given him. He'd *shouted* at her.

Worst of all, when she said she loved him, he didn't say it back. He'd just watched her ride off to an unknown fate with a stranger.

What if you never get another chance?

"Skunk?" Seto asked quietly.

Skunk took a deep breath. He looked down at the ground, his hands clenching into fists at his sides. "Seto?" he whispered as he came to a decision.

"What is it, my boy?"

"I'm going after Mom," Skunk finally said, his tail lashing at the earth. "I know she ordered me to stay. But I *can't.*" he looked up at the grieving family. He couldn't tell how they felt about him. If they hated him for what his kind did, or if they saw the fear in his eyes and pitied him. His eyes wandered down to the grave. "I was horrible to her before she left. I didn't let her say things. I was rude. I was angry. I *yelled* at her. I can't let things stay like this. Besides, There's nothing I can do *here*. At least out there, with her, I'll be useful. And I'll be with someone that I *know* cares."

He turned to look up at Seto. "And maybe she's right. Maybe I *don't* know how much I mean to her. And like you said — I have to ask her myself, don't I?"

Seto was quiet for a few seconds. Then he smiled. "Well, then, Skunk. If that is truly your heart's desire, then don't let this old bird stop you," he said plainly. "You don't need my permission."

Skunk blinked in surprise. He had been expecting Seto to caution him, citing recklessness or disobedience. But there was nothing of the sort. There was just pride. As if this was *exactly the outcome he had been hoping for.*

Oh, you clever bird, Skunk realized after a moment. It was so easy for Skunk to forget just how cunning the krauven could be. His face split with a wide grin, and he threw himself against Seto, giving his teacher a tight hug.

Seto returned the embrace gladly, patting Skunk on the back of the head. "Just promise me one thing, young man."

"What is it?"

Seto pulled back and nodded down at him. "Come back to us alive. Both of you."

Skunk pulled out of the embrace and threw a sharp salute. "I promise!" he declared emphatically, hit with a sudden surge of energy. "Thank you, gramps."

Seto smiled at him. "Why are you thanking me? I didn't do anything."

Skunk's grin grew, and both of them managed a small laugh. When it settled, Seto pat Skunk on the head between the horns. "Take care, my boy."

"I will," Skunk said, then turned and broke into a sprint through the town. He ignored the startled exclamations of the townsfolk he passed, the curious and suspicious glares. He knew he would have a *lot* of ground to make up for before he caught up with his quarry. But even with all of his aches and pains from the day's efforts so far, he felt confident he could make the journey.

He slid to a stop at the northern edge of town and stood upright. There was a moment of hesitation. The forest loomed over him, dark and imposing. He'd ventured into it many times in his life on hunts, but never once had crossing its threshold felt so daunting to him.

The hesitation passed almost as soon as it had hit him. He wasn't sitting around here waiting for things to happen. Maybe his mother didn't need his help. But *he* needed to be there for her, and he was not going to let her tell him no this time. He checked to make sure he had all he would need. Sword, check. Bow and arrows, check. A half-eaten slab of goat? Skunk quickly scarfed it down. Check.

Skunk gave himself a little shake, dropped onto all fours, and broke into a swift run for the edge of the forest. It only took him a moment to catch his mother's familiar scent, almost overtaken by the powerful and unfamiliar musk of Danica's strange mount, Lorok.

Don't get too far, you two, he thought as he barreled through the tree line. *I'm not letting you leave me behind!*

Behind him, Addernotch disappeared, swallowed by the trees.

The Leomar Forest

Danica unleashed a sigh of relief as she followed Amelia out of Addernotch. The spirited clamor of the forest replaced the depressing noise of the broken town, soothing the dwarf's nerves. She was by no means a lover of nature, but if given a choice between the high and infinite ceiling of the outer world or the suffocating, nearly claustrophobic confines of civilization, she would always choose the former. Lorok seemed happy as well, given the bounce in his step.

Neither woman spoke for some time, and Danica took the opportunity to consider her battle plans. She knew that a direct assault on the kobold burrow would be suicide. She was good, yes, but not *that* good. They would overwhelm her in moments, and that wasn't even considering that strange dragon-man, Karak.

Danica's brow furrowed as she thought of him. Karak had known her. The question was how? She would have remembered if she had ever met a creature like him.

Maybe he was simply told about me. She thought. *I've cut my way through enough smaller hordes. If any survivors reached him, they would've told their story. But he recognized who I was rather quickly...*

Now she had a headache.

"Bah!" Danica grunted, throwing up her arms.

Amelia turned to look back at her, quirking a brow. "Something wrong?" She asked.

"Just some shit not adding up. Nothing you need to worry about."

Amelia hummed and looked ahead. She led them down a narrow game trail winding through the lower forest. "I fear much is not adding up for me, as well," she admitted after a minute of quiet.

"Oh yeah?"

Amelia gestured vaguely. "Their leader. Karak. I find myself struggling to decipher how it is that he can even *exist*. I have traveled far and wide in my time and faced my fair share of kobolds. Never once have I encountered anything like him."

"Who cares? He's a dick," Danica spat bitterly. "And a coward. He turned tail and flew off the second I showed up rather than fight me."

Amelia glanced at Danica over her shoulder. There was a playful glint in her eyes that Danica decided she did not like. "I do not wish to insult you, but given what I saw of him, I fear you would not have lasted long."

Danica huffed. She would never admit it out loud, but the human was probably right. Not wanting the challenge to her pride go unanswered, however, she offered a boastful rebuke. "Bah. Like you would do any better!"

"I didn't do better. That is the point," Amelia pointed out, her grin unwavering.

"Got your ass whooped pretty bad, I remember," Danica said. "You and that kobold you keep."

Amelia lost her smile. She looked ahead to hide her face. "Yes, well, I am just grateful Skunk survived. Thank you, again."

The sudden shift in Amelia's mood threw Danica off balance. She stared at the woman for a few seconds. "Stone's blood. You mean it, don't you?" she finally asked, her voice low in disbelief. "You *really* care about that kobold like he's your son."

"He *is* my son," Amelia shot back in a biting tone as if it were a question she had long grown tired of answering. "I've raised him since he was a baby. I named him. I fed him. I housed him, and I took care of him."

Danica fell silent, letting the words sink in. She was still skeptical, but she determined that pushing the subject wasn't worth the effort. It wasn't her business anyway and had no bearing on her mission. "Whatever you say," she conceded with a shrug.

The two lapsed into silence. Danica took the opportunity to lean back and look up into the sky. Her eyes landed on the pale ring, intermittently blocked out by the canopy over her head. Its light combined with the rays from the sun, filtering through the gaps in the leaves to sparkle in her eyes like a thousand diamonds. She took in a deep breath, savoring the view and the fresh scent of the forest.

After a while, a new curiosity came to her. She returned her attention to Amelia, or rather, the woman's bow and daggers. From what little Danica had seen of it, Amelia's fighting style was as unorthodox as her family.

"Where did you learn to fight?" Danica finally asked.

Amelia did not look back. "Why is that important?" she asked.

Danica sat upright in her saddle. "Earlier, when we were talking about Karak, you made it sound like you're some master fighter. Given what I heard and saw of him, you'd have to be to survive. So, where did you learn to fight? Certainly not in the village."

Amelia was quiet for a few seconds, then shook her head. "I did not always live in Addernotch. I was given lessons on how to fight in Underbridge."

Danica leaned in. "By who?" she pressed.

"No one worth remembering."

Danica frowned. Amelia was not going to divulge the secrets of her past. Respecting the other woman's privacy, Danica fell silent and returned her attention to the sky. She allowed herself to relax, to ease into her saddle, and let the world pass her by. The steady *clip-clop* of the horse's hooves and the thumping of Lorok's clawed feet brought to mind the scrabble and crumbling of her homeland. And, without realizing it, she began to sing to herself.

She was quiet about it, and it was more a melodic mumble than anything, but it was there. The words came to her easily enough, the old guttural syllables of her native language stringing together one after another, flowing in a steady beat like the pounding of a drum. Or the strike of a pickaxe against the harsh stone.

"I didn't take you for a singer," Amelia's voice cut through the melody after a few minutes, jarring Danica out of the reverie. She looked down at Amelia to see a glint of amusement, as if she were expecting Danica to be embarrassed.

She merely shrugged. "I'm a dwarf. We're *all* singers."

Amelia blinked. "I'd heard that. I always thought it was an exaggeration, though."

"Not at all," Danica assured her. "It's how we tell stories and our histories. Even when we chisel it in stone or write it on paper, it's all lyrical."

"All of it?"

"*All* of it."

Amelia nodded along slowly. She looked ahead. "Then you and the ry'thar may just get along better than I thought. They have powerful oral traditions as well."

Danica hummed. "On that note, these ry'thar of yours. The Karjene, you called them? What should I know going in?"

Like a twig snapping, Amelia's demeanor changed almost immediately from cold and unflappable to perky and enthusiastic. "They are a proud people, but not in the ways you might expect. Many people mistakenly assume that the ry'thar are primitive barbarians or savages. But nothing could be further from the truth. Their ways are just different from those of humans, dwarves, and krauven. They tend to live in smaller, insular, and often nomadic communities. There is a powerful feeling of camaraderie between them and a deep reverence for their ancestors. They treat their territory with the utmost respect, and when they hunt, it is not a sport as it might be to human nobility, or an act of necessity as it might be for a beast. It is a ritual — a *ceremony* of sorts. I have been on a few such hunts. They are..."

Amelia paused, searching for the right words. "It is a *spiritual* matter to them. You are not an adult until you have hunted and slain your first ry'los — prey. The act of hunting the ry'los down and partaking of their flesh is one of their most important rituals. And when you join them, you can tell. I am not a religious woman, but the things I felt when I prowled across the savannah alongside those hunters must be similar to what many feel in churches. There's just this powerful sense of belonging. Unified purpose."

Danica nodded along slowly. "Hm. Sounds nice."

"Just be sure to mind your manners," Amelia added a moment later, realizing she had gotten lost in her own little world for a moment. "The ry'thar *are* still proud, and their traditions are *very* important to them. They have a strong sense of honor, and they are not fond of strangers. So in their presence, I would strongly advise you to be calm, polite, and as respectful as possible."

Danica grunted. "Great. All the things I'm good at."

Amelia shrugged. "You have the advantage of having me with you. Just follow my lead and you'll be fine."

"Hmph."

The two fell silent after that, having precious little else to discuss.

The two made decent time over the rest of the day, though not as much as Danica would have liked. Lorok, for all of his resilience and usefulness in a fight, was a cumbersome creature when compared to a horse. He could be just as fast as one when in an open environment, but out here in the forested foothills, thick with trees and exposed roots, his girth made it difficult to navigate. But leaving Lorok behind was simply out of the question, so they plodded on with the occasional need to take a detour.

The second day brought them into a different region of the forest, where the forest was broken up by a series of rocky ridges sloping down from the foothills of the Sybhrod mountains. It was even slower going over such jagged and uneven terrain, although this time, it was more because of Amelia's horse. Lorok's thick claws had no issues scrabbling over the jagged rock formations. Amelia's steed was not so well equipped, and so their pace was slow.

Once they passed the ridges, the ground sloped up steadily and easily, and the trees gradually began to thin. Amelia brought them to a halt as dusk settled. Danica frowned in confusion. "Why are we stopping?"

Amelia turned to her. "This is the last patch of relatively flat land before we reach the Leoroch Plains. We camp here."

Danica's frown deepened. "Why? We still have an hour or so before it's dark."

"I know. But beyond this point, we'll find no cover and no shelter. Anything hostile would spot us from miles away if we lit a fire, and at this altitude and time of year, we'd struggle to find meaningful sleep against the cold and the wind."

"I'm not fond of slowing our progress for the sake of a moment of comfort," Danica grunted. "But fine."

Amelia smiled and nodded before lowering herself from her horse. "Come, then. Let's make camp and-"

Before Amelia could finish the thought, Lorok suddenly lurched under Danica. She cried out in surprise, barely holding on as the shelldigger spun in place to glare to the south. It sniffed at the air a few times, then let out a low, trumpeting growl.

Something was coming.

Amelia drew her bow. "We were followed," she deduced, narrowing her eyes.

Danica nodded, jumping down from Lorok's back. She drew her bearded axe in one hand and a throwing axe in the other. "Looks that way," she said. She wondered for a moment what could have been tracking them, then decided to cast aside all notions of subtly. She bashed the flat side of her axe head against her thick chest plate, issuing forth a loud metallic clang. She followed it with a challenging shout. "Well, come on, then! Whatever stalks us, assuming you have the balls for it, come see why it's the worst mistake of your life to sneak up on Danica Flatstone!"

Amelia turned to Danica, her eyes wide and her jaw open in a look of abject disbelief. "What the hell are you doing?!" she demanded.

Danica shrugged. "Skipping to the fun part?"

She was pretty sure that Amelia's eye twitched at that, but neither said anything else, as the bushes up ahead began rustling. Whatever had followed them was approaching, slowly, but loudly. Danica drummed her fingers along the handles of her axes, expecting some manner of angry forest animal to come charging at them, or perhaps even a kobold left behind by Karak to ensure none followed him.

What emerged from the bushes, head down and hands wringing together sheepishly, was for sure a kobold, but not one Danica would have the pleasure of carving into bits anytime soon.

"Skunk?!" Amelia exclaimed, lowering her bow.

Skunk lifted his head just enough to look at his mother, and his lips curled up into an embarrassed smile. "Um... hi, mom," he greeted.

Danica lowered her axes. "Oh, for fuck's sake," she groaned, utterly disappointed.

"Skunk, what are you *doing* here?!" Amelia demanded, throwing her bow across her back and storming toward her flinching son. "I told you to stay in Addernotch!"

Skunk withdrew from her, and for a moment he appeared genuinely ashamed of himself. But then his expression hardened, and he met Amelia's glare with one of his own. "Yeah, you did. I decided not to."

Amelia inhaled sharply, her hands curling into fists at her sides. "Skunk, you... Why?! Why did you follow us?!"

"Because I belong with you," Skunk replied, unwavering. "Because I want to help you and make sure you're safe."

Amelia shook her head and ran a hand over her face. "Gods dammit, Skunk! I appreciate it, I do, but this is not the place for you. You need to go back. Right now."

"This isn't the place for me?" Skunk echoed, frowning. "Being by your side isn't the place for me?"

"Don't get smart with me!" Amelia countered, lowering her hand and affixing her son with another harsh glare. "That's not what I meant, and you know it! Now, I'm not going to ask you again. Go home. *Now.*"

"Oh, good, then I don't have to answer again. *No.*"

Amelia and Skunk stared at each other for several long moments. The tension in the air was palpable, and Danica could see now that the emotional streak Amelia had mentioned running in Skunk had not fallen very far from the tree. She said nothing, though. This was hardly her business. She leaned back against Lorok, crossed her arms, and waited for the family to be done with their pointless squabble.

Skunk took a deep breath when Amelia didn't say anything. "What good will I be back in Addernotch, mom?" he finally asked, lowering his voice to something more respectful. "When the horde attacked, I was *useless*. I could barely save three people. If the kobolds come back, I *won't* be able to keep the town safe. I'm not…" he screwed his eyes shut and shook his head. "I'm not good enough! I'm not strong enough, I'm not fast enough, I'm not *smart* enough! I'm not like you!"

Amelia took a step back, the fire in her eyes flickering. "Skunk…" she whispered, but her son kept going, unfaltering.

"Too many people I care about died or were taken in the attack. I couldn't save them, and I lost them! I can't… I c-can't lose you, too," Skunk shuddered and looked off to one side, his eyes going distant. "You're one of the only people who still cares about me. You, Seto, and Sylvia are the only ones who've ever stood up for me. And I've been taking that for granted for so long. I owe you *everything*. So just let me return the favor. Just this once. *Please.*"

Amelia was quiet for several long seconds, the anger long since faded from her eyes. Her hands clenched and relaxed at her sides over and over. She heaved a heavy sigh and opened her mouth to speak.

Thud.

The head of a crudely crafted arrow emerged from Amelia's chest. Skunk squeaked as fresh blood slapped across his face. His eyes widened. "Mom!"

Amelia's hand rose to the wound. She opened her mouth, but all that escaped her was a withering rasp.

Behind her, her horse shrieked in fear before another arrow punctured the beast's eye. It staggered to one side, then crumpled to the earth in a heap.

Danica came away from Lorok, her hands returning to her axes and her eyes darting around to hunt for their attackers. "Shit!"

Amelia fell to her knees, clutching at her chest and gasping for air. Skunk scrambled to catch her, holding her upright. "Mom!" he cried, his eyes locked onto the arrow. "Oh, no, no no! Mom! Mom, w-what do I do?!" he shouted, his hands hovering uselessly over the injury.

Amelia lifted her eyes to his. "*Fight,*" she ordered.

The advice was well given, for it was at that moment that the adversary made itself known in full. Danica turned to see a small horde of kobolds emerging from the underbrush just up the hill, jabbering and yapping at one another as they made the barreling descent. She sneered, smashing her axes together to create a spray of sparks. *They must have left some behind to cover their withdrawal,* she thought.

"Come on, then!" she roared, charging to meet the nearest kobold. It was armed with a spear. It snarled at her, its bulging muscles tensing for a thrust.

It was almost cute. It thought it had a chance.

Danica turned with the thrust, allowing it to scrape uselessly against the front of her breastplate, before bringing her right-hand axe into the kobold's skull. Scale and bone splintered, and the monster dropped dead at her feet. Another was coming up swiftly to replace it. Danica ducked its horizontal slash for her neck, hooked her arm under its leg to grab it by the groin, then used its own momentum to vault it over her shoulder. It crashed to the ground and squirmed for a moment before she crushed its head with a ferocious stomp.

A third kobold was upon her in a moment, coming at her from behind. The kobold jumped on her back, sending her staggering a few paces. Growling, she rotated her axe in her hand and swung it up, trying to strike the kobold's face on her shoulder. It was quick, swiftly shifting to her other shoulder. She just caught a glint of silver in the corner of her eye and realized it was holding a dagger, poised and ready to stab into her throat. Her heart leaped. She had no time to stop it!

Her ears rang with a meaty thud, and the kobold fell from her back with a gurgling squeal. Surprised, Danica turned to look at it. An arrow protruded from its eye. She looked and saw Amelia, bow in hand, but it was not her that had fired the arrow. Skunk stood beside her, the string of his bow still vibrating. The two made eye contact.

Danica nodded. "Keep them off me!" she ordered before turning and throwing herself at the next advancing kobolds. There were three of them. The ones on the left and right were armed with spears, while the one in the middle wielded a large, unwieldy club studded with what looked like lion teeth. Behind them, up the hill, Danica saw the archer that had sniped Amelia drawing another arrow, this one unquestionably aimed at her.

Danica pitched back and threw her first throwing axe with all her strength. The weapon flashed with each spin, catching sunlight before it found its mark between the kobold's eyes. The force of the impact was so great that blood and brains erupted out of the kobold's head. It fell to the ground, unable to even utter a cry of pain as its life came to an end.

Satisfied, Danica returned her attention to the trio of kobolds advancing on her. The one on her right snarled and lunged with a low thrust aiming for her ankle. She stepped back, bringing her axe down to catch the attack. This, unfortunately, left her side and back exposed, and the other spear-wielding kobold took advantage of the opening. It lunged with a howling roar.

It might have killed Danica, then, were it not for the furious shelldigger that plowed into it with all the subtlety of an erupting volcano. Danica smiled as Lorok's large maw clamped down on the squirming kobold, lifted it high into the air, and threw it against the ground. The kobold gasped, squirmed, and barely had a chance to scream before Lorok's stone-breaking claws tore its torso open.

Danica shifted around her current enemy's spear, keeping the shaft pinned to the earth with her axe. She lifted her bloodied boot and drove it into her enemy's knee. The joint inverted with a horrific crunch, and the kobold toppled, breathless.

Satisfied that it would not pester her any further, Danica focused on the one with the club just in time for its weapon to swing forward and catch her in the side. The breath was driven from her lungs, and she felt something shattering under her breastplate. The force of the blow knocked her off her feet. She tried to stand, but the kobold was on top of her a moment later, pinning her on her back. It snarled, clawing for her face and biting for her throat. She held it back, the muscles in her arms rippling as she put them to good use.

"Where's your master?!" Danica roared in the kobold's face. "Answer me, and I might let you live!"

The kobold said something in a language Danica did not understand, but she decided it was the wrong answer. She strained against it, managing to plant her foot against its belly. She kicked with all her might, sending the kobold off of her with a squeal. She quickly scrambled back to her feet as yet another kobold emerged from the nearby bushes, charging her with its bare claws. She turned to it. It was too close for her axe, but as she had already proven this day, she did not need her axes to brutalize an enemy.

As it charged, she turned and brought her fist into the side of its head, knocking the creature off-course and into the side of a tree. It gasped in pain as bark splintered from the trunk, then slumped to the ground. Seeing an opportunity, Danica grabbed its tail and threw it like a sack of potatoes at the kobold she had knocked to the ground a moment prior. The two bodies collided with a comical squeak before crumpling to the earth.

And then Lorok came upon them, rending their bodies with an agitated snarl.

"Good boy, Lorok!" Danica praised the shelldigger.

Lorok lifted his blood-smeared head, his nose flaring as he let out a warbling groan of delight.

Free of targets for the moment, Danica looked past Lorok to check in on Skunk and Amelia. To her surprise, the two were holding their own remarkably well. Skunk was shorter than everything else, but he more than made up for his short stature and lack of strength with sheer *speed.*

Danica watched, amazed, as Skunk drew one arrow and launched it into the chest of an advancing kobold, then turned to fire a second shot in the same amount of time it had taken Amelia to fire only *one* shot. Skunk's second shot missed his mark, she noted, but not by much. She saw a kobold emerging from behind a nearby tree, a long board of wood lined with spikes of bone clutched in its hand. It charged at Skunk, its fangs glistening.

Skunk saw it coming and ducked its first swing, his bow dropping to the ground. He rolled past his attacker, and when he rose, his sword was in his hand. His stance was stiff and awkward, his muscles overly tense, sure signs of a novice.

But again, his raw agility helped him to compensate for his lack of experience. As the kobold turned on him, he deftly avoided two swings of its board, his cloak billowing about him as he went.

"Traitor!" the larger kobold shouted in rage before lifting its weapon high, intending to smash Skunk into the dirt.

Skunk darted in, and his blade exposed his adversary's guts. At the same moment, an arrow from Amelia's bow struck the kobold in the back of the head, ending its life. It toppled forward like a felled tree, and Skunk quickly ducked between its legs and came back up behind it by Amelia's side, already moving to intercept his next target.

The kid needs practice, Danica thought idly as she turned to find her next target. *But he has a lot of potential.*

It did not occur to her just then that she was mentally praising a *kobold*.

There was only one enemy left for her to fight. It was larger than the others by a fair margin, its body marred by a handful of burns. Judging by the armor it wore on its shoulders, it was probably the leader of this party. Danica grinned. She heard Lorok snorting and starting to advance, but she held a hand out to him. "Sit, boy."

Lorok let out a confused whine but did as he was told. The earth shook slightly as the large animal plonked down onto his haunches.

Satisfied that this bout would be hers alone, Danica turned back to the kobold in front of her. She rested her axe casually on her shoulder and sized the kobold up with a low whistle. "Big boy, aren't you?"

The kobold snarled, lifting its weapon — a vicious-looking serrated sword. "The First Fang sees a threat in you, for whatever reason, and commands your surrender," he spat, advancing. "Failing that, he demands your death."

Danica quirked a brow. "Oh? You got your orders from that rolling turd, did you?" she asked before her lips rose in a bloodthirsty smirk. "Good. That means you can tell me *all* about him."

The kobold gave a battle cry and charged, the tip of his sword leading the way. Danica drew out her second throwing axe and hurled it at the kobold, but to her surprise, he managed to bat the projectile aside. The swing sent him into a spin, the momentum of which he used to swing his sword down in a diagonal slash for Danica's collarbone.

Danica lifted her weapon to catch the swing, grunting as she felt the strength behind the blow. She grinned. "Tall *and* strong? Nice!" she said before shoving the kobold back. "If you were a dwarf, I *might* think you were attractive!"

The kobold roared and charged her again. Danica braced for the charge, her axe rising to swat aside the horizontal slash. Her foe pivoted at the last second, dextrously tucking his blade back and out of the way of Danica's swing. Meeting no resistance, she over-extended, leaving her side unguarded. She quickly turned back for a clearing sweep, but not before the edge of the kobold's sword cut a burning gash down her left forearm. It withdrew as quickly as it had cut her, evading Danica's counter, and grinned.

"Imagine your repugnant dwarven male as you die!" He taunted with psychotic glee.

"Son of a—" Danica swore before charging to take the offensive. She made another swing, only for her enemy to dodge and give her another shallow injury, this time on her thigh.

The kobold grinned. "All fire, but no finesse!"

Danica felt a rising surge of rage at the insult. She took her axe in both hands and came in from the right, hoping to cut off the enemy's infuriating retreat. The kobold ducked low, parrying the worst of the diagonal slash before darting past Danica. He dragged his blade across her front as he passed. She only lived thanks to her breastplate.

She spun to face the kobold, and barely caught his follow-up slash with the shaft of her axe. The kobold's free hand flashed out to take a hold of the shaft, holding her axe in place. The kobold leaned in, grinning in her face. "No better than all the other dwarves I've killed..." he cackled mockingly.

Danica's eyes flew wide. There was a flicker of a memory, of a city plunged into darkness and screams surrounding her as the very earth of her home betrayed her. "W-what?" she asked, trying and failing to pull her axe away.

"I was there," the kobold went on, leaning in closer. "Oh, how they tried to fight. But as it always is... you fleshy things just die so very easily. It might have been funny if your screams hadn't been so *gratifying.*"

Her eyes narrowed with fury. "You BASTARD!" She bellowed, a surge of adrenaline forcing her into motion.

The kobold's eyes flew wide as Danica opened her mouth and *bit* his hand on her axe. She failed to break his hard scales, but the pain was enough to make him loosen his grip. With her axe freed, Danica shoved him back, and before he could begin another of his planned dodges, her fist swung around in a vicious backhand punch. Danica felt bone and scale crack from the blow, and the kobold was sent reeling. Taking the opening, she lifted her axe and brought it down into the kobold's chest. Blood spurted free, and he toppled back to the earth, dead in moments.

Danica took a few deep breaths, staring down at the corpse. She growled in frustration, suddenly realizing that with its death, she had lost any chance of interrogating it for information. "Son of a cow!" she swore angrily, stomping a foot against the ground.

A guttural scream drew her attention. Alarmed, she spun to face it. One last kobold, frenzied, was charging at her, an axe of his own raised high. She braced to meet it, but the effort proved unnecessary.

The kobold never reached her.

An arrow punched it in the side, sending it careening off course into the nearby bushes. Its cry was cut off by a sharp yelp, and then there was blessed silence. Looking to where the arrow came from, Danica saw Amelia lowering her bow, gasping for breath.

Danica nodded at her. "Thanks, but I had him," she said, casually wiping the blood off of her axe with a rag on her belt.

Amelia offered up a small smile. "You're welcome," she wheezed.

And then she fell.

"*Mom!*" Skunk cried, rushing to Amelia's side. It was then that Danica remembered the arrow that had struck the woman, and she cursed her casual attitude. She quickly sheathed her axe and ran to join the kobold by the woman's side.

"Mom! Mom, say something! *Mom!*" Skunk shouted, giving Amelia a hard shake.

"Move," Danica commanded, gruffly shoving Skunk back to get a look at the injury. With the fading of her adrenaline rush, Amelia had fallen unconscious. Danica winced at the many streaks of blood running down her body. "Shit. She's lost a lot of blood," she said, reaching for her pack.

"S-so get your healing pearl!" Skunk shouted. "Use it on her!"

"I'm working on it!" Danica snapped back at him. As she was rummaging through her pack, however, she felt something odd. The ringstone that powered the pearl felt smaller than she remembered. Frowning in confusion, she pulled it out.

The stone had been shattered into several small pieces, as if by severe blunt force. Danica swore, remembering when she'd felt something breaking under her armor during the fight. In the moment, she had thought it was a rib.

Skunk stared at the crushed remains of the stone. He swallowed. "Danica?" he squeaked uselessly.

"The ringstone's broken," Danica snarled, tossing the broken remnants aside. "The healing pearl won't work without it."

If the color could drain from Skunk's scales, it did at that moment. He worked his jaw up and down, hunting for words. "W-what? T-then what do we do?!" he shouted, looking down at Amelia's body. He was breathing heavily, his claws fidgeting frantically over his chest. "I don't know how to treat injuries like this! What do we do?!"

"First, calm down," Danica told him with a hard look. "Panicking won't help."

"But she's my mom!"

"Look at me!" Danica snapped, grabbing him by the collar and glaring fiercely into his eyes. He yelped, then froze as she continued. "Unless you want her to become your *dead* mom, *calm down and focus!*"

Skunk opened his mouth to rebuke, but a moment later he nodded, forcing himself to concentrate on what Danica was saying.

Satisfied that he was listening, Danica released him and looked down at the arrow. "We can't just pull it out — at least not with the arrowhead intact. We'd shred her insides. We cut off the fletching, as clean as we can, then we can pull the shaft out."

"And then?" Skunk asked. "W-won't she start losing more blood without the arrow plugging the hole?"

Danica grimaced. In truth, she was not well prepared for a medical situation like this. In all her time on the road, she often relied on her armor, her healing pearls, and Lorok to keep her safe. She basically knew nothing about treating injuries. She glanced at Skunk again. "Probably. Do you have bandages?"

Skunk shook his head. "N-no, just some meat."

Danica growled. "Shit, I don't either," she said before glancing down at Amelia's pack slung over the fallen horse's back. The animal had not risen, and it wasn't breathing. She gestured at the animal. "Check her pack. It's on the horse."

Skunk nodded and ran over while Danica took off Amelia's armor. It was thankfully easy to remove, exposing the wound in less than a minute. That done, Danica shifted Amelia into a more comfortable position for the operation. Skunk returned with a roll of bandages in hand shortly after. "It got a little squished when the horse fell," he said, kneeling on Amelia's other side. "Will it still work?"

"It's a bandage, not a crowbar," Danica remarked bluntly, taking the bandages. She reached down and took hold of the back half of the arrow, holding it steady, then looked meaningfully at Skunk. "Come on."

Skunk understood her meaning and quickly got into position. His hands were shaking as he drew his sword, his grip so tight that Danica wouldn't be surprised if his palms started bleeding. She gave him a firm glance. "*Breathe*. Try to relax."

Skunk swallowed heavily. "R-right," he muttered before closing his eyes and taking in a slow, deep breath. Danica quirked a brow, noting how remarkably practiced the motion seemed. Skunk took another and finally focused. His eyes opened and he raised the sword over his head. "Ready."

"On three, then," Danica said. She tightened her grip. "One. Two. *Three*."

With a grimace of hesitation, Skunk brought the edge of his sword down on the arrow shaft.

The cut was as clean as could be expected. Amelia was still jostled, releasing a moan of pain. Danica quickly handed Skunk the bandages. "Here. When I pull it out, tie it around her torso and cover the holes. More than one layer, and make it tight."

Skunk nodded, dropping his sword and taking the roll in his hands. Danica waited a moment longer until she was sure that Skunk was ready, counted them down again, and then pulled the arrow the rest of the way through. There was a sickening *schlick*, and the shaft came out coated in blood. Still, Skunk was dutiful in bandaging his mother, tying it off tight. He pulled back, his hands now speckled with blood. He reached a hand to where a streak of Amelia's blood was still marking him and shuddered. He brushed it away, then focused on Danica. "O-okay. Now what?"

Danica looked down at Amelia and shook her head. "Now? I pick her up and keep moving. *You,*" she pointed at Skunk. "Go home."

Skunk blinked, dumbstruck as Danica lifted Amelia and her armor in her arms, barely straining against the larger woman's weight. Skunk scrambled to his feet, picking up his sword as he went. "What?! No! No way! I'm not going back, not now!"

Danica didn't look back at him. "I wasn't asking."

Skunk ran in front of her, placing himself between her and the patiently waiting Lorok. Danica stopped and leveled an impatient glare at him.

"Move."

"I'm not leaving her!" Skunk shot back, shaking his head. "That's my *mom,* Danica! I wanna help her! *Let me help her, dammit!*"

"Don't yell at me," Danica shot back, shaking her head. "You did good, but your work here is—"

"I said I'm. Not. Leaving her!" Skunk shouted, his teeth showing in an angry growl.

Danica stared at the little kobold for several long seconds, and she began to realize that it wasn't just anger in his eyes. He was desperate. And, slowly but surely, his worry and fear for Amelia bled through his frustration. He took a pleading step forward. "Please," he begged. "Just let me make sure she'll be okay."

Danica hesitated, taken aback by the emotion in his voice. In all of her years, she had never once imagined hearing a kobold of all creatures looking at her like this. She'd imagined them begging for her mercy, sure, but this? She averted her gaze, pursing her lips in contemplation. She didn't enjoy the idea of having a kobold accompanying her, but at the same time, he *had* proven to be pretty useful in the fight just now. And there was no mistaking the fervent desire to help burning in his eyes.

Danica sighed. He reminded her of herself. Determined to a fault and impossible to dissuade.

"Fine," she relented. "You can come."

Skunk's demeanor immediately brightened. "R-really?" he questioned, surprised.

Danica grunted. "Come on. I don't know how far the Karjene are, but if you want your mother to survive, we need to get her to them as soon as possible. So no resting."

Skunk nodded, falling into step beside Danica as she made her way to Lorok. She gingerly rested Amelia on the shelldigger's back, much to Lorok's discomfort, but he dutifully carried the burden all the same. Danica climbed up after her, sitting in front of Amelia. She jerked her head back. "Sit on her other side. Keep her from falling off."

Skunk hesitated, giving Lorok a fearful look. "Is it safe?" he asked skeptically. "I've never ridden something like this before."

Danica reached down and hefted Skunk up onto Lorok's back in lieu of answering, drawing a series of protesting noises from him. Once he was secure, Danica took the reins and spurred the lumbering beast into motion.

"Yipe!" Skunk yelped as, with a resonating bellow, Lorok broke into a full run, loping easily over the ground in long, thundering strides. Danica grinned at the kobold's panicked shouting behind her, finding great amusement in his first time riding on the back of a larger creature.

Her grin faded. "To think, the day would come when I would let a kobold tag along," she whispered, only loud enough for Lorok to hear. "What foul game is fate playing with me, Lorok?"

Lorok snorted, and Danica took it to have the same meaning as a helpless shrug. She sighed and shook her head, focusing forward as the trees of the Leomar Forest parted before her.

Ry'thar

It took a while for Skunk to get used to being on Lorok's back. His stomach rose and fell with every stride, leaving him queasy and dizzy. He could feel the raw, unbridled *strength* of the animal through its shell, a humbling sensation that left him reluctant to move. If Lorok wanted, it would be a trivial matter to throw Skunk off and turn him into a thick, chunky puddle in the dirt.

As they thundered along, Skunk found himself appreciating the people who raised, bred, and cared for horses, and he made a mental note never to be mean to Lorok. Or to a horse, but those never let him get close enough for that to be a problem anyway.

When at last he was able to wrangle his stomach, he turned his attention to the world around him. With Lorok bounding along at full speed, it didn't take long for them to clear the edge of the forest. As they left the trees behind, the land that sprawled out before him stole his breath away.

"It's so empty..." he breathed in disbelief.

There was the occasional tree, sure, but for the most part, the Leoroch Plains were little more than a vast expanse of golden grass as tall as a human's waist. The quivering blades stretched for as far as the eye could see, bending in waves with the passing of the wind. The distant caps of the Sybhrod mountains encircled the plains on the north, east, and west, barely visible from this distance.

The pale ring shone brighter here. Cloud cover and mist from the ocean to the west often raced up the hills around Addernotch, leaving the ring partially obscured behind a gentle haze. But here? There was no such thing. The sky was clear, pristine, and the ring had never appeared so sharp and clear. Had he not been desperately clinging to Lorok, Skunk might have thrown himself on his back just to stare at it.

Much as he might like to, however, Skunk could not keep his attention on the ring for long. He constantly looked down at Amelia slung across the saddle, her body sandwiched between the kobold and the dwarf. She stirred every so often, groaning in pain as the speedy ride agitated her injured frame.

"Just hang in there, Mom," Skunk occasionally whispered. "We're gonna get you help. The ry'thar will know what to do."

Hours passed, and the weariness of the last couple of days of hard travel began to creep up on him. With nothing else he could do, Skunk took the chance to rest. He cuddled up to Amelia and closed his eyes, hoping that she would find comfort in his presence, even in her current condition.

Sadly, Skunk would not find any meaningful rest on Lorok's back. Between his dread and the animal's long, loping strides, he had no room to feel anything but restless and uneasy. Terrible scenarios played themselves out behind his eyelids, each one worse than the last. Questions assailed him, ones he dared not contemplate the answers to.

Chief among them being: what would he do if Amelia died?

Lorok's breakneck pace began to slow with the rising of the sun. Skunk could hear the beast panting for breath as the sun's warmth hit his scales. Stirred back to awareness, he lifted his head and looked around with a tired yawn, bleary-eyed.

"Are we there, yet?" he asked when he realized that everything looked the same.

"No," Danica answered, not taking her eyes off the landscape in front of them.

"Oh," Skunk sat up and looked down at Amelia. He winced. There was a dark red stain on her bandages where the blood had oozed through, and her face had started to go pale. *Did she catch an infection?* Skunk thought fearfully. His tail lashed behind him in an attempt to burn off his anxiety, and he couldn't keep from whimpering.

Lorok's pace continued to slow until he ambled along at a brisk walk. His shell vibrated as he warbled a protest at being pushed so hard. Danica pat him on the back. "It's okay, boy. Catch your breath," she said quietly.

Skunk wanted to argue that they should keep going as fast as they could, but he knew they wouldn't get anywhere if their sole means of transportation keeled over from exhaustion. With a quiet growl of frustration, he turned his attention to the savannah around them, hoping for distractions. They came readily.

The world was waking up. A procession of foreign sights, sounds, and smells assaulted his senses, each more captivating than the last. The distant cries of strange animals. Herds of brown-furred beasts meandering leisurely through the plains, giving them a wide berth. A flock of birds, thousands in number, scattered into the air and swirled across the morning sky in a hypnotizing dance.

The air, meanwhile, was dry and scratchy, tickling Skunk's nose and making him want to sneeze. There was no hint of the tree sap or sea-salt remnant that he was used to or the stink of human body sweat. The air was dry, crisp, almost crunchy to put a word to it. So many scents he'd never had the pleasure of experiencing before. He inhaled deeply, enjoying the foreign concoction.

"I've been meaning to ask you something," Danica's voice suddenly cut through the calming trance. Skunk snapped out of his reverie and looked at her. She was still looking directly ahead.

"What is it?"

Danica looked at him over her shoulder, a mote of curiosity in her eyes. "How did you find us?"

Skunk blinked, then smiled. "Oh, I just followed the smell," he said as if it was the most obvious thing in the world.

Danica blinked. "The smell," she echoed dubiously.

Skunk nodded eagerly. "Uh-huh! Kobolds have a *really* strong sense of smell! Like, *way* better than a blood-hounds! I know what Mom smells like, and even if I didn't, Lorok's smell is *powerful*. All I had to do was follow the musk."

Lorok shuddered, and Skunk imagined that the beast had somehow understood him enough to be offended. Danica furrowed her brow as her curiosity turned to incredulity. She shrugged her shoulders. "Remind me to give Lorok a bath next time we find some water," she stated matter-of-factly.

Beneath her, Lorok let off a moan, recognizing — and not caring for — the word 'bath.'

Danica grinned down at him. "Ah ah ah, none of the sass, mister!" she chided. "You need one."

Lorok cried in dismay and plowed his face into the dirt, kicking up a cloud of dust and scattering the population of a very unfortunate anthill. Skunk, despite everything, managed to chuckle at the childish display. He reached down to give the poor creature a pat on the side. "This guy is something else, huh?"

Danica hummed. "He's my oldest friend," she said, reaching down and scratching Lorok's neck, drawing noises from him that sounded like earthquakes. "And a massive doofus."

Skunk smiled at the display. "He means a lot to you, doesn't he?"

Danica didn't answer, and Skunk knew she didn't need to. The affection she gave Lorok was more than enough evidence of the bond they shared. He wanted to know more, but he knew that she'd only tell him if she felt he deserved to know. He turned his eyes back out to the plains. His smile slowly faded away, replaced with a grim frown.

Eventually, the monotony of the steppe was broken when they came across the lone river snaking its way through the plains. Danica nodded in approval as Lorok lumbered up to the water to slake his thirst. "Your mother said that the Karjene make camp on the river," she reasoned. "We follow it, we find them."

And so they did. Once Lorok was satiated, they continued north, keeping to the shore. Every so often, Skunk would see herds of animals gathered at the water's edge. They drank quickly, almost frantically, their bodies tense like coiled springs. They would usually bolt the moment Lorok drew near, their movements fast even by Skunk's standards.

All the while, Amelia's condition was getting worse. Her groans of pain became more frequent, and Skunk's fear grew.

At long last, the village came into sight. It started as little more than a collection of dark spots against the horizon, but as they drew closer, the shapes came into focus.

"There!" Skunk declared, rising to his feet. He placed one hand on Danica's shoulder while the other pointed ahead. "That must be them!"

Danica slowly looked up at him. "Get off me," she growled in a warning tone, her voice reminding Skunk of a grizzly bear. He obeyed with a weak chuckle.

Danica gave the reins a light snap, encouraging Lorok to pick up the pace. The mount complied, but Skunk found himself no longer content to ride on his back. The sight of civilization, and the rising hope that his mother would receive aid, drove him to leap from Lorok's back and pull ahead.

"Stay close!" Danica shouted almost as soon as his feet hit the grass. "They don't know we're coming, and you're a kobold."

Skunk paused mid-step. He looked down at the ground, his lips curling into a snarl while his tail lashed at the earth. He wanted to ignore that remark, pretend that his scales didn't mean anything. That's how he'd been thinking about them for his whole life. But that innocence was behind him now, wasn't it? Freya's scorn and the hateful glares of the townsfolk had made that pretty clear.

He took a deep breath to settle his nerves, then pushed on at a slower pace, matching Lorok's.

Once they were close enough to distinguish individual structures, Skunk spotted something on the approach. He drew up short and lifted his head. He sniffed at the air. Cooking meat and dry fur, fleas and mud and muck, rock dust and bone wax. And something more, drawing closer. He turned to Danica. "Someone's coming."

Danica nodded. "Let them come. Hands away from your weapons."

Skunk nodded and kept his hands clearly in view, fidgeting anxiously over his chest.

It was not a small group that ran out to meet them, and they were coming at a brisk pace. A solid lump formed in Skunk's throat as he realized just how *big* the ry'thar were. He had seen them before, sure, but it had been a while, and he found himself reminded that they had the nickname of lion-folk for a *very* good reason.

Each of them stood at least six feet tall, their furry bodies swollen with thick knots of burly muscle. Their heads were unmistakably feline, resembling those of lions. The males even had the lush red manes framing their faces. Tails tipped with coarse red tufts swished slowly behind them as they moved. They did not wear much in the way of clothing, and what they did wear was mostly furs and hides. All of them were armed.

At the head was a ry'thari woman. Skunk did not have any experience with their kind, so he had no way of accurately gauging anything else, but it seemed safe to assume she was in charge. Her eyes were a fierce and striking shade of orange — And they were looking specifically at *him*.

A fight-or-flight instinct came alive alongside a rush of adrenaline. It took all of his willpower to keep from turning and running the other way.

Danica, appearing unbothered, lifted a hand in greeting. "Hey!" She called to the advancing party. "We have wounded!"

If the ry'thar in the front heard Danica's call, she did not indicate it. Her lips peeled back in a snarl, revealing terrifyingly long and sharp-looking fangs. Skunk took a reflexive step back, and he was suddenly reconsidering the wisdom of keeping his hands away from his weapons.

The ry'thar broke into a sprint at him, faster than he could react. He only had time to shout before the woman's hand wrapped tight around his throat. Suddenly, Skunk could no longer breathe, and the earth fell away as the ry'thar hefted him into the air.

Skunk was vaguely aware of Danica shouting, but the words were lost. The world shifted and blurred, and his stomach lurched in his belly. There was a bellowing roar in his ears before his back slammed into the trunk of a long-dead tree at the water's edge. He opened his mouth, trying to gasp for air, but nothing got past the woman's grip.

He squirmed and thrashed, his ears ringing and his feet kicking uselessly in the air. An agonizing pressure built up in his chest, his lungs trying to push air through an utterly constricted windpipe. He felt as if he would burst.

He looked down to see the woman's face contorted into a murderous scowl. Her teeth bared, her eyes narrowed and her ears pinned back against her skull.

Panicking and desperate, Skunk took hold of her forearm and dug his claws into her skin, hoping the pain would make her release him. His effort proved fruitless. Her hide was thick and tough, her muscles even more so. All he did was make her angrier.

She roared into his face, her free hand snapping open. Skunk's eyes widened when he saw the sharp claws on the tips of her fingers glinting in the sunlight. It would be trivial for her to tear him apart. He tried to speak, to beg her to wait and hear him out, but against her hold on his throat, he was powerless.

And then an axe blade flashed up to the woman's throat, coming to a stop against her jugular. Skunk's eyes flicked down. Danica stood there, stretching her arm out all the way to put her axe to the ry'thar's throat. "Put him down," she warned, her voice low. "*Now.*"

In a flash, the other ry'thar swarmed around Danica, their spears angled at her throat. She held her ground. She didn't even flinch. Skunk couldn't decide if this was a result of confidence or stupidity.

The ry'thar woman turned her eyes on Danica, unimpressed. "Uut in'ush ka. You are brave or foolish indeed to make demands of me," she warned, her voice thick with an exotic accent. Thankfully, she loosened her grip enough for Skunk to suck in a lungful of air. "You tell me to release this abomination?"

"I do. And I won't ask again," Danica remarked, her eyes narrowing. "Put him down. We're not your enemy."

The woman barked out a humorless laugh. "Not my enemy?! In'ush, you trespass into my clan's territory, and you bring with you one of the *beasts* that assaulted my people not even a fortnight past!" she countered before turning to Skunk, leaning in so close that their noses were practically touching. "Give me one good reason why I should not crush your throat, *kalj'atla.*"

Skunk blinked, momentarily stunned. It only took him a moment to find his senses, however. Sucking in another sweet lungful of air, he met the woman's eyes. "I-It's Amelia," he pleaded, his eyes darting to Lorok. The shelldigger was being blocked from advancing by a wall of ry'thar men, their spears pointed at the furious shelldigger. Amelia was still safely on his back. Skunk nodded toward them. "Amelia Lanswel. She's hurt! She needs help!"

The ry'thar's eyes widened. "Amelia?" she questioned. "How do you know that name?"

Skunk managed a tiny smile. "She raised me."

The woman released him. He crumpled to the ground, his hands flying up to his throat as he gasped and coughed desperately for air, his head spinning with dizziness. Danica was beside him a moment later, helping him back to his feet. The world tottered and turned around him as he rose, so he leaned against the dwarf for support. Still gasping, he looked up at the ry'thar, but she had already broken away from him. Her subordinates parted around her as she came to Lorok's side. He grunted and snarled at her, pawing at the earth, ready to attack at a moment's notice.

"Lorok!" Danica snapped, drawing his attention. She pointed at the grass. "Down, boy."

Lorok looked between his master and the ry'thar for several seconds. Then, with a huff, he settled onto his haunches, though the suspicion never left his beady eyes.

The ry'thar woman cautiously circled Lorok until she reached Amelia. She looked at the groaning body for only a moment before turning back to Skunk and Danica, a new rush of outrage flashing across her face. "How did this happen?!" she demanded.

"We were ambushed," Danica replied, putting away her axe. "By kobolds. The same ones that attacked your town. We have a common enemy."

The woman frowned, her eyes settling on Skunk. "And that one?" she demanded.

Skunk straightened up, his hand resting on his chest. He was careful not to meet the woman's eyes again. He didn't know if the ry'thar had the same tendency as wild animals to take eye contact as a threat, but he wasn't willing to take the chance. "T-they attacked me, too. I'm *not* with the horde," he said before daring to look up at her. "Please. Just help her."

The ry'thari woman stared at Skunk for several long seconds, her lips pressing together in thought. Her companions shifted uneasily, awaiting her orders. Soon she placed a hand on Amelia's side and said something Skunk couldn't hear. Then she turned to bark orders at her subordinates in a language he did not understand. The warriors sprang into motion, gingerly prising Amelia off of Lorok's back and carrying her to the village.

Skunk breathed a sigh of relief, taking this to mean they had made it. Groaning with strain, he went to stand. "Th-thank you—"

"Do not speak," The ry'thar woman cut him off, turning a fierce glare on him. "You have brought me my friend, and for that, you have earned my ear. But that is *all* you have earned. You will be brought to our camp, and you will be questioned. *Thoroughly.*"

"Son of a— are you out of your gods damned mind?!" Danica shouted, throwing her arms up in exasperation. "We just said we were ambushed by the same kobolds that attacked you! We're on the same side! We came to you for *help!*"

The ry'thar turned to Danica, her lips peeling back to put her fangs on display. "Mind your tone, in'ush!" she spat, and even Danica flinched. The lion continued. "I know Amelia, but I do not know *you.* And I am not going to take *any* chances with the safety of *my clan.*"

She nodded to one of her comrades. Wordlessly, he advanced toward Skunk and Danica. He held out a hand expectantly. "Your weapons," he stated.

Danica snarled in frustration, her hands balling into fists at her sides. "Damnit," she grumbled before relinquishing all four of her axes. Skunk swallowed heavily as the ry'thar came up to him. Surrendering his bow and arrows was easy, but he hesitated on the sword. His hand rested on the hilt, feeling the leather wrapping. He closed his eyes, took a breath, and resigned himself. Without a word, he surrendered the weapon.

The ry'thar woman eyed it with interest but did not comment. She jerked her head toward the village. "Come," she commanded simply before marching away at a brisk pace.

The ry'thar behind Skunk pushed him into motion, sending him staggering forward. "Move, *kalj'atla!* And don't try anything."

Skunk did not know what 'kalj'atla' meant, but he figured it was probably an insult. He didn't feel too bothered by it, though. At this point, he was getting used to being insulted.

The remaining ry'thar formed a circle around them, blocking off any avenues of escape. Danica grumbled irritably under her breath the whole way but offered no resistance as they were escorted in silence toward the Karjene village.

Skunk took in the details with detached curiosity. Unlike the stone foundations and wooden walls of Addernotch, the Karjene village was comprised of yurts, each one built using animal matter. Hides and furs made up the walls, stretched tightly between frames of polished white bones and topped with roofs of dried grass and reeds plucked from the plains. Swirling patterns were painted on the walls in red hues, graceful and elegant. They almost made him think of cirrus clouds on a windy day.

As they walked, Skunk became aware of several things. The first was that there were not nearly as many people as the size of the village would suggest. The spaces between yurts were quiet. And no one could miss the signs of battle.

The stench of blood and death lingered thick in the air, omnipresent and oppressive. Mingling with it, choking Skunk's thoughts and churning his stomach, he could pick out the stink of the kobolds, and another scent with which he had grown distressingly intimate. Cold steel and ringstone dust. Blood and sweat, somehow wrong and twisted.

Karak had been here.

In the heart of the village, the group was divided. Skunk's heart skipped a beat as Amelia was carried away while he and Danica were guided toward an open plaza of sorts in the heart of the village. A massive pyramid of wood had been constructed there. It was surrounded by animal furs loaded with bowls, plates, pots, and jars. Those in turn were overflowing with powerful-smelling herbs, spices, and other substances.

At the far end of the circle stood the largest yurt Skunk had seen so far. It towered easily over its peers, its walls adorned with more of those curious red markings. They flowed into one another in intricate, weaving patterns that let the eyes easily slide from one image to the next.

They were ushered inside, revealing a large open space, lit and heated from the center by a blazing fire pit. The furs of massive animals were laid neatly across the floor, forming a ring around the fire.

"Sit," one of the ry'thar said, following them in. "We await the war chief."

Danica grumbled. "Fine," she said, thumping down on one of the cushions hard enough that Skunk felt the vibrations in his feet. He tentatively followed after her, finding the cushion beside her and putting a foot on it.

The fur of the cushion filled out the space between his fingers, soft and pleasant. His eyes widened, and he immediately latched onto the cushion with both hands. "Oh, wow. This is *soft*," he said almost dumbly. Oblivious to how silly he looked, he pawed at the fur as a kitten would knead at its mother's belly.

"What the hell are you doing?" Danica suddenly asked, snapping him out of his reverie.

Skunk froze, his face heating up with embarrassment. It occurred to him then that Danica had never seen him do that before. "Uh! I! Nothing!" he lied *convincingly* before sitting on his knees. He kept his hands in his lap to keep them away from that wonderful, delightfully soft fur.

The ry'thar behind them exchanged baffled looks, then took up guard posts on either end of the room, while two more stood guard by the entrance.

Time began to pass, and Skunk's embarrassment with it. His anxiety returned to him, insistent and unrelenting as ever. He shifted uneasily in place, his eyes wandering in search of something to hold his attention. Thankfully, the wait was not too long.

The woman that had pinned him to the tree strode into the room, her expression dark and her jaw set. She paused, her eyes lingering first on Skunk, then on Danica. Her eyes narrowed and her tail lashed at the air. Skunk held still, not looking up as she walked behind him and passed him by.

She made a full circuit around the room before finding a seat on a cushion across the fire from her guests.

"I am Tamaya. I am the war chief of the Karjene," she introduced herself with an aura of authority. "And you are in'ush — outsiders. Among your number, a *kobold*. A green scale at that. By rights, you should be dead already. But you brought us a friend in need of aid, and you claim we share a mutual enemy. It is for this reason, and no other, that you yet draw breath. Do not make me regret that mercy. Name yourselves and state your reasons for coming to my people."

Skunk almost jumped in fear when Tamaya's piercing glare settled on him. "I would hear from the dragonkin first."

Skunk blinked a few times, then tried to swallow the lump in his throat. It was frustratingly persistent. "Uuh, well... M-my name is Skunk," he introduced himself awkwardly, his voice quivering under the weight of Tamaya's intimidating glare. "A-and, uh... I'm here to help my mom."

"Skunk? As in the foul-smelling animal?" Tamaya asked before shaking her head. "No matter. You said that Amelia raised you. That makes her the mother you speak of?"

Skunk nodded.

Tamaya's frown deepened, but there was a visible spark of interest behind the mistrust in her eyes. "How curious that a human mother should raise a kobold child. How is it that *that* came to be?"

Skunk looked down at the floor and offered a helpless shrug. "Mom found me as a hatchling. I'd been stuffed into a dead skunk's body. I was being menaced by a bunch of slitherbounders. She scared them off and took me back home with her to Addernotch. I've spent my entire life with her, living with humans and a krauven named Seto."

Tamaya's eyes widened in surprise. "Seto? That crazy old bird yet lives?" she asked in disbelief, and Skunk heard the barely concealed note of joy in her voice.

Skunk dared to raise his head and nodded, his tail wagging slightly. "Yeah. He's getting old, but he's still kicking," he told her with a big smile. "He's my teacher, actually."

Tamaya stared at Skunk for a moment longer. Then she caught herself and her expression swiftly darkened back into a cold and skeptical glare. "I see. And how is it, then, that Amelia came to be *here?* What is it she seeks in my territory?" she asked.

Skunk's tail stilled. His eyes drifted down, the memory of the attack flashing through his mind. He shuddered uncomfortably. "She was sent to ask your tribe for help," he finally said. "See, Addernotch was hit by kobolds not that long ago. The same ones that attacked you. We never stood a chance."

Danica spoke up, leaning forward. "They were ripped apart. I showed up when the battle was almost over, and I saw the result clear as day. It was a bloodbath."

Skunk closed his eyes, his hands curling into fists over the pocket where he kept Sylvia's doll. "They took a lot of people away," he said, his voice a low whisper. "Just... *dragged* them out of town and into the forest."

He shivered, his thoughts returning to the last time he had seen Sylvia. The moment of realization as the kobold came down on her, and the panic that set in as he realized how powerless he was to save her. He looked up at Tamaya, his eyes desperate, pleading. "Even my best friend, Sylvia."

There was a moment of silence. Tamaya closed her eyes, taking in the weight of Skunk's words. Eventually, she spoke. "And so your people sent Amelia to us in the hopes that my tribe would be willing to aid them in retaliation, is that it?"

Danica grunted, shaking her head. "Retaliation? You heard the boy, they never stood a chance. Addernotch was braced for a fight and they still got picked apart."

Skunk sighed. "Y-yeah. Mom was sent here to ask for help protecting Addernotch until reinforcements can arrive from the bigger cities." He had to force himself not to mention that it was *his* desire to strike back and bring his friends home.

Tamaya hummed quietly. Her tail swished behind her in a display of agitation. "I see. I am afraid that such a request is not easily granted," she confessed.

Skunk blinked, the dread he had thought he banished earlier creeping up on him all over again. "What? What do you mean?" he asked timidly.

Tamaya pursed her lips and gestured at the door. "You saw the damage coming in, I assume. Smelled the blood on the air. We were struck with just as much ferocity, if not more. While I am confident that we fared better than you did, our losses were no less severe. We had a difficult time just taking away the kobold's bodies to bury them. We are in no condition to thin our numbers."

Skunk blinked. He couldn't believe what he was hearing. He leaned forward slightly, desperation creeping into his voice. "B-but you're ry'thar! Aren't you guys the *best* fighters around?!"

Tamaya smiled at that, but it was not the smile of someone appreciating a compliment. There was pity in her eyes, and Skunk realized how naive he was being. Tamaya shook her head. "You are right that we are mighty. We are swift. Against the lesser throngs of the horde, we were superior by all measures. After the surprise of the assault wore off, the invading kobolds fell before us one after another. But they were not alone. They had aid from something foul and unnatural. A twisted *rro'jatha*."

Skunk looked down, his expression darkening. "Karak," he breathed. "He was here. I know he was. I can smell him."

Next to him, Danica visibly tensed.

Tamaya nodded her head, and all traces of mirth disappeared like a puff of smoke. She glared into the fire, her eyes ablaze with contempt. "Such a perverse mockery of nature's designs I have never seen. His body twisted by the ring's power. A power he used to brutally subdue any and all that stood in his way." Tamaya closed her eyes, taking a slow, deep breath. When she spoke again, her voice, steady though it was, dripped with barely contained grief. "My own mother, the finest warrior our tribe has known for generations, was carved in half trying to stop him. In the end, Karak and his forces made off with more than half of my people, and we were powerless to stop him."

"By the Five," Skunk whimpered, his hands wringing together nervously over his heart. Just how powerful *was* Karak?! Did he have *any* limits? His enchantment runes gave him an undeniable edge in a fight, that much was obvious. But to cut through the ry'thar in the manner Tamaya described? Skunk shuddered, and he began to wonder if it was even possible to defeat him.

Tamaya sighed, shaking her head. "Now *I* am war chief. And I cannot place *my* people in any more danger. Our numbers are thinned, our homes are burned, and our livestock is slaughtered. We must build *our* defenses, and honor the dead we could not bury. I would send aid to Addernotch if I could — I owe Amelia much, and Addernotch has been good to us for years. But my options are limited."

"But... but she came all this way!" Skunk protested, shaking his head weakly. "We don't stand a chance on our own! And neither do you! We *need* to help each other!"

Tamaya met his gaze for a moment. There was something in her eyes, well-concealed but visible. Her whiskers wavered, her eyes sloping down just slightly. Her gaze averted for a fraction of a second. "Then I will discuss it with *her* once she is awake. But not with you. And I can make no promises."

Skunk slumped in place, his eyes screwing shut. "Damn it..." he whimpered, a hand reaching up to clutch at one of his horns as if it were a lifeline. Beside him, he heard Danica letting out a growl of frustration.

"I take this to mean that I can't expect any help from you tracking the kobolds down, then?" she asked irritably.

Tamaya tilted her head. "To what end do *you* seek them?" she asked. "You are not of Addernotch."

"No, but it'd be silly to think that Addernotch is the only place they've attacked. I have a score to settle, too. I've been cutting through green-scale hordes for years now, looking for the ones that took something from my people. This is that horde, it must be, and I mean to take back what they stole," Danica replied evenly.

Tamaya's frown deepened. "And just what is it that the kobolds could have taken from you that is of such great value that you would challenge an entire horde for it?"

To that, Danica did not have an immediate answer. She was quiet, her face contorting with indecision. Skunk looked over at her when she finally relented. She reached under her breastplate and withdrew her ringstone, the one she'd held outside of Seto's schoolhouse. He couldn't be certain, but it seemed to him that the stone was glowing brighter now than before.

Danica stared into it for several long seconds, her eyes distant. "...An important relic," she finally said. "You don't need to know more than that. All you need to know is that I have spent *years* trying to track these bastards down, I am running out of places to look, and I am *not* about to turn back now."

Tamaya nodded slowly. "I understand. That said, you are correct to assume you shall receive no aid from us. You are not known to us, and I am not going to put our lives at risk for a stranger. Especially not for a story as vague as yours."

After a few seconds, Tamaya addressed Skunk again. "If your story is true, then it shames me that I cannot do more. If you are lying, I shall know of it when roluth tha Amelia awakes. Until then, you will stay in the village and will be kept under strict watch. I will not have unknown elements parading among my people unsupervised. Is that clear?"

Danica grunted, shrugging her shoulders. "Whatever."

Tamaya nodded. "Then we are done here," she said, turning her eyes to one of the guards. "Take them to a free yurt and see they cause no trouble."

The guard nodded and advanced toward them. Before he had taken two steps, however, Skunk leaned forward. "W-wait!"

Tamaya looked up at him, her eyes narrowing. "Have you something more to add, kalj'atla?" she asked.

Skunk flinched, still not caring much for that word, but he forced himself to maintain his composure. He lowered his head in as respectful a manner as he could. He hesitated a moment before finding his words. "If it isn't too much to ask, can I stay with my mom?" he asked carefully. "I wanna make sure she's okay. Y-you can keep me under guard if you want, just... let me be with her. Please."

Tamaya considered him for a long, quiet moment. An instinct he could not name drove Skunk to lift his head to look into her eyes, meeting them fully for the first time since she dropped him from the tree.

Tamaya shook her head. "If she asks for you, you will be summoned. But I do not know you. You will receive no favors from me."

Skunk winced, but he wasn't surprised. He just looked down at the floor.

Tamaya said nothing more. In short order, Skunk found himself being escorted alongside Danica back out into the light of the sun.

Rites and Confessions

That night in the Karjene village was a dark and unpleasant one. Rare cloud cover rolled in from the south to hover over the steppe like a suffocating blanket. It smothered the glow of the ring, leaving the world bathed in shadow and Tamaya with only torches and the great bonfire to light her way.

The village was quiet, as it always was at this hour. On any other occasion, that silence would have been comforting. It would have told her that her people were safe, that any danger was past, and that the sentinels were doing their job. At most, there might have been the occasional howl or holler from the distance.

This was different. It was unsettling. It was quiet because there were so few people left. The stench of death clung to her fur like honey, faint enough to be ignored, but ever-present. It nauseated her, and she wished dearly she could be rid of it.

But there was still so much to do.

She made her way through the entire village, poking her head into every yurt she passed. Many were empty, but not all. Every so often she would find someone. A mother tending to her cubs, an injured warrior trying to treat his or her wounds, and so on. To each, she said the same thing.

"The fire is lit. We gather."

She never received a reply beyond a solemn nod. Everyone understood the gravity of her words. In the following silence, they would gather any mementos and set out for the bonfire. They would honor their dead.

As she peered into the last yurt on her route, her eyes found a huddling cluster of cubs in the back. Two girls and two boys. Her heart wept for them. They were so young, so far away from becoming adults. Their massive eyes shimmered at her from the darkness.

"The fire is lit," Tamaya said again. "We gather."

The cubs shifted uncomfortably, and one of the boys lifted his head. "W-where's our mama and papa?" he asked, a low whine coming from deep in his throat.

Tamaya hesitated for a moment. Their parents must have been taken in the fighting — it was not the ry'thar way to leave their cubs unattended. There was always at least one parent with them. For the cubs to be alone meant that their family had been taken. Alive or dead, however, Tamaya did not know.

She set her torch down and knelt before the cubs. "Taken," she said simply. "By the enemy. I do not know if they are alive or dead, but we must honor the lost all the same. Their spirits will find no rest if we do not."

The cubs lowered their faces and whispered amongst themselves for a few moments. Sluggishly, they untangled themselves and stood. Tamaya held out her hand, and the little boy took it. The others soon crowded in, finding something to hold onto, whether it be her hands or her tail. She did not mind the tugging.

It meant they were still here.

"Come," she whispered, leading the trembling children out of their home. They would be the last to arrive, but such was the custom for rites like this. It was her duty to assemble the tribe, to speak the words, to appease the dead that now lingered in the wind.

Her duty.

Not her mother's.

Tamaya's gaze fell, her ears folding back. It was a strange feeling. She had long dreamed of the day she would take her mother's place. She had always imagined it would be accompanied by a happy ceremony. Her mother, too old to carry on the task, would pass her the mantle with a smile and encouragement. She had always imagined she could go to her mother for advice in her first year as she found her footing.

Never could she have imagined that her ascension would have been so unceremonious, so sudden, and so thoroughly stained.

"War chief?" One of the boys asked her, noticing her crestfallen expression. "Are you sad?"

Tamaya focused on the path ahead. The bonfire loomed in the distance. "I am," she confessed. "But that shall not stop me."

The cub said no more.

They arrived at the plaza in front of her yurt. The bonfire was already lit, a roaring inferno that shone like the sun. The entire tribe — what was left of it — was gathered around in a loose circle. All eyes were on Tamaya as she urged the children to find a place, then made her way toward the fire.

An elderly ry'thar woman, seventy years Tamaya's senior awaited her. She was dressed in the closest thing to a robe one could get with fur and hides. A ringstone hung from a string around her neck, the shape of a lion's fang.

"Elder Annotha," Tamaya whispered to her. "That was the last of them. Are we ready?"

Annotha nodded. "We are," she said, her voice an odd blend of smooth and rough. She nodded toward the crowd. "Whenever you are ready."

Tamaya took a breath and stared up into the flames, hoping she could see the spirits in the smoke. But against the clouded sky, she saw nothing. She hid her disappointment behind a stoic mask, then spun to face her people. She spoke loud and clear in their language.

"Karjene! I thank you all for gathering here this night!" she called out, her voice firm and steady. "Several nights ago, we were the victims of an unconscionable evil. The kobolds, who have long kept to their burrows in the north, descended upon us with murder in their hearts. Against our might, they should have stood no chance. But through vile treachery, they swindled us out of our rightful victory! The consequences of their violation of nature are felt by all that are present today, for many are the warriors who fell in the defense of our home."

Tamaya hesitated for a moment, her eyes lowering. Her voice faltered, a tremble creeping into her words despite her best efforts. "Felt most keenly in my heart was the loss of War Chief Zantali. My mother gave her life to protect you all, her people."

Every head in the village had bowed low by now, hiding their faces from her. Tamaya took a shuddering breath, then turned to Annotha. The shaman smiled comfortingly at Tamaya and rested a hand on her shoulder. She stepped forward, speaking loud and clear. "The wind stands still, and the flames are lit," she called, her hands lifting into the air. "Let the lost spirits of our defenders enjoy the fruit of their labors one last time! Let them know that their deaths were not in vain and that we shall ever and always remember and honor their sacrifice! Let them know that peace, that they do not become Rro'jatha!"

With that declaration, the ry'thar began to sing. It began as a quiet hum, but gradually, it began to swell. Tamaya stepped away from the flame as the first wave of mourners approached. Each took something from the various containers — whatever they felt was most appropriate — and cast them into the flames. As they did, their hums transitioned to lyrical singing, a lullaby.

Humming along, Tamaya found the edge of the clearing to watch and wait. The war chief and the shaman would always be the last to make their offerings. It was they who guided the tribe, and so mourned for *all* they lost, not just family members or dear friends. The ry'thar believed that the spirits of the dead, released from their corpses alongside the stench of decay, would be drawn to the bonfire as if it were a beacon. The offerings made to the flame would reach them, and the scent of their labors and their memories would appease them, Then they would be allowed to depart as a peaceful breeze, rather than a vengeful demon known as rro'jatha.

Annotha stood beside Tamaya, her hand clasped around her ringstone. Her mouth worked quietly as she offered an incantation. The stone glowed between her fingers, and the flames swelled brighter and brighter with every offering. All the while, the choir of the ry'thar grew louder and louder, more and more hums turning into song.

Finally, it was Tamaya's turn. She and Annotha returned to their place before the bonfire. Tamaya stared into it, the flames sending her whiskers twitching, making her eyes water and dry from the heat. But she did not flinch. She knelt down and gingerly scooped up a small mound of green leaves from the bowls.

"To you, my mother," she whispered. "I was not there to aid you when you needed me. But I will *not* abandon *them*. I will keep us safe, I swear. Fear not for us, Mother, and may you find your peace upon the wind."

With that, she cast the leaves into the flames.

"And to all who fell in the defense of Karjene," Tamaya went on, loud enough for all to hear. She took up one last bowl, larger than all the others, filled with a fine grey powder. She rose to her full height, staring up into the billowing cloud of smoke. "To you, I give thanks. For your sacrifice, for your bravery, for your fearlessness, and for your pride."

Beside her, the shaman had taken up a similar bowl. The two shared a look, and as the singing reached a fever pitch, they cast the contents of their bowls into the fire. With a snap and a hiss, swirls of vibrant color spread through the flames, turning it all from blinding yellow to a tranquil blue. In that instant, the singing stopped.

The flames burned higher and higher, as blue as the midday sky. Everyone held still, listening and waiting. Seconds ticked by, one after another, each one feeling like an eternity. Tamaya was beginning to fear that their ritual had amounted to nothing when, at last, she heard it. Barely audible beneath the crackle was a resonant ringing, high, gentle, and soothing.

Tamaya relaxed, sighing in relief as the flame answered their song with one of its own. Their offerings were accepted. The spirits were appeased.

Slowly but surely, the fire faded away. In time, only embers would remain, and the village would fall into darkness.

No one said anything. When they were ready, they would return to their homes. Tamaya waited longer than all of the others. She stared at the darkness where the flames had once been, her mind a storm of anxiety and questions for which she had no answers.

Annotha's hand found her shoulder. "You did well," the shaman said in a soothing whisper.

Tamaya snorted, her tail lashing behind her. "You'll forgive me if I do not find comfort in that."

Annotha withdrew her hand. "It is not my forgiveness you require, war chief."

The two fell into silence for a long moment. Tamaya took a few deep breaths, allowing the lingering smell of the ashes to fill her senses. She glanced back to Annotha, her brow furrowing. "I fear I am not ready for this, elder," she confessed so only the shaman could hear her. "You served beside my mother for a long time. You are wise in ways that I am not. I will need your advice if we are to survive the days ahead."

"And you shall have it," Annotha assured her. "You need only ask. But not tonight. You are tired, war chief. You need to rest and mourn."

Tamaya resisted the urge to snort. She didn't have time to do either of those things, did she? But she didn't say as such for the time being. Another matter required her attention. "How is Amelia?"

Annotha's face wrinkled with a warm smile. "She will recover. Her wound, while serious, is nothing I cannot handle."

Tamaya relaxed, a tension in her muscles she hadn't known was there bleeding out of her. She turned, her eyes settling on Annotha's yurt. Amelia was in there, somewhere, resting and healing.

"The boy has been a delight as well," Annotha went on.

Tamaya paused and turned to her, raising an eyebrow. "The boy?" she asked. "What boy?"

Annotha's smile grew. "Why, Skunk. Who else?"

The tension returned, and Tamaya's face must have become one of aggression because Annotha's smile grew almost *mocking*.

"Did you not know? He has been in my yurt all day."

"Why?!" Tamaya demanded angrily. "I ordered him not to leave the yurt he was given! Why didn't you say anything to me sooner?!"

Annotha silenced Tamaya by poking her on the nose. "Relax, child. I said nothing to you because the boy has been no trouble. If anything, he has been a refreshing source of curiosity. He is so very much like our cubs, asking so many questions. And so eager to be helpful, too. He's a sweet little thing."

"He's a *kobold*."

Annotha quirked a brow. "And that precludes him from loving the woman who raised him?"

Tamaya wanted to retort, but the words died on her lips. She took a deep breath and turned back to the Yurt. In truth, she had pondered the young kobold all day. She did not know what to make of him. His words sounded sincere, he'd been cooperative and even polite. Everything about him ran contrary to what she knew of his kind.

She did not know if that should make her feel at ease or on edge.

Annotha pat Tamaya on the back. "He's just a boy, Tamaya," she said gently. "A little boy scared for the life of his mother. So scared he risked invoking *your* ire just to make sure he could be with her."

Tamaya sighed and brushed the shaman's hand away. "You've made your point. He can remain under your supervision so long as he causes no trouble. But don't go spreading it around that I am allowing this."

Annotha grinned and winked at her. "Do not fret. I am not in the habit of tattling on the young."

Tamaya felt her eye twitch, but she forced herself to let that go. "I will go see Amelia. Then I will turn in for the night. You should get some rest yourself," she said, projecting what authority she could.

"Don't worry," Annotha assured her. "I will take my rest soon enough. Go on, now. Go."

Tamaya gave her elder a respectful bow of the head, then turned to the yurt. She paused for a moment when she saw a pair of yellow eyes looking back at her from within.

Skunk sat at Amelia's bedside, listening to her quiet breaths and watching the steady rise and fall of her chest. Her familiar warmth and scent had eased his tumultuous thoughts, allowing him to cast his mind back to simpler, easier times. A time when he was small, innocent, and hopeful. That comfort had let him fall asleep.

Then the song woke him. He watched the entire ceremony from the yurt's entrance, curious and fascinated. He had no idea what they were saying or the words of their song. But even so, there was something beautiful about it. Beautiful, and a little haunting.

He had felt a strange tingling when that old one had used her ringstone. He did not know why, but it had made him feel peaceful.

Now, though, Tamaya was marching toward him with purpose. He withdrew to Amelia's side, staring down at her face, and waiting for Tamaya to enter.

Tamaya did not say anything when she entered the yurt. The flakey smell of ash and the dry crackle of woodsmoke joined her, making Skunk's nose itch. He heard her padded feet on the floor, and he felt her warmth as she stopped beside the bed.

"You disobeyed me," she said bluntly.

Skunk nodded. "I'm sorry, but my mom's more important."

There was a long silence before Tamaya spoke again. "Annotha tells me you're behaving yourself."

Skunk shrugged weakly. "Why wouldn't I? You're my host. I'm your guest. Besides, you're mom's friend. That means you're my friend, too."

Or at least, I'd like you to be my friend, he added silently.

Tamaya chuckled and settled down on her knees beside Skunk. "Yes, that does sound like a sentiment she would pass on to her child. She always had a good heart."

"The *best* heart," Skunk corrected, running his thumb over Amelia's hand. He stared into her face, his heart twisting in his chest as he remembered how horrible he had been to her the day she left Addernotch. "She's always been so kind to me. She gave me *everything*. A loving home, a comfy bed, tasty food..."

Skunk's smile faded, and an old feeling began to creep up from the base of his tail. He swallowed hard and shook his head to banish the memory. "I *gotta* pay that kindness forward. I *have* to. Somehow."

"Honor. A rare trait in your kind," Tamaya noted with a slow nod.

Skunk snorted, his tail thumping against the ground. "Hmph. Ya know, I could've gone my *whole life* without knowing a thing about '*my kind.*' Everything I've learned so far has made me *sick*," he stated, a low growl creeping into his voice. He closed his eyes, withdrew his hand from Amelia's, and curled his fingers together in a white-knuckle grip. "At least *now* I understand why green-scales have the reputation they do."

Tamaya hummed but said nothing. Skunk took a few breaths to calm his quivering nerves, then returned to stroking Amelia's hand. The simple motions helped his mind settle, and his anger dissipated like a puff of smoke. Tamaya was a powerful presence beside him, but after the ritual he had beheld, he found it comforting rather than intimidating. She was on his side, at least for now.

It was a few minutes before Tamaya spoke. "You're serious. Aren't you?" she finally asked. "You *truly* love her. She's *truly* your mother."

Skunk said nothing. He merely nodded.

Tamaya chuckled. "I should not be surprised. Of course, Amelia would take in the first stray baby she came across. She always wanted to be a mother."

Skunk turned to Tamaya, surprised. "Huh? She did?"

Tamaya nodded. "She would rarely speak of it, but it was never hard to see. She was a natural with children. Wherever we would go, if there were children involved in our work, her first thoughts would be of their safety, and she would stare after them when we parted ways. It did not take much intuition to sense her longing."

Skunk looked back down at Amelia, frowning. "...Didn't she have a boyfriend or something?" he asked as some questions he had never considered crossed his mind. "Or, you know, another human she could, er, make babies with?"

Tamaya did not answer immediately. "...The answer to that question is a long one, Skunk. Nor is it mine to give."

Skunk felt a stab of disappointment. He looked up at her, opening his mouth to protest. One look at the steely, unflinching wall that was her expression, however, told him it would be pointless. He looked down. "I guess that's fair," he conceded quietly. "It's just that mom never really talks about her past, you know? She gets this far-off look in her eyes whenever it comes up, but she never says anything."

"Her silence is not unjustified, I assure you."

Before either of them had a chance to continue, there was movement. A gentle rustling. Skunk felt Amelia's fingers curling around his hand.

"It's okay, Tamaya," the woman mumbled, her voice low and weak.

Skunk lifted his eyes, his heart skipping a beat. Amelia's eyes were open and staring back at him with loving warmth — and more than a little exhaustion. "Mom!" he exclaimed, instinct taking over. He lunged, throwing his arms around her shoulders in a bone-crushing hug. Amelia grunted but did not protest. Skunk's muscles eased and relaxed as he felt her arms wrapping around him, her lips brushing against the top of his head in a weak but no less affectionate kiss. Skunk shivered, burying his face into her shoulder. "You're awake!"

"Squeeze me too hard and that won't last," Amelia joked, reminding Skunk of her condition. He yipped quietly in embarrassment, loosened his grip, and moved the majority of his weight off of her. He did not release his hold on her, though. Right now, nothing could make him let her go again —save perhaps a dragon.

Behind him, Skunk heard Tamaya growling — or was she purring? — followed by a string of alien words. "Roluth tha. t' es ya k'ra za uut zen."

Skunk blinked, looking back at the war chief in confusion. "What?"

Amelia, however, did not seem so perplexed. Her face lit up with a warm smile. "Honored friend, am I? I'm flattered, Tamaya. *T' es ya k'ra za uut.*"

Tamaya's smile turned into an amused smirk. "Your *ry'thari* is rusty, I see. And your accent is as odd as ever," she teased.

Amelia shrugged, and the two shared a good-natured laugh. It only lasted a moment before Amelia's hand flew to her chest, and her laughter turned into a pained hiss. Skunk put a hand on her shoulder to ease her back down. "Woah, woah, hey, easy. You're still hurt."

Amelia nodded stiffly, taking short, sharp breaths. Once her breaths had steadied, she looked up at Tamaya. "How long was I out?"

It was Skunk who answered. "A couple of days."

"It was a near thing," Tamaya added. "Your companions did well to bring you to us. Any longer and the infection would have claimed you if the blood loss did not."

Amelia nodded quietly and closed her eyes again. Her brow creased, and Skunk knew already what she was about to say.

Tamaya beat her to it. "We will have time to speak in the morning, Amelia. But for now, you should rest. You are still tender. Besides, I believe you and your son have things to discuss."

Amelia opened her eyes. She started to protest, but a firm look from Tamaya silenced her. She relented a moment later. "Alright. Tomorrow, then." Tamaya gave each of them a small nod before stepping out, leaving Skunk and Amelia alone.

A tense silence fell over them, and free of distractions, Skunk felt his anxiety and guilt returning. Swallowing hard, he turned to his mother. Amelia stared back at him, tired and unreadable.

Skunk faltered. He looked down at his hands fidgeting over his chest. "Mom? I, uh... I'm sorry," he finally managed to say. "For how I treated you back in Addernotch. I was horrible to you. I acted like a little monster. I'm *so* sorry."

Amelia was quiet for what seemed a long time. Then she let out a quiet breath and pulled Skunk against her in a loving hug. "It's okay, Skunk. I'm sorry, too."

"For what?"

Amelia stared up at the ceiling, her eyes going distant. "For lying to you," she confessed in an almost inaudible whisper.

"You... lied to me?"

Amelia nodded. "About why I needed you to stay in Addernotch. The truth is, I knew that leaving you behind meant leaving you at the mercy of the villagers.

I knew you'd be made the scapegoat for everything that happened. I was planning on Seto keeping you safe."

Skunk flinched, unable to repress a sting of hurt deep in his chest. He looked down, his expression darkening. "I figured you weren't being wholly honest with me. I just couldn't figure out why," he muttered quietly. "Why did you want me to stay behind?"

"Because I genuinely believed you would be safer in Addernotch than you would be out here. I believed that you wouldn't be able to control yourself if we crossed paths with any other kobolds. I was *terrified* that you would get yourself killed. And I couldn't let that happen. I couldn't make myself *trust* you. And truth be told, I'm still scared it might happen."

Skunk took a few moments to let the confession sink in, and all it entailed. He was unquestionably insulted by the admission, but he couldn't find it in himself to remain that way for long. After all, he was still missing a lot of the puzzle, wasn't he?

He slowly sat up and looked down at Amelia, his eyes searching. "Mom? Why *did* you take me in?" he finally asked her. "Why did you adopt me instead of having a baby the normal way?"

Amelia winced. "Does it matter? You may not be my blood, but you're still my son."

"It *does* matter," Skunk stressed. "It matters to me! I've been learning a lot about my kobold side lately, and I *hate* it. I wanna know something about the woman who raised me. I wanna know about my *human* side. I want to know about *you,* and I want to know what *I mean to you.*"

Amelia winced as he parroted her own words back at her as if she had been struck. Skunk could see her eyes shifting under their lids as if she were actively fighting with herself about whether or not to answer him. Eventually, though, she gave a tiny nod. "Okay. The truth, then. You're old enough. And you have a right to know."

Skunk quickly rotated in his seat and propped his chin up in his hands, listening intently.

Amelia took a moment to collect her thoughts and then began. "I should start by saying I didn't have much of a childhood. Not a good one, at least. I was raised by a collector of old artifacts in Underbridge."

"Your father was a collector?" Skunk questioned.

Amelia's expression hardened. "That man was *not* my father," she corrected. "He raised me, yes. But I was not his child. I was his *tool.* He had me trained to do one thing, and one thing only. Find his enemies and kill them."

Skunk's eyes widened in shock. He looked off toward a chest tucked into the corner of the yurt, where Amelia's belongings were kept. "So *that's* why you're so good at fighting."

"It is. I had very good teachers. But no morals. It was drilled into my head for as long as I could remember. Obey, obey, obey. No questions, no affection, no games. Just *obey*. It was all I ever knew. So I obeyed. When I became an adult, he would start sending me out on missions. Usually, I was sent to acquire things to add to his collections. Artifacts and relics from old ruins, mostly. Sometimes he would send me to 'liberate' such an item from someone else. A band of treasure hunters here, a rival collector there. Those jobs often ended in someone dying.

"One day I was ordered to retrieve an artifact from someone who had refused to hand it over. I tried. And she beat me. *Handily*. It was the first time *anyone* had defeated me in a fight."

Skunk leaned forward, enthralled. "Who? Who was it?"

Amelia smiled. "Tamaya."

"What?!"

Amelia winced, lifting a hand to her ear in protest. Skunk slapped his hands over his mouth, mentally kicking himself in the butt for being so loud, then repeated himself in a whisper. *"What?"*

Amelia chuckled weakly. "I know. It's funny, isn't it? She's my best friend, and I met her by trying to drive a dagger through her back. But she beat me outright and forced me to surrender. I was convinced she would kill me. Instead, she told me that honor demanded she not take the life of an enemy who had surrendered. Besides, she saw something worth saving buried under all of the years of brainwashing, and so she saw fit to spare me."

Skunk settled back down, mesmerized. "What happened next?"

"Tamaya took me with her. Said she could use someone with my experience in the world. She was on a sort of pilgrimage at the time — she needed to know more about the lands and people around her tribe if she was going to rule one day. Now, at first, I thought she was completely mad. Mercy like that was a foreign concept to me, so I tried to kill her two more times. Each time, she bested me even more thoroughly than the last. And each time, she let me live. She wouldn't even hold it against me afterward. And in those quiet moments in between, she would question me *extensively* on my life and my decisions."

Amelia's lips slowly curled up into a tender smile. "Looking back, I realize what she was doing. She was trying to help me understand myself. She was encouraging me to shed the lies and deceptions my master had wrapped me in. She was *teaching* me how to think and act for myself while also teaching me the value of mercy and compassion — things I had never had in my life until then.

"Eventually, I came to see how rotten the life I had been living was. I cast off the shackles of my old master, named Tamaya my friend, and chose to walk beside her, rather than stalk behind her. We ventured into the world, taking odd jobs wherever we could find them. It was by no means a glamorous life, but for once, I could be content with it. Eventually, we were hired by the Arcaniun Assemblage in Underbridge. That was where we met Seto. He was our pathfinder, our guide, and in general a wonderful addition to our little team."

Amelia's expression continued to soften as she spoke. "As we took on job after job, I learned about the world around me properly. Seto and Tamaya took turns giving me long-winded lectures on history, culture, and everything else I'd missed. From our travels, I learned of everyday life for all sorts of people. And I saw children. Children laughing. Children playing. Children being smothered in the affection of their families. Children being scolded for misbehaving. Children being children."

Amelia's expression darkened into something more somber. "It was then that I realized what I had missed out on in my life. Eventually, I started to realize that, one day, when my time working for the Assemblage was over, I wanted to have a family of my own. A *real* family. A *proper* family. Not the suffocating environment the collector made me suffer through."

Skunk nodded along slowly. "So why didn't you, then?" he asked gingerly. "Why didn't you look for someone?"

"I did," Amelia said plainly. "But considering the life I had led up to that point, do you think I was *any* good at flirting with men? Or even knowing what I *wanted* in a man? Besides, we were on the road every day, fighting monsters and spelunking through ruins. That's not a lifestyle conducive to starting a family, Skunk."

Skunk opened his mouth to say something, then shut it when he realized he had no valid point to counter that with.

Amelia chuckled at his silence, then continued. "Eventually, though, that life started to wear us down. Seto was starting to show the first signs of age, and Tamaya needed to return to her tribe. So we decided this next job would be our last. Once it was done, I would remain in the city to look for a less bloody way to earn a living. As luck would have it, our final job wasn't all that far from the Karjene's lands. So we set out, Seto in tow..."

Skunk waited for Amelia to continue, but the silence continued. He leaned forward. "And...? What happened next?" he asked weakly.

Amelia shuddered. "We were ambushed. We'd reported my old master's unsavory practices some time prior, and he was executed for his numerous crimes. But I wasn't his only little helper. There was another. I suppose you could call him my 'brother.' He came after us to get revenge. He fought with a ferocity I had never seen before — and with no sense of self-preservation. In the end..."

Amelia's words caught in her throat. Slowly, she reached down and lifted the blankets and brought a finger to her lower belly. A grotesque scar ran from her navel to the middle of her pelvis.

Skunk leaned in to get a better look, his stomach churning. "I've never seen this before," he whispered.

"We cut him down, but not before he gave me this. It was the worst day of my life. The wound would have been fatal if I didn't get help. The pain was unbearable, and I blacked out from blood loss. When I came to, Tamaya had sprinted me all the way to the village. Annotha had saved my life."

Amelia's expression darkened, her fingers curling into a fist. "But some of the damage was permanent."

Skunk didn't say anything for a moment. He gingerly traced the tip of his index finger over the scar. "Permanent?"

Amelia nodded. "Tell me, Skunk. Do you know what it is that lies under that scar? What organ of the human woman's body?"

Skunk frowned. He had never received much of an education about the inner workings of the human body, save for the basics. None of Seto's classes were that advanced. He slowly shook his head.

Amelia shuddered and gestured. "Beneath that scar... that was my *womb*. Where a baby grows. My 'brother' destroyed mine. Annotha did her best, but she could only restore the shape. Not the function."

Skunk's eyes widened, and his hand drew back as if he had been burned. The gears were turning in his head, and the pieces falling into place. But he had to be sure he was understanding right. He looked into his mother's eyes. "Y-you mean you couldn't..."

Amelia closed her eyes. "I could never have children of her own, Skunk. Even *if* I found a man I was willing to have one with, I *couldn't*."

Skunk slowly sat back in shock, his eyes wide. It all made sense now. Why Amelia had taken him in, why she had doted on him and protected him so fiercely for so long. His heart twisted in his chest, his sympathy burning bright as the sun. He reached out and gingerly took Amelia's hand in his again, giving it a firm squeeze. "Mom," he whispered, his voice cracking. "I'm so sorry."

Amelia met his gaze, her eyes watering. "I stayed here for months after that, by Tamaya's insistence. I lived here with the ry'thar while they tried to mend the damage. But n-nothing worked. In the end, I left for Addernotch... Hollow. Empty. I felt destroyed."

Her fingers wrapped tightly around Skunk's, squeezing tightly. "A-and then I found you. I wished upon a falling star, and it gave me *you*. And I knew what I had to do."

Skunk leaned forward to hug her again, burying his face into her shoulder. He didn't say anything, though. He had no idea what he *could* say. Still, he could at least be there for the woman who had given him everything. Especially now that he had a better idea of what exactly *he* meant to *her*.

"Thank you," he finally whispered to her, giving her an affectionate squeeze. He felt the fur blanket being draped over them both as Amelia pulled it back into place, but he did not look up.

"No, Skunk. *Thank you,*" Amelia countered quietly. "For coming into my life. For letting me take care of you. For *everything* you've given me."

Skunk heard her sniffling, and he tightened his hold. He had no more words for her tonight, however. He held her as close as he dared, making sure she knew he was here, he was with her, and he wasn't going anywhere.

hunters

"Skunk?"

Skunk gave off a tired groan as a voice dragged him out of his slumber. He tried to ignore it, but a hand shaking him by the shoulder dashed any such hopes. He lifted his head and opened his eyes, releasing a tired groan and a mighty yawn.

Amelia was smiling down at him from alarmingly close.

"Yipe!" Skunk yipped like a puppy as he sprang out of the bed. The floor rose swiftly to meet him, and the impact drove the air from his unprepared lungs. He coughed on the floor a few times, vaguely aware of Amelia sitting up in the bed.

"Skunk, are you alright?"

Wheezing, Skunk lifted his thumb into the air. He heard Amelia laughing, equally amused and relieved. Shaking himself, he rolled to his feet and looked up to see her feeling her injury through her bandages. He rose and put his hands on the edge of the bed. "How are you feeling?" he asked, his eyes lingering on the wound.

Amelia shrugged. "Better, I think. I'm still sore, but I'll be okay," she assured him before looking down. She pulled her blanket up to hide the scar over her belly. She did not say anything, and her expression was difficult to read. Finally, she asked, "I didn't get to ask last night. What have I missed?"

Skunk's mood had been pretty high, all things considered, but that question dragged it right back down. His teeth ground together behind tightly pressed lips. "The Karjene were hit by the kobolds," he said quietly. "Before they hit us. Karak was leading them then, too."

Amelia stiffened at that, the color slowly draining from her face. "Gods... What's the damage?"

Skunk shook his head regretfully and launched into a thorough summary of what happened before they arrived. The more he said, the more troubled Amelia became, especially when Karak entered the picture. When at last Skunk had finished, Amelia had rotated to sit on the edge of the bed, a hand rubbing at her chin.

"That Karak could overpower even a ry'thari war chief, especially one as skilled and experienced as her," she whispered in horror. "What manner of monstrosity *is* he?"

Skunk shook his head. "I don't know. But just thinking about him makes me feel nauseous. He's not right, mom. He *shouldn't* exist."

The two fell into a contemplative silence for a while. Skunk couldn't stop thinking about everything Amelia had told him last night. He looked her way every so often, particularly at where he knew her scar to be. She noticed him looking and frowned. "What is it?"

Skunk bit his lip. Without a word, he stood and wrapped Amelia up in another hug. He felt Amelia return it tentatively as if confused by the sudden display of affection.

Skunk rested his chin on her shoulder. "Thank you for telling me," he said in a low murmur. "About everything."

Amelia's hold on him tightened. She let out a quiet sigh. "I'm sorry it took me so long," she apologized quietly. "It was hard to talk about. And I don't want you to think that I adopted you *only* because I couldn't have children of my own. I would *never* have left you there to be eaten by those bounders."

Skunk shook his head. "You don't have to tell me that. I know. I'm just sorry you had to go through all that," he whispered, pulling her closer. "But I'm here. And I'm not going anywhere."

There was a brief moment where Amelia did not say a word. Then she pulled Skunk as close as she dared with her injury still sore. "Yes. You're here," she echoed, running a hand down his back. "Thank you. For letting me find you."

Skunk smiled. He wanted to tell her that *he* was the one who should be thanking her, but the words stilled in his throat. He had thanked her many times in his life, always grateful for everything she had given him. He had seldom considered what *he* had given *her* beyond the tasks he volunteered for. Now he knew.

"You're welcome," he said softly, closing his eyes.

The two stayed like that for a while, enjoying one another's warmth. The pleasant haze of their newfound understanding chased away the fears and anxieties of the struggles to come, if only for that moment. Not that Skunk minded, of course. With all of the chaos and the pain of the last week, a chance to just *exist* was more than welcome.

Sadly, it could not last forever.

Skunk smelled her before she arrived. Herbal spices and mints atop a thick musk. He heard the flaps of the yurt opening, followed by a soft, elderly laugh.

"I hope I am not interrupting anything," Annotha greeted. Skunk turned to see the shaman stepping forward, her weight supported by a crooked walking staff. Her old and wrinkled face smiled back at him.

Amelia gently pushed Skunk off of her and gave the shaman a firm nod. "Elder Annotha. It has been far too long," she said respectfully. "I understand that I have you to thank for treating my injuries."

Annotha passed her staff lightly from one hand to another. "Too long indeed, cub. And yes, I treated your wounds."

Amelia bowed her head. "You have my gratitude," she said. "Thank you, elder."

"Come now, Amelia. You need not be so formal with me. We are friends, are we not?" The shaman asked before kneeling to check Amelia's wound. Skunk watched as the ry'thar peeled back the bandages with remarkable precision. As the last layer came away, Skunk could see a vertical sore lined with a ridge of freshly regrown flesh where the arrow hole had been. Annotha chewed the inside of her cheek and hummed appreciatively. "Almost done. Hold still, cub," she commanded as she took hold of her ringstone.

As the night before, she spoke in the language Skunk did not know. The stone radiated a silvery white, and bright threads of luma reached from the stone to wrap around Amelia's wound. Bit by bit, the new flesh softened and smoothed. After a few minutes, the injury was almost completely gone. The only sign it had ever been there was a tiny patch of lighter skin where the wound had been.

Annotha stopped chanting and leaned back, the glow fading from her stone. "There. It will still be sore and tender, and you're going to feel *very* hungry in a few minutes, so make sure you have a large breakfast. There is also the lingering remnant of your infection, but the worst of that has passed. You should be as right as rain by tomorrow, little cub."

Amelia nodded, standing up slowly from the bed. She wobbled for a second before finding her balance. She gave the shaman a grateful smile. "I am in your debt yet again, Annotha," she said.

Annotha snorted. "What did I *just* say about being formal?" she asked playfully.

"I'm just being polite to my elder, Annotha."

Annotha considered the response, then shrugged. "Very well. If it puts your mind at ease," she said before pointing the tip of her staff at the nearby chest. "Your belongings are stored there. Get dressed and head out when you are ready. War chief Tamaya wishes to speak with you. Just make sure you take it easy, yes?"

With that, Annotha turned and slipped out of the tent. Amelia wasted no time getting dressed. Skunk kept his eyes pointedly facing the other way until she stepped in front of him, once again clad in her form-fitting armor. The damage left by the arrow had been repaired while Amelia was unconscious, it seemed, though the brightly colored path stood out sharply against the darker leather.

She nodded down at him. "Come. Let's go see what Tamaya wants," she said.

Skunk nodded eagerly, dutifully falling into step beside his mother as they strode out of the tent.

Amelia looked around as they emerged into the sunlight, a gentle breeze whistling through the village, a whisper of grass rising from the hills beyond. The woman closed her eyes to take a long, deep breath. Skunk waited patiently, just watching her savor her return.

When Amelia opened her eyes, however, her expression darkened with equal parts fury and sympathy. Skunk could practically feel the radiating aura of malice coming from her as she beheld the state of the village and the fate of her friends.

"They're going to pay for this," Amelia whispered venomously.

Skunk wanted to say something, but an agitated voice silenced him before he had the chance to even open his mouth.

"Oh, *there* you are!" Danica's voice rang out from nearby. Skunk jumped in surprise and turned to see the dwarf storming up to them, Lorok following close behind her. She nodded at Amelia, then affixed Skunk with a stern glare. "Do you have a death wish or something, kid? What were you thinking, sneaking out like that!?"

Skunk flinched, his eyes lowering. "Sorry. I just wanted to make sure—"

"Yes, I know *why*, you're not exactly subtle," Danica cut him off. "But in the future, *warn* people before you go running off! I had to spend an hour convincing the guard I had no idea where you went."

Skunk put on a tiny, apologetic smile. "Sorry," he said again.

Danica huffed before giving the two of them a more appraising look. "Hmph. Whatever. No one got stabbed, so no harm was done, I guess. Apology accepted. Did you sleep well?"

Skunk gave her a thumbs-up. "Uh-huh! I was beat! I slept like a rock!"

Danica snorted. "Good. You're no use to anyone if you're exhausted."

Skunk's tail swished behind him a few times. "Thanks, Danica. What about you? Did you sleep alright?"

Danica waved him off. "Unfamiliar territory, stuffed in a cramped tent, surrounded by lion folk who smell like rotting meat and woodsmoke?" she asked grumpily. Then she flashed Skunk a thumbs up and a tiny smile. "Slept like a rock."

Amelia smiled and put a hand on her hip. "I'm glad to see you two warming up to each other," she observed.

There was a pause. Danica dropped her thumb and affixed Amelia with an unblinking stare. "I beg your thrice-damned pardon?" she asked, though Skunk could see the red creeping up her face.

Amelia's smile grew predatory. "You just asked if my son slept well — and even gave advice on why he *should*. Why would such a question concern you if you didn't care?"

Danica's eyes twitched. "Why— You— But— *shut up!*" she practically shouted before stomping off down the path, her arms swinging in wide, agitated arcs. As she went, Skunk's keen hearing picked out her indignant grumbling, which mostly consisted of a long string of colorful curses and swears.

Amelia shook her head, laughing. "Ah, a stubborn one, is she? Good."

Skunk wasn't entirely sure why stubbornness was a good thing in a social circumstance, but he decided that now was not the time to question it. Not that he would have the chance to do so, as a sound reached Skunk's ears from the war chief's yurt. A lion roaring.

Skunk jumped and turned to watch as a ry'thar man stormed toward Tamaya, his lip peeled back in a vicious display of sharpened fangs. He was yelling something in their harsh language. Tamaya faced him, unflinching, and answered his scream with a low, measured response.

Skunk shifted uncomfortably on his feet as they argued back and forth. "What are they talking about?"

Amelia listened to them for a moment, her expression darkening with dismay. "...He is questioning the wisdom of her leadership," she explained in a whisper. "She wants the bulk of the Karjene to fortify the village against further attacks. But he wants to launch a counterattack."

Beside them, Danica snorted. "Sounds familiar."

They watched the two argue back and forth for a moment longer. Skunk's hands fidgeted anxiously over his chest. He was about to ask another question when the man suddenly lunged for Tamaya, hands reaching for her throat. Skunk's eyes widened in shock, and he opened his mouth to cry out.

His concern was unwarranted. Tamaya turned with the lunge, effortlessly using the man's weight against him. She hauled him into a swift and vicious takedown, sending him sprawling to the dirt.

"Tamaya!" Skunk cried out, taking a step forward.

A hand caught his shoulder. Confused, he looked up at Amelia. She shook her head at him. "Don't," She said firmly. "This is their way. Do not interfere."

Skunk wanted to argue, but the firm look in her eyes cowed him into submission. He turned to watch as Tamaya dealt with the upstart. And deal with him she did. His every attack, fast and ferocious as they were, was effortlessly countered and turned against him. Curiously, Skunk noted, Tamaya launched no attacks of her own. She was redirecting the offensive efforts of her aggressor with awe-inspiring ease.

When at last she *did* take offensive action, she dipped low to drive her fist into his belly. The man doubled over her fist, his furious battle cry going silent in his throat as the air fled his lungs. Tamaya stood upright, turned, and delivered a powerful snap-kick into his face, sending him to the dirt in a crumpled heap. Tamaya spoke to him again, her voice a cold and authoritative growl. The man looked back up at her.

"You know," Danica commented in a whisper. "Displays like this are probably part of why so many people think the ry'thar are savages."

"There's an order to it," Amelia pointed. "Notice how Tamaya fought. The man was coming at her, challenging her authority. She maintained her stance and her orders. He made an effort to overpower her, but she made no effort to harm him or strike back until it was time to end the fight. Confrontations like this are meant to measure the strength of the combatant's spirits and their resolve. If he had been able to overpower her, he would have been free to disobey her command even though she is the war chief."

"So it's a type of conflict resolution," Danica surmised.

Amelia nodded. "In essence, yes. And look."

Skunk watched, surprised as Tamaya helped her fallen challenger back to his feet. She patted him down, dusted him off, and nodded for Annotha's yurt. When she spoke again, her voice was far gentler. The man did not appear pleased, but he nodded his head and turned to leave, far more respect in that one movement than Skunk had seen from him so far.

Amelia smiled. "The strength of her spirit is proven, and their dispute is settled. She sends him to ensure she did no permanent damage and he bends to her will."

"So it's a beatdown with rules and everyone walks away with respect for the outcome?" Danica noted before shrugging her shoulders. "If I hadn't seen it myself..."

"It can be hard to wrap our heads around," Amelia agreed quietly. "But then again, we don't have to. It's not our way. It is theirs."

With that, she stepped toward Tamaya. The war chief saw her coming, and any anger that remained on her face was replaced with a wide smile that almost looked out of place on her face. "Amelia! You are up!"

Skunk's chest warmed as they gave one another a tight embrace. So tight, in fact, that Tamaya lifted Amelia a few inches off the ground. She gasped, her feet kicking feebly under her. "Ow! Tamaya! Ribs!" she protested in a strangled voice.

Tamaya dropped her back to the ground and gave Amelia room to double over and catch her breath. She grinned and patted Amelia on the back. "Forgive me, roluth tha. But it has been far too long since I've had the chance."

"Doesn't mean you have to make it the last," Amelia wheezed, clutching at her chest. "Ow. You're as strong as ever."

"And you are just as fragile," Tamaya bit back. "Bones as brittle as branches."

"No, that's Seto."

"Him, as well."

The two shared another laugh before embracing once more. Skunk watched them, feeling a profound sense of whiplash at the stark shift in Tamaya's demeanor. He shook himself a moment later and quickly walked forward to join them. They were speaking in the ry'thari language now, their speech fast and animated. Skunk wanted to say something, but he couldn't bring himself to interrupt them.

Danica, however, had no such reservations. "If you two are done flirting," she said bluntly, drawing Amelia and Tamaya's eyes. Danica nodded to Tamaya. "You wanted to talk to us, and I doubt it was to play catch-up with *one* of us in a tongue only you two speak."

Tamaya frowned at the dwarf's impertinence but did not argue. She took a step back, clearing her throat. "You have the right of it, Danica," she confirmed. She opened her mouth to say something more but was cut off by the low, guttural growling of some unseen beast. There was a long quiet before Amelia's face flushed bright red.

"...Sorry," She apologized lamely, her hand coming to a rest on her stomach. "Annotha did warn me I'd be hungry."

Danica slapped a hand to her face. "Juna's tits," she swore.

Tamaya smiled. "No need to apologize. I've not eaten yet, either. Come. We can eat over breakfast."

Skunk perked up at that. He would never say no to a good breakfast.

Skunk had not given much thought to the culinary traditions of the ry'thar. He'd never had a reason to. As such, he had been pleasantly surprised to be reminded that, much like him, the lionfolk were a carnivorous people. Breakfast consisted mostly of thick slabs of wild animal meat, fatty, tough with muscle, enriched with exotic seasonings, and cooked until the outer skin had a nice, satisfying crunch.

Skunk made no effort to stifle his enthusiastic snarls as he tucked into his meal.

The group had assembled in Tamaya's yurt, making small talk for the first few minutes. Danica kept quiet, though Skunk spied her occasionally breaking off bits of meat into her pack. Probably so she could feed them to Lorok later.

Eventually, Tamaya decided the time for luxury had passed. As she washed down a thick bite of meat, she affixed Amelia with a firm look. "When you first arrived, Skunk told me of Addernotch's plea for assistance."

Amelia lowered her cup and nodded. "He told me as much before I got up this morning," she said, her voice all business now. "You declined."

Tamaya nodded slowly. "For the time being, at least. It is not a decision I made lightly, of that you may be certain. We are crippled, and I've not the hunters to spare in the defense of another town so far from my own, nor can I abandon these lands to join my forces with yours. They have belonged to the Karjene for generations. Even were I to command it, my people would never agree to such an exodus, temporary though it would be."

"Not so crippled that you're unwilling to scout out the enemy, however," Amelia pointed out, crossing her arms. "I overheard your argument earlier."

Skunk had been in the middle of taking a massive bite out of his breakfast when he heard that. He almost choked on a chunk of bone hidden in the flesh from gasping so hard. Blinking, he turned to Amelia. "Wait, what!?"

Tamaya frowned, her jaw working from side to side. She looked at Skunk a second later. "Skunk. When we spoke last night, you said something that made me question my decision. You said that Amelia showed you great kindness when she took you in, and you made clear your desire to pay that kindness forward."

Tamaya looked down into the fire, the blaze reflected in her eyes. "When the horde came for us, a great many people, yours and mine, died. Every one of them fought as hard as they could to protect themselves and their loved ones. I choose to believe that their unfaltering bravery saved many lives. And as war chief, it is my *duty* to see that my tribe is taken care of in times of war and strife."

She lifted her eyes to Skunk again. "And so I have come to the decision that I shall pay their kindness forward."

Skunk's eyes widened, his tail swishing behind him. "So we're going after the kobolds after all?!" he asked hopefully.

Tamaya lifted a hand and narrowed her eyes, silencing him. "Temper your expectations, boy. We do not possess the strength to face them in an open battle. Not with Karak leading their ranks. Your people have called for reinforcements from your larger cities, have they not?"

Amelia nodded. "Messengers were sent to Port Natha and Underbridge a few days ago. On horseback, word will have reached Port Natha by now, but it will take some time before they reach Underbridge — and even then, organizing and mobilizing a suitable contingent of troops to answer the threat may take time."

Tamaya nodded in understanding. "Well, when these armies arrive, they will need knowledge of the enemy, yes? A wise hunter knows the nature of their prey, observes them, and finds weaknesses to exploit. Their odds of success will swell significantly if they need not waste time gathering this knowledge themselves," she explained pointedly before her voice lowered to something softer. "And setting all of that aside, Amelia, I would hate for you to have come all this way for nothing."

Danica piped up, leaning forward. "So what's the plan, then?"

Tamaya turned to her. "I will be taking two of our best hunters with me. We will track the kobolds back to their lair, identify where they are hiding, gather information on what defenses we can, and return to the village without engaging the enemy in battle."

Tamaya returned her attention to Amelia, and another smile spread on her face. "If you and your companions are willing, then I would invite you to join us on this expedition, Amelia. It has been far too long since you and I have gone on a hunt together."

Amelia frowned, glancing side-long at Skunk. For a moment, he was convinced that she was going to insist that he stay behind again and was already putting together a long list of reasons why he was not about to obey that order no matter how fervently she insisted. But then Amelia nodded. "It would be my pleasure to hunt at your side again, Tamaya. It will be just like old times. Minus the old decrepit ruins, I hope."

Tamaya grunted. "If I have to delve into another Auriun undercity, it will be too soon."

"I can come too, right?" Skunk asked, standing up and raising his hand. "I got a good nose! I can track the kobolds down easy! I know their scent already!"

Amelia turned to him, her expression firm. She examined him for a few long seconds, looking for some clue or hint that he was ready. He met her gaze resolutely, standing his ground. He even made it a point to puff up his chest and hold his head high, trying to look bigger and tougher than he felt.

Finally, to his surprise — and delight — Amelia nodded. "Okay. You can come. You've come this far already. And after everything that's happened, I would be foolish to send you back now."

Skunk's heart felt as if it would burst out of his chest. The rush of validation and relief was difficult to put into words, so he voiced it as a celebratory roar instead. "Thank you, Mom!" he squealed, leaping against her in a tight hug. "Thank you, thank you, thank you!"

Amelia chuckled from the enthusiasm, then pushed him back so she could look into his eyes. "You're welcome, but calm down. I need you to understand that this is a *scouting* mission, not a *rescue* mission. That means there will be no heroics, no valiant charges, no stalwart last stands. If we are caught and dragged into battle, we fight to hide our presence or, failing that, secure an escape. Do you understand me?"

Skunk knew that of course, but it grounded him back in reality to have it reiterated. He took a moment to curb his enthusiasm before nodding. "Gotcha. No heroics."

Danica threw her hands up. "Bah. I might as well come along, too," she relented with a small smirk. "If this all goes tits up and you get attacked, you'll need some muscle to keep your asses alive."

Tamaya snorted. "I'm a ry'thar," she deadpanned.

"And I'm a dwarf," Danica rebuked.

"I've seen her fight!" Skunk added helpfully. "She's like a grizzly bear! With axes!"

Tamaya considered the dwarf for a moment. "So be it," she eventually conceded. "What is the old human phrase? Strength in numbers? If you wish to accompany us, you are welcome to do so. But I must mirror Amelia's words to her son. We are not retrieving your stolen property on this mission."

Danica grunted. "That's fine. I just need to know where it is. I can figure out the rest on my own after that."

"Well, then, if that is settled," Amelia said, hefting her slab of meat back up. "Let's finish up here and get started."

Skunk couldn't argue with that. He tore into his meal with renewed vigor, a comforting warmth settling in his belly alongside a newfound energy in his veins. Even if this mission was a few steps shy of what he *wanted* to do, he was just happy to finally get the chance to be involved — happy his mother *trusted* him to get involved.

As soon as they were done eating, Tamaya led the group out of the yurt and down a wide path through the village. They soon came to a half-circle of solidly built tents with open fronts, each one loaded to the point of bursting with weapons of ry'thari make. Long spears tipped with stone or bone, enormous bows, quivers filled with serrated arrows, and many more.

Skunk took in the armory with a small whistle before he caught sight of two other ry'thar kitting themselves with furs and arming themselves, a man and a woman. Tamaya called to them in their language, drawing their attention. The duo swiftly finished arming themselves, then moved to meet her.

Tamaya turned to Amelia and gestured at the warriors joining them. "Amelia, meet Katala and Dakar. These are the hunters I spoke of."

Katala, the woman, nodded her head respectfully to Amelia. "It is a pleasure to meet you again, *roluth tha*, though I doubt you remember me," she said slowly, tentatively, as though she was having a hard time finding the words. She must have had less practice with the common tongue, Skunk imagined.

Amelia smiled. "Oh, but how *could* I forget you? You were a cub when last we met, hiding behind your mother's leg," she said, looking the woman up and down with a warm smile and an appreciative gleam in her eye. "You've grown into a fine woman."

Katala perked up, pleased at being recognized. Dakar, however, did not share his friend's enthusiasm. His hard glare was boring into Skunk, his amber-colored eyes narrowed with skepticism and barely restrained hostility. Skunk tried to stand his ground before the imposing glare, but he found himself shrinking back anyway. Dakar turned to Tamaya, his lips twitching up to show his teeth. "War chief, we are to bring the *kalj'atla* with us?!" he asked in disbelief.

Tamaya turned to him, her eyes narrowing, but Amelia beat her to the punch. She moved quickly and quietly, interposing herself between Dakar and Skunk. She met the towering hunter's gaze with her own, unflinching. "That kalj'atla is my *son*. His name is Skunk, and he is as fine a hunter as any ry'thar I know," she stated.

Skunk's first instinct was to try and downplay the statement. He was good, and he knew it, but he doubted he could hold a candle to the people around him. But the words caught in his throat as it dawned on him that Amelia's declaration was utterly sincere. Skunk wasn't sure he *believed* it, but the compliment made him feel warm and fuzzy all the same.

"Amelia's vouched for him, and I trust her judgment," Tamaya added, putting a hand on Dakar's shoulder and lightly pushing him back. "Skunk shall be joining us. As a kalj'atla, his sense of smell is far superior even to our own. Rest assured, I will keep an eye on him."

Dakar was quiet for a moment. He gave Skunk another glance, not quite as harsh this time. "Very well. But mind yourself, kalj'atla," he warned. "If you threaten my war chief or my partner, or anyone else of the Karjene, I will not hesitate to place your head on a pike."

Skunk swallowed heavily, still not used to receiving threats from people who were supposed to be his allies. Still, he drew himself up. "I understand," he said.

Katala chose this moment to jump back into the conversation, hoping to break down the tension. "The last we saw of the horde, they were cutting across the fields moving northeast. Their eyes have no use for firelight in the darkness, and we could not track them by ringlight forever. They vanished beyond the fourth ridge."

"Then that is where Skunk shall come in," Tamaya decided, procuring a spear of her own from one of the tents. She held it for a moment, testing its balance, then slipped it gracefully into a strap across her back. She turned to face the group and offered them all a sharp nod. "*Thu kasa skaru.*"

Skunk blinked, the foreign words ringing meaninglessly in his ears even as Dakar and Katala repeated the phrase. He looked up at Amelia curiously. Her expression was grim, her jaw set.

"May the spirits guide us."

Fresh Meat

Once they were free from the forest, it only took a handful of days for Karak's band to return to the burrow. The flat terrain and lack of resistance gave them a straight shot to their mountain home. The other bands were still trickling in and would be for several days yet, but most of the horde had made it back safe and sound.

That wasn't to say that the journey had been free of concerns. Karak had worried that the Karjene might attempt to ambush his forces as they passed. Thankfully, the savage lions seemed to have learned their place, as there was no sign of them for the entire journey.

Back within the burrow, Karak allowed himself to breathe easy. He was safe here. All of the kobolds entrusted to his command were safe here.

It was a labyrinth taking the form of a convoluted network of interlocking tunnels. The kobolds could navigate the environment easily, and Karak had learned to match them with time, but it was still a headache. He still caught himself getting turned around from time to time. It was not made any easier by the near-total absence of light. The kobolds could see in the dark, but his eyes were not quite as sensitive as theirs. There was only one place in the burrow that was well-lit — and that was where Karak was headed.

It was evident that these passages were not designed for a creature of his stature. He was forced to hunch over just to avoid scraping his horns on the ceiling. His wings were tucked tight against his back, sore and stiff. Sometimes he was forced to lower himself onto all fours, crawling and scrabbling through tight spaces that did not agree with his broad frame.

He *hated* having to navigate like this. It was degrading, a pervasive insult to his pride and dignity that haunted his every step. But no matter how vexed he felt, he never spoke in protest, even when alone. He had agreed to pay this price. To moan about it now would be a waste of breath.

Karak paused briefly to glance into a feasting hall, one of many large chambers that were scattered throughout the network. A large round room with a high roof stretched before him, a space he could comfortably exist in if he wished. A massive pile of meat dominated the center of the chamber, surrounded by deep pits that spewed controlled gouts of fire. Narrow ventilation holes in the ceiling allowed the smoke to leave and fresh air to fall in.

Karak watched with satisfaction as kobolds enjoyed their meal, many of them rewarding themselves for the success of their mission. The room echoed with the snarls of the hungry, punctuated here and there by yaps and shouts as some kobolds fought over scraps of flesh. They were smeared in blood, grease, and fat, and the stench of their feast hit Karak's senses like a war hammer.

To the uninitiated, such a sight may have been horrifying. It would be difficult for a human or a dwarf to imagine that these creatures could have a culture or a history, that there was any shred of good in them whatsoever. But to Karak, it was as clear as day. He saw the good-natured grins. He heard the chuckles as some kobolds fought one another. It was like the roughhousing of brothers, the mock fighting of newborn kittens and wolf pups. He listened to their enthusiasm and energy as they talked amongst themselves over dinner, recounting their victory to those who had not been there, showing off their new battle scars and what trophies they had taken from their enemy. He saw the smaller and weaker kobolds huddling together, listening with rapt attention and cheering to their larger brothers and sisters, or scrambling as a coordinated pack to snatch up their share of food.

These little moments of delight were rare, Karak knew. The life of a kobold was brutal and often short. There was no room for weakness or doubt. But those who could make themselves useful would always have a place in the horde. There was a profound bond between each of them — a brotherhood that Karak feared he may never fully understand, no matter how long he lived among them. A fear he felt all the more keenly when one of the kobolds caught sight of him watching.

The joy in her eyes was replaced with bitter contempt and suspicion. She did not voice her distaste for the First Fang, but Karak did not need her to. He knew already that she would never consider him one of her brothers.

Karak swiftly moved on before any of the others spotted him. He did his best to put the disdain in the kobold's eyes from his thoughts. He had more important matters to attend to.

After a little more climbing and crawling, Karak arrived at his destination. He emerged to a wall of blazing green light that left him squinting in discomfort. His vision adjusted quickly, and he once again felt awed and humbled by the sight before him.

The chamber was monolithic in scope, easily able to house a small army. Piles of ringstones climbed the walls of the room, as bright as the pale ring itself in their abundance. Thin streams of luma flowed from them, glowing spiderwebs that shimmered in and out of existence like sparkling starlight. The entire horde's collection, every single stone at their disposal, all put toward a unified purpose. It was beautiful to behold and bathed the chamber with divine radiance that even now left Karak in awe.

The only places where the light did not reach were the numerous tunnels set into the walls at every elevation. This was the beating heart of the burrow, the central chamber that all others would eventually lead to. The largest of those tunnels, fifty feet high and a hundred wide, was in the back of the chamber, descending into a pit of impenetrable darkness. A smaller tunnel was set in the opposing wall, large enough for Karak to stand upright and spread his wings to their fullest.

Few of these passages saw any traffic. The kobolds knew better than to trespass in this sacred place without good reason. Only a handful were in the chamber, each one carrying out their respective duties with silent dedication.

Every so often they would cast their jumping gazes toward the dark tunnel in the back.

None of that was important to Karak right now. Instead, his gaze focused on the beating heart of the horde. A billowing inferno of green flame roared in the center of the chamber, where all the luma converged. It was a marvel of magic, burning with no fuel and emitting no smoke. A powerful enchantment had been worked into those stones not long after Karak had arrived, spawning fire in perpetuity.

Karak lifted his eyes to the ceiling above the inferno. There, secured to the roof by bone and leather and rock, was the largest ringstone he had ever seen, as large as an elephant and shining like the sun. This stone also lent its luma to the flames. But where its lesser cousins created strings and sparkles, *this* stone created rivers.

Karak took a deep breath, folding his hands behind his back. He approached one of the kobolds overseeing the chamber. She was a different color from her peers, being teal, marking her as having come from another horde. Whether she had been exiled or left of her own accord, Karak did not know, nor did he care.

She lifted her eyes at his approach, and her teeth showed in displeasure. "And the First Fang returns," she sneered, not bothering to hide her contempt. "To what do I owe the *pleasure?*"

Karak took the disrespectful tone in stride. "How are things progressing?" he asked, stopping by the kobold's side. He looked into the flames and the silhouette within.

She followed his gaze, her brow furrowed. "Slowly, but measurably. There has been some movement. I doubt we'll be waiting much longer than another week. Two, at most."

Karak nodded, pleased with the development. "Good. Keep up the good work..." he said, his eyes focusing exclusively on the object hidden within the flames.

Something pulled at him, then. It was like his instincts had been hijacked by some outside force, creating a desire that he was hopeless — and unwilling — to resist. Putting the kobold beside him out of his thoughts, he approached the flames. The oblong silhouette within almost seemed to pulse at him, inviting him to approach. Without hesitation, he stepped into the fire.

The flames hissed and bit fruitlessly at his scales, but he felt little more than a gentle tingle of warmth. He relished it.

He came to a stop in front of the object and looked it over. It was nearly as tall as he was, off-white and glossy like ice, though he knew it to be hollow and as hard as marble.

He reached out, gingerly placing the palm of his hand upon the dragon's egg.

The last egg of Azada.

It was warm to the touch, hotter even than the fire. He could feel vibrations on the surface, the dragon within shifting in response to his touch. Karak's heart beat a little faster, and he couldn't stop himself from letting out a short, anxious laugh.

"Still healthy," he whispered, pressing his forehead to the egg. "Good. Very good."

The egg vibrated again. The baby could hear him. It was reacting to him. Like a father stroking their partner's swollen belly, Karak drew circles on the egg's surface with his palm. "Ssshh, shh. It's alright. Everything is alright, little one. You are safe. I will not let anything harm you, young master," he whispered.

The child turned inside. Karak laughed again. "Are you dreaming?" he asked, turning so his ear was flush with the shell. He waited a moment, wondering what it was dragons dreamed of. Did they dream of their home? Did they dream of their parents or siblings? Did they endure nightmares of the atrocities of the past? Or did they dream of simpler things, like how a dog might dream of chasing a rabbit through an open field?

Karak would never know. And even if he did know, it would never be his place to understand. Still, it was fascinating to imagine.

"What do you see, young master?" Karak whispered, lowering himself to one knee. The egg twitched, and he heard a faint rumble within. Was the baby purring? His smile grew. "What wonders do you dream...?"

The tranquility of the moment, sadly, came to an end. A commotion sounded from one of the central tunnels, and a distressed kobold's voice called to him. "First Fang Karak! First Fang!"

Karak sighed in disappointment, pulling away from the egg. "I must go, young master," he whispered to it, seeing his face reflected in the glossy surface and wishing he could stay with it forever. He ran his thumb over the shell. "Sleep, now. You will be ready soon. Our enemies will burn, our people will unite, and the sins of the past will finally be put right. This, I swear."

Karak lingered a moment longer, then left the fire. A kobold male staggered toward him, off-balance and exhausted. He clutched a trembling hand against a festering wound in the scales on his side. Karak realized with a start that he recognized this kobold. He was one of the ones that had stayed behind to deal with Danica.

Despite his wounds, the kobold's eyes shone with frantic determination. "First Fang Karak, I bring word!" he called out between his exhausted gasps. His foot caught a ridge in the floor, and he began to fall.

With an unspoken thought, Karak invoked his gifts and ignited the runes along his calves and neck. The ringstone in the roof above him glowed to match as he called upon its power. All at once, time slowed to a crawl. Karak crossed the distance with a single, effortless stride, and caught the falling kobold before he could hit the ground.

The burst of speed faded, and the kobold looked up at the First Fang in surprise as he was lowered carefully to the ground. Karak gave him a reassuring nod. "Easy, friend. Easy. Take a moment and breathe. Collect yourself," he commanded. "What is your name?"

The kobold blinked at Karak, dumbfounded before offering a trembling answer. "Thross, First Fang. M-my name is Thross."

Karak nodded. "I remember you, Thross. Take a moment to catch your breath, then tell me what happened."

Thross stared at Karak in shock. He collected himself quickly and spent a few seconds breathing before his face scrunched up in a grimace. "We found the dwarf woman, as you ordered," he began haltingly, his voice low and timid with fear. Karak frowned, but said nothing, waiting for Thross to continue. "But s-she was not alone. She was joined by a human woman. A-and the *traitor*."

Murmurs rose from the few other kobolds in the chamber at the mention of Skunk. Tails lashed, fangs were bared, and narrowed eyes flashed with murderous rage. An uneasy feeling began creeping up Karak's spine. He did not allow his discomfort to show, however. "I take it, then, that your mission was not as easy as we had hoped," he surmised, already knowing the answer.

Thross nodded, confirming Karak's suspicion. "F-forgive me, First Fang. W-we failed. We ambushed them, and things went well at first, but they reacted quickly. I t-think I was the only one who survived. The dwarf was strong. She fought like a bear! The human woman never missed, even with an arrow lodged in her chest! I was shot with an arrow at the end of the fight. I'm only alive because I played dead."

Karak nodded along slowly. He had anticipated that Danica would prove difficult to bring down, but he had not anticipated her having any help. The news of Skunk's involvement was especially surprising. *What reason could Danica have to willingly ally herself with any kobold?* He thought.

"Did you trail them?" Karak pressed. "Do you know where they are going? What their plan is?"

Thross shrugged helplessly. He screwed his eyes shut in fear of imminent punishment. "I d-do not know, First Fang. They were venturing into the plains — to the cats, I think. One of their number was wounded, and they sought help. But I dared not track them too close to the village. Not on my own."

A moment passed before Karak pat Thross on the shoulder, much to his surprise. The kobold stared up at him in confusion, and Karak smiled. "You did well, Thross. Take your rest, see that your wounds are tended to, and get yourself some food. You have earned it," he said, meaning every word.

"B-but... b-but we failed," Thross protested, not understanding.

"You did," Karak conceded with a nod. "But *you* survived where the others perished. You showed the strength of your will and brought us valuable information. I am not in the habit of punishing those who can salvage something of worth from the fallout of their failures."

Thross stared at him, awed by the statements. Mercy was a rare thing in the horde, and it had been even more uncommon before Karak turned up. Most of these kobolds had probably gone their whole lives with barely any concept of it. Judging by the way Thross' face lit up with a warm smile, Karak felt confident it was a welcome addition.

Thross offered up a series of grateful chatterings before pulling himself to his feet. Another kobold was quick to come to his side, supporting his weight and escorting him out of the chamber. Karak watched him go, his brow furrowed and his mind ablaze.

"Our enemies band together," he mused, crossing his arms. "The people of Addernotch will seek to unify themselves with the Karjene, no doubt. A predictable outcome. They would *need* to stand together to even have a chance of repelling us. But such a force is of little concern. Danica and Skunk, however, are a different matter. Not to mention that human woman, Amelia…"

The teal-scale came up to him, her eyes boring into him with curiosity and interest. "What do you intend to do, First Fang?"

Karak hummed thoughtfully. His tail swished behind him a few times as he considered his options. This development had the potential to be disruptive, yes, but it was hardly a disaster. Still, it needed to be addressed. His first thought was that Danica and her newfound friends would just have to die.

But then Karak's thoughts turned to Skunk. Going by the report, the abandoned runt had proven himself capable in the fight, and the small scar on Karak's leg burned to remind him of the clever ruse the boy had pulled off during their encounter. Karak's hand wandered to the wound, and he found himself questioning whether killing them was the best course of action. Skunk had been abandoned for a reason — but maybe there had been something more to him that his parents had missed…

Finally, he turned to the teal kobold beside him. "It appears that I shall not be getting as much rest as I had been hoping," he decided, his wings flaring out from his back in anticipation of a long flight. "Have word sent to our sentinels in the foothills. They are to prepare a cage and be ready to receive me in the coming days."

The kobold nodded, though there was something else in her eyes. "You mean to take them alive?"

"I do. Their strength of will shall be put to good use feeding the young master."

"Even the boy?"

Karak did not miss the interest in her eyes as she asked that question. He turned to her more directly, quirking his brow. "Why does it matter to you?"

She turned away from him, working her jaw as she fished for something to say. He was about to question her on it when a different sound echoed through the chamber.

A cage was rolled into the room by a pair of burly kobolds. It was a gnarled and ugly thing, roughly assembled with scraps of rusty metal haphazardly extracted from the earth. Several prisoners, all ry'thar, had been crammed into the cage with no consideration for free space or comfort. They were bruised, battered, caked in dirt, and visibly exhausted. Frightful eyes squinted and darted about as they were rolled into the chamber.

Karak's lips spread into a bloodthirsty grin. He had been planning on departing immediately to gather a small team for his mission, but there was another, far more important duty he had to see to first. He glanced at the teal-scale and nodded for the exit.

She hesitated a moment longer, then nodded. She turned away from Karak and marched silently out of the chamber, walking by the cage as she went.

Karak watched her go, then moved to stand before the cage as it was brought to a stop. The ry'thar glared at him, their eyes ablaze with rage and hatred.

Karak lifted his arms in welcome. "Welcome, distant friends, and rejoice," he said to the prisoners. "Today, the atrocity of your birth shall, at last, be corrected! Today, by the will of the dragons, your souls shall be purified, and contribute to ending the ultimate evil!"

One of the ry'thar, a male, thrashed against the bars of the cage, roaring at Karak. He spat something at him in the ry'thar language, a guttural string of noises that Karak did not care to listen to. Not that it would have mattered regardless. Their fates had been sealed long, long ago. Their rage would not save them.

Karak lifted his arms higher, his head tilting back in praise. He called out in the language of dragons, raising his voice so all in attendance could hear him. "May this fresh meat, stained with the sins of its ancestors, serve as kindling to light the fires of retribution! May the smoke of its boiling blood clog the lungs of the guilty! May the ashes of their broken bones burn a brand onto the hearts of the villain's progeny! May the shell shatter, and the skies be darkened by the wings of good and just vengeance!"

The ritualistic words, spoken with such passion and fervor, ignited a rush of fanatical excitement within the kobolds. They raised their voices in ear-piercing cheers, and many began to stomp their feet or slam the butts of their weapons on the stone floor in a steady, thunderous rhythm.

The cage was sent back into motion. The prisoners shifted uncomfortably, and Karak stepped aside. It was then that the realization dawned on them, and even in the eyes of those who had given up the fight, Karak saw their fear bring them back to life. In defiance of their sealed fate, they began to scream. Voices laced with panic, terror, desperation, or simple fury reverberated through the chamber, drowned out by the drumbeat of the kobolds and the hungry roar of the fire. Some brave few tried to pull at the bars to escape.

One of them, a woman, managed to break her shackles in a rush of adrenaline. Karak idly mused that whoever had clasped them around her wrists had not done enough to ensure they would remain secure. She reached her hand through the bars for Karak, her eyes shining with murderous fury. Her fingers clawed at his throat, but she could not reach him. Smiling, Karak took her hand in his. His grip was firm but not forceful, and that was enough to make her pause. Maintaining eye contact, Karak bent down and planted a kiss on her knuckles. She blinked at him, bewildered.

He smiled at her, then let go.

She barely had a chance to open her mouth to curse him before the cage vanished into the flames.

Now it was the kobolds voices that were drowned out. The chamber sounded with agonized screams as fur and flesh ignited. The bodies thrashed for those fleeting seconds where they were still alive. Karak watched their suffering, watched as their bodies blackened and shriveled, and their flesh burned to charcoal in the inferno.

He smiled.

The runes along his spine glowed as he called upon a different gift. He raised his hands, chanting once more. The bodies, already crisp and brittle, cracked open like eggs, and streams of luma, tinted red by blood, emerged from within.

He stretched out his palms for the egg, and the luma obeyed his command. Wailing and screaming, the released life of the sacrifices was pulled through the shell. In mere moments, the sacrifices had been spent, and the air fell still and silent. The kobolds pulled the cage back out of the fire, revealing the blackened husks that had once been people crumbled within.

On its pedestal, the egg quivered. From the deepest depths of the mountain, hidden from sight, Karak could hear a distant rumbling that traveled up the length of his legs and settled into the back of his mind. The master was pleased.

And so was he.

Stargazing

After gathering food, water, bedrolls, and other camping necessities, Skunk and the others journeyed out of the village. Skunk took the lead, his nose to the dirt. The scents leftover from the last assault had faded over time, but there was enough for Skunk to find the trail. With his attention on the scent, he didn't have much room to engage in discussion. That did not mean he was oblivious to what the others were discussing, though.

Of particular interest were the conversations between Tamaya, Katala, and Dakar. Not because of what they were talking about, as he could not penetrate their language. His fascination came from Amelia speaking the same tongue nearly as fluently. Only occasionally was she corrected on her pronunciation. It was strange to hear her saying words that were essentially gibberish to his ears. From time to time, he thought of doubling back to ask them what they were talking about.

He resisted those temptations, though, and kept his attention on the job he'd been given. It was unlikely that he would lose the scent, but his hunting instincts were kicking in, and he was powerless to resist. They demanded he didn't take any chances.

The group marched until evening, though not as quickly as Skunk would have liked. Tamaya insisted they spend the first day moving at a slower pace, as Amelia was still tending to the aftershocks of her injury and infection. They were by no means hobbling, but they were still slowed down enough to be noticeable.

The conversations behind him had steadily dwindled into attentive silence by the time the sun kissed the horizon. Long streaks of fiery orange and red cut across the grass, and the world almost looked ablaze.

"Enough," Tamaya suddenly called, bringing the party to a stop. They had arrived at the top of a rocky bluff, giving them a clear view of the land for miles around. Skunk looked back at Tamaya as she surveyed their surroundings. Satisfied, she nodded. "We have traveled far enough today. We make camp here."

Skunk frowned. "But we still have so much distance to cover!" he said, gesturing at the vast stretch of land before them. "Every minute we waste puts more lives in danger!"

Tamaya met his gaze with a stern glare and crossed her arms. "Do not forget our mission, kalj'atla. We are gathering information, not launching a suicide rescue mission. And even if we were, we would be of no use to anyone if we were ready to collapse from exhaustion upon facing the enemy. We *rest*."

Skunk grimaced. He had to remind himself that he was, at best, a *guest* in this party. Lorok or the ry'thar could pick up the trail if he proved to be too much of a liability. And there was still the matter of his mother. Burying his vexation, he lowered his eyes. "Fine. I understand."

Amelia gave him a pat on the back, and the group set about making camp.

Tamaya ventured out to hunt something they could eat, while Katala put together a low-burning fire that would keep them warm without casting too much smoke. Dakar, meanwhile, pitched their tents.

Skunk watched them work, feeling a primal sense of satisfaction. The ry'thar worked with remarkable efficiency, cooperating in a way that pleased his deepest instincts. Skunk was impressed... but at the same time, he felt obsolete.

There was something else to it, something more. They didn't build camp in silence. There was banter, back-and-forth chatter between the two ry'thar. He did not know their words, but he could tell their tone of voice and their mood easily enough. There was a powerful camaraderie between them, a mutual sense of belonging. Once again, Skunk felt painfully out of place. He was reminded of those hours before the attack on Addernotch when the militiamen had been going about their assigned tasks.

"Hey, are you alright?" Amelia asked, snapping Skunk out of his thoughts.

He glanced at her and offered a reassuring smile. "Yeah, I'm good. Just impressed by how they work."

"They are a very intimate community," she agreed. "Every member has an important part to play, you know. A role. It is thanks to that they function so well. They have known each other their entire lives, they've had to rely on and depend on one another in all things. That familiarity, that *trust,* gives them an edge that humans, krauven, and dwarves often lack."

"Yeah, I see that," Skunk said. He watched as Dakar and Katala finished their respective tasks and sat before the fire. They kept talking, their voices casual. Every so often, though, he saw one of them glancing his way, and he would hear that word again.

Kalj'atla.

Skunk frowned. He was sick and tired of not knowing what it meant. It clearly referred to him, somehow, but beyond that...

He looked up at Amelia. "Hey, mom?"

"Yes?"

"What does 'kalj'atla' mean? Is it some sort of insult?"

Amelia blinked at him, then smiled and shook her head. "No, it's not an insult. It's just their word for 'kobold'."

Skunk felt surprised. With the amount of pure venom coating the word almost every time he had heard it so far, he could have sworn it had been an insult. He turned back to the two ry'thar, listening curiously as they spoke. "So... they're talking about kobolds?" he ventured anxiously.

Amelia hummed, listening to them for a moment. "Mostly, they are talking about you," she said.

Skunk flinched, looking down at the ground. "They don't like me, do they?"

"They are impressed by how different you are," Amelia corrected, placing a comforting hand on his back. "They hate the kobolds that attacked their home. But they've also spent the entire day following your lead, and I made sure to tell them several stories about you as we walked."

Skunk perked up a little. "Nothing embarrassing, I hope," he said tentatively.

"No," Amelia assured him. Then she gave him a small, teasing grin. "Well. Nothing *too* embarrassing, at least."

Skunk groaned. "Oh, no. What did you tell them?" he asked, already bracing himself.

Amelia's grin grew with mischievous delight. "Remember the fish barrel brought in from Port Natha that one time?"

Skunk buried his face in his hands. He let off a low whine, his tail thumping against the earth.

"I was half tempted to rename you Trout after that," Amelia went on, elbowing him in the side. "You smelled like one for *weeks*."

"Mom!" Skunk's voice rose in embarrassment.

Amelia laughed at his expense, then reached down to pull the flustered kobold against her side. She kissed him on the head. "Oh, alright," she relented with exaggerated dismay. "I'll stop. For now."

Skunk took a breath, and when he heard a few small chuckles from the others, he smiled softly. He pulled out of the hug a short time later to survey the camp.

Something was missing.

"Where's Danica?" he asked, perking up and looking around.

It wasn't just Danica, either. Both she and her trusted mount were nowhere to be seen. Skunk looked around, squinting into the deepening darkness around the fire, concerned.

Katala pointed along the edge of the bluff. "Ease your worries. She wandered off while we were preparing the fire, but she is not far."

Skunk blinked, surprised that he had missed that. He followed Katala's finger and picked out Danica's silhouette against the darkening sky. She was far enough that one would have to shout to catch her attention. "What is she doing over there? Is she okay?" he asked, confused.

"She didn't seem unwell," Katala replied, looking in Danica's direction. "But I am not knowledgeable on dwarves. Perhaps I missed something."

"I'll go check on her," Skunk decided before breaking into a jog. He turned as he went to give a quick wave to Amelia and the others. "Be back in a bit!"

"Mind her privacy!" Amelia called.

"Will do!"

Skunk slowed his pace to a walk as he drew closer. Lorok was peacefully snoozing on his side, curled into an armored ball. Danica lay on a bedroll, using an exposed portion of his squishy belly as a pillow. In one hand, she held her ringstone. In the other, that book she carried with her was open in her lap. And she was singing. Quietly, under her breath, as if she were experimenting with lyrics rather than reciting them.

As curious as he was, Skunk did not want to eavesdrop. He stood a little taller and announced his presence with a question. "What'cha doing over here?" he asked, keeping his tone casual and friendly.

Danica startled with a yelp, quickly clutching her ringstone to her chest and slamming her book shut. She turned to glare at him, her eyes narrowed with frustration. "What did I tell you about sneaking up on me?!" she yelled. "Gods, kid, I might take your head off!"

Skunk held up his hands in a placating gesture and offered an apologetic grin. "Sorry, sorry! I wasn't trying to, honest!" he said, backing off a step.

Danica looked like she was about to yell at him some more, but when Lorok snorted at the noise and pawed at her back, she thought better of it. She slumped back against his belly with a groan. "Gah. Whatever. What do you want, Skunk?" she asked, her eyes settling on the sky as she put the book away.

Skunk tentatively approached her. He sat on a small lump of stone nearby. "Just making sure you're alright. You're pretty far from camp," he said with a shrug. "I figured you'd want to be with the rest of the group. Safety in numbers, y'know?"

Danica grunted. "Too many people. Too noisy."

"You're not much of a people person, are ya?"

"Not particularly."

Skunk hummed and followed Danica's gaze to the sky. The pale ring was magnificent tonight. It was clear and crisp and *so* bright. Skunk smiled as he felt that calm tranquility washing over him, enveloping him like a warm blanket.

The two sat there for a while, just staring at the sky. It eventually dawned on Skunk that Danica was staring at it almost intently as he was. He glanced at her. "So... you like looking at the ring, too?" he asked.

"Just the sky. Sun, ring, stars. Doesn't matter."

"It's pretty," Skunk looked up again. His eye caught sight of a small piece of the ring breaking away, slowly arcing through the sky before burning away in a brilliant blue flicker as it fell to Aurus. "I dunno why, but I've *always* liked looking at the ring. It makes me feel at home, no matter where I am."

Danica hummed quietly before offering a response. "I've always liked looking at the sky. When you're out in the wilderness at night, away from civilization, it just opens up. When you look at it, it feels like you can see forever. Much better than the roof of some big cave."

Skunk blinked at her, taken by surprise. "But don't dwarves live in big underground cities?" Skunk asked.

Danica shrugged. "There are plenty of big dwarven city-states in the world below, sure. But just as many dwarves are up here on the surface. What's your point?"

Skunk hesitated, then shrugged, conceding that he did not have one. Satisfied, Danica continued. "The first time I ever saw the sky, I was just a girl. My father was meeting up with some old friends of his. They arrived at the city gates at night, and he took me to meet them. Figured I was old enough. I'd spent my entire life underground till then. I'd never seen the sky."

Her brow furrowed, her eyes dropping as she hunted for the words to convey something. "It was... strange. I felt like I was falling *up* into the sky. And I *liked* it. So much so that when I was inside again with a roof over my head, I felt trapped. And I still do. I feel like a dog in a small cage. Cramped and stuffed. Trapped. It makes me angry."

She looked at Skunk. "I don't like being angry."

"You are *very* good at it, though," Skunk pointed out, recalling how she'd acted when they first met.

Danica waved a hand at him as if to shoo away a bothersome gnat. "Oh, shut up," she grunted.

"See?" Skunk laughed before shifting onto his back, using the rock as a pillow. It wasn't particularly comfortable, but he didn't mind too much.

For a time, the two were quiet, simply enjoying the view. Skunk let his eyes trace the gradual curve of the ring, his thoughts wandering wherever they wished. Eventually, his eyes fell on Danica once again. She had lifted her ringstone, holding it up to the sky and turning it in her fingers.

At last, Skunk's curiosity won out over his restraint. "Say... what is that?" he asked tentatively. Danica shot him a look, and he was quick to lift his hands. "If you don't mind telling me, I mean! I don't wanna pry at something if you don't wanna talk about it."

Danica snorted, turning the stone over in her hand. "No, no, you're fine," she said. Skunk didn't know what she was thinking, but her face was not a happy one. He was about to tell her to forget he asked when she continued. "Tell me. Have you ever heard of Stonefall?"

Skunk considered the name. After a moment, he shook his head.

Danica huffed. "Of course not. Most people this far south haven't. You never would have had to deal with them in your tiny little town."

Skunk leaned forward. "What is it?"

Danica closed her eyes and blew out a breath of air. When she spoke, her voice lowered to something soft and somber. "Stonefall is— *was* a dwarven city-state. A fine work of dwarven ingenuity built under the Northwall Mountains near Thalgrum's Gift, protected by stone and snow and *legions* of fine warriors. Unlike a lot of undercities, we grew our own food. We grew our own *trees*. We tamed the shelldiggers of the world below, and we used them to hollow out the mountain, to make it our own."

She opened her eyes and held her stone higher as if to put it on display. "And it was all thanks to one thing. The *Sunstone*."

She said the word with the sort of reverence usually reserved for a god or a deceased loved one. Skunk leaned closer, examining the ringstone as well as he could. "Sounds important. What was it?" he asked quietly.

"A ringstone. As large as a small house," Danica explained. "Legend has it that the Sunstone was the magnum opus of a dwarven enchanter who lived centuries ago, though his name's been lost to the ages. Doesn't help that some descendant of his wound up being a traitor. The whole bloodline was condemned."

Skunk blinked. "His... *whole* bloodline?" he asked.

"Dwarf stuff," Danica explained. "Bloodlines. Honor. Integrity. All that shit's important to the purists who live underground. Sufficiently wretched crimes will stain a family for generations. Comes with a *lot* of scorn."

Skunk looked down. "But... why? If the enchanter didn't do anything—"

"I don't know all the details," Danica cut him off with a wave. "Just that the purists claim it's a necessity. Harsh punishments and strict laws to maintain order. Some leftover shit from when we were *trapped* underground instead of *choosing* to live there."

Skunk nodded along quietly.

"Point is," she continued. "The enchanter was the first man in history to ever enchant a ringstone itself. Not another object. Just the stone. No one else has managed to figure out how he did it. And it was *ours*. It gave us the warmth and light of the sun. It was the source of our dominance and prosperity. It was because of the Sunstone that my people could grow so much food underground, that we could keep ourselves so warm underground. That we could live in *daylight* underground."

She looked back at Skunk. "The other city-states can *survive* underground and have done so for over a millennia. But Stonefall? My home? My people? We *thrived.*"

Skunk listened intently, hanging off of Danica's every word with bated breath. He tried to imagine it, a great city built into the underworld and yet still receiving the benefits of daylight. "Wow. It sounds beautiful," he whispered, entranced.

Suddenly, Danica clasped her ringstone close to her chest. Her eyes closed, her jaw set with grim remembrance. "It was. The most powerful dwarven city in the world," she said. She opened her eyes, and a furious fire blazed within them. "And now it's gone."

Skunk hesitated, his mind stalling from the finality of that statement. He leaned forward slightly. "W-what? What do you mean gone?"

"I mean it's *gone!*" Danica snapped, raising her voice. Behind her, Lorok lifted his head, snorting in dismay, but Danica continued. "Stonefall does not exist anymore! It's gone, Skunk! The green scales *destroyed* it!"

Skunk sat up and stared at Danica with wide eyes and a hanging jaw. She was *shaking*. She took a series of deep breaths, and Lorok reached his head around to nuzzle his master. Slowly, Danica began to relax under his warm breath, and a concerned groan from the beast finally brought her back to a state of calm.

Skunk's hands clenched and relaxed over and over as he fished ineffectively for something to say. "What happened?"

Danica lowered her head and unclenched her fist, allowing the light from her ringstone to be reflected in her eyes. "We were betrayed," she said at last. "My father. He had friends from before he met my mother. Used to travel around, take odd jobs. He was a sellsword, you see. One of his friends was a human man. A leech named *Marus.*"

She spat the name as if it were poison on her lips. "One day, mother fell ill. Father and I tried everything to help her, but her condition just kept getting worse. Coughing fits. Pale skin. Burning fever. Delirium. We'd about given up hope when, suddenly, Marus showed up at our door. He took my father into another room. They talked. I don't know what they said, but when they were done, they left in a hurry. Father told me to stay home. Look after mother. So I did."

Danica shook her head. "They were gone for hours. And then, all at once, there were kobolds all over the place. They burst out of the ground, attacking anything and everything in sight. They weren't taking prisoners like they did with your town — this was a *massacre.* I went outside and joined the fight, cut down a few. Then it went dark, and there was a crash."

She looked at Skunk, and he could see the lingering remnants of her shock from that day represented in her eyes. "The Sunstone went *dark*, Skunk. I need you to understand, that had *never* happened before. Even at night, when we were sleeping, the Sunstone still gave off *some* light, enough to get around. But this? Total blackness. No one could see. I'm lucky I survived.

"Not long after, the kobolds left. They dove back into their holes and sealed them off with magic, leaving us to scramble blindly in the dark. I wanted to see what happened to the Sunstone, so I got on Lorok's back, grabbed a torch, and ran as fast as I could."

Danica trailed off, her eyes going distant. Skunk waited patiently for her to continue, the tip of his tail clutched tightly in his hands. Finally, Danica shook off her torpor. "The Sunstone was gone. The earth had been turned over like a freshly robbed grave where it fell. The kobolds had taken it and closed the tunnel behind them. And my father was found laying beside the clamps to release it... with a sword from the city watch stabbed into his back."

Skunk's eyes widened. "Oh, no... I'm so sorry—"

"Don't," Danica cut him off, her voice sharp as her axe. Skunk dutifully clamped his mouth shut. Danica continued. "Everyone thought my father did it. In less than a day, he was posthumously deemed guilty of high treason. His name was scrubbed from all records. Dishonor was heaped on my family. But he was framed. It was Marus, I'm sure of it!"

Skunk gaped at her in shock. "Marus helped the kobolds?" he questioned, incredulous. "Why on Aurus would he do that? I don't wanna doubt you, Danica, but are you sure that's what happened?"

"Who else could it have been?" Danica demanded. "My father held a position of honor in Stonefall. He would *never* betray it! *Yes,* I'm sure! That city had stood strong and unbroken for a millennium, Skunk. It was built to withstand any assault from any direction. The only way those green-scaled bastards could have broken through would be if they had help from the inside. Marus poisoned my mother, then blackmailed my father into helping the kobolds launch their assault in exchange for some kind of cure!"

Danica's voice was raising, her muscles growing tense with barely restrained rage. Skunk raised his hands defensively. "Okay, okay. I'm sorry, Danica. I believe you. I guess I'm just having a hard time understanding. Why would a human be in league with the kobolds?"

"Who knows? Who *cares?* It was Marus. It had to be. Mother's illness was nothing natural. It must have been poison. Besides, the man always gave me the creeps. I never trusted him, and he told me I was right not to. Said that I had 'good instincts.' I just wish I had heeded them sooner."

The two fell quiet, and the weight of Danica's story fully settled in. Skunk lifted his eyes to the ring. "I'm sorry you had to go through all that," he finally said. "I mean it. Thank you for telling me."

Danica raised her stone with a grunt. The light it gave off caught Skunk's eye and drew his attention. "You asked me what this is?" Danica reminded, glancing at him. "This is all that was left of the Sunstone. A small piece that broke away when the kobolds took it. It is all I have left of my father. It is the compass guiding me toward revenge. It's why I'm here. It is why I *fight.*"

Skunk did not know what to say. He had not expected Danica to reveal her origins and purpose to him so completely, especially given her opinion on kobolds. In the end, all he did was bow his head respectfully.

Danica pocketed the shard and affixed Skunk with a hard look. "And what of you, kobold? Why are *you* here? Why are you *fighting?*"

Skunk tilted his head, confused by the question. "Uh, I'm trying to protect my home and my pack?" He ventured haltingly, although he had the impression that was not the answer she was looking for.

Danica confirmed his suspicions when she sat up and shook her head. "That's your *goal,* not your *reason.* There is a big difference between the two."

Skunk hesitated, a lump suddenly forming in his throat. "W-what do you mean?"

Danica gestured vaguely in exasperation. "You're a kobold, kid. A *green-scale.* Your kind isn't typically known for being the good guys. Yet here you are, throwing yourself face-first at your own horde. I can understand defending your home from attack. Anyone would. But this is a step more than that, and if we're working together like this, I need to know I can trust you to stay on my side."

Skunk tried to swallow the lump, but it stubbornly refused to budge. He was starting to realize what Danica was getting at, and the answer to her question was not one he wanted to give. He felt the tingling along his gums and his tongue again, the phantom taste of blood filtering into his mouth. It clung to his teeth like the stench of his namesake. He looked away, fidgeting anxiously with his tail.

Danica stared at him a moment longer. "Is it this Sylvia girl I keep hearing about?" she ventured curiously. "You've mentioned her a *lot*."

Skunk froze, then nodded. "Y-yeah... Kinda..."

When Skunk didn't say anything for several seconds, Danica sighed and lay back down. "If you don't want to tell me, I can't force you."

"N-no, no, it's okay," Skunk said, shaking his head. "You told me your story. Fair's fair, right?"

Skunk stood and closed the distance until he was beside Danica. He lay down on the ground next to her, resting his head against Lorok's belly the way she was. Neither Danica nor her shelldigger seemed to mind. Skunk stared at the ring for a few moments, trying to figure out how best to begin. Eventually, he reached into his shirt and withdrew Sylvia's doll.

Danica raised an eyebrow. "Is that supposed to be you?" she asked. To Skunk's relief, there was no condescension in her voice at the sight of such a childish toy.

He nodded. "I wasn't welcome in Addernotch when Mom first found me," he finally began, closing his eyes and casting his thoughts back to his earliest memories. "I don't remember it. I was just a hatchling, and Mom doesn't like talking about it. But Seto told me she had to fight the rest of the town tooth and nail so I could stay. Everyone was against it at first. I didn't get why back then. I do now."

Danica said nothing. Skunk took that as his cue to continue. "W-when I was growing up, mom couldn't always be there for me. She had to work to support us, y'know? Sometimes her work would take her out of town. Hunting stuff. So, sometimes, that meant she had to leave me with Seto in his schoolhouse. I went there for my education anyway, but still, that building's like my second home."

"And let me guess. The other kids weren't kind to you?"

Skunk belted out a mirthless chuckle. "Not *all* of them were mean to me. Most of 'em thought I was neat. They mighta pulled my tail, but it wasn't because they wanted to hurt me or anything. They were kids, they didn't know any better," he said before his expression darkened. "But the ones who *did* dislike me disliked me a *lot*. There was this one kid, Bjorn. He was the worst. Had a little gang that'd follow him around and be his 'yes-men' when he decided to pick on me..."

Skunk trailed off, shuddering as the unpleasant memories came back into focus. "At first, all he did was taunt me. He never got physical. I tried to ignore him, and Seto was usually around to chase him off. But sometimes he'd catch me on my own, and he'd just lay into me. I never knew what to do. I didn't want to be enemies with anyone. All those kids were my pack. I wanted to be friends with them, I wanted to be helpful. But Bjorn was never interested."

Skunk closed his eyes, his left hand curling up tight. "Then, o-one day, Bjorn was getting *really* aggressive in his bullying. I think one of the other kids in his group dared him or something, because... he shoved me."

A cold tingle crept down Skunk's spine, and before he knew it, the memory came rushing back to him. He wasn't lying next to Danica anymore. He was cowering away from Bjorn and his trio of goons, whimpering.

"What's the matter, little dragon?! Aren't you gonna breathe fire?! Steal all my stuff?!" Bjorn demanded, throwing his arms wide, his face twisting into a confident grin. "Isn't that what you things are supposed to do?!"

Skunk shook his head, barely able to see through the tears in his eyes. He took a step back. "N-no! I just wanna help!" he pleaded in a quivering voice.

One of Bjorn's lackeys, a freckled-faced boy with messy blonde hair grinned and pointed at him. "Ha! Look at him cry! He's a freak and a coward!" he laughed, and the others all joined in. Their laughter rang loud and clear in Skunk's ears, dancing around in his skull and filling him with shame and confusion. He didn't understand. Why did these children hate him so much? What had he done wrong?

"W-why?!" he finally asked, wiping frantically at his eyes. "W-why are you so mean to me?! Why can't you just leave me alone?!"

Bjorn leaned in so he was inches from Skunk's face, silencing the backtalk. He scowled viciously. "Because you're a little monster, that's why!" he spat. "And because I want to! What are ya gonna do about it, huh?!"

Bjorn's hands flashed out, pressing into Skunk's chest. He gasped, the air driven from his lungs as he toppled back onto the earth. His head cracked against the dirt, and a spike of pain shot through his skull. He could hear them laughing above him, jeering and mocking.

Bjorn was saying something, but strangely, Skunk couldn't make out the words anymore. It was all meaningless noise. Muffled. Indistinct. Aggravating. The dull ache in his skull became a burn, his veins overflowing with the first sparks of white-hot rage.

He had been attacked. Bjorn had attacked him. The laughing flesh-thing had attacked him. It was not like him. It smelled like his pack, but how could it be? It had attacked him.

Instinct took over.

Faster than even he could track, Skunk twitched onto all fours and lunged at Bjorn, snarling like a rabid beast. In the split second before Skunk's claws sunk into fatty flesh, the bully's cocky grin transformed into a gape of terror. He barely lifted his arms in time to keep Skunk from tearing his throat out.

Skunk slammed into the bully with all of his weight. It wasn't much, but the child, unprepared for the sudden attack, toppled back onto the ground regardless. Skunk's teeth sank into the warm meat of Bjorn's forearm, his claws tore apart anything they could reach.

Beneath him, Bjorn was screaming.

Skunk did not care.

He couldn't *care.*

"H-hey! Get off him!" one of the other boys cried out, his voice trembling with fear. "S-Seto! Seto, help!"

Skunk thrashed against Bjorn, pulling with his fangs to tear away strips of tender flesh. He was kicking at him, biting him, slashing with his claws. He could taste Bjorn's blood on his tongue, and feel the wet warmth splattering across the tips of his fingers and his toes. The coppery scent of fresh blood flooded his nostrils, promising him a hearty meal if he just kept biting. The child offered feeble attempts at resistance, but they amounted to nothing.

"Help!" Bjorn wailed, his once dominating voice now a shrill squeak of panic. Tears ran down his face to mingle with his blood. "Someone help me! It's going to kill me! HELP!"

Skunk pulled the boy's arms aside, exposing his throat. He peeled back his lips and lunged, ready to put an end to the squealing prey once and for all.

A pair of clawed hands took him by the shoulders and dragged him back just before he could claim his kill. He thrashed against them, snarling and growling like he was possessed until a voice cawed directly into his ear. "SKUNK! Get off him!"

It was Seto.

It was like a candle being blown out. In one horrible second, Skunk's bloodlust vanished. His thoughts swiftly cleared, and the sight that greeted him sent a thrill of terror up his spine. Bjorn lay on the ground before him, body torn and smeared in blood. His every breath was short, a string of shallow, gurgling gasps.

"What happened?!" Seto demanded, his hold on Skunk's shoulders tightening.

One of the boys immediately pointed at Skunk accusingly. "I-it tried to eat Bjorn!" he proclaimed frantically. "It's a monster!"

Seto came around in front of Skunk and stared into his face. His eyes wandered across Skunk's blood-smeared lips and widened with shock. "By the Five..." he choked out.

"Help," Bjorn sobbed, writhing. "Help me. It hurts, it hurts, it hurts so much. I don't wanna die..."

The words echoed in Skunk's ears, joining the rapidly growing chorus of accusations from all around him. He just tried to kill Bjorn.

Bjorn was going to die.

The boy's blood was still on his tongue.

The blood of a member of his pack was on his tongue.

He was a monster.

He looked down at his hands. They were crimson. Crimson with a child's blood. He felt sick. The world tilted around him, his head filled with impenetrable ringing. Seto said something. The words did not reach Skunk. On the ground,

Bjorn whimpered again.

*"No," Skunk whimpered, taking a step back. "W-what did I...? I d-didn't...
I..." he stammered, uselessly fishing for something to say, but the words would
not come. Not that anything he said now would make a difference. There would
be no forgiving this. He knew it.*

*"Skunk! Wait!" Seto called, but it was too late. Sobbing once more,
Skunk tore himself out of Seto's grasp, dropped onto all fours, and broke into
a mad sprint. He had no idea where he was going or what he would do. All he
knew was that he had to run. He had to run and not look back. He heard Seto
calling after him, but he didn't slow down. Bjorn's screams echoed again in his
mind, louder and louder. The deafening rumble of thunder in the gloomy grey
overhead made him think of a judge's gavel deciding his fate.*

*"I'm so sorry," he gasped as he ran. "I'm so sorry, I'm so sorry, I'm so
sorry, I'm so sorry-"*

"Skunk?"

Skunk gasped as reality reasserted itself with a flash and a snap. He realized
he was hyperventilating, his heart pounding. He was still lying next to Danica,
and he could feel Lorok's damp nose pressing against his side. He sucked in deep
lungfuls of air, his hands tightening around the doll like a lifeline. Bit by bit, his
breathing began to come under control.

He looked at Danica. Her eyes were wide with surprise. It had been her
voice that had broken Skunk's trance. He smiled gratefully at her. "U-uhm,
s-sorry," he apologized.

Danica shook her head. "Don't. You did nothing wrong."

"But I did," Skunk refuted, his mind still partially trapped in the memory of
his greatest shame. "I attacked Bjorn! I almost killed him!"

Danica frowned but said nothing. Skunk ran his hands over his face, taking
another deep breath.

"I-I ran. I ran and hid in the woods. I wasn't thinking. I was too scared," he
confessed, shuddering. "I'd never done anything like that before. I didn't wanna
get in trouble, but I w-was just a kid. I didn't realize they were p-probably gonna
kill me."

Danica hummed, slowly settling back down against Lorok. "But they
didn't."

Skunk nodded, running his thumb over his eye to brush away a tear. "N-no.
They didn't. S-Sylvia saved me."

"She did?"

Skunk nodded. "Yeah. She saw the whole thing. And when I ran, s-she
followed me into the forest. She found me hiding under a fallen tree..."

The memories came again, but Skunk was ready for it this time. He closed
his eyes and braced himself, allowing the memory to take him. He tried to focus
on it and use it as a tool to help tell the story.

It had started raining at some point. Time had become loose and imprecise in the chaos of Skunk's mind. The forest canopy did little to keep the worst of the downpour off him. Every so often, the sky would flash and rumble with the boom of thunder, making him cry in fear and curl into an even tighter ball.

He had found shelter under the hollowed, rotting remains of a fallen tree that spanned the gap between two small ledges. He was pressed up against one of them, curled up as tightly as he could.

He had no idea what he was going to do. He couldn't go back, could he? Everyone would hate him. They'd yell at him, ground him forever. Maybe they wouldn't feed him? Or would they throw him in a dungeon? That was where the bad people went, right? He screwed his eyes shut at the idea, sobbing even harder.

Another blast of thunder, and another cry of fear.

"Hello?"

Skunk went rigid, his cries freezing in his throat. Slowly, he looked up to see a little girl in a plain white dress staring at him from the other side of the log. She was caked in mud and dirt and was soaking wet, but it didn't seem to bother her. He was expecting to see malice and hate in her eyes, like in Bjorn's. Or worse, bitter disappointment, like in Seto's. But he saw neither. All he saw was curiosity... and pity.

Skunk stammered fearfully and backed against the wall, his chest heaving as he tried to think of a way out. "G-go away!" he called to her. "Leave me alone! I d-don't want to hurt you!"

The girl stepped under the log, undeterred. "Then don't," she said simply. Skunk watched, baffled, as she slowly approached him. She even smiled at him. "It's okay. I'm not going to hurt you, Skunk."

Skunk swallowed heavily. "H-how do you know my name?"

The girl giggled and sat next to him. "You're the only kobold in town. Everyone knows your name," she reminded.

Skunk thought it over for a second. "Uh... y-yeah," he admitted, taken off balance. She didn't seem worried to be sitting next to a blood-stained kobold in the slightest. She didn't say anything else, either. She just sat there beside him, smiling kindly. He felt her warmth, and he slowly began to relax. "Um, w-what's your name?"

"Sylvia."

"Y-you're not afraid of me, Sylvia?"

Sylvia smiled wider and shook her head. "No. Why would I be?"

Skunk faltered, trying and failing to make sense of her. "Because I attacked Bjorn."

"He pushed you," Sylvia pointed out. "He started it."

"I guess, but," Skunk shook his head. "But I took it way too far!"

Again, Sylvia did not seem moved by his confession of guilt. "Yes, you did." was all she said. There was no accusation in her voice, no condemnation or malice. Just a simple statement of fact.

Skunk stared at her for several long seconds. He opened his mouth to say something more, but she cut him off when she took his hand into her own. He blinked, staring in confusion. She ran her thumb over his knuckles.

She giggled. "Your scales feel funny."

Skunk blinked. "Wha— no they don't!" he protested, pouting. "Your skin does!"

Sylvia squeezed his hand but said nothing more on the subject. She lifted her eyes to look into his. "Do you want some company, Skunk?" she asked, her tone lowering.

Skunk blinked, unable to look away from her. "W-why?"

"You look sad and scared. People who are sad and scared shouldn't be alone."

Skunk couldn't even begin to understand the calming effect this girl was having on him. But he was not going to look a gift horse in the mouth. He swallowed, sniffled, and gave a shaky nod. "Y-yes. Yes, please. I don't wanna be alone."

The memory began to fade. Skunk opened his eyes and turned to Danica. She was focusing entirely on him, her expression unreadable.

"So she just sat with you?" she asked eventually.

"Yeah. She just sat with me. We didn't talk a lot. We still don't. That's not the kind of friendship we have," he explained, his heart aching to have Sylvia's comforting presence beside him again. "It was always just... *quiet.* Comfortable. She always made these creepy dolls and thought about things in ways nobody else did, and I was the town's only kobold. We were both weirdos. Outcasts. And we both knew it. So we didn't need to talk. Just knowing we weren't alone anymore... that was enough."

Danica hummed, looking back up at the stars. "Sounds nice," she mused quietly.

Skunk nodded. "It is... And I'd give up anything to get it back."

Danica was quiet for a few long seconds. She looked back at Skunk, a lack of satisfaction in her expression. "What happened next? I imagine there were consequences for what happened to Bjorn."

Skunk flinched, his left hand tingling uncomfortably. "Er, yeah. While Sylvia and I were sitting in the rain, stuff was going on back in town. There was a search being organized to come find us, and Mom was at the head of the pack. She wouldn't let it be anyone else. But while they were doing that, a hungry animal found us — A wolf."

Danica's eyes widened. "A wolf?! How in the world did you survive an encounter with a wolf?!" she asked, incredulous.

Skunk grinned sheepishly and shrugged. "Would you believe me if I said I don't really remember?" he said, lamenting the blind spot in his memory.

Danica frowned. "No."

Skunk sighed. "Well, I don't. But Sylvia saw it all happen. According to her,

when it threatened us, I attacked it just like I did Bjorn. I dunno how I managed
not to die, but I held it off for a little bit. It must've been on the older side, or
maybe it hadn't eaten in a while. I dunno. But the commotion drew Mom's
group. They showed up just in time to shoot it dead, saving us. Mom hugged me,
and then they took us back to town. An emergency meeting had been called to
address... well... me.

"Over half the town was calling for me to be executed or exiled. Bjorn was
gonna live, but I'd left him with a *lot* of scars. He still has them today. His mom,
Freya, was the loudest voice calling for me to die," he recounted, shaking his
head. "I already felt dead inside. These were my people. This was my *pack*. And
they *hated* me, Danica."

"I wager I have an idea what that's like," Danica grumbled.

"Well, I probably would have been thrown back to the wolves if it hadn't
been for Mom, Sylvia, and Gothard vouching for me. Sylvia told everyone I
protected her, and Gothard backed up her story. He'd been with Mom's party, so
he saw it all going down. So, between all of that, and Mom promising to teach me
better, I was allowed to stay, *If* I worked to make up for what I did."

"So is that it, then?" Danica asked, glancing at Skunk again. "You feel like
you *have* to help them?"

Skunk nodded slowly. "I hurt my people, Danica," he said. "I don't care
about the horde. I don't care about the other kobolds. They were never there for
me. They abandoned me when I was still an egg. But Addernotch? They let me
live with them even with my kind's reputation. They let Mom keep me and raise
me as her son. They made so many concessions for me. And I spat on them by
almost eating one of them! I felt like a monster."

He looked down at his left hand. The bandages itched against his scales.
Finally, with a resigned grimace, he reached down and unraveled them. Bit by bit,
his left hand was revealed. Danica's eyes widened when she saw the grotesque
ridge of scar tissue that ran down the length of the middle digit.

Skunk stared at it and huffed. "I didn't want to hurt anyone again. I love my
people, Danica. They're *everything* to me. So... when mom and I got home... I...
found a knife—"

"Stop," Danica suddenly cut him off, placing a hand over his. It was only
then that he realized how badly he was shaking. He looked up. Danica slowly
shook her head. "Enough. I understand. You don't need to say anymore."

Skunk nodded slowly. "R-right... t-thanks for listening to me," he said,
meaning every word of it. "It's not something I ever really get to talk about all
that much. It feels good to get it out."

Danica drew her hand away and returned her attention to the stars. Skunk
did much the same, just looking. Something moved not far away, and he felt the
instinct to turn and look, but he resisted it. He knew who it was already. The
smell gave it away. A tiny smile graced his lips, and any feelings of vulnerability
he may have had at that moment were driven away.

"A good mom's never far from her kids, huh?" he mumbled, closing his eyes.

Danica glanced at him. "Huh?"

Skunk smiled wider. "Nothing. Nevermind."

Lorok let out a little snuffle, satisfied that the talking was done, and set his head down on the grass to rest.

And then a voice called out from the camp. "Skunk! Danica! Tamaya's back! She brought food!"

Skunk almost felt disappointed that the quiet had been disturbed. But almost was not enough, and the promise of some cooked meat sent him rolling back to his feet. Danica grumbled irritably but rose as well. Lorok gave a disappointed whine, but Danica silenced him with a pat on the nose.

"Just rest, big guy," she said with a smile. "I'll bring you something."

They returned to the fireside without a word, and Skunk found he did not mind. He felt easier next to her, now. More comfortable. That change must have been evident to the rest of the group, as all eyes were on the returning duo. Tamaya appeared intrigued, although her attention was divided between the two returners and the large, thick-furred beast slung over her shoulders. A very different look was on Amelia's face. A gentle, loving smile.

"Good talk," she said as Skunk came up to her side.

"Sure," Danica grunted, missing the fact that Amelia's words had not been a question. Settling down by the fire, she nodded at the ry'thar. "Make sure we get a big slice for Lorok. The big loaf needs his protein."

Skunk sat down next to Amelia, and he felt her arm drape over his shoulders. He leaned gratefully into the embrace, closing his eyes and taking a deep breath as the familiar warmth chased away his lingering doubts.

"You're not a monster," Amelia whispered to him, quiet enough that only he could hear her. "Never let anyone tell you otherwise — Especially yourself."

Skunk's smile widened, and he gently placed his hand on Amelia's. He wasn't offended that she'd been eavesdropping. He figured that she'd gotten worried after Danica snapped at him the first time. It was only natural that she'd follow and make sure he was alright. He was just thankful she'd trusted him to have that conversation himself, on his own terms.

He squeezed her hand. "I know, mom. Thank you."

The Blood Remembers

The following morning, the party set off. With the last vestiges of Amelia's hindrances fading away, their pace was brisk and steady. Once again, Skunk was in the lead, his nose to the ground as he tracked the scent of the horde. The rest of the group trailed close behind. This time, however, there was little in the way of conversation. An aura of building tension had settled over the group, in part because they were venturing further and farther into dangerous territory. But there was something else eating at them — or at least at Skunk. Something in the air felt wrong, somehow. It was as if the wind itself had become an irritant, scratching his scales, trying to get under them to his skin like a swarm of stubborn mosquitos. His entire body tingled, the worst of it gathering in the back of his scalp.

They crested the summit of a narrow ridge, affording them a view of the next leg of their journey. Skunk lifted his eyes to get a look and paused when he spotted something jutting out of the otherwise barren landscape. A massive structure made of marble-white stone and gilded in tarnished gold lay half-buried in the earth. There were plenty of signs of erosion, taking the form of crawling moss, crumbled walls, and softened edges. It looked like some sort of tower, but the architecture was unlike anything he had ever seen before.

It was elegant and graceful, beautiful even. But it carried with it an almost dominant quality as if whoever built it wished to declare their superiority. He could see artistic arches and buttresses that connected parts of the crumbling stonework and intricate geometric patterns emblazoned in the gold.

The tingling in his scalp became a painful burn, and an involuntary growl bubbled up from deep in his throat. He blinked, a hand flying up to his throat. "What the?" he mumbled under his breath, confused.

Beside him, Amelia, misunderstanding his question, nodded. "Auriun ruins. You don't see many of those on the surface," she said with mild surprise. "Most are buried deep in the world below."

Auriun.

The word invoked another tingle of hostility in Skunk's skull, and again he felt confused by the reaction. He stared at the tower, tracing its shape. Its upper half had long ago fallen away from the rest of the structure, leaving piles of rubble scattered across the fields to the east. They brought to mind the debris left in the wake of an explosion.

"Auriun?" He asked for clarification.

"The name of an ancient race that existed long before the modern age," Amelia explained. "We only know a few things about them. Namely that their empire once covered every corner of the world, and that their powers of magic were far beyond anything known today. They died out some fifteen hundred years ago, according to most scholars I've spoken to."

Tamaya hummed. "In the oral histories of my people, it is said that the auriuns abused their power to enslave our ancestors. Any who resisted were made to suffer horrific punishments. In the end, the world had enough of their madness, and brought devastating calamity down upon their empire, reducing it to ash. Our ancestors only survived because they were kept in underground slave cities."

"Which make up most of the ruins treasure hunters go picking through," Amelia added, crossing her arms and furrowing her brow. "I've been through my fair share of them. They're dangerous to explore."

Danica shrugged dismissively. "Auriuns. Whatever. That has nothing to do with our work. If the kobolds passed through the ruins, then through the ruins we go."

Skunk had nothing to say. He barely even heard the conversation. His eyes were glued on the ruins. His blood boiled with resentment he could not describe. Barely stifling another snarl, he sniffed the earth. The kobolds had cut right through the auriun ruins, much to his dismay. His tail twitched in agitation. "This way," he said, then went into motion. The others hesitated for a moment before falling into step behind him.

The ruins were far larger than they had seemed from a distance. The tower loomed over them like a guillotine ready to slice off their heads. The rubble piles were big enough that Skunk could imagine hollowing them out and turning them into modest single-room structures. Various plants grew among the rubble, climbing along the stones or peaking out from under the gaps.

The deeper they went, the more agitated Skunk became. His tail lashed behind him with increasing disgust, and he was unable to suppress his tiny snarls of anger — an anger that only served to confuse him. Finally, he heard Amelia coming up beside him.

"Skunk? What's wrong—"

"I'm fine!" Skunk snapped loud enough for his voice to echo through the ruins. Realizing what he'd just done, he clamped a hand over his mouth. Everyone came to a stop, staring at him in surprise. He looked haltingly up into Amelia's eyes. They were wide with shock.

Skunk swallowed heavily and lowered his hand. "I'm s-sorry. I d-dunno what's come over me," he said, a strange quiver creeping into his voice.

"What's wrong?" Amelia asked again, gentler this time. She knelt beside him and placed a hand on his back. He tensed under the touch, an involuntary reaction that furthered his frustrated confusion.

"I don't know!" he exclaimed, grabbing at the side of his head. "I just feel angry all of a sudden! I don't know why, but something about this place just makes me feel like... Like I've just been insulted, or something. Guh!"

Amelia pulled her hand away, then turned to the ry'thar. "I don't feel anything. Do you?" she asked, though Skunk did notice her hand wandering for her daggers.

Tamaya shook her head. "No. I feel nothing," she said, drawing out her spear.

Dakar looked around, his eyes narrowing. "Could it be some manner of trap?"

A new voice suddenly carved through the silence of the dead stones. "Oh, nothing so nefarious as that."

This time, Skunk's blood boiled with proper justification. He drew his bow and loosed an arrow at the speaker in the blink of an eye. It shot across the ruins with an almost inaudible whistle, aimed straight at his target's heart.

Karak, sitting atop a cairn of broken stones, caught the arrow right before it punctured his chest. He grinned in amusement. "His blood merely remembers."

"Karak!" Amelia shouted, drawing her own bow and readying an arrow. Tamaya barked out an order, and her associates quickly formed a defensive line with her, spears forward. Danica dismounted from Lorok, her axe flashing into her hand.

Skunk drew another arrow, growling in rage. "You!" he shouted, indulging his hatred for the moment. "Where's Sylvia?!"

Karak casually tossed the arrow aside. "The girl?" he asked, inspecting one of his claws as if looking for some nondescript blemish. "Why does she fascinate you, so?"

Skunk fired his arrow, and Karak batted it aside as if it weren't even there. Skunk screamed in frustration. "*Answer me*, damn you!"

"Skunk, calm down," Amelia instructed, her voice level and calm. "He's trying to goad you. Don't let him."

Skunk snarled, but he knew she was right. He took a moment to breathe even as he drew another arrow, ready to fire at a moment's notice.

Amelia focused on Karak. "What do you mean 'his blood remembers'?" she demanded.

Recognizing that his taunts would make no more progress, Karak leaned forward in his place, resting his arm on his lifted knee. "I suppose I cannot blame you for your ignorance on this matter. Dragonkin never forget it when they have been wronged. Every insult, every betrayal, every wound lives on in their blood, a memory passed from one generation to the next. It is but one of many gifts afforded to our kind. And the auriuns are guilty of the greatest crime in the history of this world. For their hubris, all dragonkin, kobold and dragon alike, were brought to the brink of extinction, an edge we still teeter upon."

Skunk's heart skipped a beat as Karak's eyes settled on him. "And Skunk's blood remembers. It could never forget the pain — the *violation*. And so, to merely stand in the presence of his most hated enemy, what else is his blood to do but boil with the need for vengeance?"

Skunk shook his head. "My most hated enemy is you!" he declared. "I don't care about some stupid dead auriuns or what they did a long time ago!"

Karak only smiled, a sickening expression that sent tingles crawling around the base of his tail. "And yet, your anger is very real. Just standing here, surrounded by the remnants they left behind, has left you quivering with anger. Even before I revealed myself, you were succumbing to a hatred that falls outside of your lifespan."

Skunk hesitated. He could not deny Karak's observation. He *was* angry. Far angrier than he should have been. Everyone else was fine, and Karak wouldn't stand to gain very much from fabricating such a story.

So then the question became, what did the Auriuns do that Skunk's blood would still remember it?

"Bah!" Danica shouted, taking a threatening step forward. "Who gives a shit? Just tell us where you assholes are hiding and I promise I'll take your head off in a *clean* stroke!"

Karak's smile grew wider. He tsked at Danica, shaking his head in mock disappointment. "Tsk tsk tsk. Oh, Danica, Danica, Danica. Were you never taught that you catch more flies with honey than... whatever that threat was supposed to be?"

"You're here, aren't you?" Danica countered, drawing out one of her throwing axes. "Seems to me I caught the exact fly I wanted!"

Karak lost his smile. He sighed and stood, his wings unfurling. Skunk saw the sword appearing in his hand, previously hidden from view. "I could use words to explain why you are a fool, Danica Flatstone," he lamented. "But I know how you have a hard time with words. So it shall be a *practical* lesson."

The runes along Karak's legs flared, and Skunk realized that the time for talking was over. He fired his arrow alongside his mother's while Tamaya hurled her spear. At the same moment, Karak kicked off from his perch. He shot through the air in a blur, easily swerving around the oncoming projectiles and closing the distance between himself and Danica.

The dwarf stepped back as Karak fell into their midst, his blade dipping low and angled up for a thrust at her chin. Dakar was fast, however, interrupting Karak with a thrust of his hunting spear. The dragon-man ducked back and lifted his blade to bat the thrust aside. Behind Karak, Katala dove in for the gap between his wings.

Skunk's eyes widened as Karak's tail lashed out like a whip, striking Katala's chest. The sound of crunching bones echoed throughout the ruins, and the ry'thar woman was hurled off her feet to crash to the ground nearby. Karak ducked, avoiding a swing from Danica, and his sword slid up along Dakar's spear. The ry'thar barely managed to stagger back in time to keep from being stabbed through the heart.

"As one!" Tamaya ordered, throwing all of her weight at Karak with a brutal body slam, sending him staggering forward. His runes flared again, and he spun in a clearing swipe. Tamaya sprang back, seemingly anticipating the maneuver, but she still acquired a fresh cut across her cheek.

"Skunk, at a distance!" Amelia commanded, backpedaling a few paces.

Skunk did as he was told, keeping pace with Amelia and firing another arrow, his blood pumping.

Karak was a whirlwind of movement, his blade flashing through the air with speed that should have been impossible. Tamaya, Katala, and Dakar, however, were putting up a good fight, dodging and weaving through his attacks. With their combined efforts *and* the assault of arrows from Skunk and Amelia, Karak, at last, was on the defensive.

He dropped low as Tamaya and Danica charged from different directions. His wings flapped, his runes glowed, and he flew toward them, kicking up a cloud of dust. The two had no chance to brace against his rush and were knocked to the ground on either side of Karak with cries of pain.

Dakar did not give Karak a chance to recover. He lunged as the dragon-man turned, grabbing onto the blade of his sword with one hand and his shoulder with the other. The ry'thar's claws sank into his scales, drawing blood and a hiss of pain. Behind Karak, Katala lunged with a furious roar, her spear angled at his spine.

This is our chance! Skunk thought, aiming an arrow right at Karak's head.

Sadly, it would be too little too late.

Karak snarled, and Skunk saw his runes flash right as he fired the arrow. Karak's sword arm twitched and tensed, muscles bulging, before he drew it back. Dakar's grip on the blade might have immobilized the weapon of a lesser foe, but not here. A sickening scrape of steel through flesh and bone filled the ruins, and Dakar's hand was cleaved in half. Blood and ivory splinters sprayed through the air. Dakar's eyes widened alongside an agonized roar. In the same flash of steel, Karak sliced Skunk's arrow out of the way.

Capitalizing on his momentum, Karak dug his claws into Dakar's side and hauled him along. He brought the roaring ry'thar hunter around just in time to intercept Katala's charge. There was no time to change course.

Skunk's heart twisted as Katala's spear punched through Dakar's chest and out through his back, painting Karak's face crimson. He put on a horrid, bloodthirsty grin. He was *enjoying* this.

"Dakar?" Katala choked out, her eyes wide and vacant at the sight of her brother-in-arms hanging limp from her spear.

"MOVE!" Skunk screamed.

Too late.

Karak's blade slipped effortlessly through Dakar's back and out his chest to stab into Katala's eye. She stiffened, then crumpled lifelessly to the earth without a sound.

"NO!" Tamaya screamed, rising from her place on the earth and charging Karak alongside an equally furious Danica. Karak turned to them, forced into a rapid retreat as the two warriors pressed a renewed offensive. The air rang with the clashing of steel and the guttural cries of battle.

Skunk's eyes were locked on Dakar and Katala's bodies on the earth, his heart hammering in his chest. *We had him. We had him!* He thought, his blood turning to ice.

"Skunk, focus!" Amelia snapped, shaking him by the shoulder. He looked up at her to see her eyes glistening and blazing with fury. "Mourn later! Go right, I'll go left!"

Skunk could only offer a stiff nod before obeying. He ran parallel with the melee fighters, trying to find any opening to fire more arrows at Karak.

"Keep the pressure on!" Amelia shouted, mirroring Skunk's actions on the other side. "Don't let him get away! He's fast, but he can only do so much!" Karak growled with frustration. His wings gave a mighty flap, sending him back and into the air. He rotated, his eyes latching onto Amelia. He flapped his wings and flew for her.

Amelia was ready for him. She ducked into a forward roll, avoiding Karak's plunging kick. One of her daggers came flashing into her free hand as she rose and spun into a thrust for his wing joint. He turned away from the strike, using Amelia's momentum to get behind her and kick her in the back. She tumbled gracefully into another roll, but Skunk saw she wouldn't have enough time to react to Karak's advance. He fired his next arrow, forcing Karak to deflect the shot and giving Amelia time to rise.

She spun to face Karak, throwing her dagger at Karak's heart. He shifted his weight, narrowly evading the projectile. He grinned for a split second, only for Lorok to barrel into him from the side with a furious roar. Danica was on his back, axe in hand and a fierce grin on her face. "You're dead, Karak!" she shouted.

Karak dug his feet into the earth, bracing against Lorok's charge. His clawed feet dug furrows in the earth, his muscles tensed and his runes flared brighter than ever. Skunk felt a rush of horror as Karak's strength, against all possibility, proved greater than Lorok's, and bit by bit, Lorok's charge was brought to a halt.

"How strong *is* this asshole?!" Danica yelled in outraged exasperation before jumping forward, bringing her axe down in a heavy swing for Karak's head.

Karak lifted his sword, catching the swing while the claws of his free hand raked across Lorok's sensitive nose, sending the beast bellowing and backpedaling. He was replaced by Tamaya, charging from Karak's side with another thrust of her spear. This time, the thrust made contact, albeit only as a glancing blow that left a shallow cut along Karak's back.

With another flash of light from his runes, Karak shouted and spun wide, his wings swinging to create a gust of air strong enough to throw Danica and Tamaya to the ground. Skunk fired another arrow, and Karak leaned back, barely dodging it with a grimace of effort. If nothing else, Skunk could take pride in the fact they were pressuring him this time.

Behind him, unnoticed, Amelia rushed, both daggers at the ready. She vaulted over one of the piles of rubble to drive both feet into Karak's side while he was still recovering from his dodge, sending him sprawling to the ground. She quickly straddled him and went to slit his throat.

Again, Karak's tail proved to be as effective a weapon as any other, swinging up into Amelia's side and knocking her away with a sharp smack. Skunk felt a rush of rage as Amelia fell to the earth, and he heard her cry out in pain.

Fire filled his skull and ran through his body. With a shout of fury, he cast aside his bow, drew his sword, and charged. "Don't you touch her!" He covered the distance with a guttural scream and pounced at Karak, aiming to stab him through the back.

His swing was intercepted effortlessly. Karak spun to face him in the blink of an eye, his clawed hand grabbing the back of Skunk's head.

"Pathetic!" Karak mocked. Skunk tried to swing at him again, but the world pivoted around him without his permission. His stomach journeyed into his feet, and the air rushed in his ears as Karak hurled him at Danica, who had only just gotten back to her feet. Skunk's spine collided with hardened steel and bulging muscle, driving the wind from his lungs. Both of them fell in a heap.

Tamaya went in for another attack, diving for Karak's tail and taking hold of it. She pulled, and Karak staggered back a step, grunting in surprise. It evolved into a scream of pain as Tamaya's claws dug into the flexible scales, drawing blood.

"Feral *bitch!*" He shouted. Pivoting his hips, he drove his foot into Tamaya's face, forcing her to release her hold.

"Tamaya!" Amelia shouted as Skunk stood up. He shook his head to clear away the dizziness and looked on, seeing that the ry'thar woman was still up, but blood dripped freely out of her abused nose. She growled and jumped back to her feet, spear in hand, and ready for another thrust.

Danica barreled past Skunk, axe held in front of her like a battering ram. She led her charge by throwing one of her smaller axes, forcing Karak to bat it aside before meeting her charge. He flinched from the weight of her armored rush but held his ground. Her axe swung around for his head, but his free hand caught the shaft, holding it in place.

Skunk tried to capitalize on the moment. He charged and leaped onto Danica's shoulders, using her as a springboard to tackle Karak. They roared in each other's faces as Skunk locked his fingers together behind Karak's head, his claws digging in.

Karak staggered and snarled before raising his claws to sink into Skunk's back. Blinding pain flooded his system, and even if he hadn't been sent into shock, Karak's impossible strength overwhelmed him. The taller dragonkin tore Skunk away and slammed him brutally against the wall of stone he had almost been pinned to. Skunk's vision exploded with sparks, and his hearing was replaced with high-pitched ringing. He felt gravity take him, and he fell to the earth with a thud.

He was dazed, confused. He tried to focus, but it was impossible to find details through the haze clouding his mind. He blinked and shook his head, faintly aware that every second he spent down here was a second wasted. Finally, bit by bit, the fog started to clear. He could see the other three continuing to attack Karak, forcing him into an increasingly rapid retreat. Karak's grunts and grimaces of effort were becoming more frequent, and judging by the flashes of light from his runes, he was having to call upon his enchantments more and more just to keep himself alive.

Groaning, Skunk hauled himself back to his feet. The fight had carried itself a fair distance away by this point, and he didn't trust his shaking legs to carry him that far just yet. Besides, in his current state, he wouldn't be of much help in close quarters anyway.

But his bow wasn't far away.

Staggering, Skunk made his way to his bow and picked it up. He turned back to the battle just in time to see Karak lift into the air with his wings to kick Tamaya in the chest, before springing off of her to slam his shoulder into Amelia, driving her into the earth. He didn't get to follow up on the attack, forced to step back and block as Danica came in, swinging at his chest as if he were a tree to fell.

Skunk saw a chance. He drew an arrow and fired, aiming for the back of Karak's head. His aim was a little off, sadly, but the arrow still pierced into Karak's lower back. He grunted before shoving Danica, sending her rolling across the earth. His tail swiped up to snap the arrow shaft and pull the tip out of his scales. With a mighty flap of his wings, Karak took to the air and alighted atop one of the taller piles of rubble.

The others rose back to their feet, and the fight fell into silence for a moment as the combatants took a moment to catch their breath. Karak glared down at them, his eyes ablaze. But there was something more in them. Slowly, as his rage dissipated, Skunk saw the last thing he was expecting from the arrogant creature.

Respect.

"You fight very well," Karak called out to them, audibly short of breath. "I underestimated you, I will freely admit."

"Just shut up and get back down here!" Danica barked, hurling her final throwing axe at him. Karak smacked it aside with his sword in a shower of sparks.

"If you insist," was all he said before he kicked up and into the air. But instead of diving down to engage them in melee again, he rose higher into the air. Skunk watched him, drawing another arrow, but confusion stayed his hand. "What is he doing?" he asked.

The answer came when Karak's chest began to glow, his scales turning red, then orange, and finally a blinding white. Heat traveled up his throat to pool in his clamped maw, embers spraying out of his sealed lips like spittle. With nary a sound, Karak descended onto the battlefield and opened his mouth. Flames spilled out, falling in a wide cone to blanket the earth as he passed.

"Move!" Tamaya shouted, shoving Amelia aside and rolling the other way. Danica was the last to move, and her feet were caught in the descending inferno. She screamed, rolling across the ground as the metal encasing her feet heated up. Karak arced past them and rose higher into the air while Danica pulled out her waterskin and poured the contents over her boots.

Skunk fired his shot, but against a mobile flying target, he had no chance of hitting his mark. Karak swerved effortlessly around the shot, and Skunk saw his self-satisfied grin.

"This bitch can breathe fire?!" Danica roared in fury once her feet stopped burning. She rose unsteadily, wincing, then spun to glare at Karak as he came to hover over their heads. "What's next, *magic?!*"

Karak turned to her with a grin, and his runes began to glow. He lifted his hand. More flames rose out of his upturned palm, joined by swirling ribbons of luma.

"Oh, fuck me!" Danica shouted, breaking into a run for the nearest bit of cover she could find.

The fireball shot out of Karak's hand like a meteor, tearing through the air and leaving a rippling wave of distortion in its wake. It struck the earth at Danica's heels and exploded with a flash of blinding light and a deafening boom. Skunk's eyes widened as Danica was thrown from her feet by a rising wall of flames. She sailed through the air before crashing to the earth in a crumpled heap.

Skunk's heart fell when she did not rise. He couldn't tell if she was breathing or not, but even the possibility that she might be dead sent fresh fury through his veins. Skunk turned to Karak and began firing shot after shot from his bow, trying to knock the flying enemy back down. Karak's sword was fast as lightning, deflecting each shot. Karak laughed, then flapped and flew around the perimeter of the ruins, using the mounds as cover. Skunk growled, realizing he couldn't get a clear shot.

"Where are you looking?!" Karak's voice came from behind him, the dragon-man having evaded Skunk's eyes long enough to get the drop on him. Skunk stepped back, barely avoiding being disemboweled and receiving only a shallow cut across his belly. Skunk tried to reach for his sword, but Karak's foot drove into his new injury and knocked him to the ground. The world blurred and doubled as white-hot pain paralyzed him.

"Skunk!" Amelia's voice shrieked as the aggravated mother charged Karak again. He turned to face her, parrying her thrust. His free hand snapped out to take her by the throat, and Amelia's scream went silent.

Skunk tried to stand so he could defend her, but it was too late. Karak drove his knee up into Amelia's gut with such force that Skunk almost felt it from where he lay. Amelia's eyes flew wide, her mouth stretching in a silent scream before she fell still and limp. With a scoff, Karak tossed her harshly to the earth.

Tamaya hurled her spear at Karak from afar, forcing him to dodge back. He moved lightly on his feet, hopping back a few times before his wings brought him once more into the air, avoiding Tamaya's follow-up charge. He rose above her, and flames once again gathered in his throat.

Skunk felt a thrill of panic. Amelia would be caught in the blast if Karak breathed more fire now! Spurred into motion and ignoring his injuries, Skunk scrambled to all fours and sprinted to Amelia. He took hold of her shoulders and desperately tried to drag her away.

Karak exhaled, and Tamaya was barely able to roll out of the way. The flames rolled along the ground, igniting the grass as it passed. Skunk looked back to see the wave of destruction rolling toward him like an avalanche. There was no time!

Screwing his eyes shut, Skunk did all he could think to do. Resigning himself to his fate, he covered as much of his mother's body as he could with his own, hoping and praying that it would be enough to keep her alive.

The flames washed over him, and he braced for searing agony. But it never came. He could feel the flames washing over him, he could feel his clothes igniting, and it *was* warm. But he felt no pain. Just warmth. It was *almost* uncomfortable, but not quite. The flames passed a moment later, and Skunk blinked his eyes open in confusion.

"I'm alive?" he asked, baffled.

He was alive, but he was also still on fire. With a cry of alarm, he jumped back and off of Amelia before the flames clinging to him could spread to her. He fell to the ground, dropping and rolling a few times to put out the remaining flames. Once he was confident he wasn't burning anymore, he looked to Amelia. She was a little singed but otherwise fine.

And then Tamaya slammed into him from the side, knocking him to the ground. He grunted and looked to see that Tamaya's eyes were closed. She did not move. Mercifully, though, she was still breathing.

Skunk pried himself out from under her and stood back up, trembling with fear. He looked around for Lorok but saw no sign of the beast. The injury Karak had given him and the flames must have been enough to scare him off. He looked around for Karak.

The other dragonkin came to a gentle landing not far away, sword held casually at his side. He was breathing hard and had acquired a handful of injuries, but he still looked to have plenty of fight in him. "And so it ends. As it always must," he said, his confidence returning. "With the guilty bloodied and defeated."

Skunk took a step back, then snarled and drew his sword. "I'm not down, yet!" he shouted, though he knew it was a hollow gesture. He did not have the strength or skill to beat Karak, especially considering the unfair power imbalance between them. If he fought him here, it would almost certainly end with his death.

Karak stared at him a moment, surprised. Then he smiled. "You are brave, Skunk. And more capable than I initially gave you credit for. You may be deserving of your blood after all. As a sign of respect, I will give you one last chance to surrender. Lay down your arms and you have my word that you will not come to any harm."

Skunk hesitated, his grip on his sword tightening. "And what happens then?" he asked fearfully. "What are you going to do to us?"

"You will be my prisoners," Karak explained simply. "And you will be put to use as those who came before you."

Skunk blinked and fell silent, suddenly torn. On the one hand, he had no way of knowing if he could trust Karak's word. It was possible that he was simply tired of exerting himself and wanted an easy chance to kill Skunk once and for all. But at the same time, if he *was* telling the truth about taking them prisoner, this might be the chance to get into the kobold's territory Skunk had been waiting for.

His eyes settled on the broken remains of his group, on his mother crumpled on the ground, singed and bruised. That sight was more than enough for Skunk to make up his mind. Any notions of surrendering to Karak went up in smoke.

He snarled, his fingers tightening on the hilt of his sword. Without a word, he roared and charged, hoping to at least go down swinging.

Karak did not seem surprised. As a matter of fact, he smiled. Skunk's clumsy thrust met only empty air as Karak effortlessly side-stepped the attack. He brought the pommel of his sword into the back of Skunk's head. He fell to the ground, dazed. A moment later, Karak grabbed him by the tail, and as it had been in front of the schoolhouse, Skunk was lifted into the air and spun around with centrifugal force. Skunk screamed, his pelvis burning with agony, before Karak released him, sending him high and far over the broken stones of the ruins.

He crashed into one of the cairns, and his scream fell silent. He let out a breathless wheeze as he fell to the ground below. His vision swam, darkness creeping in at the edges. He fought to keep himself awake, but it was a losing battle. Groaning, he rolled onto his belly and tried to look around, tried to stand up.

He was next to Danica. He could see her breathing. She was alive.

And on the ground in front of her, glowing brightly in his vision, was the Sunstone shard.

Time slowed to a crawl in that moment. The stone filled Skunk's vision, as if it was the only thing that existed in all the world. It entranced him, hypnotized him. He crawled toward it as if he were possessed, and as all conscious thought left him, he might as well have been. He reached out, enraptured by its singular beauty and took it.

It was warm in his hand. His scales tingled at the touch. The fire in his blood suddenly cooled, doused by the waters of something gentle and calming. It felt like coming home after a long day.

It was the same thing he felt every time he looked at the ring itself.

He heard footsteps approaching, muffled and distant. Karak.

As Skunk's mind began to slip away from him, instinct took over. He had to hide the stone. He couldn't let Karak have it, especially not after everything Danica had deigned to share with him. He had to keep it safe, somehow. And so he did the only thing he could think to do.

With the last of his strength, Skunk rolled out his tongue and drew the warm, tingling stone into his mouth. His senses spasmed at the contact, but only for a moment.

That was it. Skunk had no more strength left to spare. With a muffled groan, his head fell limp against the dirt, and the world went dark.

Actaneirum

A dull, festering ache permeated Skunk's body as he awoke. Every muscle burned, and the scales on his side pulsed with a dull, throbbing pain. That was the first thing he noticed. The second was a hard swollen sensation under his tongue, hot and tingling with pins and needles. Through the fog clouding his mind, he recalled that it was the Sunstone shard. The third thing he noticed was the world rolling beneath him without his consent. He lay prone on something cold and hard, a chilly wind whipping over him. Groaning, he dared to open his eyes.

He was trapped in a wheeled cage of crude, dark metal bars. Small spikes protruded from each, discouraging any thoughts of escape. Rust and long-dried blood decorated the bars in various places, a testimony of those who had tried and failed to flee. The cage was barely five feet from one end to the next. A cramped affair scarcely large enough to house him and the three other bodies.

Amelia was sitting against the far wall of the cage, her hands bound behind her back and her eyes downcast. Danica and Tamaya were sprawled on the floor, similarly shackled. Each of them was covered in bruises and burns, remnants of their most recent defeat. Skunk had also been cuffed at the wrists, the manacles agitating his scales with every slight movement. When he tried to shift, he yelped as sharp, tugging pain raced from the back of his pelvis to the base of his skull. He realized with a groan that his tail had been clasped to his ankle with more chains, keeping it pinned.

He didn't waste his energy trying to free himself. He would never be able to break or slip bonds this tight. He doubted that even Danica or Tamaya, with all their considerable strength, could manage it. Adding insult to injury, all their weapons and armor had been stripped away.

As his senses expanded beyond the cage, Skunk saw two kobolds pulling it along from the front, while two more brought up the rear. That was alarming enough, but the bad news did not end there.

They were no longer in the golden grasslands around the Karjene village. In the place of rolling fields was a steady incline of stone flanked by jagged ridges and twisting spikes. The sky was a deep orange, and any warmth from the sun was hidden behind gloomy crags.

"What...?" Skunk mumbled, his voice slurring through the ringstone still in his mouth. He shook his head to chase away the fog over his thoughts with little success.

The quiet vocalization drew Amelia's attention. She looked up, her eyes shining with relief. "Skunk. You're awake, thank the Five," she whispered. "Are you alright?"

Skunk struggled to sit, grunting and yelping in pain as his various chains bit painfully into his scales. Eventually, he was upright enough to meet her gaze. He nodded shakily. "I'm alive," he managed to say past the pain in his face.

Amelia relaxed. "Good. I was worried about you," she said, and Skunk could see that she desperately wanted to hold him. But between the spikes on the bars, the low ceiling, and the two bodies occupying the floor between them, there wasn't any way for her to do that.

Skunk shook his head again. He wanted to say more, but the ringstone in his jaw was becoming too uncomfortable to bear. He quickly cast his eyes about to make sure their captors were not looking. His back was to the ones in the rear, while the ones in front had to focus on the ascent. There was no sign of Karak just yet, and so Skunk took his chance. He rolled out his tongue, using it like a single finger to pull the collar of his shirt away from his chest. The Sunstone shard slid out from his lower jaw and rolled down his scales, leaving behind a trail of sticky spittle that made him cringe. Once the stone settled against his pelvis where his shirt tucked into his trousers, he shifted his weight to move it to the back, so his cloak could hide the luma shining through the fabric.

That done, he looked up at Amelia. She had turned her eyes to look over her shoulder, trying to see where they were going. She hadn't seen what he just did. Skunk wanted to say something to her, but he dared not with the kobolds so close at hand. And besides, even if he had tried to speak, another voice beat him to it.

"Ah, and the outcast awakens," Karak remarked from somewhere above them. A flap of wings and a gust of air blasted Skunk from behind, telling him that the dragon-man had just landed. Shivering in fright, he tried to turn and face Karak, but his bonds left him frustratingly immobile. He could only angle his head to look over his shoulder with wide, fearful eyes. Karak loomed before him, easily matching pace with the cage. He stared down at Skunk with a sickening smile. "Did you sleep well, Skunk?"

Skunk whimpered and tried to back away, but once again, his bonds stifled his efforts. He only succeeded in toppling over to land across Tamaya's legs. He flopped over to lay on his back so he could see Karak, his heart pounding.

Karak's smile grew, and he let out a condescending chuckle that sent tingles of terror creeping up Skunk's spine. "Come now, you've nothing to fear," he said, his voice oozing with insincere hospitality. He moved forward until he was walking beside the cage. His faintly yellowed teeth showed in the sunlight. "You aren't in any danger. Yet."

Skunk whimpered. Amelia leaned forward, baring her teeth in a murderous snarl. "If you lay so much as a finger on him, I will—" she began, only for the butt-end of a spear to pass through the bars and strike her in the back of the head. She pitched forward with a strangled grunt, her hair hiding her face like a curtain.

"No talking!" the kobold that had struck her snapped, its voice a high and guttural rasp. "Speak only when spoken to!"

"Mom!" Skunk exclaimed, turning his eyes to her.

Amelia remained doubled over for a moment, taking a few deep breaths. Slowly, she sat up and affixed the kobold with a dispassionate glare. "Bite me."

The kobold came to an abrupt stop, and the cage with it. He turned, flipping his spear in his hands and pressing the sharpened tip against Amelia's throat.

Skunk's heart skipped a beat. He rolled onto his belly and squirmed frantically against his bonds in a desperate, but ultimately futile, bid to break free. All the while, his eyes were glued onto Amelia, wide with fear. "No! Don't!" he begged. "Don't hurt her!"

Amelia, to Skunk's surprise, did not seem concerned. If anything, she looked *amused*. Her lips twitched up into a smug smile. "Don't worry, Skunk. He won't," she assured him, her voice unsettlingly calm. "Karak captured us for a reason. If this kobold does any damage to me, or anyone else in this cage, then he'll have wasted Karak's precious time. And I somehow doubt the 'First Fang' is the sort to let something like that go unpunished."

The silence that followed that observation was suffocating. The kobold glared at Amelia for several long seconds, its eyes ablaze with fury and hatred. Its muscles tensed, and for a moment Skunk feared that he was about to watch his mother's life end. Then the kobold shouted in frustration and pulled away.

Karak chuckled in amusement, his hands coming together in quiet applause. "Well said, human. You are a clever one, aren't you?" he said.

Any mirth Amelia had garnered from her moment of superiority shattered, replaced once more with an icy glare. "I'd wager I know more about being clever than you," she spat.

Karak took the barb in stride. "Maybe you do. Maybe you don't. It does not matter anymore, though, now does it? After all, You are the one trapped in a cage, not I," he reminded her.

Amelia narrowed her eyes and turned her attention to Skunk. Her features softened considerably, and she gave him a comforting smile. "It's okay, Skunk," she whispered to him. "We're going to be fine. I won't let anything happen to you."

Skunk swallowed heavily. He wasn't stupid. It was an empty promise meant to ease his fear and make him feel better. A hollow gesture reserved for gullible children. Even so, he appreciated it. He *allowed* himself to be persuaded that they *would* be fine.

"I would not make promises I cannot keep if I were you," Karak noted casually.

Amelia did not look at him. "I can keep it," she stated as if it was the most obvious thing in the world. "And I will."

Karak shrugged and continued on, pulling ahead of the cage.

Amelia said no more.

They continued in silence for some time. With a bit of effort, Skunk rolled onto his back, using Tamaya's thigh like a pillow. He watched the sky overhead, occasionally disrupted by gray stone as they climbed higher and higher.

"So where do you think they're taking us?" Skunk asked, unable to bear the silence.

Amelia shrugged. "Their burrow, if I were to guess. To do the same thing to us that they did with everyone else, whatever that may be."

Skunk nodded. There was a silver lining to that if it was true. He would be able to find out what had happened to Sylvia; assuming, of course, that she was still alive. The thought that she wasn't reared its head once more, sending a tingle of dread creeping through his thoughts. He tried to chase away that dread by focusing on the pale ring. He traced its contour with his eyes, and it did wonders to gradually calm him.

One of the other bodies stirred, and Danica let out a low groan. "Ugh. What did I *drink* last night?"

"A fireball," Amelia noted dryly.

Danica paused. "Shit, that's literally what happened," she sighed, sitting up as well as she could and looking around. Her eyes were only half open, her expression dull and distant. Skunk was about to ask her how she felt when she suddenly sucked in a sharp breath. Red flags went up in his mind almost immediately.

He hadn't known Danica long, but he'd known her long enough to realize he'd yet to hear her make a noise like *that*. She sounded scared.

Worried, Skunk rolled onto his side to see what was happening. He went rigid when he saw the look on Danica's face. Her eyes were wide, pupils dilated, the color draining from her face. She looked back and forth, frantic, almost crazed, and Skunk could see a tremor creeping into her muscles.

"Oh, *hell* no!" she suddenly shouted before throwing the entirety of her weight against the bars. Her shrieking voice echoed all around them, shrill and primal. "Let me out! *Let me out!*"

"Danica?" Skunk choked, wanting to back away but unable to thanks to his bonds. He suddenly felt like he was trapped in a cage not with his dwarven friend, but with an angry grizzly bear.

"Let me out of this thing!" Danica repeated, her breaths devolving into panicky gasps. She threw herself back against the far wall of the cage, making the whole thing wobble. She didn't seem to care about the lacerations she was picking up with every violent thrash.

"Stop it!" The kobold that had threatened Amelia earlier snapped, turning around. "I can't kill you, but I can hurt you if you don't quiet down!"

"*Let me out!*" Danica roared, ignoring him. She slammed her back into the bars again, leaving a dent in the steel.

"Danica!" Amelia barked, shifting forward as well as she could. "Calm down! This isn't helping!"

Danica didn't seem to hear her. She didn't seem to be aware of *anything* besides the fact that she was trapped. She screamed again, and again she threw herself into the bars. The cage rolled to a stop, and the two kobolds in front were readying their spears. Their expressions were twisted into severe scowls. Skunk did not doubt that if Danica made herself too much of a nuisance, they'd decide they could afford to lose at least one.

"I said *quiet!*" the kobold snapped, striking Danica in the back of the head with the butt-end of his spear. This did not serve to instill calm in the rampant dwarf. It only made her angrier. She thrust her head back into the spear before the kobold could retrieve it. The force of the movement sent him stumbling away with a yelp.

"Danica!" Amelia tried again, her voice growing more desperate. "Calm down! Please, listen to me!"

"I gotta get out of here!" Danica gasped breathlessly, her chest heaving. "Get me *out!*"

Skunk felt paralyzed, his instincts conflicting with themselves as he tried and failed to find a solution. He wanted to help Danica calm down, but with how she was acting, part of him just wanted to get as far away from her as possible.

In the end, the decision would be made for him. The other Kobold was rotating his spear, ready for a thrust, and Karak was advancing with a glare of impatience. Not knowing what else to do, Skunk forced himself forward and brought his chin to rest gently on Danica's leg.

This, finally, got her attention. She looked down at him, gasping shallowly for breath.

"It's okay," Skunk whispered to her, looking up at her while keeping his head down. "It's gonna be alright. Take a deep breath, okay?"

Danica's face twisted with confusion, but in her somewhat crazed state, she didn't have the wherewithal to question him. She inhaled deeply, and Skunk smiled.

"There you go. Deep breath in. Hold it," he instructed, remembering with a pang of bitter nostalgia how Sylvia and Seto had taught him these same steps a long time ago. "One. Two. Three. Let it out, nice and easy. One. Two. Three."

Danica did, slowly breathing out. Skunk guided her through the steps again and again, and slowly but surely, she started calming down. When at last her breathing was under control, she looked away from Skunk, her face turning red. "G-get off my leg," she grumbled.

Skunk smiled up at her, knowing what she meant. He pulled himself away and turned to the other kobold. It was staring at Skunk in confusion. He shrugged helplessly. "She doesn't like tight places," he said simply. "They make her grumpy."

"Oh, good," Karak noted in amusement. "Where we're going, it's nothing *but* tight spaces. Do try and behave yourself, Danica."

"Eat a dick, shithead," Danica growled before closing her eyes.

Karak huffed in amusement, then moved ahead. Danica spat after him, then settled in place, fuming and seething.

Skunk stared at her in pity, then returned to his previous position on Tamaya's leg. As he rested there, however, he soon realized that the woman was not as out of it as he had previously thought.

"My leg is not a pillow either, kalj'atla," she said quietly. Skunk looked up to see that Tamaya had cracked open an eye. She was smirking at him.

"You're awake?!" he yelped in alarm, pulling back so he was no longer resting his head on her leg.

"It is difficult to sleep through such a ruckus," she said simply.

Amelia managed to offer up a chuckle but said nothing.

The cage fell into silence. No one had anything else to say. Amelia's observation about the kobolds being unable to harm them would only be true up to a point, and nobody was willing to push their already straining luck with idle chatter. Besides, it wasn't like they could make escape plans with Karak and his cronies right there listening in to their every word.

Slowly, as if to remind the prisoners of their dire situation, the sky steadily darkened with reddish hues, until it was a dark, bloody crimson. Deep shadows stretched and lengthened across the mountainside, darkening into perfect blackness as night fell.

Finally, the cage rolled over a sharp ridge. Skunk heard Amelia gasp and looked to see what awaited them.

The visceral tingling of *hate* he had felt in the Auriun ruins returned, and his eyes widened in shock.

A massive valley sprawled out before them, walled in on nearly all sides by nearly vertical cliffs. The spikes and peaks of the mountains around the valley were reminiscent of teeth. It was like a carnivore's mouth yawning open as it awaited its next meal. Natural rivers born of late-season snowmelt ran like veins through the basin, gathering at the lowest point to form a sparkling lake.

In the heart of it all was another auriun ruin. But it was no mere lonely spire, but an entire *city*.

To describe the sprawl as monolithic would be a disservice. A convoluted network of streets spiderwebbed across the valley, broken in places by collapsed structures and gaping chasms. In some places, the earth had been blasted as if by mighty impacts. In others, the land and structures smoothly folded in upon themselves, melted long ago by a heat intense enough to boil the soil.

"By the Five," Amelia breathed, her eyes widening in a mirror of Skunk's shock. "I've never seen a ruin so complete before. Or so large."

"Actaneirum, it was once called," Karak said, glaring down at the city. His tail swished in agitation. "One of the few auriun settlements to leave anything behind on the surface after the fall."

"You made your home in an auriun ruin?" Danica asked, quirking a brow. "If you dragon things hate them so much, why would you do that?"

Karak gestured at the city, though it almost looked like he was trying to tear it out of the world. "So that we may never forget what they *did to us!*" he declared, and the hatred in his voice carried with it a strange resonance. Inaudible but no less perceptible. That resonance found purchase in Skunk's mind, and despite how much he hated Karak, he agreed with him.

Karak closed his eyes, took a breath, and then issued commands to the kobolds in their strange language. The cage lurched down the rocky slope, bringing them toward the city. The nearer they became, the more restless the kobolds became. They snarled, growled, and talked amongst themselves in low rasps laced with vengeful venom. And despite himself, Skunk could not resist the urge to growl alongside them.

It frightened him to realize just how *right* his voice sounded when joined with theirs...

Amelia turned to him. She leaned forward, concern evident on her face. "Skunk, no. Stop," she told him gently. "Please, calm yourself—"

"You ask the impossible," Karak silenced her. His eyes settled on Skunk with a knowing, almost pitying look. "Our blood boils just to be near these ancient stones. Skunk can do nothing to suppress that hatred. It is part of who he is."

"I- I don't hate anyone!" Skunk tried to lie, tried to make himself believe it, but the words were hollow and empty. If he were not amid these ruins, he might have been able to believe he was telling the truth. But as the few still-standing structures of the auriuns towered above him, silhouetted against the ring and the bloody red of the dusky sky, he found he had no will to resist it.

He *did* hate the auriuns.

He hated their buildings.

He had no idea what they looked like, but he knew he found them repulsive.

He did not know their language, but he knew it would be like sandpaper on chalk to his ears.

He knew nothing about them, and he hated *everything* about them.

And of everything, *that* was what he hated most. That he could despise a dead species so completely and fully, and not even know who they were.

Karak shook his head. "You lie, Skunk. You hate them," he said softly. "But it is not something for you to be ashamed of. They *deserve* your hatred."

"They're *dead!*" Amelia bit back defiantly. "There is nothing to gain from this!"

Karak's pitying eyes and gentle tone turned scornful. He turned his gaze on her. "But their evils *persist*," he sneered. "And in the service of *ending* that evil, hatred is a *very* powerful motivator."

Tamaya lifted her head to stare at Karak, her expression firm. "You poison yourselves," she said bluntly. "Your hearts blacken, as do your souls. Whatever crimes the auriuns were guilty of yesterday, you mirror their evil in your actions today. You are no better."

Karak paused, visibly tensing. Skunk flinched back from him, his instincts telling him to hide. Karak took several deep breaths, and for a moment Skunk was afraid he was about to snap. Instead, Karak slowly relaxed and shook his head. "You are ignorant," he whispered. "But I will remedy you of that ignorance soon enough."

Skunk growled deep in his throat, but this time the threatening vocalization was not meant for the long-departed. He did not get a chance to say anything, however. Karak unfurled his wings and took to the sky, vanishing into the darkness of the night like a snuffed candle flame.

As the cage rolled deeper into the city, the red in the sky gave way to purple, then dark blue and silver as night fell upon Actaneirum. Skunk looked around at the structures, awed by their sheer scale, even as his blood screamed at him to tear it all down and leave nothing but dust.

"These auriuns sure liked to build big, didn't they?" Danica mused, glancing at one building that was larger than any Skunk had ever been in. Despite that scale, it was proportionally small when compared to its neighbors. The entrance was at least ten feet tall.

"The auriuns *were* big," Amelia pointed out. "As far as we know, the average auriun stood seven feet tall. And they had four arms."

Danica grunted. "What were they compensating for?"

"Everything," Skunk replied automatically.

Amelia shook her head in disapproval. "Skunk."

Shame prickled the back of his skull, and he quickly clamped his jaw shut, looking down at the ground. He closed his eyes, trying to shut out the fire in his veins and the knowledge of where he was. Instead, he thought of Sylvia.

He was close, now. She would be here. She had to be. He would finally get to be sure that she was okay, that she hadn't been harmed. Just a little longer, and he'd know. Then they could start figuring out how to get everyone out of this wretched place.

It wasn't long before their destination became clear. At the northwestern edge of the city, perched atop a high bluff overlooking the valley, was a spire of pristinely carved stone. Its upper half was missing, not unlike the ruins they had found in the plains. But even with half of it missing, Skunk felt like an ant in comparison. Numerous supporting arches emerged from the octagonal base of the spire, securing it firmly to the clifftop like ropes tethering a sailing ship to the dock. The collapsed remnants of a stone wall surrounded the perimeter, and judging by the rubble that scattered down the slope, Skunk imagined that this spire did not originally stand on a cliff.

The cage was wheeled through a hole in the wall and up to the spire's main entrance, a towering archway nearly twenty feet high. Skunk could imagine sturdy, ornamental doors occupying the frame. The entry chamber was enormous, with a high domed roof and curving staircases on either side leading to the second floor. There were holes in the roof and walls that let in shafts of ringlight, revealing particles of dust drifting lazily through the air. Ornately decorated pillars held up the roof while encircling a gaping hole in the floor. As the cage was wheeled toward the hole, Skunk saw it was the entrance to a tunnel that led deep into the darkness of the earth.

There were murals on the walls, but Skunk could decipher nothing of their contents. They had all been blackened and charred, melted long ago by impossible fires. The only things still visible were images of mountain peaks and some sort of stylized circle in the sky. What that circle could represent, he had no idea. The sun was the only thing that came to mind — but somehow he doubted it.

And then they were plunged into blackness as the cage was wheeled into the tunnel. Gravity tilted as they began their descent, sending Skunk's stomach twisting and his mouth flying open in a startled yelp. He dug the claws of his feet into the bars to keep himself from sliding along the serrated edges. Everyone else similarly braced, but the kobolds pulling the cage did not seem disturbed by the added effort of pulling a cage downhill.

"So this is it, then," Danica grumbled. "The kobold's burrow."

Skunk swallowed heavily. The tingle of his hatred remained, but there was something else smothering it. Something opposed to what he might expect to feel when being carted toward what was almost certainly his death.

Surrounded on all sides by the claustrophobic stone walls, Skunk suddenly felt inexplicably safe. At ease. He felt at home. As if *this* was where he belonged.

His eyes adjusted quickly. It was dim, but he could still pick out the details. They passed tunnel after tunnel, more than he could count. He could imagine climbing through them all with comfortable ease. Larger passages lead to sprawling chambers of diverse purposes, and Skunk could hear the chattering voices of kobolds echoing all around him. They reverberated off the stone walls a thousand times, obfuscating direction, yet his senses honed in on them with precision. He felt acutely aware of his surroundings, even through the cage. He could hear the slumbering masses down one tunnel. He could smell the heavy musk of matted fur, spittle, and body sweat, distant but clear. He could feel the slight vibrations of kobolds scrambling through the tunnels.

There was another scent, buried under the pungent aroma of the kobolds, but present. He sniffed at the air several times, trying to parse it. Snow and brimstone, stone and ash. Charcoal, smoke, flesh burnt to a fine crisp, and steel melted to slag. Earth and Sky. Sea and storm.

So many things all at once. He had no idea what it could be. Whatever it was, it was *powerful*.

Skunk's pondering came to an end as the cage was sent rolling unceremoniously down a steep slope. He cried out in surprise as the cage slammed into a wall of solid stone, jostling them all. Skunk heard the sound of something closing back the way they had come, and he realized that they had been shoved into a chamber and left there. They had made it to their cell.

"Skunk? Are you alright!?" Amelia asked after a moment. "Where are you? I can't see."

Skunk nodded and lifted his head. "Here. I'm okay."

"Where are we?" Tamaya asked, sitting up on her knees and squinting around. "I can barely see either. My eyes are suited to ringlight, not absolute darkness."

"I got it," Skunk said, looking around to try and get his bearings. His eyes slowly widened and his heart sank at what he saw.

There were countless other cages just like theirs in the room. Each one was overflowing with people. He saw ry'thar, clustered together in cages all to themselves. But there were humans, too. A lot of them. And he recognized *all* of them.

These were the people from Addernotch.

He swallowed heavily as he took in the details. Everyone was bruised and battered, skinny from a lack of food, their bodies caked in dirt and dust. Many weren't even bothering to open their eyes, and most were huddled together for what scraps of warmth they could share. Skunk's concern only grew when he realized that some people were missing. People that he knew didn't die at Addernotch, but who were conspicuously absent. He could only hope they were being kept in a separate chamber, although this one was more than large enough to house everyone.

He tried to push the troubling implications aside and turned back to Amelia. "T-they're here," he whispered. "The hostages. The ry'thar, the villagers from Addernotch. They're all here."

And just like that, Skunk remembered the most important face. He turned around, his eyes scanning the cages. Panic steadily rose in his chest, every pump of his heart sending liquid dread surging through his veins. *Where is she?!*

"S-Sylvia?!" he called out, daring to raise his voice. Some people in the room stirred from their slumber, but none called back to him. Skunk called louder. "Sylvia?! Are you in here?!"

"Here."

The answer came from a cage beside his, pressed against the wall where Skunk had yet to look. He spun in place, his eyes flying wide with relief and his heart swelling with joy.

And then his smile died, as did any relief he might have felt.

Sylvia sat only a couple of feet away. The only thing separating them were the walls of their cages. She was smeared in dirt and bruises like everyone else, her hands bound. She smiled at him, but it could not reach her eyes. "You came for us," she whispered.

"Sylvia?" Skunk choked, his eyes misting over. He blinked rapidly, praying that what he had just seen was only an illusion or a trick of his thoughts. But when he opened his eyes again, the horrific sight remained.

Dried smears of blood ran down Sylvia's cheeks, and a bloodied rag was tied over her eyes as a blindfold. The blood made it clear what had happened.

Sylvia was blind.

"Sylvia? Oh, gods, Sylvia, what did they do to you?" Skunk whispered, unable to look away. He desperately wished to reach out to her, to pull her into a hug, and never let her go. But the metal stopped him.

Sylvia's smile became strained. She looked down. "I asked too many questions, spoke out of line," she confessed, shaking her head. "There was a price to pay for that."

"Your eyes?!" Skunk rasped in disbelief, struggling to keep the tears out of his own. "They tore out your eyes for asking too many questions?! What the hell is wrong with them?!"

Sylvia finally lost her smile. She turned in place to face Skunk more directly. "Skunk. Breathe," she instructed calmly. On any other occasion, the simple instruction might have borne fruit.

Not this time.

"I'm sorry," Skunk babbled, breaking down into sobs and screwing his eyes shut. "I'm so sorry! I couldn't protect you! I tried so hard! I wasn't fast enough! I should have gone with you, I should have tried harder, I- I- I-"

"Skunk!" Sylvia said, her voice firm but still oh so gentle. The familiar tone immediately cut off Skunk's tirade of self-depreciation. He blinked open his eyes, hoping to see hers staring back at him.

All he found was the dirtied blindfold.

Even so, he felt transfixed by her attention. Slowly, Sylvia shook her head, and her smile returned.

"You did everything you could. *None* of this was your fault, do you hear me?" she said in a reassuring whisper, and Skunk felt himself starting to relax. She leaned against the bars of her cage, wincing slightly as the jagged metal bit into her shoulder. "And besides. I think I'm starting to get used to it. The darkness isn't so bad. Not when it's all you can see."

Skunk stared at her for several long seconds, surprised. He had always known she had an iron will, but to see her bearing her new disability with such casual ease was not something he was expecting. It was inspiring, in a chilling sort of way.

If Sylvia could handle the weight of being blinded, then Skunk could handle being a prisoner.

He swallowed heavily and offered a stiff nod of his head, easing himself back from the bars. A moment later he recalled that Sylvia couldn't see him nod and spoke. "R-right."

A moment passed in silence. Sylvia turned back to him. "I'm glad you're alright," she whispered to him. "I was worried about you."

Skunk smiled, hoping it would reach his voice. "I'm glad you're okay, too."

Behind him, Danica snorted, breaking the moment and reminding him that they were not alone. "Not sure how 'okay' we can be," the dwarf snarled, barely hiding her agitation. "We're trapped in serrated cages, we're far below ground in pitch-dark caverns with a *low roof*, we're surrounded by kobolds on all sides, and to top it all off, that asshole stole my axe!"

Sylvia tilted her head, her matted hair dangling off to one side. "Who's that talking?" she asked inquisitively, not at all perturbed by Danica's tone of voice.

Skunk chuckled weakly. "Oh, uh, that's Danica. She's a dwarf. We're friends. I think?" he explained awkwardly before glancing at her. "Danica, are we friends?"

"Shut up."

Despite everything, Amelia laughed. "They're friends. Skunk worked his magic and won her over."

Danica growled but did not expend the energy to offer up a rebuttal.

Sylvia's head tilted the other way. "Miss Lanswel? You're here too?" she questioned, equal parts fear and relief in her voice.

"Regrettably, yes," Amelia replied, trying to get more comfortable. The muscles in her face pinched and wrinkled into a pained grimace. "You said you asked too many questions. Were you lucky enough to get any answers?"

Any other questions Skunk may have had died. He focused all of his attention on Sylvia.

Several seconds passed. Finally, Sylvia nodded. "Yes. Not many, but a few."

Skunk leaned forward until his face was almost pressing against the bars. "Tell us," he pleaded quietly. "Why is all this happening? What do they *want?*"

Sylvia took a breath, her expression contorting with concentration. "Karak told me that we're sacrifices," she said softly. "That we're going to be given a choice. Either we join him... or he sacrifices us to something. He wasn't clear on what, though. And he hasn't told us anything more, yet."

Skunk's breath caught in his throat. "Sacrifices?" he asked, mortified.

Tamaya sighed, shaking her head in disappointment. "Barbarism."

"He's already started, too," Sylvia continued. "Every so often, some kobolds will come in here. They either give us some food, or take away one of the cages. None have come back yet."

A wave of revulsion fell over Skunk. How many people were already dead? How many people had he failed to save? How many good, innocent people had these kobolds — some of whom must have been his own flesh and blood — murdered? How could they even be capable of something so awful? He had seen the depths of their depravity back in Addernotch, but this was far worse. If they had only attacked the down out of a sense of self-preservation, no matter how misguided, one could almost understand. But this?

This was just evil.

"The question then becomes, what are we being sacrificed to?" Amelia asked, her brow furrowing in thought.

Sylvia shrugged. "I don't know. Again, he was vague about it. He called it the 'Young Master'."

Danica grunted. "Isn't it obvious?" she asked before stating the answer no one else wanted to acknowledge. "This 'Young Master' is a dragon."

Skunk went rigid at the word. His tail twitched against his bonds again, aching to be free. But there was something more under the impulse, an emotional reaction he dared not express in front of everyone else. *Excitement.*

"As obvious of an answer as that may seem, the only dragon that is known to have ever dwelled in this land was Azada, and she was slain centuries ago," Tamaya pointed out with a frown. "Another dragon in these peaks would not have escaped my tribe's attention. They are not subtle creatures. And if Azada left an egg behind, it would have hatched by now."

Sylvia shrugged. "I'm not so sure it would have. Karak did say that dragons were on the brink of extinction. If he wasn't lying, they would have wanted to reproduce as much as possible, but they're still so rare."

"You propose that they need something more to help their eggs hatch?" Tamaya asked.

Sylvia nodded. "It's the only thing that makes sense to me."

"Something they can only get from sacrifices," Skunk noted darkly. He vaguely recalled Seto's words back in the schoolhouse on the few dragons that were known. Even the ones that were known to be actively hostile toward mankind seemed to have standards. But the green-scales didn't.

After a moment, Amelia sighed and shook her head. "Whatever the case, idle speculation will do us few favors. I propose we rest and wait for a chance to make an escape attempt."

Nobody had any objections, and bit by bit, Skunk's companions got as comfortable as they could and closed their eyes, slowly drifting off to sleep. But he was not ready to join them. Not yet. He was too afraid to even think of it. The macabre scene surrounding him persisted behind his eyelids, joined by the horrifying images his imagination concocted of what Karak was doing to the people he had abducted.

He turned back to Sylvia, hoping for a distraction. She wasn't facing him, but he knew she was listening. She inclined an ear toward him. "You've changed," she said in a tender whisper.

Skunk looked down at his hands. His eyes lingered on the scar on his middle finger. "I guess?" he mused, not entirely sure if that was true.

"You have," Sylvia assured him, her smile returning. "It's in your voice. You're braver. Stronger."

Skunk felt his cheeks warming slightly from the praise, and he found himself thankful that the darkness hid his face from everyone else in the room. Awkwardly clearing his throat, he smiled and leaned against the bars to be as close to Sylvia as possible. "I dunno. But thank you for saying so. It means a lot to me, especially coming from you."

Sylvia hummed softly, the sound like music to his ears. "Tell me what's happened," she said, her voice lowering so only he could hear.

Skunk took a few seconds to collect his thoughts, then began to recount the tale.

Sylvia barely said a word as she listened to him. She was a silent rock, a steadying presence he had been without for far too long. He clung to her as well as he could, spilling everything he had been forced to endure, everything he had done. For the time the story lasted, if Skunk closed his eyes and tried to ignore the sensations pressing in all around him, he could almost forget how bad things had become. He could almost imagine, almost, that it was just the two of them sorting books in the back of Seto's schoolhouse, the sun on his scales, the ring in his eyes, and the warmth of his dearest friend by his side chasing away his doubts and his fears.

Finally, after his story was done, and all the burrow had fallen into the quiet stillness of slumber, Skunk was able to find some semblance of rest.

The Offer

Nobody knew how much time had passed, though Skunk wagered it had to have been a few days. It was impossible to tell without the light of the sun or the ring. All they had to go on was the semi-regular basis on which food was brought to them. Skunk and the ry'thar found no issue with this, but Amelia was quick to remind him that the humans were not purely carnivorous like they were. Scurvy would set in eventually if they didn't get fruit or vegetables. Assuming, of course, they lived that long.

Adding gravity to that point, every so often, a cage would be wheeled away, just like Sylvia said. Sometimes, the occupants would scream. Other times they would simply whimper and beg. A few raged against the bars, and a few languished in silent resignation. So far, none had come back.

Skunk tried to distract himself by figuring out how many people were still alive. Most of the abducted population of Addernotch was still here, but that number was starting to shrink with every cage that was taken away. He wanted to help them, but there was nothing he could do. The oppressive sensation of powerlessness held him by the throat, strangling him as people he had known his entire life were wheeled away into the darkness, never to be seen again.

Sometimes he caught the scent of cooking meat, and morbid thoughts rebounded in his skull like a rabid bat in a cage. Relentless, incessant, and screeching too loudly to ignore.

Eventually, the vague semblance of a routine was disrupted. Three kobolds came marching into the chamber, drawing Skunk's attention. The one in the front carried an improvised lantern on his hip, while the other two flanked him with spears bearing the traditionally crude workmanship of the kobolds. The one with the light advanced on Skunk's cage, its eyes roving over him with contempt.

Skunk sat upright, wondering if it was their turn to be sacrificed. But to his surprise, the kobold instead procured a key from its belt.

"The First Fang wants to talk to the runt and the dwarf," it said, its voice coarse like burning gravel.

"Fine by me," Danica grunted, her voice raspy from a lack of water. "I'd like a chance to see Karak, too."

"Try anything and you die," the kobold told her simply, waiting for everyone to get back from the cage's entrance. Skunk backed away anxiously, his mind alight with questions. This was new, and right now, new was not welcome.

He glanced at Sylvia. "Has anything like this happened before?" he asked hopefully.

Sylvia shook her head. "No."

The cage came unlocked with a metallic clank. The kobold pulled it open, the old hinges shrieking and making Skunk's ears ring. The guards pointed their spears forward to dissuade any escape attempts. The keyholder jerked his head back and made room. "Come."

Danica lumbered forward without hesitation, clearly eager to get out of the cramped space and stretch her legs. Skunk hesitated, glancing at Tamaya and Amelia for support. Tamaya nodded at him without a word, but Amelia's expression was harder to read. After a moment, Skunk stood and made his way forward, following Danica out of the cage. The moment his feet met the stone floor, he felt a profound sense of relief and wasted no time in standing up tall to stretch his aching back.

"I said runt and dwarf *only!*"

Skunk spun around to see the keyholder shoving Amelia into the back of the cage. She grunted as her back struck the jagged bars, and the door slammed shut with a deafening clang. Skunk took a step toward her. "Mom!"

Amelia lifted her eyes toward him, then turned a hellfire glare on the keyholder. "If you think I am going to let you take my boy anywhere without me—"

"You are *meat!*" The keyholder interrupted her, baring its fangs in a vicious display. "He is *dragonkin.* Do not insult him by naming him *your boy!*"

Amelia's eyes narrowed. "You are going to die."

Skunk's throat tightened, and he suddenly found it hard to breathe. He shuddered. He had never heard his mother make such a declaration before. She said it with such calm certainty that he couldn't help but believe it — and that scared him.

"Mom..." he whispered.

"You will follow us and not say a word," the keyholder commanded simply, unfazed by Amelia's promise. He turned to leave, giving Skunk and Danica no time to even get a word in.

Skunk glanced back at Sylvia and tried to give her a reassuring smile. Then remembering her condition, he opted to call out to her instead. "We'll be okay!"

"I said to not speak a word!"

Skunk yipped in pain as the butt of a spear found his neck. He staggered a few steps before one of the other kobolds forcefully shoved him back into motion. His vision swam, his head pounding from the blow. He found Danica's side and leaned against her for support. She bore him without complaint, much to Skunk's relief.

Nobody spoke as the kobolds led them into the tunnels. Skunk had known coming in that the place was elaborate, but now that he was walking through it on his own two feet, it slowly dawned on him just how *convoluted* this place was. His jaw fell open as they walked, surrounded by tunnels that went in every direction. Each one had a different smell, a purpose all to itself.

Some were filled with dozens of kobolds just... existing. He heard them chattering at one another in that oh-so-familiar language, their voices light and friendly. It unnerved him to admit it, but when they spoke like that, their voices reminded him of his own. He saw a handful chasing each other around the room with competitive grins, cheered on by the raised voices of laughing onlookers.

Other chambers showed him kobolds eating. It was a messy and wholly impolite mess, devoid of utensils, manners, or any concept of personal space. Slabs of meat passed down lines of eager-eyed kobolds that tore into their meals with ravenous fervor.

Later he saw a larger chamber with strange animals he had never seen before. Fat, bloated things with bulbous bodies twice the height and width of an ox and three times as long. They didn't have any distinguishable facial features, and he realized that they were like gargantuan earthworms without the mucus. They were hemmed in by fences of stone and bone, but their captivity did not seem to bother them. They just lay there in their pens, nibbling quietly at cultivated beds of mushrooms and moss. Skunk realized that these were the source of the meat the kobolds had been eating in the last room.

The burrow must keep those creatures as livestock, he mused. It made sense. They would need a way to sustain themselves somehow, and he knew his own appetite well enough to deduce that if they only hunted the local wildlife, they would rapidly drive them into extinction.

But the fact that these creatures were organized and civil enough to tend to large groups of animals like this at all...

Skunk's thoughts were eventually torn away from the burrow's livelihood. He tried to remember the route they were taking, but their path was far from straight. He realized that if it were not for their armed escort, they would be hopelessly lost. Perhaps their route was deliberately obtuse to confuse their senses.

At last, they arrived in a large, natural chamber. Fire blazed up from a pit in the center, about the size of a campfire. On the other side of the flame, sitting cross-legged and waiting patiently, was Karak. He lifted his eyes and offered a smile that almost looked friendly. "Ah. There you are," he greeted as if to a friend a few minutes late to an afternoon meal. His eyes flicked to their escort, and his smile faded. He nodded, and the three kobolds peeled away from their charge to take up defensive positions by the exit. Satisfied, Karak beckoned to Skunk and Danica. "Come. There is much for us to discuss," he called.

Danica growled. "What, like the fact I'm going to use one of your horns as a beer mug?" she asked as she and Skunk advanced.

Karak huffed in amusement. "Now, Danica, must you be *so* rude? I am trying to have a civil conversation with you two," he said in mock dismay. "What would your mother and father say if they were to hear you speak that way to your host?"

"Talk about my parents again," Danica seethed, taking a threatening step forward. "I dare you!"

Not wanting to antagonize Karak more than they had to, Skunk quickly nudged Danica's foot with his. She glanced down at him, and he shook his head. She took his meaning and took a breath, then turned back to Karak again.

"You threw a fireball at me. I'm not being polite."

To that, Karak shrugged. "That is fair," he conceded.

"What do you want?" Skunk finally asked, fighting to force his fearful tremors out of his voice.

Karak's cordial expression darkened considerably at that. He eyed each of them in turn, scrutinizing them as if to evaluate the worth of an antique jewel. His gaze lingered particularly long on Skunk, making the smaller kobold squirm. Eventually, Karak leaned back and gestured. "Sit."

Skunk didn't even realize he was obeying until he was on his knees. It was that strange influence Karak had over him. His blood and his cheeks warmed with indignation and embarrassment as Skunk realized he had utterly failed to resist it.

"I'll stay on my feet, thanks," Danica stated bluntly, holding her head high, a glint of fiery defiance burning bright behind her eyes. If she in any way noticed Skunk's humiliation, she did not show it.

Karak raised his brow. A few seconds later, he spoke. "Would I be correct in assuming that you have heard my story from the human girl?"

"Yeah," Skunk confirmed, his voice thick in his throat. "Y-you're sacrificing us. To a dragon."

"That is the short of it, yes," Karak confirmed. He rolled his wrist as he spoke. "You see, the Young Master will awaken soon. For those who pledge their loyalty to his cause, there shall be nothing to fear. For those who refuse, well, the luma within them shall serve to expedite his birth, and see to it he is born strong, healthy, and fed."

"So chuck us to him and be done with it," Danica snarled.

Karak laughed quietly, mockingly. "Ah, Danica. Ever an impatient one. If you are truly so eager to die, I would be happy to cast you into the flames. But I am loath to throw away potential assets without giving them a chance to see the error of their ways."

"Error?" Skunk demanded, leaning forward. "What error?! You guys attacked us first! You started this, not us!"

Karak shook his head with a humorless chuckle. "No, dear boy. This conflict has been in motion since long before you or I were ever even conceived."

"Cut the cryptic bullshit and get to the point," Danica shot back. "I didn't come here for riddles!"

Karak frowned, his tail swishing in a clear sign of agitation. His eyes wandered over those assembled. He took a breath and nodded. "So be it. To the heart of the matter. You both deserve to know."

A creeping chill ran down Skunk's spine from the base of his neck. He shuddered uncomfortably, almost feeling naked as Karak's eyes passed slowly and quietly over them.

Karak looked down into the flames, his expression darkening. "From where you stand, my attack on your homes seems unprovoked. Your indignance and frustration are not unwarranted. But you operate under a pall of ignorance. Ignorance and righteousness make for poor bedfellows."

He stretched his hand out, the runes along his forearm flaring with luma. The flames billowed in response, flaring brighter. Danica flinched back, wincing away from the heat. The fire was hot on Skunk's scales, hot enough to hurt. Karak whispered something, an incantation. With every word that left his lips, an image began to appear within the flames. Skunk's eyes widened as the distinctive shapes of a great city made themselves visible. Magnificent auriun spires rose to pierce the heavens, their silhouettes set against the backdrop of the night sky.

Curiously, however, Skunk saw no sign of the pale ring.

"You know, of course, of the auriuns," Karak began, his eyes flicking at Skunk and Danica over the flames. "The rulers of the old world. Masters of magic. Builders of the infernal city above us."

Skunk tried to hold in his instinctual growl, but it slipped out of him despite his best efforts. Danica glanced at him from above but said nothing.

Karak continued. "None were as mighty with the gift of magic as they were. And in light of this mastery, the auriuns determined that this world was rightfully theirs to rule. They named the world after themselves and spread across the continents, subjugating all who dared to stand against them."

The auriun city vanished in a rush of embers. In its place, Skunk and Danica witnessed scenes of war and bloodshed — and scenes that by rights should not have been possible.

A city of tree-like spires built upon islands that floated above a sprawling ocean of fluffy white clouds, tended by winged figures who soared between them. Suddenly the spires were ablaze, and Skunk watched stars fall from the sky to punch through the foundations of the floating city. The land split and shattered, and the spires fell, vanishing into the clouds.

The image changed. Now Skunk saw a magnificent and sprawling forest. Humans were hiding amidst the trees, bows and arrows in hand. They wore lush greens and blacks, elegant and graceful.

Skunk inhaled sharply when he saw the unmistakable shape of the Auriuns. Their crimson robes dragged across the ground behind them, their four arms, gilded in gold and bronze, were folded behind their backs and before their navels. They marched between the trees, unnaturally smooth, as if they were floating, not walking.

The odd humans leaned out of the shadows to loose their arrows. The auriuns, in turn, lifted their hands. Tsunamis made of sunfire and ice tore from their palms to envelop the whole forest, burning away leaves and freezing what was left. Ashes and the faint suggestion of screams marked where the humans once stood.

Karak's expression darkened as more and more such scenes played out before them. "Resistance was fierce, of course. But it was ultimately futile. None could withstand the might of the auriuns for long, and many knew this.

Most threw down their arms and surrendered. But for those who dared to fight back, unimaginable suffering awaited them as punishment..."

To Skunk's shock, Karak looked *upset,* as if he was disturbed by what he was about to say. He lifted his eyes to Danica and stared at her for a long moment.

She shifted uncomfortably. "Stop staring at me."

Karak slowly shook his head. "...I am so sorry, Danica."

Now it was Danica's turn to blink. "What?"

Karak did not explain himself. He looked back into the flames. He uttered another incantation, and the images of war vanished. "In the end, the auriuns crushed all in their path. The whole of the world fell under their banner. Your ancestors, Danica, were made to bend the knee. And an age of hedonistic abundance began, with your backs serving as the foundations. For centuries, they made sport of their mastery of luma, rearranging the world to fit their delusional whims and feeding their slaves to the pits of the World Below to gather the stone and metal used in their so-called *great works*. But what they did not know was the terrible price of their abuse of magic."

A new image formed in the flames. Skunk's stomach lurched, his heart skipping a beat.

"That place..." he choked out.

Karak nodded at him. "You've seen it," he said. It was not a question.

Indeed, Skunk *had* seen it. In all of his nightmares since the attack. The world of glowing stone. Countless dragons of every color soared through its diamond-speckled, obsidian sky.

"In my dreams," Skunk confessed softly.

"Your blood remembers what it has lost," Karak reminded him, an uncharacteristic hint of longing in his voice. "What the auriuns *took* from you."

"What is it? What *is* that place?" Skunk asked desperately, lifting his eyes to Karak. "Tell me!"

Karak looked into the flames again, frowning deeply. "Your home. The homeland of dragonkin. The true birthplace of luma. Poisoned, polluted, and *devastated* by the auriuns' hubris. The spells they could work were unfathomable in scale. With each one they cast, they brought ruin. They drained the lifeblood of *our home* with every indulgence, every selfish whim. In time, when the dragons discovered the source of that rot, they sent their best to speak to the auriuns, to convince them to stop their exploitation of a power they did not fully understand — for *all* their sakes."

Karak's lips curled up into a ferocious snarl. "As you can well imagine, the 'almighty' auriuns did not heed the warning. As the dragons descended upon them, showing a mastery of magic that rivaled their own, the auriuns did what despots do."

The image of the world of glowing stone disappeared, replaced again. This time, Skunk saw another auriun city. Dragons were flying toward it, grizzled and ancient, but he could tell just from their body language that they were not hostile.

Until a ray of sunfire lanced out one of the city's spires. It struck the lead dragon before she had a chance to alter course and pierced through the scales of her chest.

"*No!*" Skunk exclaimed involuntarily as the dragon turned white, then black, then dissolved into smoldering ashes. The rest of the dragons scattered, roaring their rage and their grief.

"Yes," Karak corrected. "The auriuns saw the mere existence of the dragons as a threat and an insult. 'Beasts,' they cried, only able to see the resemblance between the dragons and a common pond lizard. To the auriuns, it was an insufferable offense that such inglorious creatures dared attempt to treat with them as equals or wield magic in the first place. The hope for peace died. So began the war."

The image in the flames flickered. The city was now ablaze, an army of a hundred dragons encircling it from the skies and breathing gouts of colored flames into its streets. Lances and waves of silver magic answered them, tearing apart all they touched. Skunk realized with a pit forming in his stomach that he could see massive skeletons littering the earth around the city.

Dragon skeletons.

"A war that the auriuns waged with yet more magic. Recklessly, indiscriminately, and heedless of the damage they were causing. With every spell they worked and every battle they fought, the imbalance they had created grew worse and worse. Until finally..."

The flames dulled, the images disappearing. Skunk blinked, snapping out of a trance he hadn't realized he had fallen into. He looked up at Karak, his eyes wide and unfocused. Karak stared back at him.

"Calamity tore across the surface of Aurus. Millions died, man and dragon and kobold alike. In the end, everyone lost, and the light of magic became a shriveled, flickering phantom of its former glory. Deprived of their power, the auriuns could do naught but vanish into extinction as the repercussions of their vanity tore the world in half. Your ancestors survived only because they lived underground — and because many dragons gave up their lives to ensure there was a world left to inhabit when the flames finally settled. It would be four hundred years before your ancestors would start to emerge from the World Below and repopulate the surface."

"So the auriuns were assholes," Danica stated, clearly growing impatient with the history lecture. "Big deal. What does *any* of this rot have to do with this, though? By the sound of things, we're victims of the auriuns just as surely as you are."

"I will not deny that the auriuns committed atrocities against your ancestors," Karak conceded. "However, you may be the victim of one crime and still be guilty of another. Given the circumstances, your guilt outweighs all else."

"How?" Skunk asked, finally finding his voice. "What have we done to deserve what you've done to *us?!*"

Karak closed his eyes. He lifted his arm, drawing attention to his runes. They pulsed and hummed with luma. "When the people of this world emerged, it was only a matter of time before they rediscovered magic. The hope was that those people would have learned from the mistakes of their former masters, and cast that power aside. But such is not the case. All across Aurus, institutions and organizations devoted to the study and the mastery of this power have sprung up. They vie for the very power that the auriuns once wielded. They exhibit the same hubris if not the same potential. Left to their own devices, mankind will repeat the sins of the auriuns and bring this world once more to ruin. And this time, it will not be able to recover."

Karak lifted his eyes to Skunk's, then to Danica's. "And that, you two, is why I am here. I had the good fortune to meet with one who graced my mind with the truth. I saw the sins of antiquity at long last, I saw the horrific crimes that persist in the blood of mankind. I saw evils that have, for centuries, gone unanswered. I saw how the men and women of Aurus have forgotten, and I said *enough*. I labor for justice. I labor to ensure that the sins of the auriuns never again come to pass. If it requires the subjugation or, if necessary, the *elimination* of the races of mankind, then so be it. But it need not be so."

Karak suddenly stood up, folding his hands behind his back. "At this point, it should be clear that you stand no chance of victory. Against the horde and my enhancements, your defenses have proven insufficient. Any resistance you offer will only end in more of your people dying. And once the Young Master is born, more hordes will flock to him. The first dragon to be born in centuries. A new beacon of hope for our dwindling species. Our ranks will swell, and in time, the nations of mankind will bend either their knees in service or their necks for the axe. But you are strong. Resilient. Those are good qualities, but you waste them on a cause borne of ignorance. It would not be so with mine — if you are willing to see the errors of your ways and join hands in common cause with me."

Skunk felt as if a mallet had just been taken to the side of his skull. "W-what?!" He exclaimed in disbelief.

Danica, meanwhile, *laughed*. She threw her head back, belting out a full-bellied guffaw that reverberated in the chamber. Skunk stared at her in bewilderment. Then the laughter stopped, and Danica's murderous eyes locked onto Karak. "Did you think that sob story was going to be enough to convince us to join you? After everything you've done?!"

"I have hope because I know you are smart, Danica," Karak offered simply, his face the picture of patience under pressure. He nodded to Skunk. "And I know the boy cares for his 'pack.' You cannot win from where you stand now. You know now why I fight. You know that mankind must be stopped before their abuse of magic brings new ruin to this world. I am offering you a chance to fight alongside me and *save* this world. We must share it, after all, and so share the responsibility of preventing a repeat of the apocalypse that brought my kind to the brink of extinction."

"I'd rather saw off my own tits," Danica stated bluntly.

Karak cringed at the obscene comment, then shook his head. "Ever a stubborn one," he said under his breath. Then he shifted his eyes to Skunk. "And you, little one?"

Skunk snapped back to attention. He blinked a few times before affixing Karak with a harsh glare. He shook his head. "If you're so insistent that we're ignorant, why did you *attack* us? You could have come to us peacefully and educated us! You could have *taught* us! Showed us *why* we're wrong! Worked *with* us to find a better way!"

"What do you think I am doing now?" Karak asked, gesturing at the fire. "I am *trying* to teach *you*. I am giving you the chance to *learn,* boy."

"But what about the rest of them?" Skunk demanded. He jerked his head back. "All those people in the cages? Or the people you've killed already? Hell, why even *bother* with us? What can Danica or I do? What can *anyone* in Addernotch do?! You could have gone to the Assemblage! Or to the king! Or *someone* important!"

Karak looked at Skunk, his eyes filled with pitying disappointment. "How naive," he said softly. He leaned forward and gently waved his hand through the flames. When he withdrew it, silver threads of light danced and weaved between his fingers. He stared at that light for a long moment, then at Skunk. "For almost a thousand years, your magi and your lords have benefited greatly from their use of magic, just as the auriuns did. In light of that, it is foolish to assume they would ever be willing to part with such power, no matter how compelling the reason that they should."

"But you aren't even giving them a chance," Skunk argued with rising confidence. "You aren't even *trying!* You're just assuming the worst about the other side and using that as an excuse to *attack* us! You're murdering us! You're *sacrificing us!* You're keeping people locked in cages and using them as *fuel* for your ambitions without even listening when someone tries to tell you that you have it all wrong! Isn't that exactly what the auriuns did?!"

Scarce had the words left Skunk's mouth before Karak's hand flashed through the flames and grabbed his throat. In the time it took his heart to beat, Karak whipped around and threw him to the floor. His nose cracked against a small jut of stone, sending his head spinning and his ears ringing. Karak's voice boomed at him through the haze. "Don't you *dare* compare me to the auriuns!" he screamed. "I have devoted my life and given up *everything* in the name of avenging what they destroyed! I will not have you question me, *child!*"

Skunk gasped for breath, then coughed a few times as ancient dust flowed down his throat. He rose back to his knees and glared bitterly at Karak over his shoulder. "See?" he asked quietly. "Exactly the same."

Karak's eye twitched. A low growl came from somewhere deep in his throat, but he did not rise to the bait. Instead, he closed his eyes and took a calming breath.

After a moment, Danica spoke up. "So this has all been *very* interesting. I couldn't even begin to tell you how invested I am in this chat. But Skunk's got a point. Why the hell are we important enough to have all this exposited at us in private?" Danica asked, turning to Karak directly. "You made it seem like everyone's gonna get this story sooner or later. Why did we go to the front of the line?"

Karak sighed. He turned back around to face Danica, his expression downcast. "I had hoped I would find receptive ears in you two. I cannot turn to the kings and queens of the world. If I could convince you two of the wisdom of my cause, the rest of your fellows might be easier to convince."

"You could do that with literally anyone else from Addernotch, and I'm not even *from* there," Danica shot back, her impatience rising. "Why *us?* Why Skunk and I? Why are *we* so special? Why am *I* so special?"

There was a long pause. Danica leaned forward, her eyes narrowing. "How the hell do you know me, Karak?" she finally asked.

Skunk watched from the floor as the two of them stared each other down. The tension in the air was thick and ready to snap. Finally, however, Danica took a single step forward.

"Who are you?" she asked with finality. "Be straight with me. Who. Are. You?"

Karak met her gaze and merely smiled. "Come now, Danica. I don't need to tell you that."

"And why not?"

Karak chuckled and shook his head. "I'm certain you can figure it out. After all, as I said the day we met..." Karak lifted his eyes, and his smirk turned downright predatory, a flicker of smug satisfaction burning behind his amber eyes. "You have good instincts."

Skunk stared at Karak, dumbfounded, then turned to Danica. Her eyes had flown wide, and for the first time since he had met her, she appeared genuinely shocked. She mouthed like a fish, her mind scrambling to catch up to the implication. "Good instincts...? *Marus?*" she breathed in disbelief.

With a fanciful, theatrical flourish, Karak offered Danica a low bow. "And at last she recognizes me. It is a pleasure to meet you again, my lady," he greeted with smooth formality.

Skunk's mind lit up with a million questions all at once. "Wait, *you're Marus?!*" he shouted.

"The very same," Karak confirmed, his teeth showing in a smug grin. "Though I must admit to being impressed that she would be open about that with you of all people."

"H-how?" Danica stammered, her hatred momentarily quelled by her confusion. "How is that possible?! Marus is a human man! Not a- a- whatever the fuck you are!"

Karak stood up and spread his arms wide, putting the countless runes etched into his flesh on display. "As I said before; I gave up everything when I learned the truth," he said. "And that included my humanity. If I was to be a champion for the cause of the dragons, then I would do so as one of their kind. Or at least, as close as I could get. My mission to steal the Sunstone was proof of my commitment, and in return for a job well done, the master saw fit to grant me my wish. The best and brightest of this burrow took magic, ringstone, and chisel to my body, transforming me into this. A hybrid between man and dragonkin — a demidragon, if you will."

Karak flashed Danica a wolfish grin. "Ah, and, on the subject of what happened in Stonefall — my sincere apologies for what happened to your mother. She was a lovely woman. I did not wish for her to suffer so."

Skunk saw the rage in Danica's eyes before she acted. Her trembling lips parted in a roar of rage. She charged, heedless of her lack of a weapon, heedless of the fact that his enchantments would make him impossible to defeat even if she had one.

Karak almost looked bored. He effortlessly sidestepped, turned, and drove his foot between her shoulder blades. Danica cried out as she was sent sprawling to the floor in a heap. She went to rise, but the three guards were already on her, pinning her to the ground and violently beating her into submission.

"Danica!" Skunk cried out, getting to his feet and advancing to try and help her. Karak's hand found his shoulder, his steel grip holding him in place. The kobolds backed off a moment later, revealing a motionless Danica. Dark bruises were already forming on her face and exposed arms, and a small trickle of blood leaked out of her nose. She was breathing, though, thankfully.

Karak shook his head. "Ah, Danica. Good instincts, but terrible judgement," he mused before turning to Skunk. "I would not advise you to try anything like that. We aren't done talking just yet."

Skunk took a fearful step back, jerking out of Karak's grip. "I have nothing to say to you!" he spat.

Karak matched his retreat. "Oh, but I have *much* to say to *you*," he said in a cold growl. "And you *will* listen. *Sit.*"

Once again, Karak's words held some sort of power over Skunk, and he obediently fell to his knees. The heat of humiliated rage crept up his face.

"Stop doing that!" he seethed through tightly clenched teeth.

Karak only smirked as he sat across from him, legs crossed. "I cannot help what your instincts demand of you, Skunk."

And then Karak was quiet. Seconds slowly ticked by. The only sound was the crackling of the flame. Skunk fidgeted in place, his anger slowly melting away, replaced by a knot of cold dread tying up his intestines. He waited anxiously for Karak to begin, wanting nothing more than for all this to end so he could go back to his cage, back to his mother's waiting arms. But Karak didn't let him go. He didn't say anything for a long while. He just sat there, staring Skunk down.

Finally, the silence became too much. "W-what do you want?" Skunk asked, his voice a low jitter.

Karak smiled, hearing the question he had been waiting for. "My offer still stands. I want to offer you a place in this horde."

Skunk narrowed his eyes. "You guys *abandoned me*. Why would you take me back now? And why would I *ever* join you?"

Karak's smile did not falter. "You were abandoned as an egg, yes. But you were taken rather far away from this burrow — *very* far. Runts rarely survive for long here, weak as they tend to be. I can only assume that your mother wanted to spare you such a fate, give you a chance at survival."

Skunk went rigid, his mind stalling. "My... mother?" he echoed in disbelief.

Karak nodded. "We do not live an easy life, Skunk. We face enemies above and below, and that means that we must always bring our best. There can be no room for weakness in our ranks. And so, much as a mother wolf would abandon a pup born with a disability or an injured horse would be left behind by the herd, runts who can not protect themselves often die young. It is not due to a lack of love for our offspring, but simple necessity. One fewer runt means one less mouth to feed, one less weakling to hold the others back."

The demidragon leaned forward slightly, his eyes lighting up with promise. "But *you* were spared that fate. Your mother went out of her way to give you a chance to survive. And survive you have. And I know who she is."

Skunk's throat constricted even more. It had rarely occurred to him to think about his biological family until recently. It had been a tiny point of speculation, flitting about the edges of his thoughts during the journey from the karjene village. Now, though? Try as he might to convince himself that he didn't care, he couldn't. He wanted to know.

Karak's smile grew when he saw the progress he was making. "I can introduce you to her, you know. And to your brothers and sisters, as well. You have several. I can bring you to them, Skunk. You can have a *real* family. You can live with your own kind."

Skunk was tempted. That was the worst part. Just a few words and already the idea was tantalizing him. He felt ashamed for even considering it, but that didn't stop him. He tried to maintain his glare, but he knew it was faltering. "W-why would you make me that offer? I'm your enemy!" he repeated, but his voice did not carry as much conviction as before.

"But that does not mean you have to stay that way!" Karak countered earnestly. "When we first met, I wrote you off as small and weak. But you have proven your abilities to me since then. You *are* small, you *are* weak, but you are *smart*. You are fast, you are clever, you are good with a bow, and you are a swift learner. Yours is a sharp mind, rich with an education that this horde desperately lacks. You understand humans in ways no other kobold I know has ever been able to. And unlike me, you are bonded to them. You love them. With your counsel balanced against my... admittedly zealous passion, think of how many lives you could save!"

Skunk lowered his eyes, his resistance to the idea faltering more and more.

Karak's smile faded. He leaned away, and his voice dropped considerably. "And beyond all of that; Tell me the truth. Do you genuinely believe that you will ever have a place among the *humans?*"

Skunk opened his mouth to say yes, of course, but he hesitated.

It would be a lie, wouldn't it?

The people of Addernotch *had* accepted him, yes. But that had been after watching him grow up and living with him for eighteen years. Now, after the attack? He recalled with a pained shudder and a twinge of grief how much they had hated him after what his kind had done.

Karak nodded when Skunk did not answer. "I thought not. You are not one of them, Skunk. You are a kobold. To them, that is all you will ever be. You will always be the *other*. The outsider. The *monster*. You have only survived as long as you have because one human woman was willing to vouch for you in a small village that could not push back against her desire. But she will not be there for you forever. One day, and it may not be so very long from now, you will not be able to rely on her anymore. Without her there to watch over you and command acceptance, how long do you believe you will last? Beyond Addernotch, you will be nothing but another kobold. Another 'evil dragonkin' to slaughter on sight."

"B-but..." Skunk said weakly. "Mom..."

"She loves you," Karak conceded with a shrug. "Only a fool would claim otherwise. She defended you as well as any good mother should. But you are *still* a kobold. Still less-than, even to her, try as she might to deny it. They will always look down on you, despise you, spit at the ground you walk on. Even your *name* is an insult!

"Skunk," Karak said the name slowly and deliberately. "The name of an animal known only for its putrid stench."

Skunk looked down, and he found he could no longer lift his head. Karak was right. Amelia was the only reason he had ever been welcomed in Addernotch, and the only way she could watch him for his whole life was if he died before she did.

His attention was drawn up when he saw Karak's hand outstretched toward him. The demidragon smiled warmly. "But here, such a name means little," he said softly. "Here, among the kobolds, your worth is measured by your ability and your commitment, not your heritage. Join hands with me, Skunk. Join your people, and I swear to you, on what little honor I have left, you will never again want for the warmth of companionship. You will be among your own kind, united in purpose, and always given the place you deserve. You will be where you *belong.*"

Skunk was silent. He looked down at the floor, his heart torn. All his life, the idea of being alone, of being without a pack, had scared him more than anything. He'd worked himself to the breaking point in Addernotch out of fear that they might reject him if he didn't. He'd forced himself to be useful, to always be helpful, to make up for what happened with Bjorn. And now he was faced with an offer to finally be with a pack that wouldn't cast him out for the smallest mistake.

But at the same time, the people of Addernotch, for all of their recent misgivings, had tolerated, accepted, and in time even loved him. He thought back on the few friends he had beyond his mother. He recalled Seto and the children of the schoolhouse. Karak had promised that Skunk could save lives if he accepted this offer. Maybe he could still save them.

But then he thought of Sylvia. He thought of long, quiet days spent sorting books or sitting by the river. He thought of peaceful moments where they sat together under a tree on the edge of town, reading in silence. He thought of her beautiful eyes that had always promised him, no matter what, that everything would be fine. The eyes that had told him she would always be there for him when he needed her. A promise that she had never once broken, and one he had always done his best to return. He had failed her when the kobolds attacked. He hadn't been able to be there when she'd needed him.

And now her eyes were gone. Stolen when he was not there. And the one responsible sat before him.

Skunk's decision was made before the thought had fully formed. He lifted his eyes to meet Karak's.

"You know, if you had come to me with all of that before the attack, I might have said yes," he stated with finality. "But you attacked *me*. *You* hurt *my* people. You *hurt* my *pack*. The moment you did that, you became my enemy. Maybe you're right. Maybe Addernotch won't keep me around forever. Maybe they *will* drive me out someday. But at least they gave me a *chance*. They *kept* me. *They* don't crush their young because they're weak! That's more than I can say of *you*."

Karak held Skunk's steadfast gaze for a moment longer, then nodded. "I see. A pity, to be sure, but unsurprising," he lamented before rising to his feet. "Your loyalty does you credit, Skunk of Addernotch. I'll see to it you and your loved ones do not suffer more than you have to."

With that, Karak nodded at the guards. They still lingered by Danica, but quickly snapped to attention. "Escort them back to their cage. See to it Skunk is given a good meal before tomorrow."

Skunk allowed himself to be guided out. He offered no resistance, but he did call out, recognizing that he had only one chance to gather more information. "And what happens tomorrow?"

"The young master is almost ready," Karak answered. "Tomorrow, we welcome him to the world."

Skunk found little comfort in the answer, and he was not given enough time to press the issue. All he could tell for certain as he was brought back into the tunnels was that if they didn't find a way out by tomorrow, none of them would be leaving this place alive.

Slumber

Skunk was dreaming again.

Once again he was greeted by the sight of an expansive silver landscape. Magnificent arches, deep canyons, and swelling mountain ranges marked the land as far as the eye could see. Above him, the black sky was endless, impossible, and so beautiful. The blue and green sphere, Aurus, hovered above him, half of its surface coated in a darkness more profound than the void behind it.

A shadow passed over him, swift and silent. Though his mind jolted with alarm, his body remained calm. He looked up, watching as a majestic green dragon soared through the cloudless sky. His heart swelled with conflicting emotions at the site of the creature. Awe and terror. Admiration and dread. Love and hate. This being, resplendent and mighty beyond anything he could ever hope to be, inspired his heart to flutter, and it drove him to kneel.

Beneath him, the ground trembled, and the sound of something hollow splitting open echoed through his mind. He heard a roar from far below, muffled by the ground. It was calling out to him, commanding him. It was fearful. It was lonely. It wanted the warmth of companionship, and it was calling on him to satisfy it. Skunk gave himself over to the command, unable to resist even if he had wanted to, and frantically began to dig. The stone was hard and dense, leaving his fingers bleeding and his arms burning with effort.

But still, he dug. He dug and he dug, tearing away thin scatterings of glowing stone with every painful scrape.

The earth trembled, and the roar came again, louder. Its demands expanded with its volume. It desired more than just companionship, now.

It was demanding meat.

Food.

A meal.

Skunk felt the impulse to obey, to feed his master. He lifted his eyes and scanned the landscape, but there was no meat to be had. It was all below, far beneath his feet where he could not reach it. He would just have to dig all the harder, he thought.

But the master corrected him. It was hungry, yes, but not for any meat from here. The master was starving, but the lumavores and the ongloreks would not satisfy. Meat alone would never be enough to make the master whole.

The cry came again, louder, desperate, furious at Skunk's hesitation. It was promising a life of agony if he did not satisfy its impossible request. Fearful, he looked around, trying in vain to find something that would satiate the growing demand. He scoured the hills and the mountains, the valleys, and the trenches of his beautiful home, but there was nothing to be found. His master needed to eat. There was nothing to eat. His master *needed to eat*.

As if in impatience, an impossible force tugged at Skunk's chin, forcing him

to raise his eyes and look above. The blue world loomed larger in his eyes. Closer.
So close, that he wondered if he might be able to reach out and touch it. If he
were to jump, would he fall into the sky toward it?

He sniffed at the air, and he smelled it. Living flesh, thriving life, and
endless vanity. It sent his stomach rumbling. Profound hunger overcame him,
joined by blinding rage. He lifted his hands out, reaching for the world. The meat
for his master was there, he knew it.

He would hunt. He would track down every scrap of flesh, and then, finally,
his master would be satisfied.

He took a step forward. His clawed toe brushed against a loose stone.
Ordinarily, he would have never given such a thing a second thought. But it drew
his attention. Curious, he looked down. A lone ringstone sat at his feet, rocking
slightly in place. He stood at the zenith of a high, narrow ridge. The stone was
balanced precariously on the edge, ready to tumble far away from him and vanish
into the indistinct landscape for the rest of time.

He teetered, and it began to roll.

Skunk took it in his hand. He could not understand why, but it felt familiar
to him, somehow. He lifted it to examine it more closely, his master's rising
demands forgotten for the moment. The stone rolled easily between his fingers,
and it pulsed softly with a comforting light. He knew this stone. It was Danica's
shard of the Sunstone. What was it doing here?

He blinked.

Danica. The dwarf woman.

He remembered her.

He recalled their chat under the starlight, and how he had confessed to her
all the reasons why he devoted himself so much to the people of Addernotch. She
had listened to him so patiently and had even stopped him when he was about to
speak of the most painful memory of all.

His left hand tingled. He looked down at the horrific scar that ran down
the length of his finger from his mangled claw. The memory of a searing agony,
of digging a knife under his own nail burned through his mind. These claws had
torn human flesh and been torn in turn. In Addernotch.

His home.

Skunk doubled over, his stomach lurching and his mind spinning.
Conflicting emotions and memories warred for dominance, leaving him dizzy and
disoriented. He looked up again, at this beautiful, perfect, glowing land. *This* was
his home. It had been for all of time. It was where he belonged. He knew this in
his heart of hearts, in his bones, in the very blood pumping through his veins.

But it wasn't.

He had no memories of this place. But he remembered Addernotch, the
men and women who had tolerated him and even accepted him for so long, even
after he had torn the flesh from one of their own. *Addernotch* was his home. It
had been for all his life. He knew this in his heart of hearts, in his bones, in the

blood that screamed in confused agony beneath his scales.

Addernotch was home.

But it couldn't be.

His home was here... wasn't it?

His master roared, and somewhere far away, the earth tore open, cracking like the shell of an egg. Skunk shook his head, his free hand rising to clutch at his temple as if that might stop his rapidly rising migraine. "What's going on...?" he choked out, barely able to find his voice. The master demanded meat. His family was meat. His master *demanded* meat.

"N-no..." He protested weakly, falling to his knees. Skunk's skull was burning. It felt hot and dense, as if filled with molten lead and soon to burst. His thoughts boiled and bubbled, two beliefs clashing behind his eyelids like armies at war. He crumpled, writhing on the cold ground in agony. He saw the world around him cracking like glass as the blue world descended. It was like the shadow of death itself had taken the form of a planet. He felt grief and rage, and the impossible desire for vengeance. His master demanded meat. His master demanded revenge!

And then he saw the face of his family. His friends. He saw Sylvia's face smiling back at him.

Meat. All meat. All viable.

His master demanded.

But Skunk refused.

If this was the meat his master wanted, then his master could starve.

The master roared in impotent rage, and the world shattered.

All that was left was the glow of Danica's ringstone.

Skunk awoke with a start, bolting upright, his breath heavy. His mind was a fractured mess of lingering contradictions, scrambling to put itself back together. His eyes darted about, wild and frenzied. He blinked, and details in his environment began to resolve into clarity.

The bars of cages. The low-hanging roof of a kobold burrow. The sounds of snoring and deep breaths. The overbearing stench of body sweat, dried blood, bad breath, and cramped occupation.

He took a few deep breaths, his heart slowing and his mind calming as he realized where he was and what had happened. He was still in his cage. Everyone else was asleep, and up until a moment ago, so had he. He had been dreaming again, though the more he thought of it, the more the events of the dream fled his recollection. All he could recall was a glow and the familiar sense of being commanded — a command that he had refused to obey, judging by the lingering pain in his skull, a pain which grew worse when he tried to think about it.

Letting out a groan, Skunk leaned back against the bars, grateful that his cloak and shirt staved off the worst of the pain from the jagged edges. He wanted to close his eyes and go back to sleep, but that wasn't going to happen. His mind was too active. And besides all of that, he'd had nothing to do but sit in one place and occasionally nibble on meat for the last few days. He hadn't been able to burn off any energy, leaving him twitchy and restless. He was practically vibrating. Not even the gradual onset of lethargy was sufficient to lull him back to slumber. Not yet, anyway. And so, grumbling with dismay, he resigned himself to his fate.

Behind him, he heard someone shifting, and a gentle voice spoke to him. "Can't sleep?" It was Sylvia.

Skunk grunted. "Nope. Sorry. Did I wake you?"

"Yes."

"Sorry."

"It's alright," Sylvia assured him. "Bad dreams?"

"Something like that, yeah."

Sylvia hummed. She was sitting with her back to his. Skunk glanced over his shoulder, catching a glimpse of Sylvia's torn dress out of the corner of his eye. "What about you?"

"My eyes hurt," Sylvia said simply. "They've been burning."

"You might have an infection," Skunk commented quietly, the uncomfortable notion making him cringe. "They never cleaned the wound, did they?"

"They cleaned the blindfold before they made me wear it," Sylvia clarified. "But I'm not sure what good that's really going to do me."

Skunk winced, his heart twisting at the reminder of just how horribly Sylvia had been treated. He looked down. "I'm sorry I couldn't protect you," he apologized again. He knew there was nothing he could have done, but he still felt the need to say it.

Sylvia let off a quiet breath. "Skunk," she said, but she didn't say anything else. To be fair, she did not have to. The meaning was clear to Skunk, and he couldn't keep himself from smiling slightly.

The two fell into a comfortable silence. It was their way, but it also came with the benefit of not waking the others. Still, Skunk couldn't be idle. He closed his eyes, focusing instead on his dream again.

Again, he found that the only thing he could remember was the glow of the Sunstone shard. He wondered why it lingered in his mind so. He wondered if he ought to ask Sylvia, but he doubted she would have any insights. So he closed his eyes and tried to sleep.

Things were quiet.

Time passed.

Skunk wasn't sure how long it was before something broke that silence. But eventually, Danica stirred. Skunk looked to see her shaking her head. She was mumbling to herself, her voice low and troubled.

"Lorok…"

Skunk blinked, recalling her mount. He had never gotten the full story on the creature, but there was no denying that the shelldigger was important to her. Skunk had lost all track of him during the fight with Karak. It was impossible to know Lorok's fate, whether the animal was dead or fled. Skunk wasn't sure which would be worse: knowing Lorok was dead, or never knowing for sure.

Danica twitched again, her grumbling growing in volume, and Skunk realized that her dream must have been more of a nightmare. He put on his best smile, not caring that she wouldn't be able to see it, and lightly kicked Danica's foot. A soft thump reverberated through the chamber, and Danica awoke with a sharp inhale. She looked around for a moment, eyes wide. They fluttered closed a second later, accompanied by a low growl.

"Dammit," she grunted.

"Can't sleep?" Skunk asked, echoing Sylvia's question from a moment ago.

Danica shot him a look, not knowing that her glare was angled a few degrees to his right. She didn't say anything. She turned her head to look away, her expression darkening.

Skunk's smile faded. "Me neither,"

Danica grunted.

Figuring that she wasn't in a talking mood, Skunk shrugged and fell silent, closing his eyes. He didn't have to wait long, however, before Danica broke the silence again.

"Karak is Marus," she said quietly, her voice laced with disbelief.

Skunk nodded. "Seems that way."

"How? I still labor to believe it's possible.'

Skunk shrugged his shoulders. "I'm no magi, but he did say they worked some sort of magic on him to make him that way. It's gotta be the runes. And mom did say he was enchanted when we first faced him, so maybe part of that made him like this," he guessed.

Danica scoffed, her brow furrowing. "Maybe. But to take a human and turn him into that… *thing,* they'd need a pretty powerful—"

Danica's voice suddenly cut off, her eyes widening in shock. Skunk came to the same conclusion a second later. "The Sunstone," he realized.

"That son of a bitch," Danica seethed, her teeth showing faintly in the darkness. "How *dare* he? That's not what the Sunstone is supposed to be used for! Is *that* why he took it? Did he steal it just so it could be used to turn him into a demidragon!?"

Skunk hummed, his face scrunching up as he thought it all over. "Karak said that stealing it was supposed to prove his commitment, right? And they need luma for the 'young master' to hatch. The Sunstone's pretty big you said, so it'd put out a lot of luma, right?"

Danica's scowl deepened. "So that's it, then. The beating heart of my home was carved out to birth a *dragon*."

Skunk nodded quietly. "That'd be my best guess."

"Fuck," Danica breathed. Her head tilted back til it hit the wall of the cage, resonating with a gentle thud.

They were quiet for a while. Skunk tried to smile and tried to find some reason to be optimistic, but none were forthcoming. His smile disappeared. "Karak talked to me some more after he knocked you out," he finally said. "He said that the young master's supposed to wake up tomorrow. I think we're out of time."

Danica looked down, closing her eyes as the unsettling realization fell over her. She took in a slow, deep breath, then let it out in a measured sigh. "So. We're dead, then."

"No," Skunk shot down almost immediately, although he wasn't sure he believed it. "We'll find a way out of this. I know we will."

Danica snorted. "Optimism is all well and good, kid," she said bluntly. "But without a plan, it won't do us much good."

"We'll think of something!" Skunk stressed. "I did not come this far just to be turned into dragon jerky!"

"Do you have a plan?"

Skunk opened his mouth, then cringed and looked away. "Uh... no, not really. Not yet," he admitted.

He'd seen more of their environment than anyone else, he felt at home in it, *built* for it, but he still couldn't see any way out, try as he might to think of one. They couldn't even get out of these damn cages, the bars were too thick. They had no weapons, no idea how this place was laid out, and they were hopelessly outnumbered. Even if they did somehow break out of their cages, the kobolds would pick them apart.

A lump formed in his throat. The imminent possibility of his death had been looming over him for a while now, but he hadn't been considering it seriously. He hadn't had the chance, or he didn't want to. But now, he had no choice, and the fear and terror that came with it was almost overwhelming. He sucked in a deep breath, starting to tremble like a leaf. "I... Oh, Gods, I don't wanna die," he whimpered.

"Skunk," Sylvia whispered behind him. He could tell she wanted to say something more, but this time, she couldn't. There weren't any words she could say that would take this fear away, and she knew it.

Something moved. Skunk looked up to see Amelia standing up. He jumped, having not realized she was awake. She closed the gap between them, gently stepping over Tamaya, and sat down beside him. "Hey," she whispered. "Come here."

Skunk knew that tone of voice. It was the same one she used to use when he was really little, whenever she needed to comfort him. He sniffled and leaned into his mother's side, screwing his eyes shut as they started to mist over. "Mom," he choked out, barely able to keep his voice down. "I'm scared."

"I know, honey," Amelia whispered to him, giving him as much space to try and cuddle up to her as possible. "I'm scared, too."

"W-what do we do?" he asked, looking up into his mother's eyes, desperate for a plan, desperate for her to come up with some kind of solution. In his mind, he imagined she already had something figured out. She had been in so many precarious situations throughout her life, whether it be hunting down relics for her old collector master or going on the prowl alongside Tamaya. She must have been in a situation at least sort of like this.

"I don't know," she whispered to him quietly, and his desperate hopes shattered like glass. She looked down into his eyes, somehow finding them through the pitch darkness. "But you're right. We *will* figure something out. Whatever happens, you'll be fine."

Skunk sniffled again. He felt like a little kid again, but he couldn't find it in himself to care how childish he sounded. He pressed himself tight to his mother's form, desperate for her warmth. "D-do you promise?" he asked, too scared to be ashamed of how pathetic he sounded.

Amelia lowered her head to plant a gentle kiss on top of his head. "I promise," she whispered to him. "No matter what happens, I won't let you die down here."

Skunk wasn't sure he believed her. It was so like a parent to lie and tell their children everything was going to be fine to make them feel better. But he had no other hopes to go off of, and so he chose to put his faith in her. She hadn't let him down yet, after all. He nodded into her, closing his eyes again. "Okay. And I'll protect you, too. We'll make it out of this together."

Amelia laughed softly. "Thank you, Skunk. I love you."

And then Amelia began to hum her lullaby.

Skunk immediately latched onto it like a lifeline, listening intently. Bit by bit, the familiar melody wormed its way into his thoughts, reawakening his oldest, happiest memories. He began to relax, and despite his fear and his dread, he was able to believe that it was all going to be okay. His mother would come up with a plan, and they would all get out of there alive.

That belief, however misguided it was, was finally enough to calm him, and slowly but surely, Skunk was able to drift back to sleep. As he did, the Sunstone shard against his scales tingled just a little warmer.

Justice for the Dragons

Amelia's lullaby filled Skunk's sleep in a way it hadn't in many years. The gentle rise and fall of the notes calmed him, chasing away his nightmares. In their place, he found himself reliving his earliest memories.

Poking his nose into Addernotch's only inn, scarfing down scraps of uncooked meat not meant for him. It had been like a little paradise, one where he could gorge himself to his heart's content. That paradise had ended when the innkeeper and Amelia appeared in the doorway. Oh, the scolding he had received that day. He might have been more upset by the event, had it not been for the spark of amusement in Amelia's eyes, and that loving, endeared smile as she laughed in exasperation.

The words said to him that day were lost on him now, little more than half-remembered mumbles contrasted against mothering love. It had sent his still-developing mind tilting in confusion. In the end, he had simply burped up a scrap of goat meat, and Amelia had laughed again.

There was nothing profound about the memory. Nothing special, nothing clairvoyant. It was just a happy memory. One of many he had the chance to revisit in that last slumber before the end. But he couldn't wander through the past forever. Time waited for no one, least of all him.

A sudden lurch dragged Skunk out of his slumber. He opened his eyes to see dozens of kobolds in the chamber. There was an excited energy about them as they split into groups of four to roll the cages away. The prisoners, realizing something was happening, began raising their voices in a fearful murmur.

Skunk shivered and pressed himself back into Amelia, who was still right where she had been before. "M-mom?" he asked, shivering slightly as it dawned on him what was happening. "*Please* tell me we have a plan?"

"I'm thinking," Was her simple response. "But whatever Karak and his goons are doing, they're doing it now."

Skunk's heart shriveled with dread. He turned back to everyone else in the cage, his eyes wide with terror. "Any ideas? Anyone?" he whispered desperately. His hands pulled instinctively at his bonds, to no avail.

Tamaya, who now sat directly across from him, grimaced. She cast her eyes about. Hers was not an expression of confidence. "None that would work now," she said grimly. "Too many guards. Any effort we tried would end before it even began."

"So we're just giving up?!" Skunk demanded.

"Skunk, calm down," Amelia cut in, her eyes firm and her jaw set. "I promised you I would keep you safe, and I *will*. But panic won't get us anywhere. Take a breath and *focus*. Pay attention. Look for an opportunity."

Skunk gaped at her for a moment, silently awed by her calm composure. Still, he did his best to follow her advice. He was in the middle of taking in a breath when, suddenly, the cage beside theirs rolled into motion. His eyes widened, and his inhale turned into a horrified gasp.

"Sylvia!" he cried as his friend was wheeled away. "No! No, no, no! Bring her back!"

Crack!

The butt end of a spear struck Skunk between the eyes, sending him sprawling back with a high-pitched yelp. Stars exploded across his vision, his skull flaring with agony. His horns banged painfully off of the bars of the cage, dazing him. He shook his head a few times to chase away the fog, then looked up at the guard that had struck him. The creature smirked at him with amusement and contempt. It cackled, then took one of the handles of his cage.

The wheels squealed, loud and maddening after days of stillness. Skunk squirmed in discomfort. Much to his envy, Tamaya's ears folded back, while to his pity, Amelia and Danica had to grit their teeth and suffer through it.

"Where are you taking us?" The dwarf asked.

The kobold answered her with a growl, making it clear that there would be no talking. The callous dismissal filled Skunk with frustration, but he restrained himself. He turned his attention to the cage ahead of his own. Sylvia sat with her back against the far wall of her cage, her head facing him. Her brow was furrowed in concern.

"I-I'm okay, Sylvia!" he called to her. "J-just hang on! We'll find a way out of this!"

The kobolds pulling his cage yapped at him, cowing him into silence. Thankfully, they did not strike him again, and up ahead, Sylvia smiled in relief and nodded. She was placing her trust in him, it seemed. He just hoped he could find a way to keep his word.

The journey through the tunnels was long and maddening. They took turn after turn, scrambling Skunk's senses the whole way, just like before. More than that, however, the prisoners were growing more fearful, raising their voices from anxious murmurs to panicking shouts. Each one that dared to speak for more than a second swiftly found themselves struck violently into silence.

Skunk kept to the front of the cage, trying to see where they were going, looking for anything they could use to get out of this. While he could see in the dark, even his eyes had their limits, and his vision did not extend forever. He imagined this was a byproduct of having spent his entire life above ground. His 'kin' could probably see perfectly fine. Either that, or they knew these labyrinthian tunnels like the back of their hands.

Eventually, the tunnel ballooned out in front of them, the ceiling sloping up and away while the walls pushed out to the sides. The long, single-file line of cages spread out into even rows. Thankfully, this put Sylvia's cage beside Skunk's, allowing him to better keep an eye on her. He wanted to reach out to her, to hold her hand and tell her it would be alright, but his hands were still bound. All he could do was watch and wait.

"Is that light?" Someone asked from up ahead. Skunk turned and followed the man's gaze. Up above, the tunnel expanded once more, this time into a monolithic chamber bathed in silver and green light. He could smell charcoal and burning meat even from here, and the musk of countless kobolds. It made his nose itch.

"Fire?" he asked in surprise when he realized the green light was flickering, and he could hear the crackling. "Is that *green* fire?!"

Amelia came up beside him, squinting into the light. "Dragonfire," she breathed in amazement.

Skunk tilted his head at her. "Dragonfire?" he echoed.

"If you believe the legends, Dragonfire matches the color of the dragon that created it and burns far hotter than any other flame could hope to match. The sort of heat that reduces bodies to ashes in moments. I've never seen it before, though. I thought it was just a myth."

"You were wrong," Danica grunted.

"So a dragon made that?" Skunk asked fearfully.

"Must have."

"But who could have done it?" Skunk asked quietly. "The Young Master hasn't hatched yet, has he?"

Amelia's expression darkened considerably, and a creeping feeling of dread blossomed deep in Skunk's guts.

The cages were wheeled into the chamber, and Skunk realized with a gasp of shock just how enormous it was. There were countless tunnels in the walls, venturing into different parts of the burrow, out of which came dozens of kobolds. They took up positions all around the chamber, clustering together into small groups. Mounds and piles of ringstones sat at the edge of the chamber, encircling the fire in a mocking recreation of the pale ring. Strings of luma flowed from each, vanishing into the flames.

On the far end of the chamber, a yawning hole in the wall vanished into an abyss of absolute darkness. A darkness so deep that not even Skunk's vision, aided by the light of the fire, could pierce it. A void in his vision, a perfect emptiness that sent his scales tingling in fear. A warm draft came from that abyss, damp and sticky, but electric in its intensity.

Above it all, suspended from the ceiling, was the largest, most beautiful ringstone Skunk had ever seen. It glowed a faint yellow, Its surface covered in paragraphs of runes, none of which he could read. Like all the others, the luma of this stone flowed gently into the flames.

"The Sunstone," Danica whispered, confirming Skunk's suspicions. "Juna's tits, they've *ruined* it."

"How?" Skunk asked.

Danica jerked her head at it. "Those aren't the original runes. They scraped them away and wrote new ones — *damn* them! Even if I brought it back to Stonefall, it'd be useless!"

Skunk looked at the Sunstone, his heart falling. It was a thing of beauty. It was a terrible shame what it was now being used for.

His disappointment was replaced by fear when he lowered his eyes. Karak was waiting for them, his hands folded behind his back. He patiently scrutinized each cage as they were arranged in a semi-circle around him. The voices of the prisoners once again rose as the people saw the face of their hated captor

Danica, in particular, came forward to slam her shoulder hard into the bars. "Marus!" she bellowed, her eyes wide and blazing. "Let me out of here, you coward! Face me properly!"

Karak smiled at her. "I fail to see what I stand to gain from heeding that request, so I think not," he droned before turning his attention to the others. He bore their words for a short time, then flared his wings and took a step forward. Skunk cringed, cowering in place as a deafening roar befitting a dragon echoed through the chamber from Karak's lips. So loud was the call that the prisoners' cries of rage and defiance turned to fearful shouts. Skunk, in particular, wished his hands were free so he could cover his ears.

When the roar ended, the chamber was left silent, save for the blazing of the fire and the amused cackling of the kobolds.

Satisfied, Karak held his arms out wide and grinned. He spun to face the surrounding kobolds and called to them. "Brothers and sisters of the Emerald Fire! For far too long have you waited for this moment! For decades, centuries, *a millennium,* you have stood deprived of direction, deprived of hope, and deprived of the chance to take vengeance upon those who have for so long spat upon and disgraced the memory of your beloved home! For too long have you been forced to watch as these ignorant mongrels take up the last remnants of your homeland and repeat the sins of those who brought you to the brink of extinction!"

The kobolds cheered, many of them stamping their feet or slamming their tails into the stone. Skunk looked around, staggered by the unity on display. These weren't pre-formed squads of soldiers, he realized. These were *friend* groups. He saw how many of them were grinning at each other, and was reminded of how he might look when something exciting happened. The similarities he suddenly saw in them were jarring, and for a moment, he wondered if he made a mistake in turning down Karak's offer. If he had accepted it, he would be out there, among the other kobolds, no longer facing imminent death.

But it only took one glance at his neighbors, friends, and family locked in cages to remind him why he had refused, and why he always would.

Karak continued his speech. "But rejoice, for your long wait is at an end! The Sunstone, taken back from the thieving hands of the dwarves of Stonefall, has answered our desires! The blood of our prey has served its purpose! Today is the final day! The shell shall shatter, and a new voice shall enter the world! Rejoice, for today, the Young Master will join his loyal servants! *Rejoice!* For today, a new dragon shall be born! Today, our mission shall, at long last, begin!"

The voices of the kobolds rose higher and higher with every call for rejoice, their manic glee almost deafening. And with every word, Skunk frantically searched for a way out. But there was nothing! He had no tools, no weapons, no keys, and Karak was right there! No effort would make it more than a step before it ended! But still, he searched.

Karak gestured to one of the cages, his grin growing. "But first, the hand of mercy must be extended! To all of you, men and women of Aurus, I offer a chance for survival — nay, not just survival, but *redemption*. Yours are lives stained with a sin you can never undo. But you are not wholly to blame for this, and you may yet be absolved! Only join hands with this horde, pledge yourself to the service of the Young Master, and not only shall your life be spared, but you shall be given the chance to make something of yourself! To stand united with a righteous crusade! All the evils of your world, all the injustices of human nobility, every ill you've ever been met with! In time, *all* shall be dismantled! And in time, those who swear fealty and serve faithfully shall have the chance to rebuild as you see fit!"

Skunk expected everyone to say 'no' right away. But there was a long silence that followed the offer, and a few people looked unsure. Skunk's heart skipped a beat as he saw some of his neighbors looking amongst themselves, fearful and unsure.

They were afraid. Some of them might do anything, literally anything, to save themselves.

Skunk would not allow that. He couldn't.

"No!" he shouted, standing up to glare at Karak. "None of us! Not one!"

"What are you doing?!" A nearby woman demanded. "You're going to get us all killed!"

Skunk shot her a glare and shook his head. "Better that than turn our backs on our homes! Our friends, and our *families* who are waiting for us to come home! Do you wanna march back down to Addernotch alongside a host of the same people that attacked us?! What would everyone think?!"

He jerked his nose at Karak. "I'm not a human. I'm a kobold. But I don't care about your stupid dragon, or your 'Young Master,' or any of your big ambitions! You, Karak, attacked us! You *killed* us! And now you're asking us to either *betray* the people we love, or die in a fire! But unlike you, I have enough faith in *my* people to see the good in them! And I don't believe *any* of us are going to side with *you*!"

There was a short silence. For a moment, Skunk feared his impassioned words would amount to nothing. But then, to his relief, many of the people in the cages nodded amongst themselves, and none rose to accept Karak's offer.

Karak nodded. "Well spoken. Such a pity it serves no purpose," he said before leveling a finger at a cage on the far end of the line. "We begin with you."

The cage housed two women and three men, all adults. Skunk recognized them. He did not know their names, but he had seen them in the village market from time to time. The solidarity of the victims crumbled, replaced by screams of panic as the cage was suddenly shoved forward toward the flames. They cried out for someone to help them, throwing themselves against the bars.

"No!" Skunk screamed, pressing himself against the biting metal. "Don't do this! Karak! STOP!"

The cage fell into the flames, and the screams of fear turned to howls of agony. The stench of burning meat struck Skunk like a hammer to the skull, sending him reeling back, wide-eyed and mortified. He could see their silhouettes thrashing about, their bodies shriveling and blackening as the flames ate away at them.

And then the Sunstone glowed brighter.

Skunk watched as threads of silver light rose out of the crumbling bodies.

Luma. It wove elegantly through the air in a manner that did not match the atrocity taking place below. The threads coiled and spun up to the Sunstone, mingled with the gentle aura of its light and then dipped down like the arc of a seagull diving for the waves. The threads vanished into the flames and something hidden within.

Skunk felt his heart quicken as the flames dulled for only a moment, allowing him to confirm once and for all what he knew already was there.

An enormous white egg, unharmed by the flames.

A dragon egg.

And it was starting to hatch.

Skunk couldn't truly understand the complexity of what was happening. He did not know how it was that Karak was able to rip the luma out of living beings the way he was, but it did not matter. What mattered was that if that egg hatched, the kobolds would have a new leader — a proper leader. A successor to Azada who would unite the scattered hordes of green scales to wreak havoc upon the people of Aurus.

And they couldn't count on a dragon with a good heart like Thalgrum to save them again.

"*You son of a bitch!*" Danica screamed, struggling in vain against her bonds. "That's not what the Sunstone is supposed to do!"

Karak grinned at her, a sickening look that Skunk could not imagine ever being on the face of a human. He beckoned at one of the kobolds, and another cage was sent rolling into the flames. Skunk's heart fell once again, guilt flooding him as more people died screaming, people he'd just talked into rejecting an offer that might have saved their lives. *Did I do the right thing?*

More luma rose to feed the waking infant.

Snapping out of his brief trance, Skunk turned his eyes back to hunting for an escape. And this time, something caught his attention.

As the third cage was wheeled into the flames, and the Sunstone flared, Skunk noticed Karak's runes glowing with it. At the same time, the Sunstone shard, still tucked away safely in Skunk's shirt, warmed up against his scales. It was getting hotter and hotter, to the point it was almost uncomfortable.

It's reacting, Skunk realized with wide eyes. Whatever Karak was doing, whatever wretched spell he was working, it was tied to the Sunstone, and that included the fragment Skunk had. *Is he drawing power from it?*

Skunk frantically scanned them both, Sunstone and Karak, and realized that the runes were the same on both of them. The words carved into the massive ringstone were the same as the runes carved into Karak's flesh. His eyes widened in realization, and he remembered something he had overheard not long ago in Seto's schoolhouse.

"The pale ring is the birthplace of all magic in Aurus. The white light it emits is known as luma — shortened from 'Luminescence'. It is this light that serves as the bedrock foundation of all forms of spellcraft. And all known forms of life have at least a tiny spark of it buried deep within them. Many great people study for years, learning how to connect the Luma inside of them to a shard of the ring. These men and women are known as magi, and by calling upon the luma of their attuned stone, they are able to bend the world around them, sparking fire where none existed before, imbuing a man's body with enhanced strength, and even granting a flightless fox the ability to soar through the skies. So long as their attuned ringstone remains intact and within their reach, a magi can work wonders."

Skunk realized what he had to do. It was a long shot, but it was better than nothing. He squirmed, trying to lift the back of his shirt up, no doubt looking like a fool but not able to care.

As he worked, a fourth cage was wheeled into the flames. The screams spurred him on. He had to move faster!

Finally, he pulled up his shirt, and the ringstone fell into his hands. He clutched it tight, feeling its warmth. A sudden surge of awareness flooded his senses as if he had just awoken from a particularly restful nap. He had no time to try and make sense of the unusual sensation, however. He closed his eyes and focused on the stone.

Another cage. More screams. The egg was shaking even more. The dragon within was stirring to life.

"Please," Skunk whispered as if in prayer. "I'm begging you, whoever or whatever you are. If you can hear me, then please, *please,* help us. Let my friends and I out of our cages."

The stone, to his shock, began to grow warmer in his hands. He heard Tamaya gasping behind him, no doubt catching sight of the stone's light between his fingers.

He ignored her.

He felt something, a tug on his chest in the direction of the stone in his hand *and* the Sunstone above. He felt torn, pulled in two directions by impossible forces even as another current tried to force him back down.

Another cage.

More dead.

More guilt for those he had failed to save.

Fire burned in his skull and pumped through his veins. His desperate pleading grew in fervor. "If you can listen to Karak, then you can listen to me!" he insisted, the stone growing so hot in his hands it was almost burning. "Even if only once! I don't care how, just set us free! Give us a fighting chance! Karak is wrong, and he has to be stopped!"

In front of the cages, Karak paused. He lifted his arm to stare at his runes as they began to flicker. "What...?" he breathed. Then, with a gasp, he spun to face the Sunstone.

Skunk's grip on the shard tightened, and he felt a tingling sensation shooting up his arms to pool in his shoulders, then his chest. His lungs ached, burning from the strain of whatever magic he was working, but he forced himself to forge ahead. His whisper rose in volume to something audible to those beside him. "Set us free... Set us free. Set us free!"

Danica turned to him, her eyes settling on the now blinding light pulsing out from between his fingers. She gaped in awe. "That's my..."

Karak spun around again, his eyes settling on Skunk. He bristled in fury. Had Skunk been looking, he would have also seen the rising panic. Karak's hand flew to his sword. "*No!*" he shouted, taking a step.

Skunk lifted his eyes. He stared at the Sunstone, and in that split second, he cast his thoughts to the people he was trying to save. His mother beside him, Danica and Tamaya, Sylvia in the cage next to his own, and everyone else. Every face, every prisoner, looking at him with wide-eyed confusion. But there was a spark of understanding, a single flicker of hope in this hopeless situation. And so, with every shred of conviction and love for his pack he could muster, Skunk shouted at the Sunstone at the top of his lungs. "*Set us free!*"

And, miraculously, the Sunstone answered.

The shard flared, burning his palms. The roar of the fire and the chattering of the kobolds were overwhelmed as an expanding dome of luma flooded the chamber. It washed over Skunk and his cage, warm and soothing, utterly harmless. But then came the sound of shrieking metal, shattering chains, and screaming kobolds.

All at once, the bonds of metal around Skunk's wrists and tail dissolved into particulates of shrapnel. The jagged metal bars of every cage were blown wide open and torn violently from their bases, clattering to the stone floor. Karak was thrown off his feet by the pulse, his wings catching a rush of power that determined he was its enemy. He cried out, soaring back into the flames.

It all happened so fast. The dome of magic rushed and expanded so quickly that Skunk might have missed it had he blinked. Every cage came undone, every shackle dissolved, and every kobold caught in the way of the blast was thrown to the ground with cries of pain and shock. Some slammed into the walls with the crunch of shattering bones, while others toppled over to be impaled upon stalagmites rising around the edge of the chamber.

For one hellish second it was chaos and screaming.

And then it was quiet.

The shard in Skunk's hands rapidly cooled. His tail swished happily behind him, glad to be free at long last, and his wrists burned with delight as he lifted the Sunstone shard to his face to look at it. The last flickering hints of light vanished from its surface. Whatever power it may have once had was now spent.

It had given them their chance, but it could do no more.

"Thank you," he whispered.

"What... happened?" Danica asked, stunned.

Tamaya, however, needed no explanation. The kobolds, disoriented and off balance, were rising to their feet. The ry'thar warrior was not about to allow them to recover.

With a guttural growl, she took up one of the fallen bars like a spear, charged the first kobold she saw, and ran the jagged tip through the beast's chest. It punctured through in a spray of gore, and the kobold toppled back with barely more than a gasp. The moment its body hit the cold earth, Tamaya lifted her head and roared, her voice echoing all through the chamber.

The meaning was clear.

It was time to fight back.

In the span of a second, the scattered prisoners rose, recognizing the call to arms for what it was. The captured ry'thar in their midst sprung into motion, claws and teeth bared. The humans of the prisoners, some of whom Skunk recognized as members of the militia back home, took up bars from their cages as Tamaya had, or the dropped weapons of their guards to join in the fray themselves.

Beside Skunk, Danica grinned, and then hurled herself into the fray with her fists, loosing a battle cry as she crushed her knuckles into the face of the first kobold she reached. It staggered back, dropping the axe it had just drawn. Danica grinned, took the axe, and took its head off with a wide swing.

Amelia took the sword from Tamaya's fallen victim and turned to Skunk. She smiled at him. "Well done. Now fight!"

Skunk nodded and gladly accepted the sword as Amelia tossed it to him. He'd rather be using a bow, but he wasn't about to be a picky beggar.

The kobolds were starting to form together, trying to organize and fight back against the sudden offensive, but the surprise of the rapid change in the scenario had left many of them off-balance and unsure of what to do. Most of the kobolds hadn't even been armed and wore no armor to speak of. This had been a birthing ceremony, after all. Nobody assembled had expected it to become a warzone. As a result, the prisoners had a chance not only to rapidly thin the numbers of their enemies but also to organize themselves.

"If you can fight, grab a weapon!" Amelia shouted as she ran to get a weapon for herself. Her target, a kobold with a mace, turned to her just in time for her to drive her knuckles into its throat. It gasped and took a step back, enabling Amelia to grab its wrist and twist, sending the mace to the floor. With a grunt, she kicked the kobold in the chest, sending it crumpling to the ground before scooping up its mace and turning to drive the weapon into the shoulder of another charging from the side. Bone and scales splintered, sending the poor wretch crumpling. That done, Amelia lifted her mace high and called out again. "Form up around anyone who can't fight and keep them safe! We're fighting our way out of here!"

Tamaya echoed the command in her language, and the ry'thar rallied to her call at once. The humans followed their lead, moving swiftly to form a protective wall around those who were either too weak or too old to fight back.

The kobolds were quickly rallying together, their shock and confusion wearing off. The guards and warriors took up their arms while those who had been here purely for the festivities scattered out through the tunnels, no doubt to raise the alarm.

Skunk looked on at it all. They weren't in the clear yet, but he couldn't help but smile. He scanned the scattering crowd, bracing for an adversary to come his way. His eyes found one kobold in particular who stood out. She was not green like all the others, but an aquatic teal.

He blinked at her. She was looking right at him. She held a sword of her own, but she was in no battle stance. Time seemed to slow as they made eye contact.

Suddenly, she reversed her grip on her sword, leaned back, and threw it like a javelin. Skunk yelped and ducked to the side, but it was not necessary. The sword had not been intended for him.

The blade plunged into the chest of a kobold that had been sneaking up behind Skunk. Its heart skewered, it fell to the floor in a lifeless heap.

Confused, Skunk turned back to his unexpected savior. She smiled softly at him, almost sadly, and shook her head. "Not you," she said simply. "I will not fight *you*. Never you."

Skunk blinked at her. He had no chance to question her, however. A new adversary arrived. A burly brute of a kobold with enormous fangs and a horned brow charged at him, lifting a gnarled axe for a swing. Skunk snapped out of his trance and quickly backstepped. He twisted his waist, allowing the downward blow to pass him by. He spied the kobold's eyes widening in shock, but the big guy had no time to reposition. Skunk took the opening left by his swing and plunged his sword deep into the kobold's gut.

The brute staggered back a step, snarling in pain as Skunk's sword ripped out of him. He raised his axe to offer a counter, but Amelia had other ideas. A low whoosh and a gust of air flew past Skunk's head as she charged by and brought her mace into the kobold's chest. Blood sprayed out of its mouth as its lungs folded under the force of the impact, and it toppled lifelessly to the earth.

Amelia spat at the corpse before turning to shout over the chaos of the battlefield. "Anyone with polearms, form an inner line! Support those with shorter weapons!"

The mass of people quickly scrambled to accommodate the command, forming up and leveling their stolen spears and serrated iron bars over the shoulders of their comrades, making any advance from the kobolds more dangerous. Skunk turned to join the formation but hesitated. He looked back toward the teal kobold he had seen a moment ago.

She was gone. He just saw the tip of her tail disappearing into one of the tunnels.

"Skunk, come on!" Amelia shouted. Skunk startled, then turned to find a place in the formation. He felt a slight tingle of discomfort when one of the bars was leveled over his shoulder, a little too close to his neck for his liking. He glanced back at the wielder and saw a human man looking down at him.

Skunk smiled at him. "Got my back?" he asked hopefully, wagging his tail.

The human swallowed heavily, then nodded. "Y-yeah," he said, then focused past Skunk at the advancing enemy.

The group of survivors was starting to make their way back toward the tunnel exiting the chamber. Skunk looked over his shoulder for any sign of Sylvia. Thankfully, she was alive and well in the heart of the pack — although visibly fearful.

"Just hang on, Sylvia!" Skunk called to her. "You'll be fine!"

She nodded weakly, but said nothing.

The kobolds were trying to cut off their escape, but Tamaya and a group of ry'thar were making that difficult, surging out to claw and bite at them every time they got too close. Injuries were numerous, and Skunk's heart twisted as more than a few ry'thar met their ends in the effort.

Even in small numbers and off-balance, the kobolds were not a foe to be taken lightly, especially when everyone was so tired and weak. Many of them had lost all of their strength to hunger and atrophy, and the unfamiliar environment gave the kobolds an advantage that was difficult to match. Several men and women were brought to the ground by blades, claws, and teeth. Their agonized screams reached his ears no matter where they were. He wanted to rush to their aid, but the line was thin and flimsy enough as it was, and he dared not leave a gap for the enemy to exploit.

The first members of the group were starting to creep into the tunnels, where the light of the fire did not reach. A voice rang out, loud and fearful. "H-how are we getting out of here?! These tunnels aren't exactly a straight line!"

Tamaya's voice answered with confidence. "Ry'thar! To the front! The humans cannot see in the dark as we can! Smell for the surface and feel for the draft!"

Skunk, at the back of the pack, opened his mouth to volunteer for that task. He was cut off when he had to block an attack from another advancing kobold.

He deflected the blow off to one side, then, remembering something he had seen Danica do, lifted his foot and drove it into his opponent's exposed knee. He did not invert the joint as the far stronger dwarf had, but he still sent the kobold toppling with an agonized squeal, right into his rising blade.

As the body fell to the ground, Skunk looked past it and the throng of enemies. Other kobolds were starting to pile into the chamber, freshly armed and ready for battle. The only saving grace in the situation was that as the prisoners advanced into the tunnels, the kobolds would be forced to come at them in small groups. Pursuit would be difficult — although it would mean that the escaping prisoners would have to fight through similarly dense clusters of enemies to make any progress, and the darkness would only make matters worse.

Adding another layer to things, Skunk saw the silhouette of Karak emerging from the emerald inferno, sword drawn. The demidragon emerged, his face contorting with unmatched fury. Skunk felt his heart skip a beat. If Karak came at them full-on, there would be no chance of escape.

As if reading his thoughts, Danica backhanded a kobold away from her as it charged, then went to advance, her knuckles whitening around her stolen axe. "Keep going!" she shouted back at the retreating masses. "I'll keep Karak busy!"

"On your own?!" Skunk shouted, his eyes widening. "Are you insane?!"

"Maybe," Danica called back to him. "Let's find out!"

Skunk stopped his retreat, his eyes darting between Danica, Karak, the egg, and the Sunstone. He swallowed heavily, suddenly torn. Everything they had suffered had happened because of that damn egg. If they retreated without doing anything about it, there would be nothing to stop the kobolds from launching another attack to take them back, and this would have all been for nothing. They needed to stop this at the source, and they had to do it *now*. If they didn't, none of them would be safe.

Skunk's expression hardened, and he advanced away from the group. "I'm with you!" he decided.

Behind him, Amelia took hold of his tail. "Skunk, no! It's too dangerous!"

Skunk glanced back at her. "We have to destroy the egg!" he shouted. "If we don't, they'll just keep attacking us! And if that thing hatches, who knows how much damage these guys could cause?!"

Amelia shook her head, her eyes set. "It's too dangerous!" she repeated.

Skunk tore his tail free from her grasp. "And letting them create a dragon that hates us *isn't?!*" he demanded, brandishing his sword ahead of him. "No! I'm not running from this! I gotta protect my people!"

The two stared into each other's eyes for a moment, and time seemed to crawl to a stop. An invisible war was raging between them, Skunk's resolve pitted against his mother's. It was a conflict that might have raged for an eternity, but in the end, someone had to give in. Amelia nodded and stepped forward.

"I'm with you, then," she said simply. "I promised I would get you out of here, and I meant it."

Skunk grinned at her, his tail swishing in approval. "Thanks, mom."

Amelia nodded, taking a place beside her son. At Skunk's other side, Tamaya appeared, caked in blood, breathing hard, but still clearly ready to fight. "My people will lead the prisoners to safety," she said, nodding to Amelia. "I'll not abandon you to fight this enemy without me."

Amelia smiled, then darted into the fray as more kobolds ran to meet them. She lifted her mace into the chin of the first kobold to reach her, sending the creature up with its lower jaw vanishing into the upper. Skunk followed up, jumping past her to skewer the next kobold in line through the chest. Tamaya, in turn, followed after him, leaping over to pounce on an advancing trio of kobolds, her claws tearing through scale and flesh with ease and leaving mangled corpses at her feet. She roared again, sending the next kobolds before her scattering in fear.

Behind them, as the last of the prisoners vanished into the tunnel, Sylvia called out. "Be careful, Skunk!"

Skunk did not look back. "Just stay alive!" he answered before throwing himself at the next kobold in line. The days of imprisonment had done a number on him; he could already feel the muscles in his arms and legs burning from exertion. Thankfully, however, most of the horde was ignoring the advancing trio to focus on the retreating prisoners.

Amelia and Tamaya fought in perfect unison, old moves they had practiced together long ago returning in the heat of battle, and Skunk was quick to find a place for himself in that coordinated dance. What few kobolds came at them were cast aside, and in short order, they were catching up to Danica.

Or rather, Danica came flying back to them after a powerful kick from Karak sent her through the air. Tamaya planted herself and reached out, catching Danica with a grunt of pain. Danica's hand clutched at her chest, her breaths heaving and ragged.

Ahead of them, Karak came to a stop. His face was the picture of impotent rage, his hand clenched so tightly around the hilt of his sword that Skunk was certain it was bleeding. But there was something else in his eyes, too.

Fear.

Karak lifted the tip of his sword toward Skunk, the runes along his body flickering in the aftermath of the young kobold's untrained spell. his teeth showed in a vicious scowl. "You. You have no idea what it is you have done!" he shouted, his typical composure all but forgotten. "You'll pay dearly for this! I swear it!"

Skunk lifted his sword and braced himself. "No. *You* will," he decided with finality.

Karak's pupils dilated. With a draconic roar that sent the air trembling, he kicked off the ground and surged forward, blade outstretched.

With a roar of his own, Skunk charged to meet Karak's attack with his companions at his side.

The Setting Sun

Danica was at the head of the charge, issuing a guttural battle cry that echoed in the chamber. Tamaya and Amelia were close at her heels, weapons poised and ready to strike at other angles. Skunk, however, took a different approach. As the group closed in on Karak, he slowed, pulling to the back and moving to one side. He remembered vividly how things had gone the last time he got in close, and he was not interested in repeating that mistake — especially not when Karak was out for blood.

Sparks flew as Danica's axe slammed into Karak's blade. Karak grunted with effort, his runes flickering, then flaring. He pushed himself back as Amelia and Tamaya came in from either side. He flapped his wings hard, buffeting the trio and forcing them to brace and hold their position. At the same time, Karak's free hand lifted into the air, curling into a tight fist. Tendrils of hissing fire appeared from nothingness, spiraling up his forearm to gather beneath his fingers.

That was when Skunk charged in. He ran in on all fours, keeping himself low and quiet. Karak saw him coming at the last second and stepped back, avoiding the thrust that would have skewered his side. Skunk did not turn to face Karak, though. He kept going, sprinting past his enemy for a ridge of stalagmites, hoping to use them for cover. Karak turned to chase him, only for a charge from Tamaya to throw him off balance.

Skunk slid behind the ridge and knelt low. A dead kobold lay at his feet, his face rent open by gruesome claw marks. Skunk cringed at the corpse, then spotted the discarded spear beside him. He picked it up. "Sorry. I need this," he whispered before rising and poising to throw it like a javelin. He had no idea *how* to throw a spear properly, but he didn't need to. He only needed to cause a distraction.

Karak threw Tamaya off with a hard shove, sending her to the ground. He lifted his blade to stab the downed hunter but was once again interrupted. Amelia came in with a wide, arcing swing of her mace. Karak turned, his free hand flashing out to catch her wrist. He snarled and lifted his blade to slit her throat.

Skunk threw the spear. It went off-center as soon as it left his hand, spinning through the air. Still, it had the desired effect. The shaft cracked into Karak's side, drawing his attention momentarily. That moment was all Amelia needed. She dropped her mace, caught it with the other, and raised the flanged head up into Karak's armpit.

Karak's eyes widened, and his hold on her wrist was broken. Amelia followed up quickly, lifting her foot to kick him between the legs. The dirty tactic did not do as much as she might have liked, considering the usual weak point in his anatomy was nowhere to be seen. Still, it staggered Karak long enough for Amelia to duck back into a roll.He slashed after her, missing her head by mere inches.

Danica charged forward as Amelia rolled back, forcing Karak to dodge her heavy overhead swing. His sword flashed out, leaving a shallow cut across her cheek, but this only served to drive her into a greater frenzy. She chased after Karak, swinging with wild abandon, driving him into a steady retreat. Skunk could tell that she wouldn't be able to maintain such a concentrated offensive for long. He took advantage of the brief moment to slip out of cover and move to a new vantage point.

Danica's momentum was finally ground to a halt when Karak ducked to one side, dodging a ferocious downswing. His weapon twitched, the sharpened tip poised to pierce her throat. She used her momentum to roll with the attack, barely avoiding it, and received little more than a thin cut in the fabric of her shirt for the effort. Still, the sharp movement left her over-balanced, and she crashed to the ground with a heavy thud. Karak was swift to drive his foot into her side, sending her rolling across the floor toward the flames. She caught herself at the edge and came up to one knee, panting for air. She looked up as Karak flapped his wings and charged her, sword aimed at her eyes.

Skunk leaped from his position, shoulder-checking Karak right before he reached the dwarf. The tackle did not slow Karak down, but his trajectory was altered so that the thrust only left a small cut in Danica's temple. She shouted in anger at the new injury and rose into Karak, tackling his belly with her shoulder. He braced to hold her charge and reversed his grip on his sword, lifting it to drive it through her from above.

Tamaya pounced on his back, her claws sinking deep into Karak's shoulders and drawing blood. She pulled, forcing him to stagger under the combined force of Tamaya's pull and Danica's push. He flared his wings to catch himself, growling deep in his throat.

"*Enough!*" he roared, and the runes along his body flared. An expanding dome of luma tore out of him like the floodwaters of a broken dam, carrying raw concussive force that sent his attackers flying.

Skunk only had time to gasp before the spell hit, driving the air from his lungs and launching him off his feet. He soared, turning like a ragdoll through the air before slamming into the ground. Pain flared somewhere deep inside, and he yelped in pain. He rolled along until his back hit one of the dead prisoners. Groaning, he looked up to see that Tamaya and Danica had suffered much the same, both now prone on the ground.

That just left Amelia on her feet — and she had found a new weapon. Her mace had been discarded, and in her hand was another sword, freshly pried from a dead kobold.

Karak turned to her, panting for breath, his runes flickering, and his lips quivering with rage. A stench of ozone filled the air, and Skunk knew what was about to happen. He scrambled to his feet, though he knew he couldn't make it in time. "Mom! Fire!" he warned at the top of his lungs, quickly picking up his sword again.

Karak's eyes snapped to him and reached out with his free hand. Skunk blinked, then gasped as an unseen force ensnared his torso. It squeezed, and yet again, he couldn't breathe. Karak lifted his hand, and Skunk rose with it. His stomach dropped, his strangled voice echoing through the chamber as he was sent head over heels into the air. His arms flailed out wildly, desperate for anything to catch his fall, or even just slow him down. In a brief moment when he was able to see the ground, he saw how fast it was rising to meet him.

Two arms flashed out, and right in the nick of time, Amelia caught him. She grunted, cradling him close to her chest as she staggered to find cover. Skunk looked up at her, shaking as his stomach returned to its rightful place and his heart determined it was safe to beat again. "T-thanks."

Another roar from Karak filled the chamber, and Skunk heard the flap of his wings. Instinct took over, and before Skunk knew what he was doing, he had squirmed out of his mother's grasp and climbed up onto her shoulders. Ignoring her protesting gasp, Skunk saw Karak flying in, wings flared and flames gathering in his maw, primed to be unleashed.

Skunk snarled, swished his tail, and leaped, using Amelia's back to propel himself at his enemy. Karak's eyes widened at the bold maneuver, flapping his wings to arrest his momentum. His tail, however, still swung forward like a pendulum. Skunk took hold of it, dug his claws into the soft underside scales, and held on for dear life.

Karak shouted in pain, and the flames in his maw were unleashed in a wild, frenzied spray that did little more than singe the long-tattered edges of Skunk's cloak. He heard Amelia calling his name but ignored it. He knew he'd be fine. When the flames were spent, he looked up at Karak and grinned. "Made ya waste it," he taunted.

Karak kicked him in the face. The world went white for a second, and Skunk felt himself falling again. Something warm, wet, and sticky clung to the tips of his fingers. For a brief moment, he recalled the night he had attacked Bjorn, but reality was quick to reestablish itself. He crashed to the floor, rolling for several feet before coming to a stop. He coughed and gasped, struggling to fill his burning lungs with air. He looked up to see Karak flying toward him, blade poised to finish him off with a deadly slice.

An axe came flying in from the side, catching the light like a shard of silver. Karak swore, swinging his sword to knock the improvised projectile off course. His clawed feet stamped down on the ground, making the stone shake. He turned to the offender, and Danica was back on her feet, prising another axe up off the ground. She smirked at him. "I thought you were a fencer, Marus!" she bellowed mockingly. "Fight with some class! Or did you give *that* up, too?"

Karak snorted out a small cloud of acrid black smoke. "You dare?" he seethed, facing her directly. Danica braced herself, and Karak charged.

Skunk couldn't focus on their confrontation. He let out another series of coughs as feeling started returning to his face, and it occurred to him just how much pain he was in. He lifted a hand to his nose, and when he pulled it away, it was smeared in blood. A tingle of disturbance ran down his spine, his vision clouding over. He felt a hand on his shoulder, shaking him, and he looked up. Through the floating darkness of his shock, he could see the face of Amelia pushing through. Her eyes were caught between relief, frantic concern, and confusion.

"Skunk! You're— y-you're okay?" she asked in disbelief, looking him over. "But he breathed fire on you."

Skunk gave her a weak smile. "Ow," was all he said, noting that his voice was a little more nasally than usual.

Despite the situation, Amelia laughed and helped Skunk back to his feet. The sounds of battle nearby drew their attention. Tamaya had re-joined the fray, fighting alongside Danica to keep Karak on the back foot. They fought with improvisational coordination, trying to cover each other as well as they could. However, although Karak's enchantments were weakened, they still gave him the edge he needed to keep them on the back foot. Skunk swallowed heavily as he began to realize that, even with their interventionist fighting style, they weren't going to be able to beat him. Maybe if they were at full strength, but as weakened as they were...

Amelia let out a puff of air, obviously having reached the same conclusion. "This isn't looking good," she said.

Skunk fiercely shook his head to chase off the remainder of his shock as he found his balance. "But we can't leave. We have to stop this *here*, or they'll just keep coming!" he said, glancing around for a weapon. His sword lay several dozen feet away, and to his disappointment, the blade had snapped on impact.

Amelia turned to him, her expression hardening. "We wouldn't be able to outrun him anyway. We're committed, but we aren't beating him in a straight fight."

Skunk frowned, looking around the chamber for something that might inspire a plan or a solution. After a moment, his eyes found the Sunstone, and how it was positioned directly over the still-trembling dragon egg.

An idea came to him. A risky gambit, but one that could work, if he hurried. He turned to Amelia. "Do you trust me?" he asked, wanting her approval, but not having time to explain.

Amelia met his gaze and nodded, without hesitating. "Yes. With my life."

For a moment, time froze. Skunk felt himself swelling on the inside, filled with a gratification he could not describe. He put on a confident smile and drew himself taller. "Then keep him busy," he stated as time resumed. He didn't wait for Amelia to ask for clarification. He dropped to all fours and sprinted for the nearest wall. He heard Amelia raise her voice in a battle cry as she went to join the others against Karak. He risked a glance and saw Tamaya receive a vicious uppercut punch to her chin, sending her into the air and crashing to the floor. Danica took advantage of Karak's posture to wrap her arms around his lower torso in a tight bear hug. Karak gasped as she squeezed. Sadly, Skunk could not see how the fight progressed from there. He had to focus all of his attention on what came next.

He climbed one of the mounds of ringstones until he reached the wall. Putting his palm to it, he found it was more or less smooth, with very little he could use for handholds. That would pose a problem. For all of his skill at climbing vertical surfaces, those had always been made of wood, or something he could easily pierce with his claws. This was denser and harder than anything he'd had to climb before. He let out a huff of exasperation, then looked down at his hands. His claws itched, begging him to put them to use. He flexed his fingers a few times, then nodded. "Don't let me down, guys," he whispered to no one in particular, before stepping forward and attempting to plunge his claws into the stone.

They bounced off with a clack, and Skunk's fingers hurt.

"Ow! Son of a— What did I *just* say?!" He complained, briefly clutching his fingers to his chest before huffing at the wall indignantly. Suddenly, he was pretty happy that everyone else was fighting Karak. It meant they were too busy to see *that.*

Fine, he thought. *We'll do this the hard way!*

He heard a clash of metal behind him, followed by a cry of pain from Danica. He did not look. He focused on one of the many tunnels in the wall. There were no such passages on the roof, but that was fine. There were stalactites up there he could hang from. He cracked his knuckles and jumped, hooking his fingers over the lip of the first tunnel he could reach. He held steady, and, feeling emboldened, began his ascent.

It was hard going, as he had to pause frequently to find the next tunnel to leap to. This meant his route was far from direct, and every diversion or branch in his path was a waste of precious seconds he couldn't get back. All the while, he could hear his companions fighting Karak. Judging by the increasing distress in their voices, they were losing.

Still, he was making progress. Not soon enough, he reached the highest tunnel, his arms aching from the effort. He took a second to look down at what the situation was. Danica wasn't doing well. A large stain of crimson was spreading across her shirt. Even so, she was charging in again, axe raised and at the ready. Tamaya and Amelia were trading blows with Karak, the former working to keep him from taking to the air by focusing her attacks on his wings.

Karak sensed Danica's approach. With a grunt, he used his tail like a whip to strike her injured side. Danica was thrown from her feet with a breathless wheeze, her axe falling from her fingers. Karak capitalized on his momentum, ducking into a wide clearing sweep that forced the others to withdraw. As he came up, he flapped his wings to buffet them with intense wind, forcing Tamaya and Amelia to back away.

Amelia briefly looked past Karak, spotting Skunk. She blinked in confusion, not sure what his plan was, but focused back on Karak. Sadly, her glance had tipped him off, and the demidragon leaped off to one side in anticipation of an attack from behind. When none came, he turned to see what she had looked at, and his eyes settled on Skunk.

"What are you— *No!*" Karak shouted, the pieces rapidly clicking together in his mind. His wings flared, and he braced to launch himself at Skunk.

Amelia did not give Karak the chance.

"Stay *away* from him!" she shouted, as, at long last, she drew blood. With a surge of adrenaline, her sword found the leathery membrane of Karak's left wing and carved it open. Blood sprayed free, and Karak howled in agony as his aerial supremacy was stripped away.

Amelia looked up at Skunk. "Go!"

Karak turned to her, and with a guttural shout, thrust his blade at her chest. She leaned back, parrying the blow, only for Karak to follow up and bring his sword down in a swift horizontal slash across her exposed thigh.

Skunk gasped, reaching out as his mother's leg buckled under her weight. He screamed as Amelia fell to the floor, and he had to fight the impulse to rush to her aid. He couldn't go to her rescue, though. Not yet. He had to finish this.

Reluctantly, he tore his eyes away and leaped to the nearest stalactite. His claws scraped down the stone spike with a sound that made him cringe. Particles of dust and small pebbles went running down his fingers and largely exposed body, scraped loose by his claws. He heard more fighting, but he did not look. All conscious thought went away, replaced with instinct and adrenaline.

He leaped to the next spike, just in time for a blast of magical force to pulverize the one he had been dangling from a moment ago. He yelped as it was reduced to rubble, loose stones from the blast battering into his back. He would have a few new bruises from that in the morning, assuming he lived long enough to see it.

If Karak was throwing spells at him, he didn't have time to gauge his jumps. Another spell was coming for him. With a frantic cry, Skunk threw himself from spike to spike in a mad rush to keep ahead of Karak's attacks.

As he got close to his destination, he grimaced. He could see a wide gap between the final spike and the Sunstone. He had no time to wait and ponder, though. He threw himself at the final spike and managed to latch on. Unfortunately, it proved more slippery than the last two. He slid down the length, holding on for dear life and barely managing to lock his grip around the tip, his legs dangling over the edge of the fire pit and the egg beneath him.

"Stop!" Karak shouted, his voice thick with genuine fear. "You don't know what you're doing! You'll kill us all!"

Tamaya's roar ended any more warnings Karak had to offer. Skunk grinned, thankful that at least one of his friends was still fighting. The Sunstone wasn't far. He could see it just ahead, he could *feel* the luma bleeding out of it and washing over him. Unlike the shard he had held in his hand, this luma felt wrong, somehow. Tarnished. Corrupted. It had been put to use for things it was never supposed to, and now it was sick.

All that he could do for it was put it out of its misery.

Skunk set his jaw, and with all the strength he had left, he swung his legs to build momentum. He heard Tamaya cry out, and he knew he was out of time. With a shout, he threw his legs forward and let go of the spike. He sailed through the air, his arms held out in front of him, his claws outstretched. His heart felt as if it stayed behind with the stalactite, and time slowed.

Skunk's claws found the side of the Sunstone and dug into the glowing material with a painful *crunch*. As his aching flesh pressed up to the massive ringstone, a strange sense of calm came over him. As if he had just come home after a long day.

The Sunstone shifted, and the air trembled with the grinding of stone. The force of his impact had loosened the Sunstone from its place suspended from the roof. Once Skunk was certain it wasn't about to fall, he pulled his head back to look at the surface. The runes were flickering sporadically, disturbed by Karak and his repeated abuses of the power it offered.

Below, Karak screamed. "*Don't!*"

Skunk did not listen. He raked his claws across the runes as hard as he could. Letters and lines were broken, and with them, the enchantment that gave Karak his power unraveled.

Karak's pleading turned into a pathetic wail of pain and anguish. The runes flickered, thrumming and crackling as they released streams of wild, uncontrolled luma. The Sunstone sparked and rumbled as its core function was ended.

Skunk grinned, satisfied, as Karak's cries echoed through the chamber. The spell was broken. Karak was beaten. All they had to do now was figure out what to do about the egg.

Then Skunk realized that he had not really thought about how he was supposed to get down.

That riddle would be solved for him as the Sunstone released a powerful shockwave of more unfocused luma. It pounded into Skunk's body, scrambling his senses into barely conscious jelly. It was only by sheer adrenaline that he was able to maintain his hold on the stone and keep from plummeting into the Dragonfire below. However, that didn't ultimately mean much. The force of the blast was enough to rip the already loosened Sunstone free from its bindings. The world suddenly began to rise around Skunk as gravity did its work, and his stomach lifted into his throat.

He looked over his shoulder as he fell. He saw Amelia, struggling to rise despite her injured leg. She reached a hand out to him, her eyes glistening as her son plummeted into the fire.

Still, despite the fact he was about to die, Skunk felt calm. He smiled at her, and if he had the time, he would have nodded.

The Sunstone fell into the flames. Something shattered, and Skunk's world went dark.

A Good Mother

Amelia cried out as Skunk and the Sunstone plummeted into the inferno. So loud was her voice, so desperate her shout, that her lungs burned. In that fleeting moment of eye contact, Skunk smiled at her—that innocent, gentle, compassionate smile. There was sadness behind it, and in his eyes was a calm, quiet acceptance. An acceptance that Amelia refused to share. But she had no time to refute it.

The Sunstone crashed into the dragon egg as the first crack appeared on the surface. The flames billowed and rose around them, and artificial sunlight spilled out of the stone, forcing Amelia to shield her eyes. The ground trembled, and the air thundered with the cacophonous crash of a rock slide. Barely audible over the rumble was a single, wet yelp that went silent almost as soon as it began. The light persisted for several long moments, blinding and terrible.

And then it was quiet. The release of luma ended. The sunlight disappeared, and the dust began to settle. The chamber fell eerily silent, the only sound coming from the slowly dying blaze. The light from the remains of the Sunstone was barely visible through the haze of dust and smoke, now no brighter than the glow of a firefly in its death roes. The mounds of ringstones surrounding them were the only other source of light.

There was movement around her, voices, but Amelia did not pay them any mind. She stood, ignoring the sharp pain that rippled up and down her injured leg. Wincing, she hobbled toward the rubble, looking for any sign of her son, desperate to keep her promise. She had said he would survive this, and she'd be damned if she went back on that now.

"Skunk!" she shouted, frantically waving her hands to clear the dust. It persisted despite her best efforts, drawing a snarl of anger out of her. "Skunk, say something! Please! Where are you?!"

She took a step forward and finally emerged from the dust cloud. She stood at the edge of the pit, the flames receding. She cringed, catching sight of the piles of lumpy, black-charred metal that had once been cages. She could see mangled limbs and piles of charred flesh fused into the cooling metal, sizzling and popping, filling the air with the stench of burning meat. Some of the metal and flesh had been buried by dimming chunks of ringstone as large as Amelia's head, while others were covered in shards of the dragon egg.

The hatchling was a surprisingly small creature. It wasn't even the size of a horse. Its body, slick with slowly cooking egg yolk, was slender and lithe, covered in iridescent scales alternating between green and teal. It lay perfectly still. Its eyes, colored like amber, were wide and unfocused. A long tongue lolled from between infantile teeth. It was half-buried in a mound of faintly glowing stones. Dark blood trickled out of its mouth, and Amelia knew that the creature was dead — crushed to death by the very stone that had just given it life.

She stared at the dead child for a moment, withering in place. An uncomfortable feeling crept up her spine to settle in her chest. It had to be done, yes, but that did not mean she had to feel good about it. This creature was one of a rare breed, and it had died before it had the chance to live. There was no good in that, only the lesser of two evils.

"Forgive us," she whispered. "I wish it had not come to this."

Any words she could offer were a meaningless and hollow gesture, she knew. The dead had no ears for the living. Even if they did, she did not imagine the corpse at her feet would care for what she had to say.

There was nothing to be done about it now. Amelia tore her eyes away from the corpse and resumed her search for Skunk. She squinted into the flames, looking around for any sign of green scales. The longer she looked, the tighter her dread squeezed her. The flames had melted iron bars into molten slag. Even if Skunk had survived falling with something large enough to crush him, Amelia doubted he could have survived flames this intense.

Amelia's legs gave out, her eyes welling over as feeling and color drained away. She felt numb. Sick. Something caught in her throat, tight and suffocating. Her chest seized, twisting as if to rip everything inside to shreds just so she wouldn't have to feel what was coming. Amelia screwed her eyes shut. Her emotions spilled over, and she began to sob.

The last pitiful crackles of the fire soon faded into silence, and the chamber was left in complete quiet. If there was anything else happening in this chamber, Amelia could not hear it. It didn't matter anymore...

But then something moved, and that *did* matter.

Amelia looked up, wiping her eyes. Though the light from the Sunstone had faded, there was still the low silver glow from the rest of the ringstones. That light was more than enough to see by. She saw a mound of rubble shifting and heard the stones grinding and tumbling. A bipedal shape, a silhouette in the dust, rose unsteadily.

Amelia blinked, thinking perhaps the shape was an illusion or a trick of her mind. But as it came closer, its eyes caught the light to shine back at her like twin suns. She knew those eyes anywhere. She choked down a sob, daring to hope. "Skunk?"

The shape took another step toward her, then another. And then, with a whine that reminded Amelia of a scolded puppy, the familiar form of a kobold tipped forward like a felled tree.

Instinct took over, sending Amelia forward to catch the falling shape and ignoring the still scorching heat coming from below. The moment she held the boy in her arms, her heart soared with relief, and a whole new wave of tears came to her eyes. There was no doubt.

"Skunk!" she blubbered in joy, hauling him out of the pit. Her wounded leg did not let her get very far, only two steps before she fell to her backside on cooler stone. She cradled him close, propping up his head in her lap so she could get a good look at him. A moment passed as he took in a deep, ragged breath.

Amelia let out something between a laugh and a sob and pulled him against her chest, over her heart. "Oh, Skunk. Oh, my sweet, sweet boy," she whispered, running her hand down the back of his head. "Thank the Five. You're okay. You're okay..."

She felt Skunk stirring in her arms as he let out a groan of pain. "Mom?" he mumbled, his voice thin.

"Hush, sweety," Amelia cut him off softly. She began to rock him back and forth in a soothing, long-familiar motion. "Don't speak. It's okay. You're okay, now. Everything's going to be okay. I've got you. I've got you. You're safe, now."

The mothering mantra had the desired effect. Skunk was silent in her arms. After a few seconds, he carefully returned the embrace. He hissed through tightly clenched teeth when he did, and Amelia realized that he was *far* from perfect health. She couldn't see the extent of the damage, but she had to imagine he had suffered at least a few broken bones in that fall, not to mention the wounds he had sustained in their battle with Karak.

Karak!

Amelia tensed, pulling Skunk closer to protect him. She cast her eyes about, looking for any sign of the demidragon. She saw him nearby, squirming on the ground. The runes that had been carved into his scaly flesh had dulled, leaving him utterly powerless. She could hear his breaths, fast and panicking. Interspaced between his inhales she could hear agonized whimpers slipping out of a tightly clenched throat. His entire body was spasming, muscles rippling under tightening skin. His wings lay limp and useless behind him, and even his tail appeared to have become little more than a deadweight.

Amelia glared at him, unable to deny the satisfying feeling of seeing him suffer. With his enchantments broken, his body was going into shock. He was vulnerable now, and not likely to recover any time soon.

If it is even worth the effort to finish him off, we might as well do it now.

That was a thought that Danica seemed to share. The injured dwarf had picked herself up after the fall of the Sunstone. She stared over at the rubble, her expression blank and unreadable. She heaved a quiet sigh, shook her head, and began a slow but steady march toward Karak. She scooped up a fallen axe on the way, grunting and holding the bleeding wound on her side with her free hand.

While Danica advanced to put an end to their fallen enemy, Tamaya came to Amelia's side. She was bloodied, battered, and exhausted, but judging by the smile on her muzzle and the sparkle in her eyes, she was in good spirits. "The boy saved all our lives," she remarked with a respectful nod. "How do you feel, young one?"

"My brain tastes like beans," Skunk supplied helpfully. "I don't like beans."

Tamaya and Amelia stared at him for a long moment, then broke out into hearty chuckles at the loopy remark. Tamaya knelt beside Amelia and gave Skunk a quick but thorough examination. Satisfied, she rested her hand on his shoulder. "I wouldn't let him walk without aid, but I do not imagine his life is in any immediate danger. Once we can get him back to Annotha, he'll make a full recovery, I am certain."

Amelia sighed in relief, the lingering tension in her chest unraveling. She looked down at Skunk and smiled. "You hear that? You're going to be fine. We'll get you back to the Karjene, and they'll fix you right up."

Skunk lifted a hand weakly into the air as if for a toast. "Wooo," he intoned in a monotone before his arm fell over his belly. He winced. "Ow."

Laughing once more, Amelia hooked her arm under Skunk's knees and stood. She hissed, her injured leg burning in pain, but Tamaya was quick to jump in and support Amelia's weight. The two shared a look once Amelia was at her full height, then turned toward Danica.

During that brief discussion, Karak's spasms had ended. He was backing away across the floor from a steadily advancing Danica. His eyes were wide with terror, and his pathetic whimpers were audible.

Tamaya snorted. "To think, he was so proud and dignified mere moments ago," she said quietly, her voice dripping with contempt. "He was a fool to put his faith in borrowed power."

Amelia said nothing.

Karak's back pressed against a mound of ringstones, and he used it to stand. He doubled over, one hand over his heart while the other, trembling and weak, supported him against the mound. He panted, staring at Danica and the others as they advanced. His lips peeled back, his teeth catching the light. "You fools," he hissed. "You've killed us all."

Danica grunted, hefting her axe up onto her shoulder. "No. Just you," she spat. "Well deserved, too."

Karak shook his head. "No, no, no. You don't understand! You have no conception of the *hell* you've just unleashed! I labored for *justice,* not genocide!"

Amelia hesitated, suddenly feeling uneasy. Karak's tone had changed. Where once he had shown nothing but bitter contempt or self-assured confidence, there was now nothing more than fear. And the more she looked at him, at the way he trembled, the more she wondered if it was them he was afraid of.

"Speak plain or not at all," Tamaya snapped, coming away from Amelia's side to advance on the trembling demidragon.

Karak opened his mouth, but something cut him off.

A thunderous jolt ran through the floor of the cave. Amelia gasped, crumpling to one knee as white-hot pain coursed up her leg. The chamber rumbled as if the entire mountain was shifting around them. Small pebbles and clouds of dust fell from the roof, and the air suddenly shifted, pulled in one direction as if a gateway into an empty vacuum had suddenly been thrown open.

In Amelia's arms, Skunk squirmed uncomfortably. "W-what was that?" he asked, his voice starting to come back into coherence and laced with primal fear.

Against the wall, Karak shook his head. "An answer to what you've done," he choked, his voice trembling. He backed away, his eyes turning to stare at something behind them.

Amelia swallowed heavily, then turned to follow his line of sight to the gaping hole in the back wall of the chamber. She hadn't had the time to give the abyss any thought during the battle. An impenetrable void of darkness lay beyond the threshold. The wind was flowing *into* that abyss, sucked in by something unknown.

"What is that? What's down there?" Skunk asked, clinging to Amelia and trembling in fear. She gave him a comforting squeeze.

Karak turned to them both, incredulous. "Think it through, *child*. What do you need for there to be an egg?" he asked in a sharp and impatient hiss.

The earth trembled again, and the air itself began quivering against their soft, fragile flesh. Amelia's heart spiked when she realized that the sound was a growl. The growl of a truly monolithic creature. And there was only one type of creature in all of Aurus large enough to create a sound like that.

The realization settled over Amelia like a blanket of suffocating despair. Any hope or joy at their victory evaporated in the blink of an eye.

"A good mother is never far from her children…" she breathed.

"Impossible," Tamaya echoed, shaking her head. She turned to Karak. "You lie! It cannot be!"

"And who are you to claim what can or cannot be?!" Karak snapped, his nostrils flaring. "What evidence did you ever have?! You never saw a body! Thalgrum told you he killed her, but in truth he only crippled her! The spineless traitor could *never* bring himself to murder his sister! So he lied, and you believed him! All this time, she has been here, nursing the wounds Thalgrum gave her and languishing in despair, afraid her only and final child would never be born. She nears the end of her life, and in desperation entrusted *me* with her child's future."

Karak's eyes turned from the abyss to glare at them each in turn. His horror turned to fury. "A future you've destroyed." The air shuddered again as if the world itself was afraid. Karak took a sobering breath and held his head high. "She will have felt the death of his blood in her own. She is awake."

From the darkness, a single glowing eye, as large as Amelia's head and as green as an emerald, rose from the shadows. A massive foot, covered in green scales and tipped with claws each as long as a human leg, fell upon the stone. The chamber trembled, and green light swelled in the legendary beast's chest, bathing the chamber in its baleful glow and revealing the owner for what it was.

An ancient green dragon, one long-thought dead, stood over them, looking down with unyielding, murderous hatred blazing in her gaze.

Azada lived.

Hers was a body marred by countless battles, with scars crisscrossing through her jagged scales. A single, magnificent horn of ivory curved up and away from the back of her head, its sibling on her right side little more than a shattered stump. Beneath that stump, a trio of ugly scars ran down her face, leaving her right eye permanently destroyed. Her left wing was hopelessly mangled, little more than tatters of thick skin and severed digits. But despite the dragon's many mutilations, the raw *power* she projected sent Amelia staggering in fear.

"What have we done...?" Tamaya whispered, staring up at the beast in terror.

Beside them, Karak suddenly called to his true master. "Azada! My emerald queen! I am so sorry!"

Azada's head moved with a speed that could not have been natural. The air cracked like a whip as her eyes focused on him, smoke billowing from her nostrils. The question in her eye did not need to be spoken.

"I have failed you!" Karak went on, pushing himself away from the wall and falling to his hands and knees. "Your egg is destroyed! The Sunstone is shattered! I tried to defend them, I fought with all of the strength you granted me! But I failed!"

Azada stared at him a moment before her massive head swiveled to look where the egg had been. She stepped farther into the chamber, emerging fully from the darkness of her concealed nest. Amelia and the others backed away, unable to do anything except stare up at the beast in wonder. None of them had ever seen a dragon before, and the majesty of the creature was beyond description.

Azada's eyes settled on the shattered remains of the egg and Sunstone. She lowered her nose to prod at the rubble, sniffing at the corpse of her child.

Karak continued. "I do not dare beg your forgiveness!" he cried, prostrating himself against the earth. "I am unworthy of it! I am unworthy of your patronage, of your trust! I am unworthy of the life you spared!"

Danica turned to Karak, eyes wide. "What the hell are you doing?!" she demanded. "Are you trying to get yourself killed?!"

Karak ignored her. He lifted his eyes to Azada as the dragon turned back to him. Her eye was wide. Karak called to her all the louder. "Your servants failed, and your enemies stand before you, caked in the blood of your unborn child! I beg of you, my queen! take your revenge! Let the weight of your wrath and our sins bury us! Let *none* go unpunished!"

"Not just himself," Tamaya whispered.

Azada's single eye, focusing on Karak, began to glisten. Amelia was shocked to realize the dragon was *crying*. But of course she would be. They had murdered her baby. She was grieving.

The dragon's grief was short-lived. In its place, rage. The air within the chamber turned hot and dry as the dragon lifted her head. Her chest glowed green as flames built inside of her before traveling up her throat to gather in her maw.

"Time to go!" Danica shouted, breaking into a mad sprint for the main tunnel. "*Run!*"

Amelia did not need to be told twice. She and Tamaya broke into a mad sprint for the exit, moving as fast as their legs could carry them. Amelia could hear Karak's voice behind them, rising even louder with insane zealotry. "Yes, my queen! *Yes!* Burn it all down! Reduce it all to ashes! Let this mountain be our tomb!"

And then Azada exhaled.

The heat was unimaginable. Superheated wind blasted into Amelia from behind, carrying with it a shockwave that sent her flying into the air. She crashed to the floor, screaming and rolling along the searing stones. The chamber rumbled around her, and more rocks fell from on high to pummel her. Skunk wailed in her arms, clinging tightly to her. She clutched him tightly, trying to shield him, and cracked an eye open.

A wall of heat stood between her and Tamaya. The ry'thar was gasping for air, eyes wide. She went to shout something, but Amelia did not hear the words. Azada roared, and the air itself pressed against her. Her ears stung, then ached, then burned, and suddenly, Amelia couldn't hear anymore. With a sharp pop, the entire world went silent, save for an ear-splitting ringing. She screamed at the top of her lungs, but even that was silent to her. Across the flames, Tamaya clutched at her ears, far more sensitive than Amelia's, and fell to her knees.

The earth shook several times, and Amelia looked back over her shoulder. Azada was advancing on her, more flames boiling out of her mouth. Chunks of the roof fell with every step the dragon took, bouncing harmlessly off of her scales like pebbles off the wall of a castle. An insult that did not even deserve an answer.

As the sound began to return, Amelia scrambled to her feet and ran through the wall of scorching air. She howled in pain, feeling her skin burning as she passed through, but she soldiered through it. She tried to protect Skunk with her body, but she could feel him thrashing in her arms. She could only imagine how loudly he was screaming. How scared must he have been?

Tamaya made it to the tunnel first. She still had her metal bar, and with no other options, threw it at Azada like a javelin. The improvised weapon scraped harmlessly off of Azada's cheek with a spray of sparks.

The attack didn't even leave a scratch.

It did, however, draw the dragon's attention.

Azada's voice reached Amelia's ears. "You barbarians killed my child!" she roared, the words echoing in Amelia's mind just as surely as they did in her ears. "Monsters! Abominations! *Demons!* Is my home not enough?! My dignity?! My brother?! Must you steal even my children?! Are there no atrocities you will *not* commit?!"

Amelia staggered, barely able to keep to her feet. The gash in her leg throbbed with pain, hobbling her. She tried to ignore it, tried to press on, but even adrenaline had its limits, and she was rapidly reaching hers.

Another gout of flame spilled out of Azada's mouth, directed at the roof of the chamber. Amelia risked a look and gasped as the flames *melted* the stone. Molted globs that glowed like the sun splattered across the floor, creating tidal waves of sparks.

"Hurry!" Tamaya shouted, backing farther into the tunnel, but still waiting for Amelia.

Amelia tried to pick up the pace. She looked down at Skunk. He was staring up at her, eyes wide. Had it not been for the impossible heat in the chamber, they would have been damp with tears of fear. He was curling in on himself. He was small, helpless, and so, *so* scared.

Just like he was the day she found him.

All of the same instincts that had driven her to save him back then came alive once more. Despite the agony in her leg and the flames stealing the air from her lungs, she charged on. She was almost there, just a few more steps and—

Something hard, heavy, and hot crashed against her back. Amelia screamed, falling forward on top of Skunk. Chunks of stone as large as she was fell all around her, making the earth jump and pelting her with debris.

A second later, as the barrage ended, she tried to rise. Her legs were weak and unresponsive, and it took far longer to stand than she would have liked. The moment she was upright, the world tilted. She staggered to the side, supporting herself against one of the fallen boulders. She took a deep breath, then regretted it as hot air burned her lungs. She doubled over, coughing up blood, which only served to make things worse.

"Mom?!" Skunk asked from her arms, his voice barely audible and thick with panic.

Amelia shook her head but did not dare answer. Oh, what she would give to have Skunk's resistance to fire just then. She lifted her eyes, determined to carry him the rest of the way. But as she lifted her eyes to their exit, her heart stopped in her chest.

A wall of rubble had fallen across the tunnel entrance, barring her path. There was no way out.

"Amelia!" Tamaya's voice came from the other side, muffled. "Skunk!"

Behind her, Amelia heard Azada's foot come down again. "You will not escape me," the dragon rumbled. "*No one* will escape me!"

Amelia did not answer, nor did she look back. She advanced on the collapsed tunnel. *There has to be a way through, there has to be!* She thought. But as she drew closer, all she found was a small gap in the cave-in. If it was a little larger, and if there had been more time, she might have been able to climb through. But she could already tell it was just too small for her. She could make out Tamaya's eyes catching the light on the other side, looking back at her.

Azada breathed in. More flames gathered.

For Amelia, the world came to a stop.

There was no time left. No options. She looked down at Skunk in her arms.

She took a moment to study his face, the face of her son. The sweet, cheerful little kobold that she had raised. It truly dawned on her then that he had grown into a fine young man. But even so, he stared back up at her, frightened. His eyes shimmered with terror, but also a quiet confidence. The confidence that she would do as she had always done before.

The confidence that she would save him.

"Mom?" he asked, his voice all she could hear.

Amelia nodded. Yes, that was who she was. She was his mother. And she had made him a promise. And she intended to keep it, no matter what.

"I love you so much Skunk," she whispered. "And I'm so proud of you."

Skunk tilted his head. "What?"

There was no time to say anything more. All she could do was trust that Skunk would be alright. And if what she had seen these last few weeks was any indication, she knew he would be. Amelia's heart slowed, peaceful.

With the last of her strength, Amelia lifted Skunk and pushed him into the gap.

"Tamaya!" she shouted. "Take Skunk and get out of here! Go! *Run!*"

"M-mom?!" Skunk called back, trying to turn to her as his head passed through the gap.

Tamaya did not argue. She grabbed him and pulled him through. Amelia watched his tail disappear into the darkness beyond. She heard him calling back to her, and his face appeared on the other side.

"Mom! What are you doing?!" he screamed.

Amelia smiled at him as she heard Azada exhale.

"Live happily."

That was the last thing Amelia said to him. The last thing she saw was his face looking back at her, before the flames of Azada consumed her.

Aftermath

Skunk stared, petrified in horror, as Amelia's face was consumed by Azada's flames. The blaze coiled around her like a million snakes, leaving nothing but a silhouette. For a fraction of a second, the silhouette remained, staring back at him. He could still see her face, hidden amid the green. She was smiling.

And then she was gone, vanishing into the inferno like a snuffed candle.

There was no time to think. The flames surged through the hole, carrying with it a powerful pressure wave. Skunk cried out as he was sent crashing to the floor in a crumpled, whimpering heap. He was numbly aware of the sound of an explosion, and the cavern began to crumble around him.

He sat up, gasping for air and holding his agonized face. When he pulled his hand away, he froze. Something was clinging to his palm and face, hot and stinking. It only took him a moment to realize what it was.

Ashes.

He was covered in ashes.

Amelia's ashes.

His mother's ashes were on his face.

They were getting into his eyes.

Into his nostrils.

They burned.

Skunk couldn't breathe. The world blurred around him, tilting and shaking. He doubled over, suddenly feeling faint. As if he wasn't entirely real. He frantically rubbed at his watering eyes to try and get the ashes out, but he only succeeded in rubbing them deeper in, making his eyes burn, making his skull sting. His heart was pounding, pounding, *pounding* against his ribs, his veins turned to ice while everything else burned.

More ashes. On his hands, on his scales. He stared at them, stared at the grey smears that had once been his mother. They dried and crumbled, flaking and falling from his body. The world was barely visible through the tears, but the ashes were clear. He watched them fall to the floor, where they disappeared, lost forever amidst the dust of the cavern floor.

Skunk couldn't move. He sat there, gasping in deep lungfuls of air that were never enough, staring at the dust as if he might find Amelia hidden in it all. But there was nothing left to find.

Voices were shouting at him. He couldn't hear them. They were nothing but muffled noise, lost to the chaos as his mind folded in on itself. Then he felt hands on him. His neck turned to look, but he hadn't commanded it. The face of a panicking lion stared back at him, her eyes glistening in the darkness with tears of her own.

She said something, her face contorted in wild desperation.

Her words meant nothing.

The lion's eyes shot to look at something behind Skunk, her ears folding against her head. She nodded, and without waiting for permission, hooked her arms around Skunk and lifted him. The world fell away, and Skunk realized she was taking him away from the rubble.

Away from Amelia.

Panic set in.

"No..." he murmured, the single word thick like old honey on his tongue. But as adrenaline began to flood his veins, he found his voice, and it rose into a shout. "N-no. No! Let me go!"

When his demand went unanswered, Skunk began to squirm. He twisted this way and that, thrashing violently against Tamaya to free himself. But her grip was like steel, indomitable against his weakened body, and he knew he'd never overpower her. He screamed and shouted, reaching out for the rubble that he could barely even see anymore. "Put me down, Tamaya! *Put me down!*"

Tamaya's grip on him tightened, and his chaotic thoughts ran red with rage. His screams turned to snarls, and before he knew it, he was biting at Tamaya's arms. She shifted him in her grasp, changing the angle and leaving him with no room to move.

"She's gone, Skunk!" Tamaya yelled, her voice thick but steady. "We must leave!"

"No! She's not!" Skunk denied, shaking his head in feral defiance. He blinked rapidly, trying desperately to clear the tears so he could see, but there were always more. "She can't be! *Let me go, dammit!*"

"Do you want her death to be for nothing?!" Tamaya snapped, squeezing Skunk tighter. "If you go back now, you will only succeed in getting yourself killed!"

"I don't care!" Skunk's reply was automatic, instinctual. He couldn't even think about the words he was saying.

Tamaya slowed and turned him so they were face to face. Her lips peeled back, her eyes narrowed. "But *she did!*" she roared in his face.

That finally made Skunk pause. He worked his jaw, hunting for words. But none came. All he could do was shake his head and repeat his denials. "She can't be gone," he whimpered. "She can't be."

Tamaya did not say anything. She pulled Skunk against her, almost as if she were hugging him, and kept running through the collapsing burrow as fast as her legs could carry her. She stopped for a split second every so often, turning up her nose to sniff at the air and find their path. Skunk barely even noticed.

"You sure we're going the right way?!" Danica's voice echoed from not far away, reminding Skunk that she was there.

"I'm certain," Tamaya replied, picking up the pace. "The scent is strong. They went this way!"

They encountered no kobolds as they ran, thankfully. Most tunnels were empty, and all the others had already or were in the process of caving in. Azada's despairing roars could still be heard echoing through the walls. Every cry was a new declaration of grief and despair that made the world shake. But each one was quieter, fading into the distance as the dragon was buried alive by the mountain she had called her home for so long. Eventually, Azada's screams disappeared into silence, and it was just the crumbling of the rocks.

"Up ahead! The exit!" Tamaya exclaimed. Skunk numbly looked up.

Sure enough, the way out into the ruins of Actaneirum was visible just ahead. The stones above were cracking, and he knew there would only be a few more seconds before it all caved in. Tamaya put on a burst of speed, and the cave walls became a blur. Skunk could hear Danica shouting behind them, but he did not have the chance or the energy to look back.

Tamaya surged out and into brilliant, golden sunlight shining down on them through gaps in the ruined auriun structure. Danica emerged a few seconds later, releasing a colorful string of expletives just as the tunnel collapsed behind her. There was a cacophonous crash, and a blast of displaced air chased her out, sending Danica stumbling forward until she fell to the ground.

But they weren't safe yet. Actaneirum, the entire city, was quivering. The tower around them swayed to and fro like a tree in a hurricane, a house of cards about to fall apart. The walls cracked and split, chunks of stone falling to smash into the already shattered floor.

Danica swore, quickly getting back on her feet. Side-by-side with Tamaya, they sprinted from the crumbling tower.

Skunk, again, barely noticed.

He barely noticed when the ancient tower fell in on itself, and massive portions of it tumbled down the cliff-side in a devastating rockslide. He barely noticed the gaping chasms in the valley widening, swallowing more of the ruined city into the depths of The World Below. He barely noticed it when the earth stopped shaking. He barely noticed when, finally, Tamaya stopped running. He barely noticed when she lowered him onto the ground.

Instinct kicked in, the need to know where he was, and he looked around without thinking to do so.

He was surrounded by a small congregation of gasping, emaciated people, villagers and ry'thar looking on as the cliffside collapsed. There were fewer of them than he remembered, proof that some had been killed in their escape.

Even more people he had failed to save.

He shuddered, trying to breathe but unable to. His chest ached, the pain so deep he was afraid he was going to burst. He would have welcomed it if he did because at least then the pain would *stop*.

He followed the eyes of the survivors, watching numbly as the last of the structure and its supports fell away. The thunderous report of their collapse was almost inaudible to Skunk over the ringing in his ears and the pounding in his chest.

As the rubble settled, and the air stilled, the world fell into an uneasy silence.

Then a voice.

"Skunk? Skunk, where are you?!"

Skunk inhaled sharply. That was Sylvia! He spun around, his eyes scanning the crowd. He caught sight of her staggering out, each arm supported by men from Addernotch. She looked none the worse for wear, and a small flicker of relief mingled half-heartedly with Skunk's sorrow.

"H-here," he croaked, his voice low and weak. Sylvia locked onto him with uncanny precision. She lurched forward, breaking away from her escorts. She made it four steps before her bare foot met a stray stone, and she toppled forward.

Skunk moved, catching Sylvia in his arms. She enveloped him in a bone-crushing hug, her weight settling against him. He bore it without complaint and buried his face in her shoulder.

"You're okay," Sylvia whispered, more to confirm it for herself. She ran a hand down the back of his neck, her fingers feeling deliberately at the texture of his scales and his horns as if to make sure he was real. "Thank the Five, you're okay."

Skunk shuddered. He *wasn't* okay. He was everything *but* okay. He didn't know if he'd ever be okay again. He opened his mouth to tell her, but all that came out was a strangled sob. He felt her stiffen, and slowly, she pulled back. She had no eyes to see him with, but he could feel her intention piercing his soul. Her hands slid slowly up his body until they settled on his face, cupping his jaw. "What happened?" she whispered.

Skunk stared into her face. He worked his jaw, his mouth opening and closing as he searched for the words that might do justice to his feelings.

"Skunk?" Sylvia asked when he didn't say anything.

Finally, Skunk was able to find a word. "M-mom," he choked out, his voice quivering. Sylvia's face began to blur, hazy and indistinct.

"Amelia did not make it," Tamaya said from somewhere nearby.

Sylvia inhaled quietly, tensing up. She was quiet for a moment, but Skunk could see the realization written plain on her face. "Oh, no, no, no," she whispered. Shivering, she pressed her forehead against Skunk's. "I'm so, *so* sorry."

The tension in Skunk's chest snapped. The feelings he had numbly been aware of hit him all at once. Years of memories flashed in front of his eyes.

Being caught in the pantry, and her endeared laugh at his innocent grin.

The lullaby she would sing to him when he was little and easily frightened.

The day she first started teaching him how to use a bow.

Stargazing with her on a warm summer night.

All of his happiest memories of her, all of them colored by the final, terrible settling of a realization he did not want to confront.

Amelia was dead.

He didn't know when he had started screaming. He didn't care. Sylvia's hands slid around him again, pulling him into another hug. She didn't say anything. There was nothing she *could* say. All she did was hold him, and pray that it would be enough. Skunk wasn't the only one weeping for the lost, he knew. But his was the only voice he could hear.

Eventually, however, a voice did break through. It was Danica. "I'm sorry, but we can't stay here. We're not safe yet. There are still kobolds all over the valley, and we don't want to be here if they start getting ideas of revenge."

Skunk's heart turned, and his mind shifted. He opened his eyes and looked up. Danica was kneeling beside them, her hair having come loose in all of the chaos. It fell around her shoulders and face in long, dirty strands. Her jaw was set, her eyes firm, but softened with sympathy.

A tingle of something besides grief settled in the back of Skunk's skull. Something hot. He sniffled. "Y-you ran," he whimpered, holding Sylvia tighter. "Y-you ran first."

Danica blinked, taken aback by the weakly uttered accusation. She looked down and to one side, her eyes falling with regret. "I did," she admitted guiltily.

"You could have helped her," Skunk pressed as that other emotion began to swell. It burned, crawling across his skull and creeping into his veins. His lips twitched, showing his teeth, and his voice lowered into a growl. "You could have *saved* her!"

Danica flinched away from Skunk. She opened her mouth, but she didn't say anything.

Skunk was about to press her, the spark in his blood turning into genuine anger. But then he felt a hand on his cheek. He went rigid, passively allowing it to turn his face until he was looking at Sylvia. She shook her head. "Skunk. Don't. Don't do this. Please."

"Sylvia," Skunk tried to speak, but the words withered and died in his throat. He stared at her for several long seconds, his mouth closing. His need for someone to blame spluttered, flickered, and died. And as it did, so too did his will to be in the waking world. He closed his eyes and fell into Sylvia's arms, shuddering and whimpering into her.

He felt a hand come to a tentative rest on his shoulder, larger than Sylvia's. It was Danica. There were several seconds of silence, and Skunk could imagine that she was hunting for something to say. In the end, she settled for a barely audible utterance of "I'm sorry," before standing and walking away.

Tamaya's voice reached him again a few seconds later. "Danica is right. We need to go. Skunk? I'm sorry, I don't want to ask this of you, but can you walk?"

Skunk wanted to say no, but he didn't have the energy left to lie. He reluctantly rose to his feet, helping Sylvia stand beside him. His entire body ached, but he was able to find his balance. He held a hand to his side, hissing in pain as a deep bruise made itself known. He met Tamaya's gaze and gave a grim nod. "I can walk," he said in a hollow monotone.

Tamaya's face twisted with concern, but this was neither the time nor the place to address his grief. She stood tall and turned to address the crowd. Skunk didn't listen to her. He looked back one more time at where the Auriun tower once stood. He bristled, the hatred in his blood stirring for just a moment before it was buried by dull apathy.

Sylvia's hands slid down to wrap around his arm, hugging it from the side as they supported one another's weight. He felt her head resting on his shoulder, felt her warmth sinking into his scales. "I'm here for you," she told him gently.

Skunk swallowed heavily and, finally, tore his eyes away from the ruins. The crowd was starting to move, the survivors arranging themselves into an organized formation to better defend themselves in case they were attacked again. Tamaya remained by his side and put a hand on his shoulder. She gently nudged him into movement. He allowed himself to be guided away from the ruins that marked his mother's grave. Around him, his pack, broken and diminished but thankfully alive, walked with him. Many looked at him with pity, sympathy, and worry in their eyes. They felt the loss of Amelia, too. But none of them felt it as keenly as he did.

She had been the most important person in his life. His caretaker. His confidant. His protector. His *advocate*.

Karak's words echoed threateningly in his ears, and he shivered in fear.

"You have only survived as long as you have because one human woman was willing to vouch for you in a small village that could not push back against her desire. But she will not be there for you forever. One day, and it may not be so very long from now, you will not be able to rely on her anymore. And without her there to watch your back and command acceptance, how long do you believe you will last? Beyond Addernotch, you will be nothing but another kobold."

Without her, would he even have a home to go back to?

That question haunted Skunk all the way out of the ruins of Actaneirum.

The journey down from the peaks of the Sybhrod Mountains was a long and quiet one. Any relief the survivors may have felt was dulled by the losses they had sustained. Of all of the men and women who had been captured by the kobolds, less than half of them remained. And all of them carried more than their fair share of scars.

Danica looked at it all from near the back of the group. She felt for them. They weren't her people, and she had never really gotten attached to any of them, with a small handful of exceptions. But that did not mean she was without sympathy. She could understand, at least to some extent, what they were going through. The tragedy of Stonefall had been different in many ways, but not the losses. Something irreplaceable had been stolen from these people, and they could never get them back.

Her eyes settled on Skunk every so often. He hadn't said a word since they left Actaneirum. He stared at the ground, his every movement stiff and artificial. It was as if he was a puppet drifting along on unfeeling strings. Sylvia and Tamaya remained at his side, offering what comfort they could. Sylvia, in particular, never took her hands off of him. Every so often Danica could hear them whispering to each other — or rather, she could hear Sylvia whispering at Skunk. The kobold barely responded. The most he'd give was a slow shrug or shake of his head.

Danica sighed. Not for the first time, her thoughts drifted to how Skunk had produced *her* shard of the Sunstone right before they were to be sacrificed. He had somehow invoked its power to set them all free. When she'd first seen it clutched in his hands, she'd felt angry. It was supposed to be *hers,* and seeing it in the hands of dragonkin only served to remind her of how she'd lost it in the first place. Now, though, after the way he'd almost single-handedly saved all of their lives with it, and what that salvation had cost them, all she could feel was ashamed of herself.

She looked down at the ground. She wanted to say something to him, but what? Even if she could find the words to express her feelings, she doubted he would even hear her in his condition. She fought the urge to curse and promised herself she would talk to him later when he'd had a chance to recover. She returned her attention to the path ahead.

The group had been walking for hours, now. They were traveling at a slower pace than anyone would like, but between their collective exhaustion and all of the wounded, they had to move slowly or risk leaving people behind. But that meant they were exposed on the slopes of the range, vulnerable to attack.

Danica did not doubt that some kobolds might try their luck. With the dragon egg shattered, and Marus and Azada buried, the green scales were deprived of their leadership. Any organization would quickly fall apart, but there would still be loyalty to their cause. If anything, such a devastating blow would only serve to enflame their passion and lust for massacre — or 'justice' as Marus had kept insisting.

She huffed quietly and wondered if this 'victory' had even made anything better. They had escaped, yes, but now the kobolds were free to act however they saw fit. Without Marus or Azada to hold their chains, would more attacks be incoming? Random raids of retribution? Bands of dragonkin stalking the countryside to pillage and slaughter anyone and everyone they could get their hands on? It was a disquieting thought, and Danica wanted nothing more than to be rid of it. Still, at least there wouldn't be a new dragon to unite the scattered hordes of green scales into a single unified army. For that, at least, she supposed she should be grateful.

After a time, Tamaya came to her side. "There is precious little shelter en route back to my people," she said, keeping her voice down so only Danica could hear. "All I know of is the sundered tower where we fought Karak. I have issued orders to my hunters to lead the way there. We can use the stones for shelter. It will also give you and I a chance to retrieve our belongings. I suspect Karak did not do anything with our weapons once we were caged."

Danica grunted, glancing down at her stolen axe. The thing was ugly as sin and about as balanced as a drunken giraffe. "Sounds good to me," she agreed simply. She looked at Skunk, her expression darkening.

Tamaya followed her gaze and let off a quiet breath. "I fear for him."

"What do you think he'll do?"

Tamaya winced. "I do not know. I fear he came to depend upon her guidance. Without that..." Tamaya trailed off, her brow furrowing and her whiskers quivering.

"You think he'll be lost?" Danica guessed.

"Everyone is lost when they lose their family," Tamaya said simply, and Danica winced. She had forgotten that Tamaya's mother had perished shortly before they had met. If the reminder had in any way upset Tamaya, however, she hid it expertly from view. She nodded her head at Skunk. "The question is whether or not he will be able to find his way again."

Danica hummed quietly. Part of her wanted to blurt out that she was sure he would. But that would be a lie, wouldn't it? And for all the things Danica was, she was not a liar.

Not like I'm in any place to talk, she thought bitterly. *I'm still lost myself.*

Eventually, she looked back up at the ry'thar woman. "And what about you? Amelia was your friend."

Tamaya was quiet a moment, then nodded. "She was a beloved friend to my entire clan. She was the only human I have ever asked to join the Karjene. The only human I would be honored to call sister."

Tamaya took a breath and looked away. She was fighting to keep her emotions in check, no doubt to project strength and confidence to the people who were counting on her for leadership. But even so, Danica could see the pain she was in.

Tamaya wiped a hand over her eyes and focused ahead. She spoke before Danica had the chance. "The loss hurts, Danica. But do not fear for me. There will be time for me to grieve, and know that I shall when that time comes."

Danica nodded, satisfied with the answer. "You're tough, I'll give you that. You have my respect."

Tamaya smiled at her, a hint of warmth returning to her eyes.

Up ahead, a voice suddenly echoed across the refugees, one of Tamaya's hunters. "Something approaches!"

At once, the refugees scrambled out of the way so those with weapons and the strength to wield them could move to the head of the pack. Danica charged ahead to join them, casting a glance toward Skunk as she went. He was looking toward the commotion, but he did nothing to join the fray. His eyes were hollow, red, and puffy, his body slouched. Their eyes met, and Danica gave him a reassuring nod.

The kid's been through enough. He can sit this one out.

She made it to the front of the pack in short order, axe raised defensively in front of her. She glared ahead, looking for the approaching enemies. She couldn't see anything just yet, however. Too many spikes of old stone blocked her line of sight. Confused, she turned to the ry'thar that had spoken, a burly man with fresh scars on his face. "Where are they?" she asked.

"Not close enough to see," the ry'thar answered, pointing his stolen spear. "But the gras — the smell — is potent. Unfamiliar to me."

Danica nodded and focused her eyes forward, bracing herself for some manner of monstrous mountain creature to descend upon the pack of blood-smelling civilians in the hopes of an easy meal. She could hear it coming, now. Stone scraped under heavy footfalls, pebbles scattering and rolling down the mountainside. Whatever this thing was, it was large and had no mind for stealth. She reared back to throw her axe.

Then the beast came into view, waddling obliviously from behind a cluster of stones, and Danica's axe fell uselessly to the ground.

"Lorok!?" she exclaimed in relieved disbelief. The shelldigger turned to her, his eyes locking onto hers. There was no mistaking him, and he did not mistake her. The light in Lorok's eyes — and the delighted warbling noise he made as he bounded up the slopes — was more than enough proof of that. Danica ran to meet her mount, overjoyed when he barreled over her. His flowering nose opened wide and sniffed her all over at the same time that he slathered her in a relentless barrage of affectionate licks.

"I missed you, too!" Danica said, releasing a rare laugh as she was buried in his affection. She didn't even mind the slobber. "I thought I'd lost you, boy! Where've you been, huh? Where did you run off to?"

Lorok whined at her, pressing his forehead into her chest with considerable force. She wheezed, then chuckled and gave the great loaf a few scratches behind the ears. She could hear his tail thumping against the earth in approval. She caught sight of a crease in his segmented armor, running along his side, and cringed. Marus had hit Lorok pretty hard, she recalled. Still, it looked like he hadn't done any lasting harm. Just a new battle scar.

The ry'thar came up to Danica, quirking a brow. "You know this creature?" he asked skeptically.

"You be nice," Danica shot back, an uncharacteristically protective edge in her voice. "This big softie's been my best friend for *years*. Isn't that right, boy?"

Lorok warbled at the ry'thar, hunching protectively over Danica like a dog protecting his favored bone.

The ry'thar stared for a few more seconds, then shrugged. "Strange one," he muttered, turning back and giving the all-clear. As the battle formation dispersed, Danica finally found a chance to stand back up. Lorok was still fussing over her, prodding his nose gently near her injured side while letting off a continuous stream of concerned warbles. She smiled, petting him again.

"I'm fine, boy. Tired and bruised, but I'm fine," she assured him. The words had no meaning to the simple creature, but her tone of voice carried all the meaning Lorok needed. He snuffed at her a few more times, then took a step back, obediently waiting for a command. Danica rolled her eyes at the display and slapped a hand to her thigh. "C'mon!"

Lorok dutifully ambled into motion, following Danica as she returned to the group. She already had an idea of what Lorok could do to help out. She scanned the crowd, quickly catching sight of Skunk.

"Hop on," she suggested, bringing Lorok over. "You need some rest."

Skunk looked at her, then at Lorok. His expression was still blank. The shelldigger, sensing Skunk's state, let off a low whine and stepped forward to offer him a comforting nuzzle. A tiny ghost of a smile played briefly across Skunk's face at the expression of affection, and he returned it with a few half-hearted pats to Lorok's cheek. He looked up at Danica, and his smile faded.

Danica nodded her head up. The kobold didn't say a word. He climbed up onto Lorok's back and curled into a ball in the saddle, hiding his face from view under his tail. Sylvia faced after him, then turned to Danica. "Let me up with him," she said softly. "Please. He shouldn't be alone."

It was Tamaya who answered. "Very well," she said before stepping forward and carefully helping Sylvia up into the saddle. She felt around with her hands for a moment before Skunk's hand found hers. She nodded her thanks before laying down, draping her arms and body over and around him. He stiffened, shuddering at the touch, then slowly relaxed when Sylvia began to stroke the spot between his horns.

Danica nodded her gratitude to Tamaya and gave Lorok a pat on the cheek. "Good boy," she whispered to him. "Take it easy for them, hm? The kids have had a rough time."

Lorok warbled softly in understanding before moving to keep pace with the rest of the group as they resumed their slow journey down the mountainside.

It was strange, the way time stopped meaning anything to Skunk. The world around him moved in a distant, foggy blur. Things happened. People talked. Sometimes, they would even talk to him. Sometimes they would hold him and whisper to him. But he couldn't bring himself to care. Not right now.

He felt hollowed out. Empty. And he *hated* it. He was used to having something burning in him at all times, a spark of motivation or enthusiasm. He had nurtured it, taken care of it, and kept it as bright as he could for as long as he could remember. But now, the spark was gone. In its place was something heavy, cold, and dreary. A thick mist that had blotted out the world and everything in it, stranding him in the middle and leaving him too tired to do anything about it.

He barely moved. When food came, he barely ate. When darkness fell, he didn't sleep.

Somewhere in his mind, he knew this wasn't healthy. He knew he should talk to someone, or eat more, or get some sleep, or even just move around a little. But he couldn't bring himself to do any of it. The energy simply wasn't there. And so he waited and allowed the world to pass him by.

He wasn't sure how long it had been when, finally, something broke him out of his stupor. Sylvia's hand gently shook him by the shoulder, prompting him to open his eyes — however heavy they felt. He looked up.

He recognized the ruins of the old auriun structure in the leoroch plains. A tiny tingle of disdain wormed through his skull, but he couldn't care enough to let it live. It died as quickly as it came. The sky overhead was gray and gloomy, the dwindling light telling him that they were well into the evening. He was still on Lorok's back with Sylvia beside him. She had stayed with him since they left Actaneirum — the only point of comfort he'd had. Tamaya stood in front of them, tired, but standing tall.

"Skunk," she said gently, lifting her hand to show him what she was holding. His eyes went wide at the sight of a very familiar sword. *His* sword. The sword Amelia had given to him as a gift.

Tamaya smiled softly. "I believe this is yours."

Skunk stared at the blade for several long seconds, unsure of what to do. He sluggishly forced himself to sit up on Lorok's back and, with trembling fingers, took the hilt in his hands. He examined the blade, noting that it had withstood exposure to the elements remarkably well. The low light was reflected magnificently off of the old steel as if it had been polished only a few minutes ago. He turned it over, and a small spark of feeling began to creep into his chest.

"She entrusted it to your care," Tamaya noted quietly, taking a respectful step back. "And I believe that is where it belongs."

Skunk blinked, finally feeling something. Confusion. He looked up at Tamaya, clutching the sword to his chest. "H-how did you know that?" he asked shakily.

Tamaya smiled sadly at him. "That was the sword she had when we first met. She wielded it for all the time we traveled together," Tamaya replied softly. "It is a fine blade, Skunk. And a finer gift."

Tamaya did not say anything else. She offered Skunk and Sylvia a nod, then moved to help set up camp. Skunk watched her go for a few seconds, then returned his attention to the sword. The memory of the day Amelia had given it to him flashed vividly through his mind.

"Wow. You sure you wanna give me this?"

Amelia just smiled. "I am. It's yours. Maybe you can put it to better use than I did."

Skunk closed his eyes tight, another surge of grief sending him doubling over. He clutched the hilt of the sword like a lifeline, holding it to his pounding heart as if somehow, someway, it might bring her back to his side.

But, of course, nothing happened.

He felt Sylvia's hand on his back, but if she said anything, he did not hear it.

The Lost

Despite his heartache, reuniting with one of his mother's final gifts helped Skunk wake up to the world. As he returned to attentiveness, he saw how everyone was bruised, bloodied, and exhausted. The stink of unwashed bodies and dried blood was thick in the air, a malignant cloud following them everywhere they went. There was also the leftover smell of the kobolds they had confronted. Sharp, spicy, and dry.

They left the ruins at first light, trudging slowly and painfully through the plains. The ry'thar maintained a constant perimeter guard, ensuring nothing threatened the survivors. Thankfully, no predators deemed it worth the effort to approach such a massive herd, and if any kobolds had tailed them, they wisely broke off their pursuit.

It was another couple of days of travel before, at long last, the village of the Karjene emerged in the distance. The sight of civilization helped unwind a tightly wound spool of tension, allowing Skunk to breathe a sigh of relief. It was evening as they approached, the sky clear and colored like fire as the sun passed under the horizon. The pale ring was particularly bright, at least to Skunk's eyes.

A band of ry'thar rushed to meet them, armed and braced for battle. Tamaya stepped forward to meet them. She raised her hands and her voice to her clan. "Send for Annotha, and make ready the bonfires!" she called out. "We have wounded, hungry, and sick in our number! They must all be received and tended to! We know not if we have been followed, but I will take no chances. Establish a perimeter guard and ensure none bare their fangs at us!"

One of the ry'thar staggered forward to meet her, eyes wide with shock. "Warchief, what has happened?!" he asked, his eyes passing over the crowd, lingering particularly on the humans.

Tamaya took a breath. "It is a long story, one I shall tell later. Our losses were many, but, Spirits willing, the kalj'atla horde will trouble us no longer."

"Were you not merely to scout them out?" the ry'thar questioned.

"*Later*. These people need our aid, and we shall give it. *Now*."

Her stern tone was more than enough to mark the conversation as over. The ry'thar bowed his head, then hurried with the rest to carry out her orders. Tamaya motioned to the survivors. "Come. You shall be our guests until you are well enough to return to Addernotch."

Skunk let out a quiet sigh, relieved. They were safe, now. Finally. They still had a ways to go before they were home, but they were *alive*. With that small pearl of hope settling comfortably in his chest, Skunk hopped down from Lorok's back. He took a moment to stretch, then held out his hands for Sylvia. "We're here. Hands," he said softly.

Sylvia reached down, her expression contorting with uncertainty. Skunk took her wrists with a firm but gentle grip and helped her make the descent.

Lorok waited patiently, having put together on his own that Sylvia was unwell.

Once Skunk was confident Sylvia was solidly on the ground, he looked to Danica. She was nearby, looking about ready to pass out. She gave him a solemn nod before taking Lorok's lead and guiding him into the village. Skunk offered her a small smile. "Thank you, Danica."

Danica waved over her shoulder at him. "Don't mention it."

Skunk watched her go for a few long moments, wanting to say more but not knowing how to say it.

Beside him, Sylia let out a quiet gasp. Turning to her, Skunk saw her face contorting in a pained wince.

"What is it?" he asked, lifting his hands.

"The stinging," Sylvia replied, tensing involuntarily. "In my eyes. It's getting worse."

Worried, Skunk reached for Sylvia's blindfold. He hesitated with his fingers inches away. "C-can I take a look?" he asked timidly.

Sylvia nodded, and Skunk carefully lifted the blindfold. His stomach twisted in a strange mixture of revulsion and sympathy. The kobolds had not been gentle when they took her eyes. Her lids were a mangled mess of swollen, puffy flesh around gaping, shredded sockets. There was a repulsive abundance of dried blood, scabs, and curdled lumps of what could only be pus. There was a putrid stench as well, rotting flesh, blood, and other unsavory things.

"It's bad," Skunk whispered, suddenly thankful that he'd had so little to eat lately. He lowered the blindfold. "You've probably got an infection. You okay?"

"Tamaya said we're going to see a healer. I'll be fine," Sylvia replied, leaning into him to share her warmth. "I'm not the one who should be answering that question, though. Am I?"

Skunk winced and looked away. His tail swished behind him in agitation, his chest tightening with emotion. He did not speak.

"Skunk, you need help."

"I know," Skunk finally agreed, his despondent voice thick in his throat. "But not right now. You're the one with the missing eyes. Let's get you taken care of," he suggested, tugging at her hand to lead her into the ry'thar village.

Sylvia kept her head down, allowing her hair to hide her face. In some ways, Skunk was glad for that, guilty as it made him feel. Every time he saw her blindfold, he felt like it was glaring at him. Accusing him.

And there were a *lot* of things to accuse him of, weren't there? Failing to protect Sylvia in Addernotch. Failing to keep them from taking away her eyes. Failing to keep the kobolds from shooting his mother. Failing to save more lives from Karak and that damned egg. Worst of all, incurring Azada's wrath and getting Amelia killed.

He shook his head with a miserable moan. He tried to convince himself that he didn't know what would happen, that he couldn't have predicted things would go so wrong, that he couldn't be held responsible. But the notions sounded hollow. He *should* have known that the mother was still nearby, he should have *known* she'd take revenge if her egg was destroyed! So many things he *should* have known, *should* have considered, *should* have done. But he didn't, and now...

"Skunk? You're crying," Sylvia's voice cut through his thoughts.

He blinked, realizing that she was right. He choked down a sob and rubbed the back of his hand over his eyes. "Sorry, I'm sorry," he mumbled weakly.

"No, Skunk," Sylvia whispered, pressing herself closer to him. "Don't apologize."

It took far longer for Skunk to compose himself than he wanted, but Sylvia was patient with him. The ache remained, but he had other things he had to focus on for now.

"Come on," he said quietly, trailing behind the procession of the wounded for Annotha's yurt. "Let's get fixed up."

Annotha received her patients with the patience and grace of a saint. Even though half of the people coming to her for treatment were not of her tribe, she accepted them all with a smile, provided thorough explanations of what she was doing, and offered countless assurances that all would be well. Some of the survivors from Addernotch were resistant to her at first, harboring superstitions about either the ry'thar or magic, but few held out for long.

Skunk and Sylvia found a place off to one side and settled down to wait. It wasn't long before Annotha got through the most dire cases and came to them. She smiled comfortingly down at him, carrying herself with courtesy and dignity. She knelt before them. "Hello, children," she said softly. "Where are you hurt?"

Skunk shook his head. "Forget me. Sylvia first," he said. "They... t-they took her eyes, Annotha. We think there's an infection. Is there anything you can do?"

Annotha turned to Sylvia, and her smile disappeared. She reached out with a hand. "May I see?"

Sylvia nodded without a word, and Annotha lifted the blindfold. Skunk looked away, unable to let himself see the injury again.

"An infection indeed," Annotha confirmed thoughtfully. "Though for how old this wound looks, it could be far worse. You are lucky. Your name was Sylvia, yes?"

"Yes."

"That is a very pretty name. Now, Sylvia, please hold still. You will feel *intense* itching. You must resist the urge to scratch or move. Are you ready?"

Sylvia nodded, and the shaman went to work. Skunk kept looking away, but he could hear the gentle hum of magic, and Annotha speaking under her breath. He heard Sylvia gasp and felt her tensing beside him when the itch set in. He had half a mind to rake his claws across Annotha's face then and there, but he held himself and his spiraling protective instincts in place. After several seconds, Annotha lowered the blindfold back into place. "There. You'll want to get some food in you and get plenty of rest, but the worst of the infection has been averted."

"Thank you, miss," Sylvia said quietly.

Skunk, determining it was safe to look, faced Annotha again. "What about her sight?"

Annotha's smile vanished, and Skunk's hope went with it. The ry'thar shook her head. "I am sorry. Healing magic such as this can only accelerate a body's natural ability to heal itself. Without the eyes that were taken from you, I am afraid there is nothing I can do."

Skunk felt his heart dropping into the pits of his stomach. "S-she'll never see again?!"

"If a means of restoring her sight exists, it is beyond my power. I am sorry."

Skunk took in a deep, shuddering breath before dropping his face into his hands. "Dammit!" he whimpered, shivering and hunching. "Gods *dammit!* I'm so sorry, Sylvia."

"It's okay, Skunk," she assured him, running her hand down his back. "I told you. The darkness isn't so bad. I'll adapt."

"You shouldn't *have* to!" Skunk protested, lifting his head to look at her in disbelief. "It's not right!"

Sylvia, despite everything, just smiled. "I'm not worried. I have people to help me."

Skunk just stared at her, dumbfounded. "How? How do you *do* that?" he asked as if in a trance.

Sylvia tilted her head. "Do what?"

"That—that *thing* you're doing. How do you live with what's happened to you and not... n-not..."

Sylvia cut him off by taking hold of his hand and squeezing it. "Because my life's not over, yet," she whispered. "Is yours?"

Skunk blinked, not sure how to answer that. He was still alive, obviously, and he wasn't going to die tonight. But he had the feeling that wasn't what she meant.

"She speaks with wisdom, Skunk," Annotha said with a clear note of respect in her voice. "Now. Are *you* hurt?"

Skunk was quiet for a few moments, then tentatively lifted the tattered remains of his shirt. "I, uh, I think I have a few broken bones. Lots of bruises, too," he mumbled dumbly, looking down at the swollen bruise along his torso. He touched a hand to his snout and cringed as it flared with pain. "Ack! A-and my nose. I got beat up a lot."

Annotha gave Skunk a thorough examination, scrutinizing each of his wounds, then placed a hand against him while the other gripped her ringstone.

She uttered a quiet incantation. As the words flowed, so too did the ringstone glow with luma. A warm tingling sensation began to seep under Skunk's scales, deeper than any massage or oil ever could.

And then it became a maddening itch, and he fought the urge to gasp. He squirmed slightly while the magic did its work, slowly but surely healing his injuries. After a minute, Annotha pulled her hand back and nodded in satisfaction. "There. That should do it. You will still be tender, so don't do anything strenuous for at least a few days if you can help it, and make sure you eat something *substantial*."

Skunk lowered his shirt. "T-thank you. Um, d-do you mind if we stay here?" he asked. "I- I don't wanna get up."

Annotha nodded in understanding and rose to her full height. "You may stay as long as you wish," she told him before bowing her head and saying something in ry'thari. Skunk did not know the meaning of the words, but her tone was comforting. With that, she drifted away to tend to her next patient, leaving Skunk and Sylvia alone.

Skunk looked down, toying with his fingers and allowing his thoughts to wander. Sylvia rested her head on his shoulder, and he gave a slight smile. "Clingy today?" he asked, trying to sound teasing.

Sylvia nodded into his shoulder. "I want to make sure you're alright," she whispered.

Skunk closed his eyes. He leaned into her embrace, enjoying the contact. "Thank you, Sylvia. I mean it. Thank you so much. I dunno what I'd do if I lost you, too."

"You would live," Sylvia told him.

Skunk wasn't so sure, but he didn't debate her on it. He closed his eyes and rested his chin on her head. "I guess."

The two sat in silence, and at long last, the exhaustion of the last few days caught up to him. The last thing he felt was Sylvia's arms cradling him and bringing him to rest in her lap before he drifted away to sleep.

"Skunk. Hey, Skunk. Wake up," Sylvia's voice echoed through the black fog of Skunk's dreamless slumber, slowly rousing him. "Something's going on."

Skunk, groggy, lifted his face from her lap. He felt stiff, sore, and altogether too tired to deal with the world. There was a deep-seated ache in his spine, however, which told him that it would be unwise to stay like this any longer. He gave a big yawn as he rose and looked around.

The healer's yurt was deserted, with only a handful of the more critically wounded survivors resting in the few beds scattered around. Everyone else was gone. The candles had gone out at some point, leaving everything cast in shadow. The only light came from the flickering glow of torches beyond the tent, and the light of the pale ring barely penetrating the roof.

Skunk grunted as a few of his stiff bones popped, then turned to Sylvia. "How long was I out?"

Sylvia shrugged. "A couple of hours, I think. I don't know."

Skunk hummed and stood. He stretched languidly, a few more satisfying pops sounding from his back and tail. "Here, lemme help you up," he said, holding out a hand to her.

Sylvia took it and slowly rose to her feet. She wobbled unsteadily, her grip tightening on him until she found her balance. Worried, he opened his mouth to ask if she was alright, but she cut him off before he had the chance. "I'm okay, don't worry. My legs are asleep, that's all."

Skunk stared for a moment before a certain heat began to fill his cheeks. It occurred to him that his scales weren't exactly the *softest* thing in the world for someone to keep in their lap for 'a couple of hours.' "Oh... uh, sorry," he apologized sheepishly.

Sylvia giggled and gave him a playful nudge. "You're fine," she assured him. "But something's going on outside. Tamaya came by a minute ago. She wants us to meet with the tribe in front of the bonfire. She said you'd know what it meant."

Skunk stiffened as any semblance of a good mood he had melted away. He took a slow, deep breath. "Y-yeah, I know. They're going to hold a funeral," he said quietly. "For e-everyone that didn't make it."

Sylvia's expression remained unchanged. She took his hand in hers, their fingers lacing together. "Do you want to go?" she asked. "If not, we can stay here."

Skunk shook his head and started for the exit. "I'm not going to sit this out," he decided. He licked his suddenly dry lips and blinked away the moisture building in his eyes. "Mom deserves to have me there."

Sylvia smiled in sympathetic approval. "Of course. Lead on."

It was surprisingly warm outside, but eerily silent. All of the other lights of the village had gone dark, save for the bonfire. The rest of the village — those well enough to attend, at least — were gathered around it. Several of the people from Addernotch were here as well. They looked about at the strange ceremony with curiosity. Even Danica was there, lingering by the edge of the firelight with Lorok.

Tamaya and Annotha stood before the fire, speaking in hushed whispers. Skunk held his head up high and walked toward them. Tamaya spotted his approach and respectfully pulled away from her discussion with Annotha to meet him. "Roluth tha. You're up," she said, keeping her voice low. "How are you feeling?"

"Like crap," Skunk replied before shrugging his shoulders. "But I'm alive."

Tamaya examined him quietly. "There is no shame if you wish to rest," she told him. "After everything you've endured—"

"I'm fine," Skunk lied. "It's okay. I want— I *need* to be here for this."

Tamaya studied him a moment longer, not entirely convinced. In the end, though, she nodded her assent. "Very well. Find a place," she instructed before patting him on the shoulder. Skunk watched as she returned to Annotha, then guided Sylvia to an empty spot off to one side. He turned to face the fire and settled in to wait.

Tamaya and Annotha exchanged a few more words in their language before the war chief stepped forward. As she had when Skunk had watched the ceremony before, she projected her voice loud enough for all in attendance to hear her loud and clear. This time, though, she spoke in the common tongue. "Brothers and sisters of the Karjene, and our friends and neighbors from Addernotch, I thank you all for being here. We have come together this night, under the ringlight, to honor our friends and families who were taken from us by the mutant Karak and his perverse ambitions."

Tamaya folded her hands behind her back and began to pace before the fire. Her every step was slow and deliberate, her eyes passing over every gathered soul, one at a time. "When my hunters and I set out, it was not to confront the beast, let alone within the beating heart of their lair. But such is what transpired. We were bested in battle by the abomination, and to my eternal shame, we were taken prisoner. We lost many loved ones in that place. Friends. Brothers and sisters. Sons and daughters. Mothers and fathers."

Skunk kept the pang of hurt in his chest from displaying on his face. Sylvia must have sensed it, though. She squeezed his hand tightly, helping him to keep grounded.

Tamaya paused for a moment, collecting herself, before turning to face the crowd. "All had seemed lost, and I will confess, I was afraid. But had it not been for the bravery and quick thinking of the kalj'atla named Skunk Lanswel, *none* of us would have been able to return."

Skunk went rigid as, all at once, countless pairs of eyes were on him. Put on the spot, he looked around, wondering if he should say something.

Tamaya gestured at him. "Where I had surrendered to fate, *he* found a way to break our bonds. Where I had given up against an impossible foe, *he* found a way to deprive that foe of his strength, allowing us all the chance to fight back and *survive*."

Skunk opened his mouth, stammering. He wanted to refute the claims, to call back that all he did was make Azada angry and get his mother killed. Tamaya continued before he had the chance as if she knew what he was going to say and wanted to shoot down his argument preemptively.

"He is small, yes. Small, and he lacks strength. But unlike the enemy we faced, Skunk is possessed of a good heart, a keen mind, and the unshakable resolve to do what is *right* for those he walks beside. So though we gather tonight to mourn and appease the dead, let us also give thanks to this kobold, for it is thanks to him that we may enjoy the gift of those who yet live. Let all in attendance know that, as of this moment, Skunk Lanswel is named roluth tha - honored friend - of the Karjene!"

Skunk again opened his mouth to protest, but the words died on his tongue as the voices of the crowd washed over him. He stood there, dumbstruck into silence as all of these people raised their voices. Cheering. For *him*. Even the humans of Addernotch were calling out to him, offering him gratitude.

"But..." he choked out, but over the calls of the crowd, the word was inaudible. Part of him wanted to believe he was imagining this, that it was all some form of bizarre hallucination. How could it be that these people were singing his praises? Before, all he had received were glares of scorn and suspicion — and even calls for his execution. This was...

His vision blurred with tears again. It was different this time, though. These tears were warmer. Happier.

Sylvia's hand squeezed him, a silent gesture of reassurance. She didn't say a word.

After a few seconds, the whoops of gratitude began to die down, and the smile on Tamaya's face fell away. Annotha stepped forward to continue the ceremony. "Come, friends. Let us not leave the souls of the dead to wallow in uncertainty. The flame shall guide them to us. Let them know that they live on in our memory, and us in theirs. Let those who fought to defend those who could not defend themselves know that their sacrifice was not in vain. Let the dead know that we *live* — and that we shall live well, with their names and deeds burning bright in our hearts, until the day we join them upon the wind."

With that, Tamaya began humming. The rest of the tribe was quick to join in, and as Skunk heard the first few notes, he expected it to be the same song that he had heard last time. He even prepared himself to sing along, not wanting to be insensitive to their culture. But it was a very different lullaby that reached his ears. He knew it. He'd heard it countless times when he was young — and most recently, in a cold iron cell, in a dark cave.

It was his mother's lullaby.

The ry'thar stepped forward, offering whispered words to their departed loved ones and casting their gifts into the flame. It wasn't long before the humans, catching on to the ceremony, stepped forward to join them. With every gift and every offering, the flames surged, and more voices joined in the choir. Skunk listened as the wordless song Amelia sang to him so long ago turned to words.

Tamaya came to Skunk's side and faced the flame. He looked up at her. "This song," he whispered only loud enough for Tamaya to hear him.

"We do not sing only one song for the dead, roluth tha," Tamaya whispered back, misunderstanding his surprise. "We have many."

Skunk swallowed heavily, his eyes misting over. "W-what do the words mean?" he choked out.

Tamaya looked down at him for a moment, then turned back to the flames. She folded her hands behind her back, her lips pressing tightly together, her whiskers twitching in thought. "It is difficult to translate directly," she admitted. "But it is a song about... trust, I suppose. And gratitude. We are thanking the spirits of our dead for all of the good they brought into our lives while they were with us. We are telling them that we trust them to be fine without us, and we ask that they, in turn, trust *us* to be fine without *them*."

Tamaya's eyes fell, as did her ears. Her tail swished behind her a few times. "Your mother. She loved this song. She would hum it all the time when she was with us," she said at length. "She said it was beautiful, even if it was sad."

Skunk nodded quietly. "She used to hum it to me when I was little."

There were not very many people left who had to make their offerings. It was his turn. Tamaya placed a hand on his back. "Then come. It is time she knew your answer," she told him softly.

Skunk, on stiff legs, allowed himself to be escorted toward the fire. Sylvia clung to him the entire way, a comforting presence warmer than the inferno could ever be. To his surprise, Danica met them halfway, her jaw set and her eyes focused. Skunk tilted his head at her.

"I didn't know her long," Danica explained curtly. "But I owe her this much."

That was all the answer Skunk needed. He smiled at Danica, however briefly, before looking up into the flames. They burned brightly, to the point they were almost blinding to his sensitive eyes. He could see the embers dancing, the coils of flame slithering through the air like agitated snakes.

Tamaya whispered to him. "Speak your heart."

Skunk didn't look at her. He felt silly, staring into these flames, taking part in this ceremony. What difference would his words make? Amelia was dead. She couldn't hear him anymore. He'd be wasting his breath on the wind... wouldn't he?

But then again, Amelia had lived among these people for quite some time. She loved them. To her, they may as well have been a second family. And that meant they may as well have been family to him, too.

What could it hurt?

Taking a breath to steady himself, he gently pried Sylvia off of him and took another step forward, so he was closer to the flames than anyone else could be. He looked up into the billowing smoke cloud, looking for some sign, some hint.

It might have just been a trick of the light or a moment of coincidence. But for a second, just a fraction of a second, he thought he saw a face looking back at him in the smoke.

It was smiling.

It was probably just his mind playing tricks on him. An illusion of desperate desire. But for the moment? It would be enough.

"Mom, I," he whispered, his voice catching. He swallowed hard and tried again. "I'm okay. I made it out of the caves. We made it back to the Karjene. Not everyone made it, but, w-we're okay. Y-you saved my life."

He looked down, balling his hands up into tight fists at his sides. "Um, I, I don't know what to say. Just, T-thank you. F-for finding me. For taking care of me. F-for *everything* you gave me."

He screwed his eyes shut, trying in vain to maintain his composure. The tightness in his throat returned, and he had to sniffle before he could keep talking. "I w-won't ever forget you. I p-promise. And I'll be o-okay. I'll live my life, a-and t-try and be happy, just like you asked. I'll m-make you proud of me."

There was a pause, a moment of quiet, and Skunk recalled that there was one more part to this ritual. Sniffling again, he touched a hand to his chest. He knew what his offering would be.

With a twitch of his fingers, the clasp holding the charred, tattered remnants of his cloak came undone. The black fur fabric fell loosely from his shoulders, bunching up in his left hand. He stared down at it for a moment, his eyes going over the rips and tears the garment had acquired in all of the recent chaos. He could barely even see the white stripes running down the length anymore. It was barely recognizable.

It would have to be enough.

"I-I'm going to miss you," he whispered to the flames. "A-and I know you'll miss me, too. S-so, here. H-have this."

With that, he rolled up his sleeve and pushed his hand into the flames. In the blink of an eye, the cloak ignited, the smell reaching him immediately. He winced but did not pull his hand away. He held it there in the blaze, feeling the fur of the cloak as it wrinkled and burned in his fingers. In time, it turned crisp, then brittle, and at last crumbled in his hands, reduced to ash in the flames. A large plume of smoke rose from the destroyed clothing, ascending and vanishing into the night sky. Skunk watched it go and pulled his now naked hand out of the flames.

"A little piece of me," he said quietly, then touched the hilt of Amelia's sword at his belt. "And a little piece of you. So we'll never be far apart."

With that, Skunk stepped back. He had nothing else to say. Tamaya nodded in approval, but it was Sylvia who spoke next.

"Your son is one of the greatest people I have ever known, miss Lanswel," she said gently. "You've raised a wonderful person, and the world's a better place for having him in it."

Next, Danica. She stared into the flames for a long moment, an awkward frown on her face. She was just as uncomfortable with the ritual as Skunk had been, if not more. Still, she found her words in the end. "I didn't know you long," she confessed quietly. "I don't know if I ever earned the right to call you my friend. But we fought side by side. I'm happy to call you my sister-in-arms, and you have nothing but my respect. And the girl is right. You raised a good kid."

Finally, it was Tamaya's turn to offer words. She knelt before the flame and closed her eyes. "I wish I could have saved you, my dearest friend," she said, and Skunk's keen hearing picked out the beginning of a tremble in the whispered voice. For the first time in all the time he had known Tamaya, she was allowing her grief to show. "But know that your sacrifice was not in vain. My people still live. *Your* people live. Your *son* lives. He saved us all, and he will be honored by my people until the end of time. If ever he should need me, I promise you, I will be there for him."

With that, they stepped back, their parting words said, and Skunk joined his voice to the song. He did not know the words, but the melody had been in his heart for his entire life. He hummed to it, hoping that it would be enough. No one seemed to mind. All the humans were doing much the same.

Finally, Tamaya stood alone before the fire. She whispered something under her breath before casting the final offering into the flames. As before, they flashed and snapped, turning a vibrant shade of blue. At once, the singing came to an end, and silence fell over the village.

A moment later, the ringing came. A gentle, melodious noise that reverberated across the village, heard clearly by all in attendance. With that, Skunk knew that the ceremony was done.

He looked down quietly. Without a word and with Sylvia at his side, he turned and walked away.

Skunk and Sylvia walked out of the Karjene village and headed north. They didn't go far, Skunk just wanted some privacy. They found a fallen tree by the riverside, granting them a pristine view of the hills. Skunk plonked himself down on the log with a heavy sigh and buried his face in his hands.

Sylvia sat beside him. "What are we doing out here?" she asked him.

"Just— I dunno," Skunk confessed, lifting his eyes. Under the light of the ring, the fields seemed to stretch on forever. A cool breeze blew by from the northern mountains, sending the grass wavering and filling the air with a soft, meditative rustle. The fresh smell of disturbed dirt reached him. "I just wanted to get away from everything for a bit."

Sylvia hummed quietly. She took his hand in hers for what must have been the hundredth time. "Are you feeling any better?"

Skunk pondered the question for a little while. In the end, he shrugged. "I dunno. I'm too tired to know. I just feel kinda numb now."

Sylvia hummed, and once again leaned against him, lending her warmth. He was able to smile this time, and wrapped an arm around her, pulling her closer.

There they sat for what felt like an eternity, basking in one another's company as they had done since the day they had met. Neither of them said a word. Neither of them needed to.

Skunk looked up at the pale ring, allowing the light to draw him in as it always did. He stared for a long, long while, and for the first time since this began, it felt like he had a moment to just *relax*. Be still and process everything.

Eventually, he looked down, and his smile disappeared. "So what happens now?"

Sylvia tilted her head.

"What happens? What do we *do?*" Skunk clarified. "Hell, what do *I* do? After everything that's happened, everything we just went through. What happens next? I mean, do we just go home? Back to Addernotch?"

Sylvia nodded. "I think so. It's home. It needs us."

Skunk wasn't so sure. He lifted his left hand, inspecting it. His bandages had been destroyed in the bonfire, leaving his scar on full display. He flexed his fingers a few times, frowning. "I dunno, Sylvia. It just feels weird. The idea of going back, after all of this? Trying to live normal lives again? Can we *ever* really live a normal life? Especially without...?"

He trailed off, but Sylvia picked up on his meaning.She squeezed him closer but said nothing.

Skunk sighed and leaned against her, closing his eyes. Once again, the duo fell quiet, and Skunk returned his attention to the land around them. A flock of nocturnal birds flew through the air in the northern skies, a thin cloud standing out brilliantly against the pristine silver of the ring. He watched them fly to the south, and his eyes fell back on the Karjene village.

He blinked in surprise when he saw Danica and Lorok heading their way. The dwarf raised a hand in greeting. "There you are!" she called. "Was wondering where you two went."

Skunk and Sylvia rotated to face her, surprised by her sudden appearance. Lorok lumbered up to Skunk ahead of his rider and offered the kobold an affectionate nuzzle. Skunk laughed quietly and reached out to pet the beast, then turned to the dwarf. "We wanted some privacy," he said.

Danica nodded. "Fair. Mind if I join you?" she asked before nodding up at the sky. "Sky's clear. Would be a shame to waste it."

Skunk stared at her a moment, then smiled. "I don't mind. Sylvia?"

"I don't mind."

"Good, 'cause I wasn't going to take no for an answer," Danica rumbled before knocking her knuckles on Lorok's shell. He immediately and obediently flopped over onto his side, kicking up a small cloud of dust and leaving his squishy belly exposed. Danica lay down and rested her head on him with a satisfied sigh.

Skunk snickered at the display, but his mirth quickly died away. He stared at Danica for a few seconds, noticing that her eyes were trained squarely on the ring. She wore no smile, and her thumbs fiddled with one another over her belly. After a moment, she closed her eyes and let out a sigh. "Well. Guess we're just about done, then, huh?"

Skunk looked down. He had figured this was coming. "I guess so. What'll you do now?"

Danica shrugged. "No idea. Wander, I guess?" she said, sounding genuinely unsure of herself. "Getting to the Sunstone's been my entire goal for a good few years now. I haven't taken the time to think about what I'd do when that was done."

Skunk twitched guiltily, remembering the destruction of the relic. He looked away in shame, his tail thumping agitatedly against his seat. "Yeah, uh, I'm sorry about that, Danica," he apologized.

Danica scoffed. "Nah. Don't. You did the right thing. Karak ruined it beyond repair by the time we showed up. Even if I somehow lugged it back to Stonefall, it wouldn't fix things. Better to just destroy it."

Skunk relaxed somewhat. He still felt guilty for destroying such a precious and unique artifact, but he recognized the truth in her words. Still, there was at least one thing he could do to make amends. He reached into his pouch and procured the shard. It still let out a gentle light, but only barely. He turned to Danica and hefted it up. "Here. Catch."

Danica looked and snatched the shard as Skunk tossed it to her. She looked at it for a second, then smiled at him. "Thanks, kid."

"You're welcome. Sorry for stealing it."

"Five's sake, kid, you *need* to stop apologizing. Again, you did the right thing. If you hadn't taken it, we'd all be dead," Danica reprimanded him, though he did not miss the smile on her face. "And you didn't *steal* it. You just borrowed it without asking permission."

Skunk looked away, smiling a little. "Sorry," he apologized automatically before slapping a hand to his face.

"What did I *just* say?" Danica accused him in a jovial tone.

The two broke out into a fit of laughter a moment later, the happy sound helping to lift Skunk's spirits.

As their laughter died down, Sylvia spoke up. "Danica, if you don't have any other plans, maybe you could stay with us in Addernotch for a while?" she suggested, leaning forward in her seat.

Danica paused, her brow furrowing. She rolled the shard between her fingers as she considered the suggestion, then pocketed it and put her hands behind her head. "Meh. Why not? I can stick around for a few weeks. You know, lend some muscle while you folks get your balance," she said before flashing Skunk a smile. "Besides. The little guy's...*fun*, I guess."

Skunk was, understandably, taken by surprise by the sudden compliment. He leaned toward Danica, his lips quirking up slightly. "I'm *fun?*" he parroted knowingly.

Danica turned her head away to hide the fact she was blushing, but he'd seen it already. "S-shut up your face," Danica grunted.

Skunk laughed again. "Ha. Thanks, Danica. You're a good friend."

"I just told you to shut up, and you're calling me a friend?!" Danica asked incredulously. "When did that happen?"

Skunk just smiled and stared up at the sky. "When you heard me out," he said. "When you listened to what I had to say. And you didn't judge me for it."

Danica was quiet for a few long seconds. At last, she conceded with a shrug and settled more into Lorok's belly. "Alright. Fine. You win, we're friends."

Skunk's tail tapped on the log a few times in a sign of victory.

With that, the group fell into a comfortable silence. Skunk slid down the log to sit on the ground. Using the log like a pillow, he looked up at the stars and closed his eyes again. His heart still ached for his lost mother, but he felt somehow lighter. Maybe there had been something to that ceremony after all? And even if he had lost an advocate in Amelia, he still had two good friends with him now, and there was always Seto back in Addernotch. He would never stop missing his mother, and he knew he was far from done weeping over her. But for now? For this moment? He was content.

And then he wasn't.

All at once, a chill ran up his spine from the base of his tail, pooling at the base of his skull. His eyes snapped open, and he bolted up to his feet as a powerful fight-or-flight instinct awakened within him. Sylvia stood as well, a hand lifting to her chest. Behind them, Danica and Lorok rose.

"You feel that, too?" Danica asked, her hand going for her retrieved axe.

Skunk nodded, a lump forming in his throat. "Y-yeah," he said, taking a step back. Something was wrong. They looked around as a terrible feeling, oppressive and powerful, crawled across them like an army of flesh-eating worms. The air shifted and trembled as if the world itself was suddenly afraid. Overhead, the pale ring itself almost looked to be glowing brighter — but the light was anything but comforting.

It felt *angry*.

And then Skunk heard it. An earthquake, but not the steady rumble one might expect. It was repetitive, the pounding rhythm of a wild drumbeat. With every beat, the earth shook. Skunk turned his eyes north to the source of the sensation. His blood turned to ice in his veins.

"It can't be..." Danica gasped, walking forward to stand beside Skunk.

In the distance, a massive shape had come into view and was thundering across the plains with great loping strides. Its form was obscured by the cloud of dust it created with every step, but even its silhouette was distinct enough to identify it.

Four legs.

A long neck.

Two flaring wings, one of them mangled to the point of uselessness.

A single emerald green eye that glowed with a malice that defied description.

Skunk's tail tucked low, his heart withering in his chest. "It's her," he choked out as the realization settled over him.

Azada was alive.

And she was coming for them.

Wrath

In all of his life, never before had Skunk been as afraid as he was right now. His body trembled with panic, and it was almost impossible to think through the screaming chorus of instincts telling him to *run*. Not even the anticipation of being sacrificed had inspired such a profound, all-consuming *terror* in him.

"We need to get back," Skunk declared, spinning toward Danica. *"Now!"*

Danica nodded, patting Lorok and urging him to rise. The great beast warbled in fear, shrinking from the approaching dragon like a scolded puppy.

Taking Sylvia's hand in his, Skunk tugged her toward the village. They only made it a few yards before she staggered and fell to her knees, tripping on the uneven terrain.

"Dammit!" Danica cursed, sprinting over and lifting Sylvia in an awkward underarm carry. "Lorok!" The shelldigger didn't need to be told twice. He dutifully lowered himself, and Danica tossed Sylvia on, barely giving the poor girl a chance to protest the harsh handling. "Hold on to something and do *not* let go!"

All Skunk heard from Sylvia was a terrified whimper as her searching fingers curled tightly around the leather.

It took less than a minute to make it back to the bonfire. The rumblings of Azada's approach were already audible, and Tamaya's sentries had already brought word. The warriors barked orders to one another while shepherding the frightened humans toward the southern side of the village.

"Tamaya?!" Skunk called, looking around desperately. "Where are you?!"

"Here!" Came the reply from nearby. Tamaya jogged to meet them, a spear already in hand. "I heard from my scouts. It's her. The dragon. Azada."

"How did she survive?!" Danica demanded, glaring back over her shoulder. "A *mountain* fell on her!"

"There's a reason the dragons survived where the auriuns did not," Tamaya replied with narrowed eyes.

"What do we do?!" Sylvia asked, her voice quivering. Skunk's heart skipped a beat at the sound. She had always been such a sturdy and stalwart rock for him. Even when she was scared, she maintained her composure. To see her now, shivering so fiercely...

"We run is what we do!" Danica offered quickly. "My axe is good, but it isn't cutting down a dragon!"

"I agree, but that will not be enough," Tamaya said, nostrils flaring. "Just as your axe cannot penetrate her scales, our legs cannot outrun hers! If we flee, she will run us down long before we see the treeline!"

"There's gotta be something!" Skunk shouted, his fingers twitching.

"I'm working on it!" Tamaya snapped before turning to Annotha, who had followed close behind her. "Annotha, round everyone up. Lead them south with all speed!" she ordered, then turned to the rest of the crowd. "Those of you with the strength to fight and run at length, find a weapon and form up on me! We need to keep that beast occupied until the others can make it to safety!"

Skunk blinked, staring up at Tamaya in wide-eyed horror. "W-what?!" he shouted, grabbing her wrist. "Are you insane?! You'll get yourself killed!"

Tamaya pulled her wrist from his grasp. "If that is what it takes to fulfill my duty to my people, then so be it," she stated. Before Skunk had a chance to argue, she turned and ran off to organize her doomed resistance. He reached after her, watching in despair as a small team of nine ry'thar and a handful of humans came together.

"They'll die," Danica noted grimly. "It'll be a miracle if they even manage to slow that thing down."

Skunk shook his head, his mind scrambling. There *had* to be another way! But try as he might, he couldn't think of one. Everyone was exhausted, wounded, lacked training, or lacked equipment. Any fight against Azada would inevitably end in everyone dying.

And that meant Tamaya was going to die.

Skunk's heart twisted. He didn't even realize he was chasing Tamaya down until he caught up to her. "Tamaya! Please! Your people need you alive more than dead! You're useless to them as a corpse!"

Tamaya shook her head, her eyes fixed on her work as she took up a second spear from a rack. "I know. But I see no other options. As Addernotch is your home, this is mine, and I will give my life to defend it."

Skunk reached out to her, but she brushed his hand away. Still, he spoke. "Let someone else lead the distraction! We need you!"

Tamaya scowled at him, her lip curling up into a vicious growl. "I am *not* a coward, Skunk! I will not send someone else to die in my stead against their will!"

Finally, Skunk gave up any pretense of selflessness. He shut his eyes and raised his voice into a desperate shout. *"I can't lose anyone else!"*

For a brief second, the clamor of the panicking village seemed distant and unimportant as all eyes fell on him. It was for less than a second, but that moment of stillness felt like an eternity. Skunk held Tamaya's gaze, his vision blurring.

Unfortunately, if Tamaya had anything to say in response, she didn't get the chance.

A stream of emerald flames tore through the heart of Karjene behind her. A concussive blast created by superheated air punched into Skunk's gut. Deep pain blossomed in his core, driving the air from his lungs as he was thrown back against Danica even as she braced against Lorok.

Skunk had to close his eyes against the blinding light, but when he opened them again, the world slowed to a crawl.

An entire swath of the village was just... gone. There were only ashes left. Ashes, flames, and the silhouettes of what had once been people. Humans. Ry'thar. Men and women. The elderly. The young. Skunk blinked, and the silhouettes were gone.

The screaming, however. The screaming lingered.

There, above the flames, a shadow loomed. It strode through the cone of annihilation its exhale had created, its bulk and shape blocking out the sky and bathing the world in the deepest blackness.

Azada had arrived.

Her voice rolled across the land, a low rumble that made the heavens themselves shiver. "Where is he?" she hissed. Her eyes fell on the blue bonfire. She grunted and brought her claws down upon it, snuffing the funeral pyre with a sound like thunder, sending splinters scattering through the air. Her great wings, damaged though they were, spread and flapped, buffeting the ry'thar, who had only now gotten to their feet and forcing them back down.

"Fragile creatures," Azada continued, taking a single, threatening step forward. The earth jumped, and the air pushed out from the dragon with her every move. It was like the very fabric of creation was retreating from her. And rightly so.

If only mankind had the good sense to do the same.

"*Die, monster!*" Some idiotic man screamed, a human. He picked up a discarded ry'thari axe and stepped forward to attack Azada. His eyes were wide and manic, unfocused. Skunk couldn't tell if it was madness, fear, or bravery that drove him to act with such stupidity.

Azada scowled at him, raised her clawed foot, and brought it down on the man. The earth cracked under the force of the step, and the air thumped as the poor fool was reduced to a splatter of blood and powdered bone dust. Azada snorted, acrid smoke rising from her nostrils.

"Time to go!" Danica proclaimed, getting back to her feet and hefting Skunk onto Lorok's back next to Sylvia. Skunk nodded, his hand finding Sylvia's shoulder to steady them both. His eyes, meanwhile, flicked up to Azada, and he almost fainted when he realized she was staring directly at him.

"There you are," she purred. More smoke rose from her nostrils, and the armored scales of her chest glowed green. Embers and sparks dripped from her maw like spittle, as if she were drooling at the idea of killing him. "*Murderer!*"

"Run! *Run! Hya!*" Danica shouted the moment she was mounted. He warbled out his agreement and began to run.

"What about Tamaya?!" Sylvia asked, shouting to be heard above the screaming. Skunk, also worried for the ry'thar, glanced over his shoulder. Thankfully, she and her volunteers had not been caught in the first surge of fire. Tamaya was scrambling to her feet, reaching for a spear.

"I'm sorry! We can't help her now!" Danica shot back. "If she's smart, she'll run, too!"

The ground lurched under them, and Lorok stumbled with a cry of fear. Skunk and Sylvia screamed, clinging to one another to keep steady.

And then the world went dark.

Skunk looked up. Azada had jumped, eclipsing the sky with her immense size. Her wings flared, slowing her descent and creating another powerful gust that pressed Lorok into the earth. She landed in front of them, her back facing them, the ground sundering under her weight. Her tail whipped around, and Skunk saw numerous bony spikes protruding from the tip.

Acting on instinct, Skunk grabbed Sylvia and leaped from Lorok's back at the last second. He heard Lorok's agonized wail as the tail smashed into his side.

Skunk grunted as they hit the ground, then looked up to see Danica striking dirt as her mount rolled away amid a spray of blood. There were several puncture marks surrounding a new and impressively sized dent in Lorok's armored plating.

"Lorok! Danica!" Skunk shouted, reaching out after them.

Azada turned to him, her mouth opening wide. Recognizing what was about to happen, Skunk sprang to his feet and ran, pulling Sylvia along with him. He heard the rush of flames as Azada exhaled. His heart jumped.

Sylvia was vulnerable to the fire!

Desperate, Skunk turned to shield her fragile form with his own.

Mercifully, Azada's attack was interrupted when a spear found a gap in the scales on her shoulder. Her head reared up, issuing a deafening roar of rage and releasing her fire into the sky. She looked down at the ry'thar warrior that had *dared* to attack her. He was rearing back to throw a second spear. He didn't get the chance. With barely even a moment, Azada stomped down on the soldier, reducing him to crimson paste.

Danica rose unsteadily to her feet, running after Lorok. "Lorok! Shit, *shit*! No!" she screamed when she reached his side. The shelldigger released a long and miserable wail, advertising that he was alive, much to Skunk's relief. But he feared he might not stay that way for long. There was so much blood...

"*Murderer!*" Azada repeated, and Skunk turned his eyes back to her. She was barreling toward him, teeth bared and eye shining with madness. He reacted on reflex, shoving Sylvia out of the way. She gasped as she hit the ground, but Skunk had probably just saved her life.

The dragon's claws slammed into Skunk with such force that, if he hadn't been running along with it, it probably would have killed him. The world fell out from under him, gravity became a suggestion rather than a rule, and a storm of wind howled in his ears. Then it all stopped when he collided with the wall of a yurt. It created and folded under the force of the impact, and the whole structure caved in on top of him. Skunk thrashed as he was buried in thick hides and leathers, leaving it hard to breathe — or maybe that was because of the sudden trauma his torso had received.

The earth spasmed under him three times, each time accompanied by the sundering of stone and soil. Then the weight was lifted. Skunk blinked as the yurt was torn off of him like a wet bandage, and he was greeted by the sight of Azada looming over him, her eye blazing with hateful contempt.

He tried to get up and run, but Azada's claws came down on him, pinning him and leaving only his head exposed. He gasped, unable to find enough air to scream. He thrashed and squirmed desperately under the elder dragon's strength, but to no avail. He was like a mosquito trying to move a mountain.

Azada leaned in close, inspecting him with her one eye. A low growl rumbled deep in her throat, and Skunk felt the instinctual need to cower and grovel before her.

"You. Do you have *any* idea what you have done?" she seethed, her voice like the streams of lava from a volcano. "Do you have any concept of what it is you have *stolen* from me?!"

Skunk did not dare speak, his voice strangled by terror.

"My child. My *only* child!" Azada bellowed, her voice so loud Skunk was afraid it might deafen him. "My *baby! My future!*"

Skunk squealed as her claws wrapped painfully around him and lifted him into the air. His feet and tail dangled out of her grip, kicking feebly as she held him up toward the pale ring. "You will suffer," she promised him, and he believed her. "Every agony. Every sorrow. Every violation. Every suffering you can imagine, and more! You shall endure them all for what you have done!"

"W-what I've done?!" Skunk finally managed to say, forcing himself to meet Azada's glare. "You're the one that ordered an attack on innocent people!"

"Innocents? There *are* no innocents!" Azada screamed, driving him down into the earth. The momentum was so great he felt his stomach almost leave his body, and the impact with the ground sent him screaming in agony.

Azada continued. "Not among these vile creatures! These *abominations*! How can you not see them for what they are?! They are rotten! They are heartless! They have driven our people to the brink of extinction, and they spit upon the names of our ancestors! They abuse *our* gifts, and they hoard *our* relics like cheap baubles! You would *dare* call them *innocent?!*"

Her claws squeezed. Skunk's screams grew as his bones began to bend and crack. He knew she could pop him like a grape whenever she wanted with barely even a thought. The fact he still lived meant only one thing.

She was torturing him. And he could see in her eyes how she delighted in his suffering. It inspired both terror in Skunk, and hatred. His blood shivered at the idea that this evil being could be in any way connected to him.

It shivered. It boiled.

And it remembered.

He lifted his eyes to meet Azada's gaze. "More innocent than *you.*"

Azada was quiet. It was strange, though. For a fraction of a second, Skunk thought he saw something else under her hatred. Was that *respect?*

He had no time to contemplate it. Azada reared back, flames gathering in her maw, and somehow, Skunk knew that even his considerable resistance to fire would not spare him from the pain.

Suddenly, he could breathe again. He sucked in a deep lungful of air as Azada abruptly released him, roaring and throwing her head wildly about. Skunk wasn't sure what had hit her, but he was glad for it all the same. He took the chance and quickly rolled to his feet. He turned to see Azada spinning around, and he realized with some satisfaction that the tip of her tail had been cut off. Standing where it had been, axe dripping with freshly spilled dragon blood, was Danica, breathing heavily.

"Get away from the kid," she said, lifting her axe in front of her. "He's been through *enough*."

Skunk's eyes widened. "Danica, RUN!" he screamed, his hand reaching for his bow. Thankfully, the weapon hadn't been destroyed by Azada's wrath just yet. He turned and fired an arrow at the dragon's head. His aim was off, unfortunately, the arrow scraping harmlessly off of the scales beneath Azada's eye. Still, even if he hadn't hurt the dragon, he got her attention off his friend.

Azada snarled and charged Skunk again, her mouth flying wide. Even from this distance, he could see how sharp her teeth were. Instinct and reflex took over yet again, sending him rolling to her blind side as Azada's maw snapped shut where he had been, creating a deafening crack and a pulse of displaced air.

Azada grunted, lifting her head to try and find him. Skunk saw a chance to capitalize on her handicap and ran under her belly. He spotted an old wound that had never healed properly, leaving an ugly gap between two of the armored plates of her underbelly. Sensing an opportunity to do some damage, he drew Amelia's sword and thrust the blade up into the gap. He was rewarded with a spray of blood.

Above him, Azada roared and thrashed before leaping away with a flap of her wings. Skunk was crushed into the ground by the gust, but he still managed to smirk. He had just hurt a dragon. Not a lot of people could claim that. If there was an afterlife, he could take those bragging rights with him.

"Wretch!" Azada bellowed, the air pulling toward her as she sucked in another breath. Skunk's moment of triumph ended as soon as it had begun, as Azada breathed another wide cone of flames toward him. This time, there was nowhere for him to go.

Swearing under his breath, Skunk dove to the ground and covered his head. The flames fell over him, and unlike normal fire, it *burned*. An agony unlike any he had ever known pierced every scale in his body. He howled in agony, thrashing and rolling in a desperate effort to put himself out. But even after the torrent ended, and another massive swathe of the village was reduced to ash, his scales still burned.

It hurt *so much*.

Azada chuckled ominously at the wailing kobold. She rose onto her hind legs, the kickoff from the ground sending another tremor through the earth. Skunk managed to open his now dry eyes to look up at her.

Azada's eye shifted colors. The glow of emeralds was replaced by the unmistakable silver of luma — magic. She looked ahead and narrowed her eyes.

The air tingled, the ring glowed brighter in the night sky, and Skunk realized that she was casting a spell.

And then the world was shaking. Stone and soil split apart, reduced to ash as a ring-shaped wall of green fire rose around them, hot beyond description and blocking all possible means of escape. His eyes fell on Danica, Sylvia, and Tamaya, who had assembled nearby. They were checking on Sylvia, making sure she was alright. They were trapped in here with him. It was just them versus the fury of a dragon avenging her murdered child. Beyond the roar of the fire, Skunk couldn't make out anything else.

If anyone else had survived, they were gone now.

Azada came back down on all fours. "No running," she commanded in an almost playful tone. "No hiding."

Skunk, whimpering in pain, pulled himself up to his feet. The pain was more than he could describe, but the adrenaline in his veins let him focus through it. He looked at Azada, then threw his arms out wide. "Don't you see what you're doing?!" he screamed at her. "I'm the one that killed your child! Punish me! But leave them out of this!"

"I will punish *everything*," Azada countered before surging forward. For such an impossibly huge creature, her speed was staggering. Skunk yelped and threw himself to the ground, hoping to get under Azada again. She saw through the tactic this time, however, and with a single flap of her wings, drifted back far enough to reveal him and stomp down on him.

All Skunk could do was roll out of the way as Azada pummeled the earth, trying to crush him into paste. Every stomp, every earth-shattering blow sent his bones rattling and his lungs burning with terrified screams. He tried to run, but she had him blocked at every turn.

"Yes! *Yes!*" Azada squealed, her voice rising higher with delighted madness. "Grovel! Cower! Beg! Scream! Suffer! Suffer, and *know your folly!*"

Finally, her claws swiped across the earth, slamming into Skunk once again. He couldn't even gasp as he was sent rolling along the ground. His back met the wall of flames, and the burning returned. He rolled away from the wall as quickly as he could, shrieking in pain. He tried to stand, but his muscles refused to obey.

"Skunk!" Sylvia's voice reached him. He looked up to see her and Danica rushing his way while Tamaya moved to draw Azada's attention, spear in hand.

Skunk reached out for the ry'thar before something burned in his chest. He doubled over, hand over his heart, and coughed at the ground. Flecks of blood splattered against the earth, sizzling and popping from their proximity to the flames. He forced himself to stand, blood dripping from his mouth, and staggered for Sylvia. He only made it a few steps before his legs gave out under him, and he fell forward. He felt hands on his bare scales for a moment. They had barely touched him when they jerked away, their owner squeaking in pain. It was only now that Skunk realized that his clothes were gone. It had all been incinerated in the fire, leaving nothing but his sword clutched in a death grip in his numb hand.

"By the Five," Sylvia whimpered, enduring the heat radiating off him to roll him onto his back. "Y-you're burning up."

"Fire does that," Danica noted bluntly before glaring back at Azada. She suddenly reached down to pick them up. "Shit, *move!*"

Skunk barely had time to register the command before Azada's foot beat down on the earth where they had been. Cracks spiderwebbed out from the point of impact, and Danica, try as she might, could not hold her balance. She fell forward, bringing her passengers with her to the ground.

Azada slithered over them, flames gathering in her mouth again. "You killed my child," she seethed at him. "My only creation. The *only* thing left for me to love in this miserable world. They were *everything* to me. It is only just, then, that I take *everything* from *you!*"

"Stop!" Skunk begged, trying to shove Danica and Sylvia away. "Just leave them be!"

Azada did not listen. She reared back, the flames about to be unleashed.

A lion's roar heralded Tamaya's arrival. She came in at a sprint and leaped, latching onto Azada's side. Her claws found the gaps between the scales, giving her purchase, and prompting Azada to turn her attention away from her victims. Her growl turned to a grunt of curiosity. She pivoted back, turning to try and get at Tamaya. The ry'thar was quick, climbing up Azada's side and heading for where her good wing met her back.

"Time to move!" Danica instructed, getting back to her feet and hauling Skunk up after her. "Get out of here, kid!"

Skunk turned to her, appalled. "What?!"

"Look, clearly we aren't killing this thing!" Danica shot back, pushing him for the flames. "But at least *one* of us can walk through fire! So do it and get out of here!"

Skunk shook his head, bracing himself against Danica's shove and holding his ground. "No! I'm not leaving you!"

"I was *not* asking!" Danica snapped before hooking her arms under Skunk's armpits. He blinked, then yelped as she lifted him and carried him for the wall. "Someone's getting out of here alive, and it might as well be you!"

"No! *No!* Put me down! *Danica!*" Skunk screamed, thrashing against her grip. But her hands were like iron, and in his weakened state, he was powerless to resist.

Sylvia's voice reached him, drawing his attention. She was facing him, her hands clutched over her heart. "Just run, Skunk! Live! Please!"

Behind her, Skunk watched as Tamaya finally reached Azada's wing. The dragon had reared up on her hind legs and was reaching back with her claws to rip the ry'thar away. Tamaya saw the attack coming and jumped away along Azada's wingspan. She drove her spear through the leathery membrane, arresting her momentum and drawing a spray of gore out of the wing.

Azada roared, coming back down onto all fours. With a stomp of rage, she tucked her wings close to her torso, then shoved herself into a roll across the ground. Under the dragon's bulk, Skunk lost all sight of Tamaya, and his heart almost stopped.

And then Danica threw him into the fire.

As he passed through, his scales once again burned with agony. But then he hit the surprisingly cool ground on the other side and rolled to a stop. Gasping, he rose to his hands and knees and looked up. Danica pointed at him.

"*Run!*" she commanded before turning to face Azada and brandishing her axe.

Skunk stood up and ran for the wall of fire, desperation driving him on. "No! No no no! Danica!" he shouted. He yelped and backed off when he reached the fire, unable to make himself brave the pain again. He watched, mortified as the dwarf charged the dragon with a battle cry.

She was charging to her death.

Azada rose back to her feet before Danica reached her. Tamaya lay in the broken earth, squirming, but alive. Azada glared at her, then turned to the charging dwarf. Her teeth showed, and she reached out to stomp Danica into the earth. She managed to roll aside, avoiding the blow. As she rose, she turned, bringing her axe around in a rounding swing. The blade bit into Azada's wrist, but not very deeply, drawing barely a trickle of blood. The dragon hissed and jerked her wrist, backhanding Danica through the air. She crashed to the earth several yards away.

Skunk watched, his heart sinking with despair. As Danica hit the ground, his eyes returned to Sylvia. She stood on the other side of the fire, facing him. Her hair and tattered dress were billowing in the heated air.

She smiled.

Even after all of this, she smiled at him.

"Go," she whispered. "Please. Live."

It was almost the same thing Amelia had said to him just before she died. Everyone was telling him to run and live through this waking nightmare. But none of them outranked Amelia in his heart, and she had told him to live *happily*.

How could he be happy if his friends died in front of him, and he did nothing to stop it?

He looked up. Azada was behind Sylvia, looking down at her with contempt.

Skunk's eyes widened, and he took a step forward. "Azada! Please! I'm begging you, don't do this!"

Sylvia's smile gained a sad quality.

Azada reached down and picked Sylvia up off the ground, the tips of her claws finding the back of Sylvia's dress. She screamed, thrashing against Azada's claws, trying to free herself even as she ascended to heights where a fall would kill her.

"Put her down!" Skunk screamed, falling to his knees. "Please! Don't hurt her! I'll do whatever you want, just don't hurt her!"

Azada scrutinized Sylvia for a few seconds, turning the girl this way and that in her grasp. "*This* child is important to you?" she asked. She glared down at Skunk, meeting his gaze. He didn't need to answer her question, he knew that. She found her answer in his pleading expression.

Azada smirked a horrible, blood-curdling smile that made Skunk's heart stop before she casually tossed Sylvia over her shoulder. Skunk watched her sail through the air, spiraling wildly and shrieking in fear. He stood, reaching his hand out after her, screaming her name.

She hit the ground. There was a sickening crack. She fell perfectly still.

She did not rise.

She did not move.

"Sylvia...?" he choked out.

Above him, Azada chuckled in malevolent amusement. "Does it grieve you? To lose one you love in such a manner?" she asked him, her voice rich with murderous glee.

Skunk looked up at her, his expression blank as his mind fell into a strange silence.

Azada smirked. "Good."

At that moment, time seemed to freeze for Skunk. In his mind, images of all of the deaths he had seen since Karak arrived in Addernotch flashed before his eyes. The soldiers in the field. The civilians in the streets. The ry'thar hunters who had joined them to find the kobolds. The men and women wheeled into the flames, sacrificed to this dragon's child. The survivors who had been incinerated in her charge. Amelia.

And now Sylvia.

Azada was saying something more, but Skunk couldn't make out the words. Everything was muffled. Indistinct. His skull burned, his blood boiling with white-hot rage.

No more.

Enough was enough.

This thing had attacked his pack. This laughing, sneering *beast* had hurt his people. His friends. His *family*.

It shared his scales. It shared his blood. But it did not share his scent, and it did not share his mind. It was not his pack, and it had hurt him.

Skunk didn't even realize he was moving until he was through the wall of the flames. They burned.

He didn't care.

Azada, surprised by the unwise charge, took a step back. Skunk burst through the wall, wreathed in a cloak of billowing flames. He thundered across the dirt, and with a roar befitting a dragon, he leaped and sank his claws into the gaps in Azada's scales as Tamaya had done. Azada took another step back, frowning in irritation. She lifted a claw to scrape Skunk off as if he were a spot of dirt. He saw the claws coming and moved first. He threw himself higher up

Azada's chest scales, growling all the way.

"Such insolence," Azada seethed, almost sounding offended. Smoke billowed out of her nostrils. "What do you hope to-"

And then she roared, throwing her head back as something attacked her again. Skunk briefly got a look behind Azada and saw that Tamaya had plunged her claws into the bleeding stump where the tip of Azada's tail *had* been. She was covered in a spray of gore, and she was gasping for air, but she was up and alive.

Azada turned to her, then roared again. This time, it was Danica who had abused one of Azada's physical weaknesses. On her blindside, the gap in her scales that a ry'thar had earlier speared was a prime target for one of her throwing axes. The dragon wobbled in place as pain surged into the muscles of her shoulder, and her agony allowed Skunk to continue his climb.

"How dare you! Beasts! *Monsters!*" Azada seethed, thrashing wildly. Her tail raked itself over the ground, her feet stamped and swiped, but the pain of her injuries slowed her just enough for the attackers to evade the worst of it. And all the while, Skunk kept climbing. And any time he found a loose scale, he violently ripped it away before plunging his claws into the moist, crimson flesh underneath, drawing even more blood and more wails of agony from the dragon.

Down below, Tamaya and Danica were beginning to properly coordinate their efforts to keep Azada busy from beneath. "Don't let her inhale!" Tamaya shouted. "If she can breathe fire, we're finished!"

"On it!" Danica replied, lifting her second throwing axe and hurling it at Azada's head. She had hoped to hit the dragon's good eye and leave her blind, but she could settle with the blade finding a new home in the exposed flesh of the ruined eye. Azada staggered back, screaming wildly as another spray of blood flew free from her head.

"Demons! Abominations!" Azada shouted, and this time, there was actual strain in her voice. Distress.

Once again, her tail swept over the ground, accelerated and empowered by her own adrenaline. Danica and Tamaya were unable to dodge it, and both were sent sprawling to the earth with cries of pain and the crack of breaking bones.

Above, Skunk saw his friends getting hurt again. His fury renewed a thousand times over, burning in his blood like the sun itself. "Stop it!" he roared, finally hauling himself onto the back of Azada's head. He grabbed her one good horn to keep himself steady. "Stop hurting my friends!"

Azada reared up onto her hind legs, roaring in rage. She lifted her claws to try and brush him away. In his rage, he didn't even hesitate at the sight. He ducked down across the dragon's face and hooked his claws into the bloodied flesh of her injured eye, eliciting another scream from her.

And then he *pulled.*

With a satisfying rip, a long strip of flesh came away from Azada's face, accompanied by a visceral spray of blood that coated the entire front of Skunk's body. The smell of it reached his nostrils, and his raging instincts spurred him on.

He reached in deeper, took hold of even more flesh, and dug his claws in.

"Stop! *Stop!*" Azada wailed, throwing her head around wildly in a desperate bid to throw him off. His arms jolted, his joints screaming as they almost dislocated. But he held firm, determined to see this done. He pulled his claws out, taking as much meat as he could. Again, Azada screamed.

Down below, Danica pulled herself back to her feet. She saw Skunk struggling with Azada, clawing at her head and digging his arm elbow-deep into her eye socket. Her eyes then fell on one of Azada's feet planted on the ground, and Skunk's sword discarded in the earth nearby. She got an idea, and for want of anything better, decided to try it.

Danica ran for the sword and scooped it up. Then, with a bellowing battlecry, she charged the dragon's foot and brought her axe around in an arcing swing against the tendon with all the strength she had. The blade met resistance but managed to pierce the scales and sever Azada's equivalent to a hamstring. The force of the blow, regrettably, snapped her axe in half, but that was a small price to pay for the prize. Azada slumped to one side, her ability to stand impaired.

Satisfied, Danica looked up at Skunk and whistled at him. He looked down at her. She gave him a nod and reared back. "Catch!" she called, throwing Amelia's sword at him like a javelin. His eyes latched onto it. His hand pulled out of Azada's eye and snatched the sword out of the air by the hilt. The motion jolted him, and he almost came loose as Azada again began thrashing. He held firm.

"I will not die!" Azada roared, her voice high and rising with fear. "Not to you! I cannot die! *I cannot die!*"

Skunk growled as Azada reared up on her hind legs again, and then screamed as she unleashed a torrent of emerald flames into the heavens, bathing the landscape for miles around in its glow. This close to the heat, Skunk almost let go as snakes of fiery agony licked at his abused scales. He couldn't feel his claws holding onto Azada's brow anymore, and he knew he wouldn't get another chance.

Gritting his teeth, Skunk planted his feet in the scales of Azada's cheeks, his clawed toes finding purchase in the gaps. He drew back Amelia's sword and aimed the tip at the gaping, bleeding socket. With a final scream of rage, he plunged the blade into the gaping wound as far as it could go.

Azada's voice went silent, cut off with little more than a gasp and a gurgle. The flames emerging from her maw spluttered away, leaving a few wandering embers to fall to earth, and a plume of smoke rising from her throat to vanish among the stars.

The dragon remained motionless for a few horrible seconds, her body twitching as the last sparks of her brain and body desperately tried to keep her alive. Then, in unnatural silence, Azada toppled to the earth, bringing Skunk along with her. He held on for dear life and screwed his eyes shut, bracing for impact and accepting whatever came next.

With a sound like thunder, Azada hit the ground, and a dragon died.

Danica watched Azada in shocked silence. Even though she had thrown the sword to Skunk, she hadn't expected her hair-brained scheme to work. It had been a desperate gambit, a last-ditch effort. And yet, it *had* worked. Azada was defeated. An ancient dragon, old enough to be near the end of her lifespan, was dead. Slain by a kobold, of all creatures.

When Azada hit the ground, Danica took a few steps back, throwing up her arms to shield herself from the tsunami of dust kicked up by the impact. She dug in her heels, barely withstanding the initial gust. As the wind died down, the cloud lingered over the remnants of the Karjene village like the haze of a distant, half-forgotten memory.

All was silent, now. The screams of the fleeing survivors were too distant to be heard, and the ring of fire conjured by Azada's magic died with her. All that was left was Danica's exhausted panting, the pounding of her heart, and a gentle breeze that whipped across the plains.

Is that it? Is it over? Danica thought. Her eyes remained locked on Azada's silhouette, waiting for the terrible monstrosity to get back up. She never did.

Danica's attention would be pulled away by a whimper from nearby. Turning to look, Danica's eyes landed on the prone form of Sylvia.

The girl stirred.

Hit with a new spark of adrenaline, Danica sprinted to her side. Sylvia was curled on the ground, gasping rapidly for breath with her hands clutching at her chest.

"You're alive?!" Danica asked, equal parts relieved and baffled.

Sylvia sniffled, tilting her ears toward Danica. "...I think?" she said through tightly gritted teeth, then cried out in pain. Danica, realizing that Sylvia was only alive by the bare minimum, knelt to check her injuries. The girl was in bad shape. Her legs and chest were swelling, and judging by her labored breathing — and the flecks of blood spattering the ground by her mouth — she had suffered broken bones everywhere. She would only live with significant medical attention.

Annotha had better have made it out of all this in one piece, Danica thought.

Tamaya came jogging up to her, favoring one leg and sporting a limp arm, but alive. She crumpled to her good knee by Sylvia's side and gingerly helped the girl up into a sitting position. "There you go. Nice and easy. Have no fear. You will live," she said softly.

"W-what happened to Skunk?" Sylvia asked in a barely audible rasp, turning to the ry'thar. "W-where is he? W-what happened—" She suddenly doubled over, coughing up more blood. Danica put a hand on her back and looked helplessly at Tamaya. The ry'thar shook her head slowly before focusing on the girl again.

"Hush, Sylvia. Try not to talk. Save your energy."

"Where's Skunk?!" Sylvia demanded the moment she could speak again, though there was no strength to her voice. "Where is he?! I need to know he's okay!"

Danica and Tamaya stared at one another for a moment, then turned to the fallen dragon. Without a word, Tamaya nodded to Danica, then stood and limped for the massive corpse. Taking the hint, Danica picked Sylvia up, careful not to hurt her, and walked slowly across the devastated landscape as the dust began to clear.

Danica felt a lump form in her throat. Tamaya was knelt by Azada's head, trying to lift it with her only good arm. Pinned to the earth under Azada's face, eyes closed and not moving, was Skunk.

"Damn it, damn it!" Tamaya grumbled, crumpling back to one knee. "Come on, come on, come on. Don't die on me, don't you *dare* die on me, too. I couldn't save your mother, I'm not failing you as well!"

Sylvia swallowed heavily, her grip on Danica's shoulders tightening. "Skunk...?"

Danica stared at the fallen kobold's form. He looked like hell. His scales were blackened with burn marks, and it was impossible to tell which splatters of blood belonged to him as opposed to the dragon. It was bad.

Tamaya looked at Danica, her eyes shimmering in the low ringlight with desperation. "Help me!" she pleaded, placing her hand on Azada's head and once again trying, and failing, to lift it off of Skunk. She let out a long, agonized groan before folding back. The earth rumbled just slightly as Azada's head settled. Tamaya screamed in frustration and slammed her fist into Azada's forehead before trying again. Her every motion was frantic, desperate.

"Stay put a second," Danica ordered, setting Sylvia down on the ground by Tamaya.

"Is there anything I can do?" she asked, trying to rise, but her wounds stopped her.

"Just don't move," Danica instructed. "The dragon's dead, but its head fell on Skunk. He's pinned and he's hurt. We'll haul him out, then we'll get the two of you some help."

Sylvia nodded weakly, clearly unhappy to be sidelined like this, but unable to dispute it. She listened for a moment, then her lips quirked up into a small smile. "He's breathing. I can hear him," she whispered. "He's alive."

"Then let's keep it that way," Danica said as she knelt beside Tamaya and hooked her arms under the dragon's brow. "I'll prop her head up. You pull him out."

Tamaya nodded. Then, as one, the two lifted with all their strength. The dragon's head was impossibly heavy, and all of Danica's muscles were already at the point of exhaustion. But after everything, she was not about to let down her new friend. The last dregs of her adrenaline let her power through her breaking point.

Together, grunting with effort and straining against Azada's impressive heft, Tamaya and Danica lifted the dragon's head. Little by little, bit by bit, but surely. It was only by a few inches, but it was enough. Danica used herself as a wedge, keeping Azada's head propped up, and nodded at Tamaya. "Now!"

Tamaya didn't have to be told twice. As quickly as she could, she reached under Azada's head and hauled Skunk out. She grunted with the effort and pain, but after a few seconds, the kobold was safely out from under the dragon's head.

Danica let Azada's head drop with a gasp and fell on her back.

"Okay. I'm done," she declared, barely able to focus through her exhaustion. She stared up at the pale ring, gasping for air. Her mind was a fuzzy mess of non-thoughts and half-ideas. She could have fallen asleep right there and been perfectly content to sleep until the end of time.

A few seconds later, Lorok, limping and whimpering, lumbered up to her. His side was still bleeding, and she knew he'd need to be looked at too, but the mere sight of her oldest friend and beloved companion alive put a smile on her face. "Hey boy," she said at length, reaching out to half-heartedly pat his nose. "You look like shit."

Lorok whined and snuffed at her side.

"Yup, I know," Danica chuckled before letting her hand thud to the ground. A spike of pain ran through her nervous system, and she immediately announced her regret for that action with a long, pitiful 'ow.'

"Skunk?"

Danica took a deep breath, then released it with a heavy groan. She wasn't done just yet, was she? "Ah, shit. Right, alright, lemme just—" she grunted, hauling herself up to a sitting position. Lorok helped her as well as he could, snuffling and warbling in concern for her all the while. Using his muzzle as a perch, Danica picked herself up and turned to look at the others. Tamaya had helped prop Sylvia up, sitting beside her as the two jointly cradled Skunk's body between them. He was flat on his back, one hand held in Sylvia's, his eyes closed and his mouth hanging open.

Danica inched forward and fell to her knees beside them to get a better look. There was even more damage that she could see now that the rest of him was in the open. He was alive, but there was no guarantee he would stay that way. Reluctantly, she looked to Tamaya. "Well? Will he live?" she asked hopefully.

Tamaya stared at him for a moment. She opened her mouth to say something, but it was another voice that answered.

"Owie..."

All eyes zeroed in on Skunk as, finally, the boy opened his eyes. He looked around for a moment, groggy and unfocused, until his eyes settled on Danica.

His lips opened up wide into a massive, dopey grin. His tail thumped against the ground a few times. "...Did we win?"

Before anyone could answer, Sylvia fell over Skunk, wrapping her arms around him in the tightest hug her destroyed body could manage. She wept into his shoulder, and he looked more than a little dumbfounded. "Sylvia..." he breathed, wrapping his arms around her as it finally occurred to him that she was alive. "You're okay?"

Sylvia nodded, pulling back so he could see her face. She sniffled. "I will be."

Skunk's lip was quivering. He lifted a hand to her face, touching her cheek to make sure she was real. When her soft skin met his fingertips, he choked. "I thought— I thought I lost you, too," he said, his eyes watering with tears.

Sylvia shook her head. "Not today, it seems."

Skunk stared at her a moment longer, before something between a laugh and a sob burst out of him. Trembling, he pulled Sylvia against him as tightly as he dared. The two friends held onto each other for dear life, weeping tears of joy and relief.

Danica watched them for a few seconds, before putting on a tiny smile. "Gods, Skunk, you have got to be the luckiest bastard I have ever met," she said, shaking her head.

Tamaya nodded, adding in her own two cents. "You have done the impossible... *again*. Your mother would be proud of you."

Skunk took a few deep breaths, fighting to get a hold of himself, before lifting his eyes to Tamaya. He sniffled. "R-really?" he asked.

Tamaya smiled at him. She reached out and gently wiped away his tears with her thumb. "Really," she whispered to him.

Skunk stared her down for a few seconds longer. He sniffled again. "Tamaya?" he finally asked, his voice growing quiet.

She took hold of his hand. "Yes, roluth tha?"

"Can I take a nap?"

Tamaya stared at Skunk for a second and then started laughing. Danica couldn't help but join her. It was such an innocent-sounding question as if asked by a little child, but she could relate to it *so much* right now.

Tamaya nodded. "Yes, Skunk. Take a nap. Get some rest. You've earned it."

"Thank you," was all Skunk said before closing his eyes and going limp. For a moment, Danica leaned forward, worried he might have just expired. She quickly relaxed, however, for as he curled up in the joined embrace of his friends, Skunk smiled.

home

It was strange being back in Addernotch. Skunk sat atop a pile of large stone blocks that would eventually be used to lay the foundations for several new homes around the devastated village. Men and women moved about, bringing wagons and wheelbarrows loaded with supplies and tools wherever they were needed. Many of these were people he did not recognize, having come with the contingents from Underbridge and Port Natha.

He still remembered with some satisfaction how surprised the reinforcements had been. To say they had been incredulous when they heard that a *kobold* of all creatures had saved the day would be an understatement. They had tried to dismiss the tale as utter nonsense at first. But when they were shown Azada's carcass out in the plains, courtesy of the ry'thar, their tune quickly changed. Tamaya, in particular, had been steadfast in backing up the truth of things. As far as she and her people were concerned, Skunk was a *hero*, and they made sure everyone knew it. The reinforcements didn't believe the story, even with all of that, but they accepted it all the same.

A majority of the soldiers had returned to their respective cities once it was clear the greater threat had ended, but enough were left behind to keep the town safe as reconstruction got underway. Search-and-destroy missions through the woods were routine at this point, hunting for any signs of the horde regrouping. There had been a few scattered skirmishes with lingering kobold packs, from what Skunk had been told, but most had scattered and fled the moment they were seen.

Deprived of their leadership and their home, Azada's horde was doomed to scatter across the land. Surviving members would likely find new holes and hordes to settle into. Local pests more than the regional threat they had been before.

Skunk looked down at his swinging feet. It was hard to believe that it had been two weeks since Azada's death. The days that followed had been a chaotic blur, most of it passing him by. He had spent the first several days receiving extensive medical treatment from Annotha, and then a few more traveling back to Addernotch. Once the people here had been brought up to speed on what they had missed, the old agreements between the Karjene tribe and Addernotch were revisited and revised. Recognizing their mutually crippled status, the ry'thar and the humans were collaborating closer than ever before as they rebuilt their homes and their lives.

Things were going well, so far. Progress on rebuilding felt slow, but entire sections of a town were not something that could be built up in just a couple of weeks. It would take months. And then there was the matter of homes that had been destroyed, and whose owners no longer lived to rebuild them. There was going to be a lot of empty land in the future.

But through all of that, save for when he had been first called upon to recount everything that had happened, Skunk had been given almost nothing to do. Some said that he just wasn't built for this sort of manual labor. Others told him that he should rest and recover after the hell he had been forced to endure. And then some of them just *looked*.

He glanced up to see a child catching sight of him. A little girl, probably not even ten years old. She let out a high-pitched squeak before quickly running to hide behind her mother's skirt. The woman looked at her child, then turned to Skunk. He tried to give her an apologetic smile and wave, but he didn't even get the chance before she, too, flinched and ushered her child down the street. He watched her go, and his heart sank into the pits of his stomach.

This was nothing new, unfortunately. Many people in Addernotch had not been there to witness what happened in the burrow. They accepted the story, perhaps, and the amount of hostility aimed at him had gone down dramatically. But the sorrow felt over the fallen was not so easily replaced, and neither was the memory of *who* had done it. As much as it grieved him to recognize it, Skunk looked exactly like the monsters that had ruined so many lives.

He knew they didn't mean it — at least, he hoped they didn't. He told himself it was a natural reaction, and that it would go away with time as the dead were buried, mourned, and the survivors put their lives back together. And he was probably right. But he had no idea how long it would take, and every time someone looked at him like that, or a child ran away, he felt a stab of hurt in his chest, accompanied by a throb of guilt. The idea that his people, his pack, could look at him and feel fear...

The day they put all of this sorrow behind them could not come soon enough.

He was drawn from his ruminations when he spotted Tamaya and Danica approaching him. Tamaya was sporting a few new scars, but she held her head high and proud. Danica's armor had been replaced, and a brand new ry'thari axe was strapped to her belt. Lorok lumbered along behind her, his armored shell largely healed, but still bearing the scars of his injuries.

The shelldigger spotted Skunk, and with an excited warble, bounded up to him. Skunk chuckled, accepting the nuzzle the moment it was offered. He ran his fingers through the fur between Lorok's eyes, and the beast's tail thumped happily against the ground. "Ha! Hey there, boy! How are you doing?" Skunk asked happily, grateful for the affection.

Lorok licked him, and Skunk laughed. That was a pretty definitive answer, he felt.

Tamaya smiled. "Hello, Skunk," she greeted. "Do you have a minute to talk?"

Skunk gently nudged Lorok back and hopped down from the pile of rocks. He offered both of them a warm and friendly smile. "Yeah, sure. What's going on? Need me to do something?" he asked, hoping to finally get his hands dirty and help build something.

Danica shook her head. "Just to talk."

Skunk tilted his head, an uneasy feeling creeping up on him. "About what?"

Tamaya's smile disappeared. She turned to look to the north, her tail swishing in slow, looping circles behind her. "I am afraid Danica and I are leaving, Skunk," she informed him after several long seconds.

Skunk deflated, his hands starting to fidget over his heart. "What?" he asked weakly.

Danica shrugged helplessly. "I've done what I can to help out around here, Skunk," she said before leaning against Lorok. "Rebuilding efforts are getting along just fine, and you all seem to be in good hands with these people from the cities. I think it's time for Lorok and I to move on."

Skunk looked down and heaved a heavy sigh. He knew Danica wasn't going to be sticking around forever, but the news still pained him. "Right. I understand," he mumbled dejectedly.

Tamaya spoke next, her voice low and soothing. "And I am needed back in the plains. It will take a long time for my people to rebuild what Azada and her horde destroyed. I fully intend to nurture the good relations between our peoples, but my place is with my tribe."

Skunk gave her a small smile. "Right. I can still come and visit you at least, right? And you'll come to visit me?"

The lion woman, who had once tried to strangle the life out of him, knelt to be at his eye level, her smile warm and caring. She placed a hand on his shoulder. "When time allows it, yes," she said affectionately. "I do not know when that will be possible, however. The days ahead promise to be long and challenging for both of us. I do not imagine we will have many chances to meet face to face for quite some time."

Skunk's smile fell away. "Right."

Tamaya's smile grew, and she carefully drew the kobold into a warm embrace. He returned it happily, enjoying the feeling of her fur on his scales. It was coarse, rough, and scratchy, and against easily irritated human skin, he imagined it might have been unpleasant. But for him, it was nice. As they embraced, Tamaya spoke to him in a hushed whisper.

"Your mother would be so, *so* proud of you," she told him. "You must be growing tired of hearing people say that, but *never* let anyone tell you otherwise. I do not believe she could have raised a better son. Never forget that."

Skunk closed his eyes. "I won't."

The hug persisted for a moment longer before Tamaya stepped back. Skunk looked between his two friends, a lump forming in his throat. His eyes eventually settled on Danica, the one he would not be seeing again. "Will you write?"

Danica shrugged. "I can try."

Skunk smiled at her. "Guess that's all I can really ask of you, huh?"

"Pretty much."

Skunk snickered and stepped forward to hug Danica. She yelped, her hands flying wide in a display of confusion and alarm. "What the— hey! Can you not? I don't do hugs!"

"Well, I do," Skunk murmured, hugging her tighter.

"Son of a— gah, fine," Danica relented, patting Skunk awkwardly on the head.

"I'm gonna miss you, Danica," He murmured, squeezing her closer.

Danica grumbled out a string of disgruntled but ultimately meaningless syllables. After a few more seconds, Skunk figured she had had enough and pulled away.

Tamaya gave the dwarf an amused smirk before refocusing on Skunk. "Be well, roluth tha Skunk. And if you ever need me for any reason, you know where to find me."

Skunk nodded up at her, smiling as wide as he could. "I will. Don't worry, Aunt Tamaya."

Tamaya blinked, taken aback. "Aunt?"

Skunk didn't say anything. He just grinned.

A moment later, Tamaya's shock turned into a proud smile as she accepted the new role. Sadly, before she had a chance to comment on it, another voice called out from nearby, speaking in the ry'thari tongue.

All eyes turned to look. The voice had come from a collection of ry'thar at the end of the street. Skunk took a quick head count and determined that this was not all of them, but it was most of them. A few would remain to help with things here, no doubt, just as a few humans would be helping the Karjene.

Tamaya nodded to her people. She turned back to Skunk and gave him one last smile. "It is time. Until we meet again, roluth tha," she said. Then, with her head held high, she turned and walked to rejoin her companions. Skunk watched her go, a part of him wanting to follow. He remembered the glow he'd felt when the ry'thar had sung his praises around the bonfire, the validation of finally being seen as more than just the 'weird neighborhood kobold.'

But, as tempting as the urge was, he resisted it. He had a duty to the people here, after all. Addernotch was his home. It was where he belonged.

...Right?

Tamaya met with her companions, speaking to them in their native language. They nodded in unison, and as one, the party of lions turned to begin the long trek north. Tamaya looked at him over her shoulder and then disappeared behind a building. With that, Tamaya was gone.

Skunk let out a heavy sigh, then turned to Danica. She had hoisted herself up onto Lorok's back and was now looking back down at him, her expression unreadable. Eventually, however, it turned into a strained smile. "You're a good kid, Skunk," she finally told him. "Never thought I'd say that about a green scale, but here we are."

Skunk returned the smile. "And I never thought I'd meet a dwarf," he told her. "It was good to meet you, Danica. And thank you."

Danica snorted. "For what?"

"For being my friend."

Danica paused, not able to meet his eyes for a long few seconds. He saw her thumbs rubbing back and forth across the leather of Lorok's reigns. At last, she gave him a respectful nod. "Yeah. You, too."

There was a brief, awkward silence. Lorok warbled, and Danica took that as her cue. She turned her mount to the east and nodded back at Skunk over her shoulder. "See you around, kid. Take care." She said before starting down the road for the east. The crowds parted around her, some people giving her respectful nods or shouting their thanks for her part in recent events. She ignored them. Skunk watched her go, and bit by bit, she disappeared amid the crowd, and then into the distance.

And then he was alone.

Skunk shuffled uneasily, loneliness already starting to build in his chest like a puddle in the rain. He looked up and to the side on reflex, a habit he still hadn't been able to shake. Once, he would have found Amelia there, offering him that kind-hearted smile and a well-worded instruction or bit of advice to get his mind off whatever was troubling him. But now, there was no Amelia. No smile. No advice. No instructions. He was on his own.

Nothing had terrified him more.

People were starting to stare. He could feel it. Eyes upon eyes, all around him, boring into him. He was just standing there, feeling sorry for himself. He wasn't doing anything. He wasn't helping. He looked around. So many were looking back at him. He suddenly felt unworthy.

A man wandered in front of him, his arm marked with scars leftover from a kobold's claws. Not far away, there was another man who had lost a hand to one of their swords. Over there, a child who had been burned when the village was on fire stared at him through a window. The moment the child saw him looking, he ducked out of sight.

More and more eyes. More and more faces. Staring. Some judged. Some pitied. But all were singling him out.

The unique one.

The 'other.'

The kobold.

Karak's words echoed hauntingly in his ears, and he couldn't contain a quiet, strangled whimper. He took a few steps, then broke into a run.

He was being irrational, he knew. He was letting his emotions control him, letting his trauma muddy the world around him, but he just couldn't help it. In his mind, he saw the injuries these people, *his people,* had suffered, and he could only feel guilt. So many were still afraid of him or what he resembled. He wasn't even doing anything, and still, he was hurting them.

He heard voices raise in surprise as he ran, but he ignored them all. He let his stride carry him, his mind spinning too wildly to think clearly. He uttered apologies as he scrambled around people, the world a blur. Before he knew it, he was bodily shoving his way through a wooden door. His foot caught on the threshold, and he toppled to the floor in a heap.

Grunting, Skunk drew himself to his feet and slammed the door behind him. His breath was coming in rapid, panicky gasps, his heart pounding in his chest. The lingering image persisted in his mind, the image of all those eyes staring at him, glaring at him, *fearing* him. He remembered with vivid clarity the day he had attacked Bjorn and the meeting that had been held to decide his fate. It had taken years to earn their trust after that, and even longer to earn their affection. It had taken him *his whole life* just to be accepted, and that was *with* Amelia's help.

As he leaned against the door, the quiet of his surroundings settled over him. The lack of stimulation and the familiar scent allowed him a chance to focus and bring order to the chaos of his emotions. Bit by bit, the world resolved and came into focus.

He was back in his house. It was quiet. There was no crackling in the fireplace. No creaking of wood as someone moved around in another room. There was nothing here. It was just him. Alone.

Skunk pushed away from the door and half walked, half stumbled through the house. His pace was slow and lethargic, with no destination in mind. He walked first to the far end of the house, where his eyes passed over his room and the nest-like bed within. Then his feet brought him to the empty dining room. Phantom images of himself, Amelia, and Gothard discussing the disappearances of the farmer at the edge of town appeared before him, floating in his vision like afterimages from staring at the son for too long.

It felt like it was so long ago, now.

The phantoms left, and he was moving again. His feet carried him up the stairs to his mother's room, the wood faintly creaking with every step, impossibly loud in the otherwise silent house. It was as if the walls were weeping alongside him, missing their former occupant as much as he was.

He paused by his mother's door, his hand stopping a few inches from the handle. He had not been here since she'd given him the sword. He hadn't wanted to disturb her things. And he still didn't. But there was something he needed to do, while he still had the chance.

With a deep breath, Skunk stepped inside. Everything was right where she had left it. The chest where she had stored the remnants of her old life. Her bed against the wall, neatly made and waiting for someone to lie down in it. The window across from the door shut tight.

And there, faintly buried under the smell of dust and stagnation, was

Amelia's scent. It was faded and muted, but unmistakably *her*. Skunk inhaled through his nose, long and deep, savoring the last remnant of her presence as well as he could, before slowly walking forward and sitting down on the edge of her bed.

How long would it be, he wondered, before he couldn't smell her at all anymore? That last bit of her would disappear one day. It probably wouldn't even be all that long from now. In the rest of the house, his scent had already eclipsed hers. One day soon, he would never smell her again. To a human who did not have such a strong sense of smell, maybe the thought would be strange, or the loss a trivial one. But to Skunk, the idea of never finding her scent again was almost as terrifying as never seeing her face. Whenever it had been there in the past, it had meant he was safe because *she* was with him.

He stayed there for a long, long time. Just breathing. Slowly in, slowly out, just like Sylvia taught him. Sadly, on this occasion, it did little to help. The all-consuming silence that had helped him find his focus now allowed his thoughts to wander, and new anxieties began to make themselves known.

There was so much he didn't understand. So many questions he had no answers for. How was it that he had been able to cast that spell with Danica's Sunstone shard? What were those strange dreams that had hounded him since before the initial attack, but stopped when the threat had ended? Why had he been so easily coerced into obeying Karak's commands, especially when they had first met? Why did it take so much luma to hatch a dragon egg? Who was Azada's mate? *Where* was Azada's mate? What was the calamity the Auriuns caused that brought the dragons to the brink of extinction?

All of these and so many more nibbled ravenously at the back of his mind like hungry ants. The worst of them was whether or not the people he fought so hard to protect would ever be able to see past his scales again. Or, he supposed, if he could ever convince *himself* that they could.

Skunk growled in bitter frustration, then shook his head, biting back a sob as a fresh twinge of grief stabbed through his chest. It did not bite as fiercely as it did before. But in these moments, alone in the empty home, surrounded by the memories of what *he* had lost, it became all he could think about, and the pain blossomed.

"Mom," he whispered, bringing his hands up to his chest, his fingers curling tightly into the fabric of his shirt. "What do I do? Where do I go from here?"

He waited and listened, desperate for an answer. But the dust had no answers for him. Only silence.

He curled in on himself, hugging his legs against his chest and resting his chin on his knees, his tail curving protectively around his shins. "What do I do?" he whispered again, closing his eyes. "What do I do...?"

He stayed there for what must have been hours, thinking and fearing and wondering. As time passed, his breaths became slower and deeper, calling back on Sylvia's lessons again. He tried to concentrate on Amelia's scent, on her voice, and his memory of her. He couldn't rely on her to guide him anymore, but that didn't mean he had to make his decisions in complete isolation.

He imagined her voice in his mind, tried to imagine what she might say to him if she were here now. He gave no conscious effort to direct the words. He let his mind and memory do the work in the hope of finding inspiration.

"I don't think we're finished, Skunk. There is too much we do not know. Karak was a monster, but I do not believe he lied to us. He was even right on a few points — mankind and dragonkin do not *get along. From the day our ancestors returned to the surface, we've often been at odds with them. But I could not tell you why. Someone must have cast the first stone, and now neither side is willing to* stop. *Maybe we were defending ourselves this time. Maybe Addernotch did nothing wrong. But Azada was not acting in a vacuum. She was reacting to something done against* her. *How far back does it go? How many stones have we used to build this mountain of hatred?"*

A sound drew Skunk's attention — a laugh. From outside. He lifted his head to the bedroom's sole window. He was momentarily startled to see that the sky had turned orange, the sun dipping down for the horizon. Curious, he slipped off the bed and peeked outside.

Children were playing in the street. Two boys and two girls. The oldest of them couldn't have been more than ten. They managed to smile and laugh, chasing one another through the streets with sticks despite the sorrow that had befallen them.

"They don't even know why," Skunk breathed, his tail lashing slowly across the floor. "Hell. I *barely* know why."

How many people had died not knowing why they were the villains in Karak's story? How many people fought without even understanding the nature of their enemy? How many more would die getting caught up in a fight without knowing where it all started?

"Too many," Amelia's voice whispered. *"So tell me. What can you do about it, Skunk?"*

Skunk closed his eyes. He listened to the playful shouts of the children as they battered one another with sticks. He listened to the quiet ramble of the people of Addernotch going about their work, talking amongst themselves as they rebuilt their lives and their homes.

"You told me to live happily," Skunk said quietly, once again imagining that Amelia was there in the room with him. "But how can I do that? How can I be happy when there's so much I don't know? How can I be happy when the people I love are hurt just by having me around? When there's a chance that this same tragedy might happen again somewhere else?"

"I can't answer that for you."

Skunk sniffed, pressing his palm to the glass. He lifted his eyes to stare over the rooftops into the distance. He could see the canopy of the forest and the distant peaks of the mountains to the north. He could see the main road that divided Addernotch in two, heading west and east. Over it all, ever and always, was the pale ring, shining down.

He traced the ring's contour until it slid from view, and his eyes eventually settled on the horizon to the east.

"I can't live happily with all of that," he finally said quietly. "You're right. I'm not done yet."

He closed his eyes again, imagining Amelia's hand coming down on his shoulder to reassure him.

"Then go."

Skunk shuddered, his tail swishing along the ground. "But. Addernotch. My pack. I can't just leave them, can I?"

"That depends. Do you trust them to be fine without you? More importantly, do you trust yourself to be fine without them?"

Skunk inhaled sharply, his mind reverberating with the memory of the ry'thar funeral song. He stared at Addernotch for several long seconds, not just looking, but *seeing*. He saw the homes his people had built up years before he had ever been born. He saw the road traveled by a million feet before he had ever been conceived, and he knew would be traveled by a million more long after he was dead. He saw the men, women, and children who had survived the fury of a dragon. He saw Addernotch.

He saw his home.

And once he saw it, he decided. "I do."

"Then you know what to do."

Skunk drew himself up taller. It would be a lie to claim he wasn't afraid of the choice he was about to make, but he knew it was the right one. Addernotch had been fine before him. It would be fine without him. Given recent events, it might be better off without him, at least for the moment. And he would be of more use to his pack finding answers than sitting here, twiddling his thumbs and feeling sorry for himself.

He took one last deep breath, looking for the last traces of Amelia's scent.

He found only himself.

His mind made up, Skunk turned and walked away, closing the door behind him.

Fond Farewells

Seto's schoolhouse had been one of the first buildings to be fully restored, as it was still serving as a shelter for displaced children. As Skunk looked up at the building with a warm glow of nostalgia, he couldn't think of a better place for them to be.

Three children were loitering outside as he approached, and he recognized them. They had been among the survivors of Azada's rampage. He gave them a small smile and wave as he passed. To his surprise, the three suddenly snapped to attention, whispered amongst themselves low enough that even he couldn't hear it, and then ran off behind the schoolhouse. Skunk paused, watching them go with a pang of hurt. Had they joined in on fearing him, too?

He shook his head. *Just one more reason to go.* Doing his best to keep his expression level and neutral, he opened the door. He cast his eyes about the room and noted that Seto had acquired more and better amenities for the children. Plentiful bedding and fresh clothes were folded neatly on tables in the back, while the shelves were stuffed with boxes, jars, and small pots of preservable foodstuffs. Seto sat at his desk in the back, his weary eyes focused on a sheet of parchment spread on his desk.

Skunk cleared his throat, and Seto looked up. His face glowed with delight, and he rose, perhaps too quickly for his old bones if the pops and winces were any indication. "Skunk!" he called, stepping around the desk and quickly closing the distance between them. "I've hardly seen you since you got back my boy!"

Skunk allowed himself to be drawn into a hug, returning it happily. He took a moment to take in Seto's scent — probably for the last time in a long time.

Road dust and feathersweat. Tree bark and springtime flowers. Ink and parchment. Book leather and candle wax.

Seto pulled back a second later to look into Skunk's eyes. He was as perceptive as ever, his eager smile shifting to a look of concern. Skunk did not resist when Seto's knuckle gently ran under his eye.

"You've been crying," Seto whispered. "How are you feeling? Is there anything I can do?"

Skunk wagged his tail, appreciative of the sentiment. "No, not really," he said honestly. "But I was hoping we could talk. In private. You, me, and Sylvia, if she's available."

Seto tilted his head, clacking his beak in curiosity. He did not question him, however. "Of course. She's having her dinner right now. Come on."

Skunk followed Seto into the backroom, trying to brace himself for what was coming. The room was a cluttered mess when compared to how it used to be. All of the books and scrolls that once dominated the front room had been relocated here. With such little space on the backroom's shelves, there were numerous piles and precariously balanced towers of tomes shoved into the corners.

Sylvia sat at the desk in the back, nibbling quietly at her lunch — boiled eggs wrapped in thin strips of bacon. She looked up at the sound of the door opening. Skunk paused for a moment to take in her appearance. Her wounds had healed nicely, though she was not as swift or as graceful as she used to be, and she would never walk unaided again. A well-made walking stick leaned against the table beside her, proof of her new disability.

Some damage was just too much for even Annotha's magic to heal completely.

Her long-tattered white dress was gone, replaced with a new, dark blue one. The rag that had been her old blindfold had been replaced with a high-quality black cloth.

Skunk smiled, hoping it would reach his voice. "Heya, Sylvia."

Sylvia swallowed her mouthful and returned the smile. "Skunk. How are you?"

"Crappy," Skunk declared honestly. He stepped forward and gave Sylvia a careful hug. Her scent reached him, and he committed it to memory.

Thin metal and unspooled thread. Dry wool and damp cotton. Wooden buttons and nail polish. Tulips and sliced watermelon.

She returned the hug, her familiar fingers running down the back of his neck. He hummed quietly, pleased by the touch, and savored it for all it was worth. When he withdrew, he could see by the way Sylvia's brow had furrowed that she already knew something was off.

"What's wrong?" she asked, grabbing her walking stick.

"That obvious, huh?" Skunk asked with a crooked smile, taking a step back.

Seto closed the door, his brow furrowing to match Sylvia's. "What's bothering you, young man?" he asked, his voice as kind and gentle as always.

Skunk took a deep breath and looked out the window at the darkening sky. This was it, then. If he started talking now, there'd be no taking it back. For a moment, just a moment, he hesitated, wondering if this was really the right thing for him to do. But his doubts were short-lived, and he started talking.

"I've, uh. I've been thinking. A *lot*," He began, finding a seat in the room's spare chair. His hands locked together between his knees. "About the attack. What Karak said. The Auriuns. The people we lost. Just— *everything* that's happened to us lately. And the more I've been thinking about it, the more I've come to realize that I'm not done yet."

"What do you mean?" Seto asked, finding a spot next to Sylvia and giving Skunk his undivided attention.

Skunk scratched at the back of his head. "Kay, so, see, we don't really know why all of this happened. Not really. Karak told us a few things, but he was pretty vague about it, ya know? It just feels like we're missing something — like we're looking at a tiny piece of a really big puzzle that nobody's trying to solve. Or, maybe, it's more like everyone thinks they've solved it already, but they've only put corners together? I dunno, just— something's not right about this, and it's eating me up."

Seto hummed thoughtfully. "I am inclined to agree with you, Skunk. I've pondered this relentlessly since you all came home, and I am no closer to piecing together the full picture myself," he said before narrowing his eyes. "Where is this going?"

Skunk looked down at his hands, his expression darkening. "So many people died, you guys, and it wasn't just a random slaughter. It was all *for* something. It *meant* something. And I want to understand what that something is, and I *don't* mean Azada's egg. That felt more like a symptom, not the cause. I need answers, but I can't find those answers here. So..."

He lifted his eyes to look at them, his dearest friend and the only family he had left. He took one more breath as a tightness began to form in his chest, and forced himself to speak. "And so... s-so I've come to say goodbye."

Skunk was expecting them to look shocked, or to loudly protest the moment he said as such. Part of him was even hoping for them to try to talk him out of it, to give him an excuse to remain. He had not taken into consideration the possibility of them just staring at him in patient silence.

This is almost worse, honestly.

Licking his suddenly dry lips, Skunk pressed on. "I've been thinking about it all day. And I think Addernotch might... might be better off without me for a little while. I'm no good at manual labor, and right now I'm just a reminder of the monsters that ruined everyone's lives. Right here, right now, I'm *useless*. And I *hate* being useless. I *need* to do something to help my pack. And out there? Looking for answers? Maybe something good can come of all this. Maybe I can make all the deaths mean something! Maybe I can stop it from happening again, Maybe— I— I don't know."

Skunk dropped his head into his hands, his fingers curling around his horns. "I'm sorry, I probably sound really stupid right now."

"Not at all," Seto assured him, drawing a glance from Skunk. To his surprise, the old bird was *smiling* at him. "In truth, I am very proud of you, young man."

"You mean you *aren't* going to try and stop me?" Skunk asked in confusion.

Seto shook his head. "Why would I? I am not your master, Skunk, and you are nobody's servant. If this is the path you wish to walk, then far be it from me or anyone else to stop you. More than that, you're right to seek answers. Far too often, men and women of means will rest on their laurels once the moment of danger has passed. They take our world one day at a time and rarely cast their thoughts to the future. Even rarer do they do so with the *right* questions."

Seto knelt on one knee so he was at eye-level with Skunk. He lifted his cheeks in a warm smile and placed a comforting hand on his shoulder. "That said, I would be derelict in my duty as your teacher if I did not ask a question of my own."

Skunk tilted his head. "What's that?"

Seto's expression hardened. "Are you *certain* this is what you want? You've thought it through? Action taken without thought is almost as bad as no action at all, in my experience."

Skunk swallowed heavily. "I'm sure," he said shakily, as convinced as he could be. "At least, I *think* I'm sure. I'm as sure as I *can* be, you know, considering."

Seto smiled wider and ruffled the scales between Skunk's horns, drawing a small laugh out of him. "I guess that will have to be good enough for me," he said before standing up.

"When are you planning on leaving?" Sylvia asked, leaning forward in her seat.

Skunk turned to her, hesitating. "Uh, before sundown, if I can," he finally said. "The sooner the better. I don't wanna give myself a chance to change my mind."

Sylvia nodded quietly. "I see."

There was a long moment of quiet. Sylvia slowly stood from her seat, and Skunk reached out to help her find her balance. He pulled back when he saw there was no need. She had adapted to her disability remarkably well and carried herself with a crooked elegance on her walking stick. Seto stepped aside to give her some room, and she knelt before Skunk. She reached out, taking his hand in both of hers. Skunk savored the touch, feeling the softness of her skin under his thumbs.

"Just promise me one thing," she whispered.

"Anything."

Sylvia smiled. "Come back to us. Alive. And *happy.*"

Skunk returned the smile. "I will. And I'll write every chance I get! I promise."

Sylvia seemed satisfied with the promise. Without another word, she leaned forward and planted a gentle kiss on Skunk's forehead. His face began to grow hot from the unprompted display of affection, but he took it in stride.

Beside them, Seto spoke up a moment later. "Where do you plan to go?"

Skunk froze, not entirely willing to admit that for all of the thought he had put into this decision, he hadn't actually made it that far yet. Thankfully — or unluckily, depending on one's perspective — his sheepish grin told the tale better than he ever could.

Seto chuckled and pat Skunk on the shoulder. "Then might I make a recommendation?"

Skunk looked up at him, curious. "Sure, what'cha got?"

"Go to Underbridge," Seto suggested. "Head for the Arch, and look for the Attuner's Spire. That is the headquarters of the Arcaniun Assemblage, and you'll not find a better hub of knowledge and information in all the known world.

I have a friend there, a magi and archivist named Jeta Birkmont. He's a krauven like me, although many years my junior. He would be happy to help you."

Skunk thought it over for a moment. It seemed like a logical place to start. But there was also the fact that Underbridge was to the east.

The same direction Danica was going.

"Underbridge," Skunk conceded under his breath, already starting to make a plan in his head. "Alright. I can't think of any better ideas, so I guess that's where I'm headed first."

Seto nodded sharply, then turned for the door. "In that case, there are things I need to get for you. Wait here."

Skunk watched Seto leave, curious, then focused back on Sylvia. She was smiling, but there was a tension behind it. A lump formed in his throat, and he had to fight to swallow it down. "Do you, uh, do you think you guys could walk with me? To the edge of town, anyway?"

Sylvia nodded. "I was already going to."

Skunk felt more relief at that than he had been expecting. With a quiet hum, he leaned forward to press his forehead against Sylvia's. "Thank you."

The two were quiet for a few minutes, and in that time, the world seemed to fade away. There was a moment, a fleeting collection of precious seconds where Skunk almost felt the way he used to. The way he did before everything had gone wrong. Just him and his best friend, silently together. Of all the things he was leaving behind, he would miss this feeling the most. He cherished it while it lasted, anchoring it along with the scents in his soul.

Eventually, the feeling had to end, as Seto returned to the room. He held two folded envelopes in one hand, while the other was conspicuously hidden behind his back. He handed the items to Skunk. The scales tingled uncomfortably in his hands.

"Here you go," he said as Skunk took them. "These are letters of introduction. They carry a seal from my time working for the Assemblage and should serve as sufficient proof of your identity and peaceful intentions. They'll get you inside, at the very least. Once you're in the city, head for Bradigen's Workshop in the upper city. He's an enchanter of some renown, an associate of the Assemblage, and a friend of mine and Jeta's. He can help you set up a meeting, and if you're lucky, get you a place to sleep at night. I should warn you, however, that you may have a hard time of it in the city."

Skunk turned the envelopes over in his hands, scrutinizing them before looking back up at Seto. He frowned deeply. "Because I'm a kobold. Right?"

"Not just a kobold. A green scale," Seto clarified. "Word of the attack on Addernotch will have spread far and wide by now, as well as word of Azada's death. But I cannot be certain that word of *you* will have spread. And even if it has, most people will not recognize you on sight alone. Be careful, young man."

Skunk nodded gratefully. He'd figured that would be the case, but it was good to have it confirmed. "Thanks for the heads up," he said before jerking his nose at Seto's other hand. "But you've got something else. What is it?"

"Keen as ever," Seto noted, a sparkle coming into his dark eyes.

Skunk blinked, tilting his head in curiosity as Seto settled down before him. With deliberate slowness, he revealed the hidden item. Skunk's eyes widened. It was a ringstone, bright and brilliant.

"Here. This belongs to you," the krauven said, pressing the stone into Skunk's free hand. It was warm to the touch, and the same awareness he had felt when he had taken up the shard of the Sunstone came over him once again. An expansion of his inner self, as if his mind and body were swelling with a new volume of free space.

"Wow... Where did you get this?" he asked, lifting his eyes to Seto.

Seto's smile persisted, but it did not quite reach his eyes now. He pointed at the stone. "You know that the day your mother found you, she was helping me locate a fallen ringstone, yes?" When Skunk nodded, Seto continued. "This is that stone. We found it the day she found you. I was meant to send it back to Jeta in Underbridge. But, well... after Amelia brought you home, it didn't feel right to send it away. So I held onto it. But after everything we've learned, and everything you've endured, I believe it was meant for you all along. And if one ringstone was willing to obey you, I am sure this one will as well."

Skunk's eyes widened. He looked down at the stone with a new feeling of longing and reverence. He traced a sharper edge of the stone with the tip of his finger. His scales tingled at the contact, and it ran down his spine. He smiled sadly and held the stone to his heart before meeting Seto's gaze. "Thank you. I'll cherish it, always."

"I know," Seto said.

The trio spent a few minutes talking and waiting for Sylvia to finish her meal before they left. During this time, Skunk listened as Seto rattled off a long list of instructions on everything Skunk would need to keep in mind when traveling the world. Most of these tips were things he already knew, but the refresher course was welcome all the same.

Once all was said and done, they left the schoolhouse and returned to his home so he could pack what he needed. It didn't take him very long. A blanket and a pillow, some flint and steel, and as much dried meat from the pantry as he could stuff into his pack.

Once the survival essentials were squared away, he armed himself. A bow and a quiver of arrows, obviously — but more importantly, the sword. He had left it resting on the dining room table, undisturbed. He stood over it, eyeing the blade for a long while. Once again, he found himself recalling the day Amelia had first given it to him.

"Put it to better use than I did."

Skunk took the sword in his hand and drew it from the scabbard to inspect the blade. It was shining and radiant, as always, untarnished even after all the fighting. He could see his face reflected in the shiny metal. With a small huff, he pressed the blade against his forehead and closed his eyes. He took a deep breath, then opened his eyes to meet his gaze. "Come on, Amelia," he whispered, calling the sword by its new name for the first time. "We're going."

He sheathed the sword and secured it to his belt. As he went to leave, he paused in the doorway, giving his home one last look. He had lived his entire life in this house, and now he was leaving. He did not know when he would be back. So many memories were made here, and he tried to recount them all in his mind, but there were too many and not enough time.

"Thank you," he finally whispered. "For everything. I'll be home someday. I promise."

With that, he shut the door and turned the lock, sealing the door until he returned. He turned to Sylvia and Seto, both of whom had waited patiently outside. He handed Sylvia the key. "Mind holding onto this for me?" he asked.

Sylvia took it and held it close, nodding. "I'll keep it safe."

"Do you have everything you need, Skunk?" Seto asked. "It would be very embarrassing if you got halfway to the city and had to turn around because you forgot something important."

"Don't worry. I got it covered," Skunk assured him. He looked down the road to the east, toward Underbridge. He took a deep, heavy breath. Danica had a massive head start on him. Loaded down as he was with travel gear, it would take a lot of effort to catch up. But he didn't feel the need to start running right away. He didn't know how long he would be gone, and he wanted to make the time he still had count.

Sylvia held out a hand for him, and Skunk took the offer, lightly intertwining his fingers with hers. Seto stood on his other side, and together, they began the slow walk to the edge of Addernotch.

There were still people out and about, but oddly enough, they felt thin and far away. Skunk could occasionally feel their eyes on him, but he didn't feel the fear and suspicion that had characterized them for so long. All he felt from them was curiosity or a solemn understanding.

They knew he was leaving. He didn't have to say it.

Part of him wanted to make the rounds and say goodbye to everyone. But he decided against it. He needed to catch up to Danica, and if he took any more time saying his goodbyes, he might get second thoughts.

No, he had to do this now, while it felt right. And so he forged ahead, Sylvia and Seto at his side.

Soon enough, they came to a wooden archway that stood over the road, marking the official edge of the village. Skunk looked up at it with a sense of apprehension. "So, this is it," he whispered. "Last chance to turn back, right?"

"It's your choice to make, Skunk," Sylvia said.

After a few seconds, Skunk took in a deep breath. He was about to release Sylvia's hand and step through, when the sound of small feet running up from behind them caught his ear, accompanied by a vaguely familiar scent. Skunk turned around. "Huh?"

The children he had seen outside of Seto's Schoolhouse earlier were practically sprinting to catch up to them. They were carrying something with them.

"Mister Skunk! Waaiiit!" the child at the head of the pack called. He and his friends came staggering to a halt a few yards away, the leader doubling over to catch his breath. "Don't— *guh*— don't go yet!"

Skunk exchanged looks with Seto and Sylvia, baffled. To his growing suspicion, neither of them looked particularly surprised. In fact, Sylvia looked *pleased*, as if she'd been expecting this.

Skunk turned back to the children. "Er, yes? Can I help you?"

The boy took a few more seconds to catch his breath, then rose to his full height. He looked at the ground for a few seconds, then looked at Skunk with massive blue eyes. "Um... we wanted to thank you," he said.

Skunk blinked. "Wha— huh?"

"You saved us all from that dragon!" one of the other children, a girl, explained. "We all hid when it came and attacked the ry'thar! We watched it burn everything up!"

"But then you climbed it!" the third child, another boy, continued. "You fought it! You *beat* it! You were *so cool!* And you saved all our lives, too, which is even cooler!"

"Uh, that's not really—" Skunk began, wanting to tell the kids that it was not, in fact, 'cool' that he had brought dragonkind one step closer to extinction, but he was cut off.

The lead boy puffed up. "Uh-huh! And we saw how you've been going around town since then, and you were always looking all sad and stuff, so we decided we wanted to do something nice for you! It was gonna be a 'thank you' present, but, well..."

The boy looked past Skunk at the open road, and his expression soured. "I guess it's a going away present, now, isn't it?"

"They've been working on it all week," Sylvia whispered to Skunk, drawing his attention.

"You knew about this?!"

"She *helped*," Seto replied. "Did damn near half the work herself."

Skunk stared back and forth between the two of them, thrown utterly off balance. At a loss for words, he turned to the lead boy as he approached. He held out the thing they were carrying. It was a large package wrapped in paper and bound with string. A present, complete with gift wrapping.

"Uh, t-thank you," Skunk stammered, taking the package awkwardly.

"Open it!" the girl urged, pumping her fists. "We worked real hard on it! We just finished it a little bit ago, too!"

Skunk, still feeling a little unsure about all of this, decided to just run with it. With a shrug, he tore away the paper to see what lay beneath.

What he saw put a lump in his throat, and a tightness in his chest. But instead of the grief and sorrow that had characterized the last several weeks, this was a different feeling. Happy. Joyous.

Reaching into the package, he carefully extracted a brand new, black-fur cloak, large enough to cover his entire body like a blanket. The fur was soft and exquisite, the inner lining dense and firm. Turning it over, he saw the familiar white stripes of a skunk's back running down the length.

"We saw that you lost your cloak," The second boy explained. "It was always your whole thing. You didn't look right without it, so we thought we'd make a new one for ya."

"Do you like it?" The girl asked.

Skunk stared at the cloak for a long while, his eyes watering over. It was a silly thing to get so sentimental about, he knew. But he couldn't help it. With quivering lips and a warming heart, he smiled at the boy. "Thank you. All of you," he said. "And you're welcome. Living with you all has made me so happy."

"Are you going off to fight more bad guys?" the second boy asked.

Skunk glanced at Sylvia for a moment, then at Seto. He shrugged. "That's not really the plan, but if I meet any, I'll give 'em a smack or two."

"You'll win," the lead boy told him with a truly staggering amount of confidence.

Skunk chuckled weakly. "Thanks, you guys."

The lead boy smiled brightly, then ran forward to quickly hug Skunk around the waist. The kobold barely had time to register the embrace before the kid broke away and went running back into town with his friends. Skunk stared after them, feeling just that little bit lighter.

Beside him, Seto clacked his beak. "Are you ready, lad?"

Skunk looked down at his cloak. Then, with a nod, he swung it around his shoulders and clasped it into place.

It fit perfectly.

"I am now," he said confidently.

"You are," Sylvia agreed.

Skunk took the encouragement as well as he was able. Then, with a nod more to himself, he turned to face the road. He cast one last glance back at Addernotch and smiled. "I'll be back," he said, just loud enough for Sylvia and Seto to hear.

"We'll be here," Seto replied. "Take care on the road, Skunk. And as a word of advice from your teacher: Never forget who you are. Nobody else knows you, but we do. Make it a point to show them, won't you?"

Skunk nodded. "I will."

He looked at Sylvia and Seto one last time. Then, with a parting wave, he dropped to all fours. He would have to go fast if he was going to catch up to Danica.

With a flick of his tail, Skunk launched himself forward. His clawed hands and feet kicked up small clouds of dust as he hurried along the road to the east, his tail lashing around in the air behind him.

Sylvia listened to him go, both hands clutching her walking stick. A chill wind rolled by, sending her dress and hair drifting in the air.

"Goodbye, Skunk," she said.

Epilogue

Danica blew out a long puff of air between pursed lips, her mind drifting as she stared into the flames of her campfire. She lay on her back with her head against Lorok's soft belly. Her book lay open in her lap, and she held a quill in one hand. She nibbled softly on the tip of her free thumb as she tried to find the next words to write down. She hummed softly under her breath, trying to make the lyrics flow, make them fit. But the songwriting her people put so much effort into never came to her as naturally as others might have wished. She was trying to write of Amelia, trying to put into song the impact of that woman in this chapter of Danica's life. But the words would not come.

She sighed and closed the book. "Damn it," she mumbled before looking into the fire. She pondered the road ahead, knowing it would be a couple more days before she was out of the forest, and that was assuming she wasn't moving at a slow, leisurely pace. That meant she had plenty of time to try and figure out what her next move was going to be.

It was *very* frustrating. She was in no hurry, but she still felt the pressing urge to *find* something to pick up the pace for. A mindless stroll across the realm was not something she particularly wanted to do. In the past, she'd always had a destination in mind. Whether it was taking care of a job to earn herself some coin or tracking down a kobold den, she *always* had a direction. But now all she could do was hope something came along that caught her interest.

And yet, despite her desire to press forward, her thoughts kept turning backward for Addernotch. It wasn't that she had any particular attachment to the village. She had helped undo the worst of the damage Azada's horde had done, but there was only so much she was capable of helping with. She was a warrior and a wanderer at heart, and spending her days hammering in nails was just not for her.

Even so, she couldn't help but feel a little uneasy about leaving it behind. And, as much as she did not want to admit it, even to herself, it was specifically because of Skunk.

Danica's eyes fell. She looked over her shoulder at Lorok. He was happily chomping down on a pile of mushrooms and some bread Danica had bought before she left. "None of this bothers you, huh?" She asked. "You'll just keep ambling along wherever I tell you. Not a care in the world."

Lorok briefly lifted his face from his food to snort at her.

Now that she had his attention, she reached over to scratch behind his ear, drawing a pleased rumble from him. She sighed. "Lorok? Are we doing the right thing?" she asked in barely even a whisper.

Lorok tilted his head, warbling curiously. Her words might have had no meaning to him, but she had raised him ever since he was born. She trusted him to know when she was troubled.

"I'm worried about Skunk," she went on, looking up at the pale ring, its light dappled by the forest canopy stretching over the road. "I know what he's going through. Losing his family like that. Having his people practically turn against him through no fault of his own…"

Lorok shook his head from side to side, then pressed his snout into her palm.

Danica smirked at him. "Yes, I *did* have you there, you big loaf. But Skunk?" her smile faded. "Who does he realistically have left? Sylvia and Seto, I suppose. But that's about it. And Skunk's soft at heart. The days ahead are going to be hard for him."

Lorok let off a low whine, and Danica took that as an agreement. She sighed, leaned forward, and plopped her chin into her palm. She tossed a stray pebble into the flames and watched them roil. "I don't know, boy. I almost feel like we should turn back around just to keep an eye on *him*. Help him through it."

Lorok snuffed. Danica rolled her eyes before lightly swatting him on the belly. "That is *not* helpful, you lummox."

Lorok warbled in protest, and Danica was quick to pat the spot to soothe any discomfort. Not that she had caused any; Lorok just liked to complain.

After a few seconds, Danica pulled her hand away. She stared into the flames again, her brow furrowing. "Maybe we *should* go back," she muttered at length, rolling it over in her head. "Stick around, just for a few more days. Give Skunk some pointers. Walk him through how I dealt with it."

Not that I have much in the way of good advice. She had handled her version of this situation by packing her bags, hopping on Lorok, and leaving to get revenge. She had *run*. That was no way to deal with trauma. At least, not for someone as emotionally and socially driven as Skunk.

Danica had half-resolved to turn around first thing in the morning when the decision would ultimately be made for her. A sound reached her, echoing between the trees. It was a voice, one she recognized instantly, calling her name.

"Danica!"

She turned to look, Lorok lifting his head behind her. The source of the voice had come from well beyond the light of the fire, but she could hear it approaching. The familiar scrabble of scaled feet and clawed digits on cobblestone tickled her ears in a way that would otherwise be unpleasant. Soon enough, the familiar form of Skunk came bounding into the firelight, a new black cloak fluttering across his shoulders. For a brief moment, the corner of Danica's mouth twitched up into a smile. "Speak of the kobold," she whispered to herself. "And he shall appear."

Skunk came sliding to a halt a few yards away, before doubling over to plant his hands on his knees and pant for air.

Danica looked him over for several long seconds. She was glad to see him but also confused. She frowned, doing her best to hide her concerns behind a stoic mask. "Skunk. What are you doing out here?" she asked simply.

Skunk looked up at her, and only now did she see the relief in his eyes. But there was more to it. She saw fear in them, along with a fiery conviction she'd only seen when he'd demanded to accompany her and Amelia in the past.

He opened his mouth to speak, but his words came out a jumbled, stammering mess of broken syllables and half-sounds. "Uh. W-well, uhm... y-you see, I was wondering... I, uh... i-if you don't mind, I was hoping you... um..."

"Juna's tits, Skunk," Danica grunted, rolling her eyes. "Just spit it out!"

Skunk quickly stood bolt upright, his eyes shooting wide. "C-can I come with you?!" he blurted out, faster and louder than was strictly necessary. A few birds, startled from their peaceful slumber, scattered from the nearby trees, filling the air with offended chirps.

Danica stared at him for several long seconds. *So he is running,* she thought soberly. She eyed him up and down, taking measure of what he had brought. Judging by the straps over his chest, he had a pack slung over his shoulders under his cloak. He had a bow, arrows, and Amelia's sword. He looked ready to travel — or as close to ready to travel as the inexperienced youth imagined he needed to be.

"Why?" Danica asked, glancing past him toward Addernotch.

Skunk was quiet for a long moment, his expression falling. His hands lifted over his chest, wringing together in a display of nervous energy. "I... I love my home, don't get me wrong," he said at length, his voice low and shaky. "Addernotch is everything to me. Its people mean everything to me. They're my pack. All I want is what's best for them..."

"Then stay with them. Help them rebuild." Danica urged, gesturing back the way he'd come and raising an eyebrow. Skunk flinched, his tail swishing behind him a few times. Danica could already see that he wasn't backing down. *Stubborn little boy.*

"Look. All I want is what's best for Addernotch. And right now," Skunk's hands tightened around each other, his knuckles whitening. "Right now... that isn't me."

Danica didn't say anything. She held his gaze, waiting for him to continue and explain himself.

He took a deep, shuddering breath. "They need to heal. They need to mourn everyone and everything we lost, and they need time for the pain to go away. They need to rebuild their homes and their lives. And I can't help them with *any* of that. At best I could shoot at animals getting too close to town, but they have people for that already. And besides all that..."

Skunk looked down, sagging in place. "There's so much we don't know about the attack. So much I want to understand! I wanna find answers, Danica. I *need* answers. And I'm not gonna find 'em in Addernotch. S-so right now, the best thing for me to do is leave them."

Skunk shuttered, tearing his eyes away from Danica again. "B-but at the same time, I don't wanna be alone. Even just the idea of it scares me to death.

I've *always* had someone. Mom, Seto, Sylvia, and the kids at the schoolhouse. *Someone.*"

Danica looked down, her heart twinging just a little. On that, she wasn't entirely sure she could relate. Kobolds were pack creatures in a very different way to humans or dwarves. She could only imagine how horrifying being truly alone was to someone like Skunk.

Skunk took a pleading step forward. "S-so can I come with you? Please? I promise I won't slow you down! I brought my own food, I can pull my own weight, and I can help you fight if you get into trouble! I won't slow you down! I won't be a burden!"

Danica lifted her hand to stop Skunk before he could work himself up into a fit. She didn't want him to humiliate himself like that, especially not in front of her. She stared at him for a few long seconds, trying to gauge his resolve.

"Are you sure?" she asked gently.

Skunk frowned, taken off-guard by the question. But he nodded sharply a moment later. "Yes, I'm sure," he said, his voice firm and steady with resolve despite his anxiety.

Danica held the silence for another few seconds, waiting to see if the conviction would waver.

It did not.

That was all the convincing she needed. The last thing the kobold needed was to be alone right now. *I'll keep an eye on him for you, Amelia,* she thought. *At least until he's ready to go home. I promise.*

Danica lowered her hand, then nodded at the fire. "Come on, then. I was just about to break out some dinner."

In the beat of a heart, Skunk's features shone with joy, and the light returned to his eyes. He grinned and threw himself against Danica in a tight tackle hug, much to her chagrin. "Thank you, Danica!" he practically squealed into her breastplate. "Thank you so much!"

"Off," Danica commanded, trying to keep the smile from making it to her face and her voice.

Skunk released her promptly, a sheepish grin replacing his ecstatic one. "Sorry, sorry," he apologized.

Danica pat the ground next to her. "Sit down and catch your breath, kid. You must've run like crazy to catch up to me so fast," she said, reaching into her pack at her side to pull out a handful of travel rations. Skunk took a position beside her, sitting cross-legged on the stone next to her. "Unless you were stalking Lorok's musk the whole time again?"

"Ha! No, not this time. I ran," Skunk confirmed, reaching into his own pack and withdrawing a handful of dried meat, his tail swishing eagerly behind him. "Honestly, I wasn't expecting to catch up to you tonight."

Danica shrugged. "I'm not in a hurry and I stopped early."

"Where were you headed?"

Danica shrugged. "No clue."

"So, you left Addernotch without even knowing where you were going?" Skunk asked, baffled.

"Yup," Danica replied. "It's not like I have anywhere *to* go. Without the Sunstone, I can't go home and fix things up there. Even if I could, I wouldn't stick around. I'm not keen on sleeping in a big cave again surrounded by people who shamed my family."

Skunk hummed quietly. "Well... would you mind if we went to Underbridge before anything else? That's where the Arcaniun Assemblage is. That's my best bet for finding answers."

"That, or they'll stuff a ringstone in your hand and make you a mage," Danica noted with a small smirk, imagining the kobold flinging spells left and right.

She had been joking, but apparently, Skunk had other ideas, if the way his face lit up was any indication. "Oh, I already have one."

Danica blinked and watched as he reached into his pack and reverently withdrew a ringstone. He set it down in his lap and leaned back so she could get a good look. She stared at it for a second, baffled. "The fuck?"

"Seto gave it to me," Skunk clarified. He looked down at it and traced it with the tips of his fingers. "He and mom found it the day they found me."

"Do you even know how to use it?"

"No clue!" Skunk chirped with a wag of his tail. "D'ya think I can figure it out, though?"

"Skunk, you almost single-handedly killed an ancient dragon," Danica replied, giving him a grin. "At this point, anything is possible."

Skunk's grin returned with gusto, but he said no more.

Danica rolled her eyes. "Right, then. To Underbridge?" she asked.

Skunk pointed ahead dramatically. "To Underbridge!" he answered, his voice echoing off the trees.

With their destination set, the two tucked into a humble but filling fireside dinner. Come the dawn, the open road would beckon them to Underbridge, and the beginning of their next adventure.

Dragonkin Saga

9 781968 826017